FATAL PATTERN

BOOKS BY KATE ANGELO

THE KING LEGACY

Girl Lost

Fatal Pattern

THE KING LEGACY #2

FATAL PATTERN

KATE ANGELO

Revell
a division of Baker Publishing Group
Grand Rapids, Michigan

Published by Revell
a division of Baker Publishing Group
Grand Rapids, Michigan
RevellBooks.com

Printed in the United States of America

Library of Congress Cataloging-in-Publication Data
Names: Angelo, Kate (Romance fiction writer) author
Title: Fatal pattern / Kate Angelo.
Description: Grand Rapids, Michigan : Revell, a division of Baker Publishing Group, 2026. | Series: The king legacy ; 2
Identifiers: LCCN 2026001947 | ISBN 9780800746643 paperback | ISBN 9781493455492 ebook
Subjects: LCGFT: Romance fiction | Thrillers (Fiction) | Christian fiction | Novels
Classification: LCC PS3601.N554426 F38 2026
LC record available at https://lccn.loc.gov/2026001947

Cover design by Mumtaz Mustafa

Baker Publishing Group publications use paper produced from sustainable forestry practices and postconsumer waste whenever possible.

26 27 28 29 30 31 32 7 6 5 4 3 2 1

To God,
who fills me daily with
unimaginable peace and joy.

To Jerry,
my prayer warrior, trusted adviser,
biggest supporter, and best friend.

And to those living among the wheat and tares,
take heart—the harvest will reveal what only God can see,
and his hand will separate light from darkness.

Jesus told them another parable: "The kingdom of heaven is like a man who sowed good seed in his field. But while everyone was sleeping, his enemy came and sowed weeds among the wheat, and went away. When the wheat sprouted and formed heads, then the weeds also appeared.

"The owner's servants came to him and said, 'Sir, didn't you sow good seed in your field? Where then did the weeds come from?'

"'An enemy did this,' he replied.

"The servants asked him, 'Do you want us to go and pull them up?'

"'No,' he answered, 'because while you are pulling the weeds, you may uproot the wheat with them. Let both grow together until the harvest. At that time I will tell the harvesters: First collect the weeds and tie them in bundles to be burned; then gather the wheat and bring it into my barn.'"

Matthew 13:24–30

1

THE COLD EDGE OF THE BLADE kissed Tori Crew's throat, drawing a rivulet of blood that began its descent down her neck.

"Don't move." The whisper brushed against her ear.

Tori tasted bile at the back of her throat, and for one horrifying moment, she thought she might throw up. Her pulse thumped against the knife pressed to her carotid. Each beat reverberated through the steel and deep into her bones.

The parking lot at the Kingdom MMA Gym stretched dark and empty around her. It was her stupid idea to meet at 4:30 a.m., and now here she was all alone. No witnesses. No help.

Stryker should be here. Setting up folding chairs in a circle near the boxing ring, brewing that industrial-strength coffee that could wake the dead, preparing for morning Bible study with the kids who lived in the residential program.

But Stryker wasn't coming.

Stryker lay unconscious in a hospital bed, his salt-and-pepper hair loose around his pale face instead of tied back the way he always wore it. Some lunatic had tried to kill her mentor. One of the greatest men she'd ever known, and now—

The blade pressed deeper. "I said don't move."

Her knees wanted to buckle, but she locked them straight. Stryker had taught her that. Stay strong. Stay focused.

The fighter in her knew what to do. Elbow to solar plexus. Heel to instep. Grab the wrist. Twist. Three seconds and he'd be on the ground. But he had the knife pressed just right. She couldn't make a move without him slicing through a major artery. One wrong angle, and she'd bleed out before she hit the pavement.

She forced her breathing to slow. Fought the adrenaline that wanted to flood her system and make her do something stupid.

Assess. Analyze. Act.

The mantra from Krav Maga training steadied her racing thoughts. Observe first. Plan the attack. Strike when the odds shifted.

"You're bleeding." His breath was hot against her neck. "I've always liked the color of blood."

She cataloged details. Male. Less than six feet tall, based on the angle of the knife. Maybe 5′9″. Right-handed. Gloves. No discernable accent. No alcohol on his breath. Not impulsive. Calculated. Educated.

He drew in a breath. "Such a pretty shade of red, don't you think?"

"Who . . . who are you?" She worked to keep her voice steady despite the tremors threatening to overtake her body.

"I'm the one who watches. I'm your . . . shadow. A part of you." His free hand clamped around her chest, crushing her arms against her ribs. The blade pressed deeper, stealing her breath. "You've been busy. Two new cases, six trips to the gym, and you changed your coffee order to vanilla instead of caramel."

Her stalker. The one who'd been leaving notes on her car. The one who'd been calling and hanging up. The one the police wouldn't pursue because the "non-violent harassment" apparently didn't meet the threshold for a credible threat.

He'd been watching everything.

Her stomach twisted, not with fear—she could handle fear—

but with fury. "You think that makes you powerful? It makes you pathetic."

The knife pressed deeper. Not enough to do serious damage, but enough to elicit another drop of blood. His gloved finger caught the droplet sliding down her neck, then traced it back up to the wound.

"Ah. We mustn't lose too much. Not yet."

She analyzed his posture. The way he held the knife. How his chest rose and fell against her back. "What do you want?"

"To show you that I can kill you anytime I want." His laugh was soft, almost tender. "This is just the beginning, Dr. Crew. I'm not done toying with you yet."

Fight instinct coiled through her muscles, but her mind weighed the odds again and overrode them. *Information. Get information.* Every criminal had a pattern, a motivation. Understanding him meant catching him. And catching him meant ending this nightmare.

She strained her eyes to the right, trying to catch even a sliver of his face in her peripheral vision. "Why me?"

"Because you think you understand the darkness," he said. "But you don't. Not like I do."

A pair of headlights sliced through the blackness, white light stabbing her retinas. The blade lifted from her throat.

She spun, fist cocked for a power jab at his face, but she only struck air. Gone. The coward had melted into the shadows along the wall, black clothing swallowed by the darkness as he disappeared into the alley beyond. Her chance—blown. She could have ended this right here, right now. Could have put him down and dragged answers out of him. Instead, she was standing here bleeding while he slipped away like the roach he was.

A car screeched to a halt beside her. The driver's door flew open. Detective Blade St. James erupted from his unmarked Charger with his hand on his holstered weapon. "Tori? You okay?"

Her fingers went to her throat and came away sticky with

blood. She stared at the crimson smear. A savage anger bubbled up inside her chest. He'd touched her. Cut her. And vanished like smoke.

"What the—" Blade's eyes widened at her blood-slick fingertips. "You're bleeding."

"It's just a scratch." Her knees felt shaky. She'd had every skill and training to handle situations exactly like this, and she'd let the stalker get the drop on her.

"What happened? Who was that?"

"My stalker." She pressed the cut to stem the bleeding.

"Stalker?" His voice rose in disbelief. "What stalker? Since when do you have a stalker?"

"Three weeks, give or take." A crimson droplet had dropped on her knuckle. Perfect. Round. Like a bead of glass.

"I've always liked the color of blood."

Ice slid through her veins.

"And you didn't think to mention this?" Blade had his phone out. "We need to call this in. Get you to a hospital."

"No." She caught his wrist. "The locals are aware, but you know stalker cases. Nothing they can do."

"Tori, he had a knife to your throat." His voice ticked up. "That's attempted murder."

"It's not that simple."

"It *is* that simple. Let's do this right. Get an officer out here. Take your statement, photos, dust for prints, canvass witnesses—"

"There are no witnesses at four thirty in the morning!" She swept her arm toward the deserted street and empty parking lot. "And he wore gloves, so no prints. We've got nothing."

"All the more reason to report it. You say this guy's been watching you for weeks, and now he's crossed the line to physical assault. He's escalating."

"You think I don't know that?" She dropped her hand from the cut and stormed over to Blade's car.

She hadn't seen a hint of the stalker in the last week, but she couldn't shake the feeling that she was being watched. Even now, standing in the dark parking lot, she sensed he was still nearby.

"Look, I didn't see the knife or his face, but we've got footage from the security cameras. We've got four hours in the car to fill out a police report. I'd rather do it myself than stand around here being told how many things I did wrong."

Blade's eyes lost that hard detective edge. His thumb, calloused from a thousand hours lifting weights at the gym, lifted her chin. The touch was feather-light, but it sent a jolt straight through the icy shock that encased her. Heat, unexpected and unwelcome, pooled in its wake. The urge to lean into that warmth warred with the instinct to pull away from a closeness that suddenly felt . . . dangerous. More dangerous than the man who'd held a knife to her throat.

His gaze dropped to the cut, his focus so absolute the world seemed to narrow to the few inches between them. "This needs medical attention."

"It's superficial." The words came out breathless. She stepped back, breaking the contact. The sudden loss of his touch left her skin cold, but she needed the space. Not just to think. To breathe.

Blade stood there in his rumpled slacks and dress shirt, his hand working the change or keys in his pocket. The look on his face said everything his mouth wasn't.

"Don't make that face at me, Blade. I'm a big girl."

"You are the most stubborn—" He caught himself. Shook his head and looked around the parking lot as if he expected the stalker to lunge at her again. "Fine. But we're not done talking about this."

"I figured." She resisted rolling her eyes.

She'd known Blade since they were teenagers, young and stupid, throwing punches at heavy bags in the Kingdom MMA Gym where they'd both been court ordered to live and attend the Warrior program.

Back then, Blade's restless energy had matched her desperation to hit something—anything—until her knuckles bled and her mind went quiet. Unlike her, he processed everything out loud. Their talks turned into him working through problems step by step while she listened.

He flicked a hand at his ride. "Get in the car. I'm gonna check the area."

"Don't bother. He's—"

But Blade was already moving, his flashlight sweeping across the shadowy spaces around the building where her attacker had disappeared.

"Gone," she said.

Long gone by now.

She slid into the passenger seat and shut the door. Pulled down the visor and flicked open the mirror. An amber light illuminated the red parenthesis at her throat. Not deep enough to kill, just deep enough to remind her he could. Her mouth went dry. She couldn't generate enough saliva to swallow. If Blade had been even a minute later, she might be dead. Instead of pulling up to pick her up, he could've found her bleeding out in that alley.

"Thank you, Jesus," she whispered, digging through her work bag for her travel first aid kit.

One of many items she lugged in her work bag. Foster care had taught her that. Always be prepared. Always have what she needed to take care of herself.

The driver's door opened. Blade got in.

"Nothing. No footprints, no evidence. The guy's a ghost."

"Not a ghost." She dabbed an antiseptic wipe on the cut and winced. "Just careful. A planner. He wants to be in control, so he's been watching. Learning my patterns."

"And you didn't think to vary your routine?" he snapped. "Basic security protocol, Tori. You of all people should know better."

The criticism stung. Mostly because he was right. She'd been careless, overconfident. Told herself she could handle it. That she wasn't afraid.

But that was before she felt the cold steel against her skin. Before she heard him whispering threats in her ear. "I know. I screwed up. Won't happen again."

She peeled away a Band-Aid's backing and pressed the adhesive over the cut. The flesh-colored circle was amazingly discreet.

Something in her tone must have registered with him, because his voice softened. "We'll catch him. I promise you that."

"Let's focus on today." She flipped the visor closed. "We have a four-hour drive to Union Correctional, and I need coffee."

Blade didn't start the car. He turned in his seat to study her with those piercing blue eyes that always seemed to see more than she wanted them to.

"Are you sure you're up for this? We can reschedule. Damien Sullivan isn't going anywhere."

"I'm fine," she insisted despite the tremor in her hands that she couldn't quite control. "It's just adrenaline."

"Tori—"

"I said I'm fine!" She gritted her teeth, wishing she hadn't yelled at him. The look of hurt on his face made it worse. He'd seen her through just about everything in life; it made sense he'd want to do that now. "I'm really okay. Promise. I need this."

He didn't look convinced, but nodded anyway. "Okay. But if you change your mind—"

"I won't," Tori said, tucking the bloodied wipe into a small plastic bag and sealing it. Evidence. Just in case. "Now drive, Detective, before the morning traffic turns our four-hour trip into six."

He started the engine, casting one last glance her way before easing out of the parking lot. She turned to look out the window, watching as the gym where she'd learned self-defense receded in the side mirror.

She absently pressed her fingers to the wound on her neck, feeling the sting of it. A reminder that she was dealing with someone dangerous. Someone who had gotten close enough to hurt her. Someone who had promised he wasn't done.

"He said that I think I understand the darkness, but I don't."

Blade glanced over. "What?"

"It's what he said." The hot breath in her ear. The pressure of the knife. His fingers digging into her arm. "He's wrong. I understand darkness better than most."

"So, what are you thinking? Profile?" Blade shifted into work mode.

She exhaled, taking a few seconds to create professional distance. "Male, late twenties to early thirties. Comfortable with weapons."

"That narrows it down to about half the men in Florida," Blade muttered.

"He's also controlled. Educated. Narcissistic, with delusions of grandeur," she continued. "He sees this as a game between us. He's not just stalking me, he's on a mission only he understands."

"A mission for what?"

She stared at the road ahead. The sun began to peek over the horizon, casting long shadows across the asphalt. "That's what I need to figure out."

Blade pulled into a drive-through and ordered his usual coffee and sausage biscuit. Tori asked for a double Americano, extra cream.

"You want anything to eat?"

"Nah." Her stomach churned at the thought of food. Food meant chewing. Swallowing. Basic functions that required her throat to work normally.

Blade paid and pulled back onto the highway. "So, you want to tell me what really happened back there? Because I know you. You're a third-degree black belt. You teach self-defense classes. There's no way this guy got the drop on you unless you let him."

The question she'd been dreading. The car suddenly felt ten degrees warmer. "What are you saying?"

"I'm saying you weren't fighting back. Not really." His eyes flicked to her, then back to the road. "Why?"

For a moment, she considered deflecting, making a joke, changing the subject. But this was Blade. He deserved honesty, even if it made her sound crazy.

"I needed to understand him," she admitted. "I needed to hear his voice, feel his presence, gauge his confidence."

"You risked your life for a psychological assessment?"

"I took a calculated risk." She sipped her coffee. "And now I know things about him I didn't before. He's escalated and injured me. Things the police can't ignore."

Blade shot her a look that was half concern, half grudging amusement. "You really are something else, you know that?"

"So I've been told." She leaned back in her seat, trying to ignore the phantom sensation of cold steel against her skin and the whispered promise of more to come.

"Should I be worried about you?"

"Remember when I ankle-picked you at the gym last month? I think I can handle myself, chico."

Blade laughed, and she felt her smile reach her eyes this time. "Now quit driving like a Florida snowbird. We've got a killer to interview, and it would be rude to keep him waiting."

He shook his head. "One of these days, Dr. Crew, your curiosity is going to get you killed."

"Maybe." She smiled again. "But not today. Today, the only thing that matters is what Damien Sullivan knows about my parents' murder. And not even a knife-wielding stalker will keep me from hearing what he has to say."

2

THE HIGHWAY STRETCHED AHEAD, four lanes of asphalt cutting through Florida scrubland toward Union Correctional. Blade kept the speedometer steady at seventy-five, watching the landscape shift from coastal palms to inland pines. Each mile took them closer to Damien Sullivan's cell, where the man spent twenty-three hours a day in protective custody, holding secrets that might finally give Tori answers about her parents' murder.

Blade had argued with himself for days about whether to make this trip. Tori insisted she didn't need a babysitter, that interviewing dangerous inmates was part of her job. But something about Damien Sullivan set his teeth on edge.

Blade glanced over at Tori, who sat with her laptop balanced on her knees, fingers flying across the keyboard. She'd caught her lower lip between her teeth, a habit she did whenever she concentrated. The Band-Aid on her neck showed a pinprick of fresh blood seeping through the center.

What would have happened if he hadn't shown up when he did? That maniac had a knife to her throat, and she'd stood there analyzing him like he was a case study instead of a predator who could have killed her.

"Eyes on the road, Detective," Tori said without looking up from her screen.

"I *am* watching the road."

"You've glanced over here six times in the last five seconds." She looked up, eyebrow raised. "Something on your mind?"

"Just making sure you're not planning any more psychological experiments with knife-wielding psychopaths."

"We don't call them psychopaths. They're individuals with antisocial personality disorder. And I told you, the only reason I'm riding shotgun is so I can work."

"Work?" He shot her another look. "You're supposed to be filing a police report about your stalker." Was this woman trying to give him an ulcer?

"I haven't made it that far. I'm reviewing everything we know about Damien Sullivan before we walk into that prison."

Blade couldn't blame her for that. She had a lot riding on this trip. More than just catching a lead on her parents' cold case. "Remind me again how you managed this trip as part of your research sabbatical?"

Her fingers paused on the keyboard. "The book I'm writing is on behavioral patterns in familial homicides. Part of that means consulting on active cases, gathering real-world data."

"How exactly does interviewing Sullivan fit your research? He isn't a family annihilator."

"True, but Sullivan's case is textbook workplace violence with underlying family dysfunction. Plus, if he can provide a connection to my parents' case, I'll have material for my chapter on perpetrator psychology in cold cases." She closed the laptop and leaned back against the headrest. "The FDLE encourages field research. Keeps me sharp while I'm technically on academic leave."

"Academic leave." Blade shook his head. "Most people take sabbaticals to write poetry or learn French. You're chasing down murderers."

"Different people, different hobbies."

"You know, I should turn this car around and haul you straight to the station." He pointed at her bandage. "Document that knife wound with photos."

"Ease up a little, Detective. I'm fine with the photos, but I can snap them myself."

"I swear, woman." He flicked a look at her. "You're the reason I'm losing my hair. You know that, right?"

"That's not my fault. You've been thinning since college. I just help the process."

"Very funny. At least you admit you're a walking disaster."

"I prefer magnet for adventure."

"Yeah, well, I'd prefer adventures that don't involve knives at four thirty in the morning."

She stuck her tongue out at him then smiled.

The jokes and easy conversation didn't cool the rage simmering beneath his skin. A man had attacked Tori. Held a knife to her throat. One different angle, one deeper slice, and he'd have found her body cooling in that parking lot.

He took his eyes off the road for a second. "I'm sorry for what happened back there."

She dismissed him with a wave of her hand and opened her laptop again. "Look, if you'll stop yapping, I could actually fill out this report."

Classic Tori deflection. Fine by him.

He reached over and flipped to a classic rock station. Guitar riffs cut through the car, drowning out the lecture he'd been building in his head about proper threat assessment and the wisdom of actually filing police reports before they became obituaries. The opening chords of a song from his middle school days drifted through the speakers. Since when was this song classic rock? He drummed his thumbs against the steering wheel, singing along under his breath.

"You're getting all the words wrong," Tori said, not looking up from her laptop.

"Am not."

"It's not 'can't find the pyramids.' It's 'can't find a better man.'"

He shrugged. "Pyramids make more sense. Who goes around looking for better men anyway?"

"Women who date cops?"

"Ouch." He grinned. "That one stung."

"I speak the truth."

"Hey, I have a girlfriend. Unlike some perpetually single profilers I know."

The jab was meant to be easy. Another shot in a game they'd been playing for years. But he watched the comeback die on her lips. For a half second, the light in her eyes just . . . went out.

"I'm a behavioral analyst." She turned her head, giving him nothing but the sharp line of her jaw.

The "perpetually single" crack must've hit a nerve. He was about to apologize when she let out a short huff and turned back, her expression all familiar armor.

"And please. Give it a month, and you'll have found something wrong with poor Kiara just like all the others."

There it was. Same old Tori.

"Hey, five months is a new record. Cut me some slack."

Her eyes flicked up, and he caught the flash of—what? Disappointment? Relief? Gone before he could pin it down.

She went back to typing. The quiet click of the keys was the only sound in the car, each one a tick on a clock measuring the distance she'd just put between them.

But Tori had punched back with the very thing he'd been avoiding.

Five months with the pretty records administrator. Longer than any relationship since high school. He hadn't told Tori how serious things were getting with Kiara. He wasn't sure why. Maybe because saying it out loud would make it too real. Or because he might be the one left behind when Kiara realized she could do better than a swamp rat with a badge. For once, he found himself dating a woman who offered a future he wasn't sure he deserved.

Sure, he couldn't needle Kiara the way he did Tori and expect her to dish it right back. Kiara didn't snap back with quips that could slice through steel or roll her eyes when he cracked jokes that fell flat. But Kiara listened, and her calm, earnest nature was the kind of gentleness he'd never experienced in a relationship.

Tori's fingers paused over the keyboard. "What time did you pull up at the gym? I need it for the report."

"Four thirty-seven." At least she'd document the stalker properly instead of pretending a knife to the throat was just another Tuesday morning.

He heard her sucking air between her teeth as she peeled the bandage off her neck. "Ay, that hurts worse than the knife did."

"Wimp."

She angled her phone's camera at him and snapped a photo. "That fairy princess filter suits you. I'm sure Luna and Harlee will love it."

Luna King would have a field day with that photo. The former CIA operative had married Corbin six months ago, but she still found time to roast Blade at every opportunity. And Harlee Bay, the ATF intelligence specialist with tattoo sleeves and a stare that could freeze lava, would probably print it out and tape it to his locker at Kingdom.

"Delete that." He swiped for the phone, but she pulled it out of reach.

Tori tapped her phone. "Too late. Already sent."

"You know they're going to make that my contact photo."

Tori grinned. "That's the plan."

The smile dissolved as she flipped the camera around and tilted her chin up, exposing the thin red line across her throat. The phone clicked. She studied the screen, adjusted the angle, took another shot.

The laptop keys clicked in rapid succession.

She snapped the laptop shut. "There. Happy now?"

"That wasn't so bad."

Tori fished a fresh Band-Aid from her bag and pressed it over the cut. She crumpled the wrapper and stuffed it into her bag.

"Says the man who's never had to photograph his own wounds."

"That's not true. Remember that time in college when I had to put myself between you and your psych professor?"

"That wasn't a knife, it was Professor Bernstein's nails."

The guy had claws longer than most women Blade knew. "Dude needed a manicure."

"Or he should take a class at Kingdom and learn not to hit with an open hand. Bernstein was a hack. He had it coming."

"Maybe so, but leading with your fists is a quick way to lose a scholarship." Blade massaged his jaw. Bernstein's talons had raked furrows deep enough to warrant campus police documentation. "I spent three hours convincing the dean you were having a PTSD moment."

"He gave me a C, Blade. He stood there in front of the whole lecture hall and insisted that criminal behavior was purely environmental. That people like *me* were just products of a bad zip code. I proved him wrong."

"By proving you were violent?" He slid her a look.

Tori looked away. Her bravado flickered. "Yeah, not my best moment."

"You were nineteen." He softened his voice. "You were a kid who'd grown up believing you were less than everyone else. You didn't have a fuse back then. You just had a detonator."

"I've learned containment since then. Most days anyway." She exhaled through her nose. "Speaking of criminal behavior, how's the task force going? Any closer to finding who's at the top of the organ harvesting ring?"

Last year, he'd played a supporting role in an undercover mission where Luna and Corbin infiltrated a biomedical research facility and uncovered an organ harvesting operation straight out of

Frankenstein. The arrests of Dr. Forest and his daughter, Elizabeth, had only scratched the surface. Forest had been the surgeon, sure, but someone else had been bankrolling the enterprise. Someone who'd made sure every witness disappeared before they could talk.

"Things are a little weird right now." He tapped the brake for a red Ferrari cutting into the HOV lane. The supercar passed a minivan, then darted back into regular traffic. "They replaced Brown at the local FBI office with Special Agent in Charge Sebastian Wells. He's taking over the task force. No interviews. No evidence moving. Nobody touches the file until he reviews everything himself."

"Uh-oh. Is he cleaning house?"

"Not exactly. He seems like a great guy. Very encouraging. He spoke highly of the work we've done so far."

"Sounds like the old school FBI move," Tori said.

"He's not that old. Early forties, maybe." He glanced over his shoulder and switched lanes. "Back to your question; everything's on hold until SAC Wells decides what happens next."

"That's frustrating," she said. "You've put in a lot of hours on this case."

Not to mention how personal it had become. Every fiber in Blade's body demanded he tear apart whoever orchestrated the whole sick operation that had killed countless innocent people and nearly killed his friends. They had Forest and his daughter locked up, but somewhere out there, a puppet master still pulled strings from the shadows, and he wanted to find him.

"Sounds like Wells is making the right call. We've got too many suspects, and every lead dies before we can follow it. Maybe with fresh eyes, the case will gain traction."

"I'm guessing that's why you're here with me instead of working the case."

He reached over and turned the radio down until the music faded to background noise. The speedometer needle held steady at seventy-five, but his mind shifted gears to the case that had been eating at him.

"Actually, I caught a homicide a few days ago. It's not sitting right with me. I could use an extra brain. Mind if I walk you through it?"

Her smile said he had her attention. "Hit me."

"Male victim, forty-eight years old. Found stabbed to death inside his home. CSU traced the killer's movements by how the blood spatter painted the living room walls in arcs."

"Ay. That couldn't have been an easy scene to process."

"One of the worst I've ever worked. Furniture overturned. Glass from shattered picture frames crunching underfoot. The victim's face was unrecognizable." Blade flexed his fingers and tried not to picture it. "Took the crime scene team twelve hours to document everything."

"Run down the vic for me."

"Donald Florek. Corporate attorney. Worked for one of those big firms out of Ft. Lauderdale that charges a thousand dollars an hour to read contracts."

"Family?"

"Divorced. Ex-wife lives in California with their teenage daughter. Both have solid alibis." He'd spent hours on the phone with the Riverside County Sheriff's Department, confirming their whereabouts. "No current girlfriend. No close friends that we can find."

"Enemies?"

"None that anyone admits to knowing about," he said. "Florek's colleagues described him as quiet, professional, and unremarkable. The kind of man who went to work early and stayed late."

Tori nodded. "Okay, so that leaves the scene itself."

"Looks like the attack started in the foyer and ended in the living room. No signs of forced entry, so either the killer had a key and waited inside, or Florek let him in willingly. The unsub got Florek the second he walked through the front door. Blood trail leads to the living room, where the killer continued stabbing, even after Florek went down." He switched lanes and passed a VW bus with a surfboard strapped to the top, then continued, "CSU is still working the evidence, but so far nothing useful. No prints. No murder weapon."

"That's a lot of blood for such a tidy exit. Usually the handle gets slick and the killer ends up slicing their own hand when the knife hits resistance."

"A few drops of the killer's blood mixed in with all that carnage? It'll take the techs a while to test every sample. Like finding a specific grain of sand on a beach."

"If Florek is such a loner, who found the body?"

"Dog walker. Florek has a pitbull mix, and with his corporate attorney hours, he had a dog walker who handled morning and afternoon walks. She's taking care of the dog for now." Or maybe the dog was taking care of her. The woman's screams had brought three neighbors running, and she was still clinging to the dog when Blade arrived.

"Anything taken from the house?"

"Not that we can tell."

Tori sipped her coffee and slid the cup back into the holder. "Without seeing the scene, I can only hypothesize. The close-quarters violence and weapon choice signal rage." She shifted in her seat, warming to her analysis. "Knife assaults are intimate. The killer wanted it up close and personal. He wanted Florek to fight. Otherwise, he might have used a gun. But the lack of prints or even a shoe print indicates some level of control."

"That makes sense. The repeated stab wounds, especially to the face, are generally a sign of rage."

"Yes, or a fused mix of anger, possessiveness, power, or a desire to humble or debase the victim," she said. "There could also be ritual elements, but again, I'd need to see where Florek was attacked and the subsequent staging to verify. What about defensive wounds?"

"All over Florek's forearms where he'd tried to block the knife. Bruising too. The man had fought hard before going down."

"Which means your unsub had to be strong enough to overpower Florek and knew it," Tori said. "As you run down a suspect, look for cuts and bruises."

"Thank you, Captain Obvious," he said, grinning.

"Hey, do you want my help or not?"

They laughed.

"Of course I do," he said. "Care to take a look at what we've got later today?"

"Sure. But I'm not telling you anything you don't already know on some level."

"Your brain works differently from mine. You see evidence and connect it to patterns in behavior. Right now, I'm staring at a dead end, so I'll take any direction you can give."

The GPS announced their exit, and Blade guided the car onto the off-ramp toward Union Correctional. Pine trees lined both sides of the two-lane road, their branches creating a canopy that filtered the morning sunlight into scattered patches.

"Two hours, twenty-three minutes until destination," the GPS said.

Tori yawned. "I think I'm gonna take a nap. I got up way too early." She reclined her seat and closed her eyes. "Wake me when we get there."

Within minutes, her breathing settled into the deep, even rhythm that meant she'd actually fallen asleep. The woman could drop off anywhere.

He kept his eyes on the asphalt rolling toward them, white dashes clicking past the windshield in hypnotic succession. Finally, he could let his brain work the Florek case without interruption. Two hours of pine trees blurring past the windshield, exit signs counting down the miles, and the steady thrum of rubber meeting asphalt lay between them and Damien Sullivan's cell.

3

TORI STRETCHED, working the kinks out of her neck from sleeping against the window. The movement pulled at the bandage on her throat, sending a sharp pinch through the shallow cut. The sting brought back his voice, his breath on her skin. She sat up straighter. Fear didn't get to win today. Not here.

The first gate clanged open, jarring her more awake. She'd made this drive too many times for inmate evaluations, consults, and behavioral profiles. Every trip meant sitting across from men who lied without conviction and who smiled while describing murders. Normally, she could stay clinical, let the fascination of unraveling a criminal mind keep her from thinking too hard about the constant threat of violence. But today, she couldn't stop the nervous flutter in her chest.

Blade pulled into a visitor parking space and parked between the yellow lines. She left her laptop bag and phone in the car and climbed out into the humid Florida air.

Union Correctional was one of the largest prisons in the Florida system and housed no fewer than thirteen serial killers in its time. It was where monsters came to pay for what they'd done.

And she'd have to sit across from one and pretend she wasn't shaking.

"This place gives me hives." Blade stared at the guard tower like the sniper might pick him off for sport.

Big tough guy reduced to jelly by a penitentiary. She couldn't blame him. Probably dredged up memories he'd rather keep buried. "Want me to tuck you in the car with snacks and a blankie?"

The corner of his mouth twitched upward. "Don't tempt me."

"Then move."

Inside, the tang of chain-link and pine-scented disinfectant hit her nostrils. She would never get used to that smell. Or the way the armed guards at the security checkpoint tracked her every move. Professional paranoia at its finest. She'd been here dozens of times, yet the guards never seemed to recognize her. Fresh meat or familiar face, everyone got the same treatment.

"IDs," the guard said, extending his hand.

Tori pulled out her FDLE credentials and Blade handed the officer his Broward County detective shield.

"Purpose of visit," the guard asked with the flat tone of someone who'd asked the same question a thousand times.

"Inmate interview," Tori said. "Damien Sullivan."

The guard examined both sets of identification, comparing photos to faces, checking expiration dates, running the credentials through his computer system. Prison security didn't rush for anyone.

"Service weapon?" The guard's gaze flicked to Blade.

Blade unholstered his Glock and handed it over, along with his spare magazine. The guard locked both items in a numbered locker, then slid a plastic bin across the counter. "All personal belongings go in the bin. Weapons, cell phones, watches, electronics, pens, keys, everything."

Tori dropped her notebook in the bin and waited as Blade emptied his pockets, dropping in his notebook, pen, wallet, phone, keys, and the coins he seemed to always carry.

"Don't forget your watch. And belt."

"Right." He removed both and dropped them in the bin. "I think that's it."

The metal detector's arch waited beyond the checkpoint, its sensors calibrated to catch everything from belt buckles to dental fillings. Blade stepped through first, arms raised. A beep confirmed he'd cleared the scan, but he looked ready to bolt through the nearest exit.

She made it through and pulled him aside to wait for their escort. "What's with you?"

"I don't know, maybe it's all the bars and wire mesh. Or could be the big red panic buttons lining the walls." He swiped at a bead of sweat sliding down his temple. "Why's it so hot in here?"

"The AC's broken?"

The joke fell flat. This had to be difficult for him. Walking through these corridors, hearing the electronic locks engage, breathing air that tasted of sweat and desperation. His time in juvie might have been years ago, but some experiences carved themselves into your bones, and she could kick herself for not considering how this place would affect him.

"Detective St. James? Dr. Crew?" A correctional officer approached, keys jangling from his belt. His uniform was a khaki shirt with brown pants. Instead of a gun, the CO had pepper spray and a steel baton. "Name's Trussler. I'll be escorting you to the interview room."

They followed the CO through the first set of electronic doors. The heavy steel slammed shut behind them, sealing them into the institutional maze. Black eyes mounted in armored housings swiveled to follow. The cameras recorded every second for guards who probably ate donuts while watching visitors navigate this cinder block labyrinth.

Each secured door required Trussler to swipe his card and wait for an invisible hand in the control booth to buzz them through. The metallic clang of locks disengaging bounced off concrete walls painted that particular shade of institutional gray that existed nowhere else on earth.

"Well, this is unexpected."

Tori turned. Warden Maggie Quick stood near the control center, in her usual brown pants and white uniform shirt with her badge pinned above the left shirt pocket. She wore her black hair styled in a shaggy pixie cut, and Tori noticed the gray strands streaking through her part.

"Warden Quick." She hadn't expected to see the warden, who had a reputation for staying off the cell block and behind her desk. "Good morning. This is Detective—"

"St. James. Yes, I know. I've seen you on the news." The warden offered a nod at Blade in place of a handshake. She turned back to Tori. "You're not scheduled for evaluations today. What brings you in?"

"We're here to see an inmate," Tori said.

Warden Quick's dark eyes shifted between them. "Which inmate?"

"Damien Sullivan," Trussler interjected.

The warden's spine straightened as if someone had pulled a wire taut through her vertebrae.

She speared Tori with a stare. "What's the purpose of the visit?"

Tori started to speak, but Blade jumped in. "We're hoping Sullivan can remember some details from his time on the force. Following up on old leads."

Warden Quick's skeptical expression suggested she wasn't entirely convinced, but she nodded slowly.

"Fifteen minutes. Sullivan's in confinement, and I don't want him out of his cell longer than necessary."

"Understood," Tori said. "We'll keep it brief."

"See that you do." The warden nodded once to Trussler and waved to a guard behind the bulletproof glass.

The electronic buzzer made Tori flinch. Steel bars groaned open ahead of them, and they stepped into the corridor that would lead them deeper into the heart of the prison.

Trussler's heels clacked off the polished concrete like gunshots. Blade's shoulders stayed locked beside her. Some genius had cranked a morning talk show loud enough to wake the dead. The cheerful chatter about celebrity gossip crashed against the walls until it dissolved into meaningless noise. Probably the point. Keep the inmates distracted, keep them from thinking too hard about the bars.

They passed the commissary, where inmates lined up for their weekly purchases. Ramen noodles, instant coffee, and soap that cost three times what it should. A few faces turned toward them. Some curious, some bored. Some calculating. She recognized Aruajo from D-block, a lifer who'd been nothing but respectful during his sessions. He lifted his chin in greeting, and she returned the gesture.

Trussler motioned to the intersection ahead. "Sullivan's been moved to Interview Room C around the corner here. He's been cooperative this morning."

Cooperative. Prison speak for not throwing feces or threatening to kill everyone in sight. Sullivan's file painted a picture of a man who'd lost everything to alcohol and rage, taking the lives of four officers in a workplace shooting that had made national headlines. How he'd managed to avoid the death penalty, she wasn't sure.

They stopped outside the interview room, and Tori's pulse thudded as she peered through the reinforced glass rectangle in the door. Her stomach twisted so hard it nearly folded her in half.

There he was. Damien Sullivan. The man who claimed to have found her that night. A corrupt cop. A convicted killer. Probably a liar. And yet, her only shot at the truth.

He sat stiff at the metal table, shackled at the ankles and wrists. A chain snaked from his waist to a ring bolted in the center. Salt and pepper stubble covered hollow cheeks, and his skin had the gray pallor of someone who hadn't seen real sunlight in years.

If he found her that night, what else had he seen? What else had been buried along with her parents?

Trussler shifted and hooked his thumbs on his duty belt. "There's a panic button on the wall. Standard response time is fifty-two seconds. If something goes sideways, you'll be on your own until we breach."

"You ready for this?" Blade's blue eyes searched her face.

Ready? She glanced at Damien through the window. She'd been carrying her parents' unsolved murder her entire life like a stone on her back. Ready didn't factor into it. "No. But I'm going anyway."

"You heard the warden," Trussler said. "Fifteen minutes." The door buzzed open with a metallic shriek.

Sullivan straightened, drawing his chains across the table as he put his hands in his lap. She pulled out the chair across from him and sat. Blade slid into the one beside her.

This was it. Twenty-six years of questions but no answers. No leads. No witnesses. No hope. She'd read every detail that had trickled into public record. A mention here, a court filing there. Not once did she read a mention of Damien Sullivan.

"Mr. Sullivan, I'm Dr. Crew. This is Detective St. James." She laced her fingers on the cold metal. No aggression. Just control. "Corbin gave me your message. He said you specifically asked for this meeting. You said you were the responding officer the night my parents were murdered. You claimed you found me. We drove four hours for the rest of the story. Don't waste our time."

"What happened to your neck?" Damien didn't even try to hide his smirk.

Her fingers found the bandage before she could stop herself. Shoot. The stupid Band-Aid screamed weakness. She should've known better in this place.

"I guess I cut myself shaving." She dropped her hand. "I'm not here for small talk, so get to it."

"Sure you did." Damien's gaze slid to Blade. "I know you." He tilted his head, studying him like a specimen. "Yeah. You were that chubby kid I booked for the pier stabbing. Funny how that works. Me in chains, you with the badge."

Blade crossed his arms and leaned back. "Yeah. Hilarious. I'm not the one in shackles."

She wasn't about to let Sullivan yank them around. "Spit it out, Sullivan. Say what you have to say, or we walk."

"Ah, the feisty ones always made interrogations interesting. I miss that." He drew in a deep breath and pushed it out slowly. "But know what I miss most?"

"Whiskey? Beating your wife and kid?" Now it was her turn to smirk.

"Art." His voice didn't rise, didn't react. That was worse. "There's no color in this place. Even outside. It's all gray. Gray sky, gray concrete, gray . . . everything." He looked up at the ceiling. A gray water stain hovered overhead like a rain cloud.

He was stalling. Winding up to something.

"You wouldn't think a guy like me cared about art, would you?" Damien rested his shackled hands on the table. His index finger moved in slow circles on the steel, always returning to the same point. "But I've studied it. Not the paintings. What's underneath. The way the greats used patterns. Da Vinci knew it. Ever heard of the Divine Ratio? The Vitruvian Man?"

"Yeah." Tori's patience stretched thin as piano wire. "What's it got to do with my parents?"

"I'm getting there." The chains rattled as Damien shifted forward.

"Art isn't just pictures, it's patterns," he continued. "Messages hidden in plain sight. Divine architecture. Plato said that God geometrizes, that everything follows math. There's even a thirteenth-century manuscript with an image depicting God as the cosmic architect. Six hundred years later, a man named Benoît Mandelbrot used that image in his book *The Fractal Geometry of Nature*. Don't you see? All creation is governed by mathematical laws."

Good gracious, the man loved the sound of his own voice. She felt Blade shift in his chair. Fidgeting. Ready to shut this down. She caught his eye and gave the slightest shake of her head. Not yet.

"Three minutes. Then we walk," she said. "Get to the point."

Sullivan's stare bored into her. "The point is patterns, Dr. Crew. Your parents weren't random victims. Their deaths were part of a design. Mathematical precision. Divine geometry, you could say."

The words zinged through her bloodstream like a live wire. Finally. Something useful.

"What kind of design?"

His eyes went to the corner of the ceiling, then back to her.

"The kind that repeats. Over and over. Like fractals." He rolled a finger. "Your parents were part of something much larger than a simple home invasion. And it's still happening."

Blade's tapping foot stilled. "Fractals?"

Sullivan lit up with a smile. "Ah, you caught that. Very good. A fractal is a geometric shape that repeats itself at every scale. Zoom in on any part, and you see the same pattern repeated infinitely. Fractals appear everywhere. Art, medicine, technology. All over nature. From clouds to blood vessels. Fractals are God's fingerprint on creation."

She caught Blade's quick brow lift. He was as hooked as she was.

"There was this medieval monk," Sullivan said, animated now. "Udo of Aachen. Copyist, poet. Forgotten by history until a mathematician spotted something strange in one of his illuminations. The Star of Bethlehem. Drawn with fractals! Six centuries before Mandelbrot's mathematical equation."

Damien was pontificating again, and Tori wanted to grab his shackles and shake the words out of him.

"Corbin brought me a Bible, and I can see how it all connects. God's creation follows these same mathematical principles. Take the number seven. It repeats throughout Scripture as a symbol of divine completion. Seven days of creation, seven churches in Revelation, seven seals, seven trumpets. Patterns. Everywhere."

A siren split the air, stabbing her eardrums. Red light strobed across Damien's face, painting him in crimson. Blade shot to his feet as the door slammed open. Trussler rushed in with another corrections officer.

A voice over the intercom cut through the sirens. "All inmates return to cells immediately. Lockdown in effect. All inmates return to cells."

"Interview's over," Trussler barked, reaching for Damien's chains. "Situation on C-block."

"Wait." Tori was on her feet too. Four hours in the car for this? For Damien to ramble about Renaissance painters and mathematical theories? No. Not when she was this close. "We need two more minutes."

"Lockdown. No exceptions." The second CO, a thick-necked man with sergeant stripes, grabbed Damien's arm.

"The pattern—" Damien tried to twist back toward her.

"Move it, Sullivan." Trussler unlocked the chain from the table ring and hauled Damien to his feet.

"Our fifteen minutes aren't up," Blade said, stepping toward the officers. "We drove four hours for this interview."

"And you can drive four hours back," the sergeant said. "Lockdown means lockdown."

The pressure behind her sternum built to an unbearable point. All that buildup about patterns and divine geometry, and now they were dragging Damien away before he could tell her anything useful.

"Please." She hated the desperation in her voice, but she couldn't stop it. "The pattern. What is it? What happened that night?"

Damien struggled against the guards, chains rattling like wind chimes in a storm. "Give me one minute!"

"Not happening." The sergeant jerked Damien's other arm.

The toes of Damien's prison-issued shoes scraped against the floor as they pulled him away.

He strained to look back at her. "It started with them. Your mother. She knew about the fractals."

"Move it," the sergeant said, jerking his arm.

Sullivan's face flushed red as he struggled against the chains, against the officers, against time running out. The veins in his neck bulged. "It wasn't just me there that night! It was the start of the pattern! Barclay lied!"

Barclay? Millie Beach Police Chief Barclay?

"Lied about what?" she demanded.

The officers shoved him through the doorway. He twisted in their grip, eyes wild and locking with hers one last time.

"The report is a lie! A cover-up! Barclay created a whole second story—there's a second murder book!" Damien fought against the guards, desperate now.

The door slammed shut, cutting Damien off midsentence, but his words hung in the air like gunpowder smoke. She felt her hands begin to tremble. Her knees went loose, like the floor had dropped six inches without warning.

A second murder book.

4

A VOICE DRIFTED through layers of darkness. Muffled. Sound through water. Male. Familiar, but . . . blurred in the fog that had become Stryker's world.

Move. Open your eyes. Do something.

Nothing. His body remained a prison. Unresponsive to every command his mind screamed.

"I'm sorry, Stryker." The voice carried regret. "This wasn't supposed to go this way."

Who are you? What happened?

He tried to force his eyelids open. *C'mon, muscles. Respond.*

The effort exhausted him. Consciousness began to slip away like sand through fingers.

Fingers. Move your fingers.

Were they moving? He couldn't tell. The disconnect between intention and action had become absolute. His toes. Could he feel them?

The question dissolved, and darkness pulled him deeper.

Twenty-six years melted away.

"Third donut, King? How do you stay so skinny eating like that?"

Stryker glanced at Damien Sullivan across the patrol car's center console. His partner's gut strained against his uniform shirt, the buttons working overtime. Steam rose from their coffee cups in the October chill.

"Maybe you should trade beers for dumbbells," Stryker said. "Then you could lift more than your cup, there."

Damien snorted into his coffee. "Funny. Real funny." He gestured at the donut box between them. "Seriously, though. Your metabolism's unnatural. You eat twice as much as me and look like you stepped off a magazine cover."

"Yeah, *Mad* magazine maybe." Stryker pushed the last bite of donut into his mouth and wiped his glazed fingers on a crumpled napkin.

Damien laughed, and Stryker listened to the dispatch chatter. Three a.m. in Millie Beach meant mostly quiet streets, domestic disturbances, and the occasional drunk driver. This time, dispatch reported a shift change.

"How'd your fight go last weekend? You never told me," Damien said.

"Good. Real good." The buzz of the fight hadn't worn off. The crowd. The lights. That perfect combo of leg kick, jab, teep, and overhand right that dropped his opponent in the second round. He'd trained that combo a thousand times, but man, it felt incredible to watch it land just like it was supposed to. Earned him another interview with *Martial Arts* magazine. His fourth in the last year.

"That thud when the guy hit the mat? Best sound in the world."

"Ah dude, wish I'd been there. It must be cool to watch a guy go down like that and know it was your fists that did it."

Stryker had to admit, some part of him lived for it. But underneath sat something else. Something he didn't want to examine too closely. Better to focus on the last glazed chocolate. Two bites and it was gone.

"Scouts showed up. International promotion." He brushed crumbs from his uniform pants.

Damien's coffee cup froze halfway to his lips. "Scouts? What kind of scouts?"

"The kind setting up a meeting Thursday." The words tasted better than the donut. "They want to discuss opportunities."

Damien whistled. "That's big time. Like, pay-per-view big time."

"Could be." The empty street stretched ahead through the windshield. A streetlight flickered overhead, throwing broken shadows across the cracked asphalt. On. Off. On. Off. The rhythm matched the uncertainty bouncing around his head. "They're talking contracts. Travel. Real money."

"What about this?" Damien's thick fingers swept toward the dashboard, the radio, the badge clipped to Stryker's chest. "Your career? You're good police, King. Better than most of the nitwits we work with. You just gonna quit?"

The question had been chewing at him for weeks. He'd pinned on this badge to make a difference, to stand between decent people and the garbage that preyed on them. Some shifts, he walked away knowing he'd done exactly that. Lately, though . . . Too many nights like this one, sitting in a patrol car eating donuts while the real problems festered in places his badge couldn't reach.

He took a sip of coffee that burned down his throat, buying him a few seconds to sort through the mess in his head. They caught the dealers. Locked up a few wife beaters. Pulled drunk drivers off the road before they killed somebody. But every arrest felt like slapping a bandage on a severed artery.

"We're catching bad guys, keeping people safe. But . . . I don't know . . . There's got to be more than just arresting perps and putting them behind bars."

"More how?"

"Reaching people before they become criminals. Helping the ones headed down the wrong path. Kids especially."

Kids like Aaron. Thirteen years old, already running drugs for his older brother. Three more years and he'd graduate to adult prison. Where was the intervention for kids like that?

Damien's eyebrows climbed toward his receding hairline. "And you think full-contact combat sports is the answer?"

A piece of sugar glaze clung to his uniform shirt. He picked it off and dropped it in the donut box, watching it land among the crumbs. One scout had talked about marketing himself through community outreach programs and youth training centers. Places where kids could learn discipline instead of destruction. Better to strap gloves on their fists than wait in a cruiser for the next body to drop. If character took root while he was at it, even better.

"I just feel like my heart isn't completely in this anymore." He shrugged. "Like God's preparing me for something different."

"God." Damien huffed but kept his thoughts to himself. For once.

"Unit 47, this is Dispatch. Do you copy?"

Damien grabbed the radio. "47, go ahead."

"Unit 47, respond to 5486 Flores Drive. Possible burglary in progress. Neighbor reports male subject fleeing residence."

"10-4, Dispatch, 47 en route." Damien shoved the shifter forward, tires spitting gravel as the cruiser lunged into the dark.

Less than ten minutes later, Stryker stepped out of the patrol car. One hand on his service weapon, the other holding his heavy-duty flashlight. He scanned the exterior while Damien radioed their arrival.

The house on Flores was a single-story ranch with a two-car garage. Standard white stucco with black colonial hurricane shutters. It sat dark except for a yellow porch light throwing a jaundiced glow that pulled in moths and gnats, wings pattering against the bulb. Windows showed nothing. The air held nothing. Driveway bare. House sealed tight, waiting.

"Back door." Stryker jerked his flashlight toward the rear.

Damien dipped his chin once. No extra talk. They'd run this play too many times to need it.

Stryker cut along the siding, heels rolling soft, body low under the windows. Curtains hung still. No movement. He eased to the corner where the fence met the stucco and lifted just enough to scan over. Pool water caught the rear porch light in a dull shimmer. Empty deck. Empty yard.

He pushed through the gate, cleared each corner, then stopped at the sliding glass door. A gap no wider than a fist cut the black frame. An invitation no homeowner ever meant to give.

His radio crackled. Damien's clipped words came through: "In position."

Stryker raised his weapon, tracked the sight line across the frame, and closed the last feet to the door. The glass threw his outline back at him. A black figure, gun leveled. He tipped his head to the narrow gap, listening.

Nothing. The house held its breath.

He thumbed the mic. "Ready."

A pause. Then Damien: "Three. Two. One."

Stryker shoved the door wide and slid inside, muzzle up, flashlight braced beneath the barrel, weight pitched to the balls of his feet.

The dining room opened in front of him. A polished wood table, six stiff-backed chairs aligned like soldiers. China stacked behind glass, untouched. Nothing broken. No overturned chairs. No rush of violence had swept through here.

He moved on. Boots groaned against tile as he cut around the corner into the kitchen. Square room, the island dead center. Stove jammed into the counter run on the right. Refrigerator sunk into the wall on the left, its white face smudged with handprints. Beyond it, the sink cut into the counter, positioned to stare out over the inky water of the pool.

Stryker paused in the kitchen. Something was off. Too still.

The radio crackled. "Living room clear."

Stryker moved down the narrow hall linking front to back. His shoulder brushed bare drywall. The hall ran narrow and undecorated, the kind of stripped quiet that came before something terrible. No family portraits. No framed school pictures. Just nail holes and bare paint, like someone had scraped the life off the walls.

The carpet muffled his bootsteps as he slowed at the first door. Bunk beds against the wall. Picture books spread belly-down on the floor. Plastic dolls and dinosaurs frozen mid-battle. The air tasted of crayon wax. He yanked the closet open. Ran his hand over the child-sized clothes on hangers. Nothing.

The second bedroom held a crib against the far wall. Changing table lined with folded blankets. A rocking chair angled in the corner like it had been set in place and left. Everything spotless. No bottles tipped over, no toys dumped, no faint wail cracking the silence. Empty crib. Empty room. Where was the baby?

"Stryker," Damien yelled. "Master bedroom. Now."

He rushed down the hall, drawn to the thin wash of light leaking from the open doorway. The copper stench struck before he crossed the threshold.

Blood. Lots of it.

The bedroom reeked of iron and death.

Damien braced a hand on the bed, bent over the woman sprawled across the mattress. Blood soaked the sheets and pooled beneath her torso, then ran off the mattress edge in a slow ribbon, spreading across the hardwood in a glossy black sheet. Stryker's boots stuck a half-second with each step. Knife wounds striped her back in jagged slashes, the flesh torn open. Black hair clumped in wet strands spreading across the pillow.

"She's gone." Damien straightened, his hand flexing once before he pointed to the floor. "Other side."

A man lay collapsed on his back, body twisted as if he'd fallen mid-struggle. His chest hitched, shallow draws dragging air in and out. His throat was hacked nearly through, and the cut yawned wide from one ear to the other. Blood seeped with each faint throb of his heartbeat, pumping onto the hardwood, stretching the pool wider.

Stryker shoved his weapon into its holster and dropped to his knees beside him. The man's skin had gone slack and colorless, and his pulse flickered at the edge of nothing. CPR would blast the rest of his blood onto the floor. Pointless. He snatched a blanket from the bed's footrail, crushed it against the wound, and leaned his weight into the pressure. The cloth drank the blood instantly, blooming red beneath his hands.

"This is Unit 47." He jammed the transmit button, his other hand locked on the wound, blanket squelching blood through his fingers. "Need paramedics, homicide, and backup. Two down. One critical."

The man's lids twitched open. No focus in them, just a cloudy glaze. Bubbles leaked at his mouth, a guttural gurgle sliding out before his chin sagged. Still breathing. Barely. The pulse under Stryker's fingers fluttered like moth wings against glass, but it was there.

"No." Stryker shoved harder. "Breathe. Stay with me. You don't stop here."

Across the room, Damien's voice cut sharp. "King. Over here."

Stryker flicked his gaze up. Damien stood planted at the closet door, his stare locked past the dangling clothes. Hands loose at his sides, jaw bunched. Not much rattled Damien, yet his skin looked bleached in the lamplight.

"I can't leave him," Stryker said, still grinding down on the pressure.

Damien crossed the room and dropped to a knee beside him. He pressed two fingers to the man's neck, held them there a beat too short, and pulled Stryker's hands off the wound.

"He's already gone, King."

Stryker felt the faintest twitch under his palm before Damien's grip pulled him clear. A breath. Maybe. Or the body unclenching, as Damien said it was over. He couldn't tell anymore.

Abandoning the man somehow still felt like desertion. But Stryker couldn't save him. No one could. He stayed on his knees a beat longer, then rocked back, rose, and crossed the room.

Stryker froze.

The closet wasn't empty. A girl—tiny, no more than four—was curled into the corner, swallowed by hanging clothes. Her knees vanished beneath stick-thin arms. She rocked, steady as a pendulum, back and forth, back and forth, as if the motion alone kept her anchored.

He sank to both knees again, close but not crowding her. "Hey, sweetheart. You're safe. Nobody's going to touch you."

No flicker in her eyes. No shift in her rhythm. The world beyond her rocking didn't seem to exist.

Stryker cut a look at Damien. The man stood stone still, saying nothing. The house pressed in with silence, broken only by the fan whirring overhead and the ghostly hiss of air escaping the dead man sprawled on the floor.

5

BLADE DRILLED HIS FOCUS into the asphalt, but every shift in Tori's posture registered in his periphery. She remained anchored in the passenger seat, head down, eyes on her computer.

Four hours of near silence. Four hours of tension cracking between them like humidity before a thunderstorm. The only breaks came when his phone rang. Sergeant Acker calling twice about the Florek case, then the lab tech with preliminary blood work results, then Acker again reminding him of the evidence chains that needed documenting. Each call dragged him back into the machinery of the job.

Between calls, Tori's fingers moved across her laptop keyboard in steady bursts. *Click-click-click,* pause*, click-click-click.* She'd claimed she needed to get Sullivan's statements down before they blurred. Now she typed like the memory might vanish if she stopped.

The brief flashes he caught of her screen between glances at the road showed lines about Sullivan's tangents, cross-links to fractals, pattern theory, and a bulleted list capped with one phrase that snagged him every time: *a second murder book.*

The GPS announced they had twelve minutes remaining to Millie Beach. Almost back where they'd started this morning. Back to the parking lot where some psychopath had pressed steel against Tori's throat. The bandage on her neck caught his eye every time she turned her head.

His phone buzzed against the center console. Acker again. He let it go to voicemail.

Tori shifted, finally lifting her head from the screen. She closed her laptop and sat back. Dark circles rimmed her eyes. She looked like someone had twisted her emotions through a wringer and hung her up to dry.

"You good?" he asked.

She nodded without looking at him. "Yeah."

The single word carried the weight of everything unsaid. No, she wasn't good. None of this was good. But she was Tori, and Tori didn't break down in passenger seats. She processed. She analyzed. She built walls around the damage and kept moving forward.

The familiar outline of Kingdom MMA appeared ahead. Home base. Neutral ground. A place where they could finally hash through what had happened back there without the road noise and phone calls creating distance between them.

The rush of the gym hit the second they stepped inside. Warm air thick with sweat and testosterone. Rubber mats giving underfoot. Runners drumming on treadmills, a steady grind of metal plates, the bag in the corner taking hits in a hard, steady rhythm. The place breathed work.

FDLE Special Agent Corbin King stood behind a bench station, one knee braced on the floor, steady hands spotting a younger kid pushing through his last rep. Sweat darkened his navy FDLE T-shirt, clinging across the defined lines of his shoulders. His eyes caught Blade's from across the room in one glance.

Corbin tapped the kid's shoulder, said something quietly, then lowered the bar.

"How'd it go?" Corbin's tone stayed light, but the pinch in his brows told Blade he already suspected the answer.

Blade hiked a thumb over his shoulder. "Let's take it upstairs."

Corbin swiped a towel off a rack and wiped his hands as he turned to the kid. "I'm out. Hit your cooldown and log your weights."

The younger man nodded, towel swinging as he waved them off.

Blade's boots clanged on the metal stairs. Tori climbed ahead of him, one hand grazing the rail. Corbin came behind them, his heavier step setting the steel treads rattling with each rise.

At the top, Blade pushed open the thick door marked "Private." Stryker's office ran more like the nerve center of a surveillance unit than a gym. Three desks, each lined with curved monitors glowing in soft blues and whites. Screens streamed footage from the weight stations, the front lot, even the alley cameras Jett had installed for "situational awareness."

"What's that smell, chica? Did you burn the coffee again?" Tori hoisted herself up on the table beneath the wide one-way glass overlooking the gym floor and sat cross-legged.

"ATF motto, Crew. Burn it. Test it. File it. Coffee's just field research." Harlee Bay leaned back just far enough to cut Tori a look, mouth tilting in that near-smile she rarely let out. The black hoodie she wore had the Kingdom MMA crest printed in red along one sleeve. Strands of blond had slipped free of a half-knot on her head.

Blade propped a shoulder against the doorframe, glancing at Harlee's ultrawide monitor setup. Data crawled across one screen like ants after sugar. "You still even work for the ATF, Bay? Or they just pay you to haunt that keyboard?"

Harlee's head turned half an inch, enough for the warning in her eyes to hit him straight on. "Keep talking. I'll enter your social into the national forfeiture database. Let's see how long your condo stays yours."

Before he could fire back, Jett Nu rose from the desk beside her. The tech billionaire was dressed in his usual. Slacks, vest, French cuffs rolled to the forearms. His dark curls pushed past where a collar would've been, and Blade couldn't tell if he needed a haircut or if he'd shelled out two hundred bucks for that look.

"She does work," Jett said, voice calm as ever. "Intelligence Research Specialists operate anywhere they have a secure system. And she's got the best one here. ATF headquarters can't touch our encryption."

Harlee arched an eyebrow, pleased but pretending not to be. "Translation, I've got better toys here."

Blade grinned. "You're too smart to be in the field anyway. Let the rest of us catch shrapnel."

"Yeah," Corbin added as he crossed the room. "Why waste a mind like hers dismantling bombs when she can save the world from here?"

Luna spread her arms, gesturing to the stack of color-coded binders containing the Warrior kids' case notes. "What am I then, chopped liver?"

Corbin stopped in front of her. "Of course not," he said quietly. "You're saving the world too." He bent and kissed her. Slow, certain, like a man who'd finally learned what love was.

Blade watched them and let his breath settle. Same two kids who used to sneak outside after sparring, leaning into each other like nothing else existed. Married now, but the same them. They'd come so close to losing everything. Blade's attention cut to Tori perched on the table before returning to Corbin's hand tracing along Luna's dark hair. Maybe love like that belonged in real life after all.

Blade cleared his throat. "Hey, Jett. You get Tori's text this morning? About checking the exterior cameras for the guy who jumped her?"

"Sure did." Jett gestured toward Harlee with a flick of his pen. "We've got something."

Harlee's tattooed hands worked the mouse and keyboard simultaneously. One monitor flashed through feeds of the front lot, side entrance, and a dark sliver of alley beyond the dumpsters.

"He parked two blocks east," she said. "Walked in like he owned the place. Hoodie up. Kept his head tilted down every time he passed a camera."

"He knew where the blind angles were," Jett said. "Never let his face hit full frame."

Blade stepped nearer and braced a palm against the desk to study the loop. "So, he did his homework. Never let us see his face."

"Fact." Harlee toggled to a magnified frame. The man crossed under a parking light. "But here's his mistake." She jabbed a finger at the image. "My baby doesn't need a face."

Tori watched Harlee's screen from the table. "Your baby?"

Jett chuckled. "She's talking about our motion-based biometric capture. Every frame pulls a signature. Stride rhythm, skeletal alignment, limb rotation. Within 87 percent confidence, we can ID a person walking through a fog bank at midnight."

Blade buried a hand in his pocket and raked the loose change. "Translation?"

"It reads how you move," Harlee said. "Like a fingerprint in motion. Might take a while to scour through local surveillance footage, but we'll get him."

"Still can't get over the fact we've got CIA-level tech sitting in a gym office," Luna said.

Jett's grin widened. "Who do you think the government licensed it from?"

"You nerds and your tech toys," Tori said. "Don't waste too much time on it, okay? We've got bigger fish."

Like Sullivan's stunt at the prison.

Blade nodded, coins and keys clinking in his pocket. The motion helped him think, same as the rhythm of writing in his notebook. Little cadence loops kept his brain wired in usable lanes.

"Work it anyway," he said, dropping into the worn leather armchair.

Harlee yanked a drawer open and tossed something across the room. "Here."

Blade caught it one-handed. A green rubber ball, covered in soft spikes. He squeezed. The thing gave under pressure and expanded again like memory foam. Small, firm, almost satisfying. "What's this?"

"Sanity," Harlee said. "Yours and mine. You keep rattling change, tapping desks, and clicking pens like you're sending some secret code. I'm one minute away from hurling your keys out the window." She pointed at him with her pen.

"It's a stim ball," Luna said. "Use that instead of turning every room into your own drumline."

He turned it in his palm. Felt weirdly good, holding something meant to channel the restless current always working through him, that too-fast hum in his head that never really found neutral. "Thanks," he said. "Guess I owe you one."

"Thank her for my sake too," Tori said with a half smile. "The last hour in the car, you were clicking the cruise button like a percussion section."

He smirked. "You really want me quiet? Not sure I'd recognize myself like that."

"Try me," she said.

The corner of his mouth hitched. He squeezed the ball and let the room settle. His mind kept circling back to that concrete visitation room. Sullivan spitting out Barclay's name and accusations about a second murder book. If any of it was true, someone had kept those files buried for decades.

If Sullivan was telling the truth.

Tori's reflection ghosted across the one-way glass overlooking the gym. Shoulders slumped. Hands limp in her lap. The woman who'd razored him with jokes that morning—the skilled analyst who could stare down a killer without flinching—had vanished. He was looking at the fourteen-year-old girl he'd pulled out from under a pier in the dark, the one whose scream had been the first thing in his life he'd ever run toward.

She'd needed him then. She needed him now.

He was going to find that second book for her.

"The stalker in the lot wasn't the only excitement today," Blade said. "We made our little field trip to Union Correctional."

That got everyone's attention.

He leaned his elbows on his knees. "Damien Sullivan gave us the runaround at first. Started quoting math formulas and talking about fractals and God's divine pattern. Claimed he was at the Crew house the night of the murders."

Every head turned toward Tori. She uncrossed her arms and slid off the table edge. "He said the official report on my parents' murder is a lie. A cover-up. And that there's a second murder book somewhere—one that proves it. He said Millie Beach chief of police Dean Barclay is involved. But lockdown cut him off before he could give us details."

The room went quiet for three heartbeats.

Jett frowned, spinning the pen between his fingers. "Murder book? Someone built a whole second case file?"

"Everything from crime-scene photos down to the janitor's statement. The whole life story of a homicide investigation. Only detectives touch it." Blade rolled the ball between his hands, the nubs dragging faint lines across his skin. "If he's saying there's another one, that means someone built a second record and buried the first."

"But why would there be a second one?" Luna asked. "If Barclay was covering it up from the start, why keep any record at all?"

"Because no record is a red flag," Blade said. "A double homicide with a surviving child? You can't just pretend that never happened. Something has to exist on paper. Something that answers the basic questions and lets the case look finished."

He turned the spike ball in his palm.

"Barclay wrote the first book as the official story. Anyone who came digging would find a clean file and stop there."

"And the second one?" Luna asked.

"Damien's," Tori said quietly. "The real version. What actually happened that night. He kept it as leverage. If Barclay ever turned on him, Damien had proof."

"One book for the lie," Blade said. "One book for leverage."

"You believe him?" Corbin asked.

Silence filled the space between them. Tori's gaze found his, steady, searching. Blade saw the question there too. The same balance of doubt and need that had followed them since the interview room slammed shut.

"Not sure yet," he said. "But if he's telling the truth about that second murder book, I want it in my hands. Now."

"You know, I gave him a Bible." Corbin sighed. "I was hoping God could break through that mess of a heart."

Fractals. Divine patterns. All that talk from Sullivan clicked now.

"Don't write him off. Seems like he was actually reading it," Blade said. "When'd you see him last?"

"I haven't seen him since I brought him that Bible. That was the same day he asked me to have Tori come see him. Since then, he's refused to see me," Corbin said.

"Maybe this confession is his way of showing he's changed," Tori said. "Damien's warped way of owning up to the corruption everyone suspected he had his hands in."

Blade didn't think Sullivan's grip on Scripture was about devotion. Neither was his confession. It was survival. He twisted verses into formulas, equations of blame and redemption, like a man trying to calculate a way out of his own damnation.

He didn't voice that opinion, though. "We can't just take him at his word. We'll have to prove Barclay's police report is a lie."

"How?" Corbin asked.

Blade tossed his spikey ball straight up and caught it. "By finding that second murder book."

Harlee swiveled her chair so her back was facing her monitor. "Where do you even start with something that buried?"

"We start with the one that's filed. The original Crew murder book. That's the first thing we do," Tori said.

Blade nodded. "The problem is access. Millie Beach Police handled the investigation and never requested outside help from Broward Sheriff's Office or FDLE. No invite, no jurisdiction."

"Can't Tori get the file? As a witness, she has standing," Corbin said. "They might not give you everything, but if you put in a formal request for your own statement and the initial report, they'd have a hard time stonewalling you."

"You think I haven't tried?" Tori shook her head. "I've put in requests. I've had FDLE brass push them up the chain. Every time I get the same answer. The case is technically still open, and I'm the surviving witness. Never mind that I don't remember a thing from that night. They won't let me within ten feet of the murder book."

Blade saw her frustration bubbling up. Of course she'd tried. She'd tried everything.

"Maybe I can get access," he said. "Broward's not FDLE. If anyone at Millie Beach PD asks, I'm working an active case with a potential connection. Might get me in the door."

"Make the call," Harlee said.

Blade looked at Tori. Her chin lifted in a slight nod.

He punched in the number for Millie Beach PD Records and hit speaker.

Tori didn't take a chair. She circled the room, arms locked across her chest.

"Millie Beach PD, Records Division."

"Detective St. James, Broward. I need a homicide file, 1998. Nikos and Ji-Yeon Crew."

Rapid keystrokes rattled through. "That file's flagged. You'll need my supervisor."

"Transfer me," Blade said.

Tinny hold music bled from the receiver, some looping track no one cared enough to update. He rolled the ball beneath his thumb, pressing hard until the plastic teeth bit into his skin. He could get used to this thing. Perfect tool for calls and conversations when people stretched sentences, spoon-feeding details his head had already stacked, labeled, and shoved aside three thoughts back.

"Supervisor Corso," the man identified himself, sounding annoyed. "You're after the Crew file?"

"Correct," Blade said. "Working a related case. Need to see originals."

"No can do, Detective. File's sealed under court order. Protection on the surviving child."

Bureaucrats blocking him was one thing. A judge's seal? Whole other beast.

He glanced at Tori, who pinned him with a look that said, *I told you so.*

"Supervisor Corso, the surviving victim's grown. My case ties in—"

"Detective, I'm staring at the status on my screen." Keys tapped on his end. "It isn't only sealed. It's Internal Affairs flagged. Sensitive probe. Locked down."

Internal Affairs? That made zero sense. Unless it had something to do with Damien Sullivan.

"When was the IA flag added?"

"Same time as the judicial seal—1998."

That didn't have anything to do with Sullivan's workplace shooting. Someone had locked this case down from day one. Wrapped it in enough red tape to strangle any future investigation.

"Which commanding officer requested the judicial seal and IA probe?"

"That would be . . ." A pause. "Detective Dean Barclay."

The ball slipped from his fingers and bounced to the floor. Sullivan hadn't lied. At least not about Barclay's involvement. No sense battling it over the phone. It would take a hefty authority to bulldoze Millie Beach PD into releasing those records.

"Appreciate your help." He ended the call and rose from his chair, snatched the green ball.

"A judicial seal. An IA flag. Sounds like a wall of red tape," Corbin said.

Blade stared at the blank whiteboard at the opposite end of the room. Every official door was slammed shut.

"That sounded like a dead end," Jett said.

"Worse." He fired the ball across the room, and Tori caught it between her palms. "It's a fortress. Judicially sealed, requested by Barclay himself to protect you. Flagged by Internal Affairs to keep any cop from touching it. He's got us completely boxed in. We can't get to it. Not officially."

"Told you." Tori rolled the green ball between her fingers. "I'm stealing this."

"Oh no you're not," Harlee said. "We're not going back to Mr. Jingle-Jangles."

Tori smiled and lobbed the ball back, then climbed back onto the table and folded herself cross-legged, like always.

For a heartbeat, she wasn't Dr. Crew, the FDLE's newest behavioral asset with seven years of post-grad and a dissertation on predatory impulse. She wasn't the expert who could strip a killer's psyche down to the bone in under an hour. She was just a fourteen-year-old girl again. The one whose screams had ripped across the pier that night. The one he'd hauled out of the dark and refused to let go.

Luna hooked a finger around the handle of her coffee mug and locked eyes with Corbin. "There's truth in what your father said."

Corbin's shoulders stiffened. His gaze cut toward Blade. "Barclay was there that night. Question is, what did he bury?"

"We still don't know if Damien was there. All we have is his word." Tori looped a shoelace tight around her finger, skin blanching, then let it loose. Air hissed out between her teeth. "The whole trip was pointless. He dragged me out there just to watch me squirm. I should've left all this buried in the past where it belongs. I feel so stupid."

Blade leaned across the table to her. He set his phone on the table and placed a palm on her shoulder. "You are not stupid. You deserve answers about your parents."

Tori snapped her shoelace again, the welt already red on her finger. "Yeah? I don't see how I'll ever get them short of solving the case, which we can't do because we can't access the files, and I can't remember that night at all."

"There's a way around it," Blade said. "Kiara's a records administrator. She handles sealed files every day."

Her head jerked. "No."

"Why not? She could walk into the evidence warehouse, pull the Crew file, no roadblocks."

"She'd lose her job. I-I don't even know her, Blade." She shook her head, strands of hair brushing her cheeks. "No. Absolutely not."

"You wouldn't be the one asking," he said. "I will. She's a smart woman. Let her choose."

Her eyes cut around the room then back to him. "You'd risk that? For me?"

"Especially for you."

The phone buzzed against the table. Tori scooped it up before he could move, shoved it into his hand. The corner of her mouth curled with something that wasn't quite a smile. "Speaking of."

Honey-blond hair caught the light in the thumbnail, a frame of sun across her face. Green eyes crinkled mid-laugh, frozen bright. Tori had always teased him about his taste in women, but Kiara was knockout gorgeous in a girl-next-door kind of way.

"Give me a second." He swiped his thumb across his cell to take the call, heading for the exit. "Hey, you."

"Detective Blade St. James, world changer! How's my guy doing? You heading home yet?"

"No." He sighed. "Still at it." He propped a shoulder against the wall.

"Oh no. My tireless hero. Everything okay?"

"Yeah, it's just been one of those days."

"Oh that's too bad," Kiara said. "I hate it when you have rough days, but I know you're investing your time in what matters."

"Listen, need to ask a favor. Case-related."

"You know I'm always happy to help. We can go over it at dinner."

Dinner. Right. The beach picnic. The one she'd set up and he'd forgotten all about. He pressed a palm against his forehead. "Yeah, sure. We can talk then. I might run late. That work?"

"Of course. And hey, even if you can't make it tonight, I'll understand. Just shoot me a text."

How did she always pull that trick, lobbing him an exit like missing plans was a public service instead of him letting her down? "Thanks. I'll call you soon."

The line died. Kiara's photo glowed from the screen. World changer. Hero. She actually believed that. She gave him a free pass and somehow made him feel bigger for taking it.

Before he could shove his phone back in his pocket, the screen lit up again. Acker.

"St. James."

"Blade, hey. Listen, I was wondering if Dr. Crew could consult on the Florek case. We're dead in the water, and I need to see some movement."

"That's actually a great idea." He straightened off the wall. "I'll ask her right now."

"Appreciate it. Sooner the better."

The line went dead. Perfect timing. Tori needed something to focus on besides Sullivan's games and dead-end files.

He pushed back through the door. "Hey, I gotta get going." The team looked up from their screens and conversations. "Tori, you willing to take a look at my crime scene? Acker's asking for a consult."

She uncrossed her legs and pushed off the table, already reaching for her bag. "Yeah. I could use the distraction."

They headed for the stairs. The gym noise swelled around them. Weights dropping, someone calling out rep counts, the steady thump of gloves on heavy bags.

Outside, the late afternoon sun cut harsh angles across the parking lot. Tori stopped beside his Charger, arms crossed. "So what'd your girlfriend say about helping us access the file?"

Girlfriend? No, Kiara wasn't his girlfriend. She was the girl he was dating. Different thing entirely.

"I figured asking her to access the case files would be better in person. We'd planned a beach picnic at sunset tonight."

"Fun," she said, but the smile didn't reach her eyes. She opened the door. "We'd better hurry. You don't keep a woman like Kiara waiting." She dropped behind the wheel of her Range Rover and slammed the door.

Blade dug out his phone. He typed quickly:

Case running late. Rain check on the picnic? I'll make it up to you.

Her response came immediately:

Of course. Be safe. Love you.

The words on the screen—*Love you*—should have thrilled him. Instead, they sat heavy. Kiara meant safety, the kind of soft place a man like him wasn't supposed to get. Gardens, books, quiet nights that stretched forward like a promise. A future he wasn't sure he deserved.

But his gaze tracked Tori checking her cut in the mirror.

No pause, no hesitation, he'd picked the case over Kiara. He wanted the crime scene. Wanted Tori at his side. Even knowing Kiara waited with sunsets and takeout, he stayed with the mess.

What did that say about him? He shoved the thought down before it could take root. Some questions didn't need answers.

His phone vibrated with a new text from Kiara:

Don't forget to eat something. 😘

He tucked the phone in his pocket and climbed into his car.

6

THE REAR DOOR of Donald Florek's house opened into Florek's kitchen. Tori stepped into the open-floor-plan home behind Blade. Granite countertops gleamed under the afternoon light streaming through plantation shutters. Everything pristine, untouched. The contrast hit her before they'd even entered the living room.

"Gloves," Blade said, pulling a pair from his jacket pocket.

Tori snapped them on and followed him down a hallway lined with expensive artwork. The house whispered money. Persian rugs, crown molding, furniture that cost more than most people's cars.

The smell hit her.

Blood had its own signature. Metallic, organic, impossible to mistake once you'd encountered it as many times as Tori had. But this wasn't just blood. This was violence soaked into carpet fibers and drywall, the kind that lingered weeks after the scene had been processed.

Tori stopped in the doorway and let her eyes adjust. The blood spatter painted the walls in arcs that told a story of movement, brutality, and overwhelming force. Dark burgundy streaks climbed halfway up the cream-colored walls, some reaching toward the ceiling in perfect parabolas that mapped the killer's swing patterns.

An overturned coffee table lay on its side, one leg snapped clean off. Glass from shattered picture frames crunched under her feet as she stepped carefully into the room. A broken lamp sat askew near the fireplace, its shade torn and hanging at an odd angle.

But something felt wrong.

She crouched near the largest blood pool, where Florek's body had been found. The stain had darkened to an almost black color. She studied the spatter patterns on the wall above it, noting the height and angle of each arc.

"Blade, how tall was Florek?"

"Five ten, according to his driver's license."

She stood and moved to the opposite wall, where more blood had sprayed in a different pattern. Lower. More horizontal. "And the killer was swinging down at him?"

"That's what the ME figured. Defensive wounds on Florek's hands and forearms suggested he tried to block the blows."

Tori walked the perimeter of the room, tracking the destruction. The overturned furniture, the broken glass, the blood covering nearly every surface. The scene screamed rage, a chaotic frenzy. But it was a performance. She could feel it. The rage was real, but the mess was for show.

"You said no forced entry?" she asked.

"Front door was unlocked when the neighbor found the body. Back door was still locked from the inside."

"So Florek either knew his killer or—"

"Or the killer picked the lock and waited until he got home."

Tori knelt beside the coffee table and examined the broken leg. Clean break, recent. She looked up at the blood spatter on the wall behind it, then back at the table's position.

"This is overkill," she said, more to herself than to Blade.

"What do you mean?"

She stood and brushed off her knees. "Stabbing someone this many times, that's a crime of rage. It's about making someone pay."

"Pay for what?"

"That's the question. Whatever Florek did, the killer believed he deserved every single blow. But look at this scene. It's too messy. Too . . . theatrical. Like someone wanted us to think it was a crime of passion."

Blade moved closer, and his gaze swiveled around the room. "You think it was staged?"

"Not staged exactly. But . . ." She trailed off, trying to put her finger on what bothered her. She walked to the front window and peered through the blinds at the quiet street beyond. Coral Gables. Upscale neighborhood where people minded their own business and paid for privacy.

"Corporate attorney, you said?"

"Yeah. Divorced. Clean record except for a few speeding tickets."

She turned back to the room. "What kind of law did he practice?"

"Medical malpractice defense, mostly. Some corporate litigation."

"The same fields that would intersect with organ trafficking and illegal research."

Blade's expression sharpened. "You think Florek was connected to the organ ring Corbin and Luna exposed?"

She didn't answer. Her attention had shifted to a section of wall where the blood spatter looked different. Instead of the violent arcs that covered most surfaces, this area showed something else. Individual drops that had fallen straight down in a neat vertical line.

She crouched and studied the pattern. "Blade, look at this."

He joined her beside the wall. "What am I looking at?"

"Drip pattern. See how these drops fell straight down? No impact spatter, no directional spray." She traced the line with her finger, careful not to touch the dried blood. "Someone stood right here and bled."

"The killer?"

"Most likely. Florek's defensive wounds were on his hands and forearms—he wouldn't have been standing here bleeding. This is where the attacker paused after the assault."

"I'll make sure they get tested." He took out his phone and tapped a message.

Tori stood and moved toward the kitchen, following the logic of the scene. On the counter, she spotted Florek's keys and cell phone.

"Blade, does this look right to you?"

He examined the items. "What do you mean?"

"A man comes home, gets attacked in his foyer, fights for his life through multiple rooms, and his keys and phone end up neatly arranged on the kitchen counter?"

Blade's jaw tightened. "Someone moved them. Officers know better."

She nodded. "The killer took time to move them." Tori pulled out her phone and snapped photos of the kitchen, the living room, and the hallway. "That's not rage behavior. That's control."

She noticed a hardcover book on the floor near the couch, face down with its pages splayed open. Blood had smeared across the back cover, obscuring part of the title, but she could make out enough letters to read: *Medical Ethics in the Modern Age*.

"Very interesting," she murmured, crouching beside the book.

"Find something?"

"Maybe." She pointed to a blood smear. "Looks like someone dragged a bloody finger across the title."

"Medical ethics. Not exactly subtle for a malpractice attorney."

Blade led her into Florek's home office. Leather-bound volumes lined built-in shelves and a hand-carved desk dominated the center of the room.

"We found blood in here," he said, gesturing to evidence markers across the room.

"I'll get there." First, she had to see the room as the killer did. Her gaze swept the desktop items—brass letter opener, crystal paperweight, Montblanc fountain pen stand. Empty. The pen was gone, but an indentation pressed into the leather desk blotter caught her attention. She switched on the banker's lamp and leaned closer.

Someone had written with enough pressure to leave an impression in the leather beneath.

"What is that?" Blade asked. He was standing close. Too close. Her concentration scattered.

"You're breathing down my neck."

He stepped back, palms raised. "Sorry. Just watching you work."

"I know. But I need space to think." She handed him her phone. "Take some photos of that blotter, then have someone collect it for evidence. Could be important."

She crossed to the far wall and crouched beside the evidence markers. Tiny blood droplets formed a perfect circle. Was this intentional? Why here? The killer had taken time to arrange some things, clean others, but leave this blood behind.

Calculated. Controlled. Nothing about this scene suggested someone who'd lost their temper or acted on impulse.

Blade leaned over the table on the opposite side of the room, camera clicking softly, his weight braced on his palms.

"Medical malpractice defense attorney. Defending doctors who made mistakes," she said, processing out loud.

"Or doctors who did exactly what they intended," Blade said.

Evening light had gone gold by now, the shutters laying long honey-colored bars across the bloodstained carpet. Hours. They'd been at this for hours. She made one final sweep of the office, cataloging details that might matter later.

Back in the living room, she waited while Blade called the Crime Scene Unit to come collect additional evidence.

He disconnected and said, "They'll be here in fifteen. Done in here?"

She nodded and followed him toward the back door, stripping off her latex gloves. The snap of rubber against skin felt final, like closing a chapter.

Blade pressed her phone into her hand without a word, and she walked out behind him into air that smelled like rain coming. The normalcy of Florek's neighborhood slapped her. Manicured St. Augustine grass, blooming bougainvillea cascading over privacy fences, the distant hum of a leaf blower maintaining someone's perfect landscape. Life continuing its predictable rhythm while violence festered behind closed doors.

The house's exterior revealed nothing. No broken windows, no signs of struggle, no indication that brutality had unfolded inside these walls. The killer had counted on the assumption of safety in Coral Gables's manicured streets.

"Well, Doctor." Blade leaned against his car's hood. "First thoughts?"

Sweat prickled the back of Tori's neck. She pulled her hair back and secured it with an elastic hair tie from her wrist. "The blood patterns, the staged furniture, even that book placement, it's all too intentional. It feels like someone wanted us to see specific things while missing others."

"Like what?"

"The killer bled in that living room for at least thirty seconds. That's not adrenaline-fueled escape behavior. That's someone taking time to survey their work." She looked back at the house. "And moving Florek's keys and phone to the kitchen counter? That's control."

The medical ethics book nagged at her. Too obvious, like a breadcrumb dropped. But breadcrumbs led somewhere, and whoever killed Florek wanted them to follow a specific trail.

"We need to dig into his coworkers and his client list," she said.

Blade nodded. "You thinking this connects to his work?"

"I'm thinking someone wanted Florek silenced before he could talk."

The white CSU van rounded the corner and parked at the curb. Tori checked her watch and grimaced. Six fifteen. She'd promised the kids she'd be at the gym by seven.

"I gotta bounce," she said, fishing her keys from her purse. "Warrior class tonight."

Blade grinned and shook his head. "Still teaching those teenagers that size doesn't matter in a fight?"

"Yes, and they still don't believe me until I prove it." She looked him up and down, taking in all six-foot-four of him. "Matter of fact, I'd use you as my demonstration dummy if you didn't have that hot date with your girlfriend tonight."

His laugh came out easy, but something flickered across his face. "Yeah, well."

That was it? Yeah, well? She waited for him to say more, maybe tease her back about how she'd never actually take him down, but he just stood there adjusting his car keys.

"Have a good night," he said, already turning toward the CSU team. "I'll forward you the CSU file when they're done shooting it. Body and all. Whatever they pull, you'll have it tonight."

She walked to her Range Rover, the dismissal stinging more than it should have. She slid behind the wheel and started the engine, watching Blade in her rearview mirror as he approached the crime scene techs. She pulled away from the curb and headed toward Kingdom MMA, but her mind stayed stuck on that weird moment.

Like he couldn't wait to get away from her.

Maybe she was imagining things. Blade had always been protective of his personal life, keeping work and relationships in separate boxes. But they'd been friends for years. She'd saved his life, he'd saved hers. They had history that went deeper than professional courtesy.

So why did it feel like he was building walls?

The traffic light ahead turned red, and she braked. He'd been with Kiara for five months, and Tori had only met her once. A brief introduction at a coffee shop where Kiara had been polite but distant, like she was sizing up the competition.

Which was ridiculous. Tori and Blade were friends. Colleagues even. Nothing more.

But as she accelerated through the green light, she couldn't shake the feeling that something had shifted between them. Maybe Kiara didn't want her around. Maybe Blade was choosing sides.

The gym's neon sign came into view, and she pushed the thoughts away. She had teenagers to train, kids who needed to learn that strength came from more than just size. That was something she could control.

Unlike whatever was happening with Blade.

Two hours of sweat and grit did the trick. Class had been brutal, and the Kingdom MMA throbbed with leftover energy. Bodies moved through cooldown drills while laughter and glove slaps bounced off the black steel beams. Strands of Tori's hair stuck damp against her neck, and her arms felt heavy from rounds of demonstrating holds and escapes. The teens had emptied their frustration onto the mats. Andre driving double-legs with grit. Jordan grinning as he sprawled and countered.

She drained the last of her water and cut toward the women's locker room. Time to change out, shut the night down. Rot at home on the couch with spicy Thai food and a mindless TV show to scrub away the day.

Tori dragged the duffel free from the metal locker and yanked the zipper. Her body locked.

Her clothes weren't sitting right. She always placed them in the same order out of a habit born of a childhood where she owned very little. Bra laid smooth at the top, shirt sharp-folded beneath, shorts squared on the bottom. Now the stack looked off.

She dug through, retracing the order, and halted. Down against the canvas, something waited. A clear plastic baggie.

She pinched it out. A square of gauze was pressed inside. A quarter-sized maroon stain in the center. Blood.

Flat beneath that, folded paper.

Her fingers worked at the crease, bracing for the words.

The first cut wasn't deep enough. Let's try again.

The bag slipped from her hands and smacked the tile. Plastic skidded, the square of gauze glaring through clear wrap. He'd stood here. In her gym. In this room where the walls should have meant safety.

She crouched, pinched the bag shut again, and locked the seal with more force than needed. Her training shouted, *Don't smudge, don't contaminate.* Evidence. That's what this was.

Not that she could tell anyone. Not yet. Blade was already watching her six every second, and if he caught a whiff of this, he'd chain her to his squad car. He needed her steady, not spooked.

She shoved the baggie inside, yanked on clean clothes, and zipped the gym bag closed. The stalker case was already open at Millie Beach. She'd drop it to the detective on record tomorrow, quiet, no Blade involved. Let the evidence work through proper channels while she kept moving.

Her phone lit up. Blade's name. The vibration rumbled against her palm as her thumb hit accept.

"Hey."

"I was thinking about taking a run at interviews at Florek's law firm tomorrow morning. You up for a drive?"

She pressed her back against the locker, the plastic baggie in her gym bag feeling like it weighed ten pounds. "Yeah, sure. What time?"

"Eight. I want to catch the partners before they disappear into depositions and billable hours."

"You haven't interviewed Florek's coworkers?"

"Patrol deputies handled initial witness interviews. This is follow-up. Standard procedure."

"Oh yeah. Right." She wasn't thinking.

Blade paused. "You sound weird. Everything okay?"

Her throat tightened. The concern in his voice almost broke her resolve to handle this alone.

She forced a laugh. "Weird? That's my natural state, remember? I'm a behavioral analyst who talks to criminals with mental disorders for a living."

"Fair point. Though I was thinking more like you sound tired weird, not your usual crazy-smart weird."

Despite everything, a genuine smile tugged at her lips. "Such a charmer. No wonder you're finally taken."

"Heh, yeah. Guess I finally found someone who appreciates my sparkling personality and devastating good looks."

"Good luck with that. Hope you remembered to brush your teeth before that picnic."

Blade chuckled. "Ouch. Remind me why I keep you around?"

"Because I make you look smarter by comparison." The banter steadied her, pushed the fear back into manageable territory. This was normal. This was safe.

"Hardly." He laughed. "Eight tomorrow morning. I'll bring coffee."

"Make mine a double. And none of that gas station swill you call coffee."

"Cuban coffee from that place you like. I'm not completely hopeless."

She ended the call and stood at the locker room sink, eyes locked on the mirror. The face staring back gave nothing away. Skin a shade paler, maybe, but anyone passing would see normal. Fine. Steady.

Her gaze slid lower. The strip of flesh-colored tape clung to her throat, almost invisible against her skin. Almost. It covered the cut where his blade had kissed her. Covered the message he wanted etched into her head.

The corner of her gym bag caught her eye. The plastic bag hidden there. His little trophy drop. Proof he thought he was circling tighter, pressing her into a corner. Creeping into her places, breathing her air. He believed that meant leverage.

It didn't.

She pressed a fingertip against the bandage and winced at the bruised sting beneath. He wanted her hearing him whisper through every cut: *I can reach you. Anywhere. Anytime.*

Her jaw locked. *No. Not this girl.*

She wouldn't fold. Wouldn't run.

Let him step closer.

She was already waiting.

7

THE HIGH-RISE MAIN-FLOOR LOBBY, with its security desk, turnstiles, and elevator banks, stretched before them like a marble cathedral, all gleaming surfaces and calculated intimidation. Blade followed Tori toward the reception desk, their footsteps echoing off polished floors that probably cost more than his annual salary.

The receptionist glanced up from her computer screen with the kind of smile that never reached the eyes. Polite, professional, and completely disinterested in their existence. Her nameplate read "Madison Vigliotti" in sleek silver letters.

"Good morning. How may I help you?"

Blade pulled out his badge. "Detective St. James, Broward Sheriff's Office. This is Dr. Crew with the Florida Department of Law Enforcement. We'd like to speak with someone about Donald Florek."

Madison frowned. "Oh. Yes, of course. Such a terrible tragedy." She picked up her phone. "I was told to call HR for any interviews."

Blade stepped back and looked around while Madison spoke in hushed tones. Behind her desk, a massive canvas dominated the wall. Layers of paint splattered and dripped in random patterns, yet somehow forming a cohesive whole. The colors bled into each other, creating smaller swirls within larger ones, repeating endlessly inward. His eyes traced the swirling blues that morphed into greens, then yellows, each layer revealing new details the closer he looked.

"Interesting artwork," Tori murmured beside him.

"Yeah." Blade tilted his head. The painting pulled at his attention, those repetitive spirals drawing his focus deeper into their mathematical precision.

Madison hung up and stood. "If you'll follow me, please."

The elevator climbed silently to the fifth floor, where Madison led them down a hallway lined with identical abstract pieces. The conference room she ushered them into commanded a spectacular view. Floor-to-ceiling windows overlooked the Atlantic on one side, while the other wall offered a bird's-eye view of the lobby below.

But Blade stopped dead when he saw the painting at the far end of the room.

This one covered most of the wall, a riot of blues and greens that seemed to pulse and shift when he stared at it. The same technique as the lobby piece, but larger, more complex. The patterns repeated at different scales, each section containing miniature versions of the whole.

Tori walked straight into his back. "Ay. A little warning next time?"

"Sorry." Blade steadied her with one hand, not taking his eyes off the canvas. "Just—"

"There's just something about it, right?" Madison smiled. "I don't know what it is, but I could stare at that thing for hours. It's . . . soothing."

Blade nodded. He couldn't describe the pull he felt, the way the painting seemed to draw his attention deeper into its layers. "Yeah. I can't put my finger on it, but there's something . . ."

"Well, someone will be with you shortly." Madison backed toward the door. "Can I get you coffee? Water?"

"Coffee would be great," Tori said. "Thank you."

After Madison left, Tori dropped her work bag, the one that never left her side, into one of the leather chairs and shook her head. "You look like you're about to propose to that painting."

He moved closer to the canvas, studying the way the paint created depth and movement. "Doesn't it do anything to you? Emotionally, I mean?"

"Yeah, it makes me nauseous thinking about how much they probably spent on that thing." She pulled out her notebook and settled into a chair. "Probably could've fed a small country with whatever they paid some artist to splash paint at a wall."

"It's more than that." He traced the air in front of the painting, following one of the larger patterns. "Look at how it repeats. The same shapes but different sizes. Layered over each other like—"

"Blade, focus. We're here to solve a murder, not critique the interior decorating choices of overpriced lawyers."

He forced himself to turn away from the painting, though something about it lingered in his peripheral vision like an itch he couldn't scratch. The conference room felt different now, charged with an energy he couldn't name.

"You're right." He took a few steps back and let his eyes trace the lines. "But doesn't it strike you as odd? A corporate law firm with this kind of art?"

"Rich people spend way too much money on weird, expensive things. Not exactly breaking news." She clicked her pen and opened her notebook. "What's our approach here? Good cop, bad cop, or are we playing it straight?"

"Straight. For now. Let's see what they volunteer before we start pushing."

The door opened behind her. Madison eased in with a black lacquer tray, three white mugs steaming, a small pitcher of cream, and a bowl of sugar packets tucked along the edge. She set it on the conference table without a word and was gone before the door finished closing.

Tori picked up a mug and offered it to Blade, but he passed with a shake of his head. As she finished pouring some cream, the conference room door opened again. He turned to find a man in his late fifties striding in with an air of confidence that came from winning cases and commanding courtrooms. Expensive suit, direct eye contact, two-hundred-dollar haircut. Everything about him screamed law partner.

"Detective St. James? Rich McCrary." Even the man's grip fit what Blade had expected. Solid.

"Thank you for meeting us," Blade said. "This is my colleague, Dr. Tori Crew."

"Pleasure." McCrary shook Tori's hand. "I'm sorry for your wait. This is Yevonne Mellas, our director of HR."

The woman beside him carried an iPad and wore the kind of neutral expression that came with years of managing difficult conversations. She nodded politely as they settled around the conference table.

Blade pulled out his notebook and clicked his pen. Most detectives used their phone to record and transcribe notes, but the act of writing always grounded his scattered thoughts. Gave his hands something to do while his mind processed information.

"We appreciate you taking the time to speak with us," Tori said.

They got comfortable in the soft leather chairs, and Blade got right to it. "We're investigating Donald Florek's death and hoping to get a better picture of his work here."

McCrary leaned forward and laced his fingers on the table, showing his French cuffs and gold cufflinks with a crest. "Don was a solid attorney. Ten years with the firm, mostly handling medical malpractice cases. He was thorough, professional, and kept to himself."

"What kind of medical malpractice cases?" Tori asked.

"The usual range. Surgical errors, misdiagnoses, pharmaceutical issues," McCrary said.

Blade listened, though his peripheral vision kept catching the painting's swirling patterns. Something about the repetitive nature of the brushstrokes made his eyes want to follow them deeper into the canvas.

A sharp pain shot through his shin. He glanced over to find Tori's eyes boring into him, her foot still pressed against his leg under the table. *Right. Focus.*

"So no recent cases that might have generated threats or unusual attention?" Blade asked, forcing himself to look away from the wall.

McCrary shook his head. "Nothing out of the ordinary. Most cases never make it to trial. They settle out of court. Don wasn't the type to make enemies. Which is why this is all so . . . strange. For someone to murder Don so brutally, it doesn't make sense."

Blade kept his pen moving. "We'll need a list of every case Florek was working in the last year. Especially anything still active."

McCrary's gaze slid to Yevonne, then back. "I'm afraid that won't be possible. Attorney-client privilege."

Across the table, Yevonne gave a quick nod and tapped something on her iPad.

McCrary leaned back, folding his hands. "Even internally, we're careful about access. I'm sure you understand."

Blade didn't answer. The page in his notebook stayed open, pen hovering.

Yevonne's head lifted from the screen. "Richard—" She angled the iPad toward him. "They're asking for you now."

McCrary frowned at the message but was already pushing back his chair. "I'm sorry. Apparently, I'm needed rather urgently." He straightened his cuff. "Detective, Doctor—it's been a pleasure. Drop by anytime."

Blade stood with him. "We just might."

McCrary's smile never touched his eyes. He exited with the same confident gait he'd entered with.

Blade wrote one word in his notebook—*stonewalling*.

The painting on the far wall caught his attention again, pulling at the edge of his focus until Tori stood, breaking the line of sight.

“If you’ll follow me,” Yevonne said. “I’ll take you to the attorney handling Florek’s case load.”

Yevonne strode ahead, spine straight as a ruler, heels punching out a steady tempo down the corridor. Blade tracked motion through the glass-front offices they passed. One guy racked up steps circling his office with a phone pressed to his ear. Another leaned into his desk, chewing the arm of his glasses, eyes locked on a tower of briefs. Most sat hunched over monitors and files, pens twitching, fingers moving across the keyboards like lizards darting across hot pavement.

They stopped at a corner office whose door was already open. Inside, a massive conference table ran the length of the space, covered in open files, legal pads, and color-coded binders. Three people clustered there, mid-discussion, bright yellow highlighters moving in unison. The wall of glass behind them showcased the downtown skyline all the way to the ocean, blue haze blurring the horizon.

The guy at the head of the table stood, flashing a grin fit for a billboard. Tall, broad across the shoulders, sun-bleached hair swept just messy enough to pass as casual. Blade’s first thought was “Ken doll meets Malibu surfboard,” only this one wore a tailored navy suit instead of board shorts.

“Ryan,” Yevonne said crisply, motioning toward Blade and Tori. “Detective St. James and Dr. Crew are here about Don Florek.”

“Ryan Petersen. Pleasure to meet you, sir.” Ryan’s handshake was firm. “Y’all can call me Ryan,” he said, the easy drawl stretching vowels just enough to give it away. “Always had the utmost respect for law enforcement, Detective. If I hadn’t gone the law school route, I’d probably be doin’ what you do.”

Beside Blade, Tori tilted her head, already pegging it. “That accent. Louisiana?”

“Yes, ma’am,” he said without missing a beat. “Born and raised. But I went to law school here in Florida. Fell in love with the beach, and of course, golf. So I never left.”

He took a closer look at Ryan's face. The black eye wasn't fresh. Yellow bruising at the edges, deeper purple in the center. A shallow cut marred his cheekbone. Lower down, a fading bruise along his jaw traced in clean lines, like it had come from a single, direct impact.

Blade kept it casual. "Rough weekend?"

Ryan reached up, thumb brushing his jaw with a sheepish grin. "This? That's what I get for walkin' too close behind somebody on the driving range. Colleague of mine whacked me good on the backswing."

Sure he did. The symmetry of those marks looked more like fists than a nine iron. He pressed, just enough to feel for a seam. "What's your friend's name?"

"Harris Zirinsky in contracts. He's probably still mortified about it. Happened Thursday morning."

Blade scribbled it into his notebook, quick and neat. Plenty for someone at the station to run down later. "Funny," he said. "My deputies didn't note those injuries."

"That's because I wasn't here." Ryan leaned on the back of a chair. "I was at Holy Cross with my mother Wednesday night. Kidney stones. They admitted her around nine and didn't release her until past midnight. The hospital records can verify."

Tori's eyebrow went up. "With Florek gone, I imagine there might be some opportunity in the firm."

Ryan laughed at that, shaking his head. "Generous of you, ma'am, but no. I'm years away from that. Plenty more time carryin' water for these guys before I see my name on that wall."

Each "ma'am" earned him the barest flicker of narrowed eyes from Tori. Blade had to stifle a smirk and filed it away for later ammunition.

He nodded toward the two others at the table. "And them?"

Ryan glanced over his shoulder, then chuckled like he'd broken some personal rule. "Pardon me, where are my manners. Let me introduce you to my team. Leslie and Gary are paralegals. They've been helping me dig through Don's old cases, making sure nothing slips through the cracks."

Leslie gave a polite nod without looking up from her highlighter work. Gary kept his focus on a stack of depositions.

Blade let his gaze linger on the files spread across the table. At Ryan's end, a yellow legal pad covered in tight handwriting sat on top of a messy pile of folders. A manila tab stuck out just enough to snag his attention.

Psychiatric Research Institute.

Ryan's hand came down on the legal pad. He slid it over the folder.

"Sorry." Ryan's easy smile didn't waver. "Confidential client matter. You understand."

Blade did. They weren't going to get anything from a few stolen glances at someone's chicken-scratch notes.

He kept going down the list. Last time he saw Florek (Tuesday morning in the break room), any disagreements (none he knew of), clients that caused trouble (plenty, but none that stood out). Every answer came quick and smooth.

Yevonne stepped into the doorway and checked her watch. Ryan gave another politician's handshake, thanked them for their time, and was back in his seat before they'd stepped into the hall.

In the elevator, Tori nudged his elbow. "Hey. How'd your date go last night?"

He bumped the back of his head against the steel wall, staring at the panel lights as they counted down floors. "Didn't make it."

"Oh?" Her tone carried the exact level of feigned innocence that made him side-eye her.

"Case work." It wasn't exactly untrue, but it still pinned a little weight across his chest.

"Uh-huh. So you stood her up."

"Not stood up. I texted her to let her know I couldn't make it."

"That's practically the same thing."

"You're supposed to be helping me solve a murder, not grading my social life."

She arched a brow. "Multitasking."

They stepped into the parking garage, and Blade dug the keys from his pocket. The Charger's headlights flashed twice as he hit the unlock button.

A shadow shifted between parked cars. Blade's hand shot to Tori's shoulder, pulling her behind him before the thought fully formed. His other hand hovered near his hip.

The receptionist from the lobby rounded a pillar.

"Madison." He sighed and let his arm drop but didn't step back.

The twentysomething woman hurried toward them, stopping close enough that Blade caught the tremor working through her jaw. A stack of file folders sagged in her grip. Mascara smudged beneath her left eye. It hadn't been there upstairs.

Her gaze darted past his shoulder toward the elevator bank, whipped left to scan the exit ramp, then locked back onto his face. Whatever she had to say, she didn't want an audience.

"Detective." Madison snapped a glance over her shoulder. "About Don." A swallow stretched her throat. "It might connect to why he's dead."

8

TORI'S JOKES about Blade's dating life died somewhere between the elevator and Madison Vigliotti's face. For a few seconds, Tori was too surprised to do anything but stare.

Madison lifted the file folders and pressed them to her chest so tight that her sharp acrylic fingernails left clean indentations in the back. The woman's eyes hadn't stopped tracking back and forth since she'd rounded that pillar. She was obviously nervous and scared.

Tori had stood in Donald Florek's living room. Madison was right to be afraid.

She spoke as gently as she could. "Start from the top and tell us what you mean."

Madison's glance flicked again toward the elevators. "This can't get back upstairs. I could lose my job."

Blade shifted, planting his bulk in front of the elevators. "It's just us here."

"Okay." Madison's chin dropped slightly.

"Pretend we're not law enforcement." Tori slid in front of Blade and spoke to Madison like they were just girlfriends. "Were you and Don . . . involved?"

Madison's head shot up, eyes wide. "No. Nothing like that." She hugged the folders tighter. "It wasn't . . . look, we were friends. Work friends. And sometimes we'd bump into each other outside of work."

"Where?" Blade asked.

Madison hesitated and shifted her weight before she pushed the words out. "We . . . shared the same therapist."

Tori's mind pinged in ten directions at once. She didn't bother asking why they were in therapy. "Which therapist?"

"Dr. Anton Stone. His office is in Palm Beach."

Tori didn't break her gaze. "Why would that have anything to do with him ending up dead?"

Madison hunched into herself, lifting one shoulder in a shrug. "He was different lately. Paranoid. I suggested he see my therapist because, you know, he'd been helping me with my anxiety. But Don kept asking if anyone had been looking for him or saying anything about him. No one had. At least not to me. When I asked what was going on, he got even more jumpy. He finally told me he'd called some people out and they wanted him gone."

"Any names?" Blade asked.

Madison shook her head. "No specifics. Just . . . he acted like someone was out to get him. I thought he was being insecure. Typical office politics where associates climb over each other's backs to get to the top. But after he was . . . you know." Her eyes cut to the ground. "After I heard what happened, I wondered if it had something to do with the firm."

Tori ticked through a checklist as the young woman spoke. Madison's hands stayed still, her eyes steady. No liar's tells. If anything, she trimmed the edges, handing over only the basics and nothing more. She wasn't about to spill her guts in this parking garage. If they wanted more, they'd have to talk away from this place.

"I have to get back." Madison shifted the files. "Told them I was making copies. They time how long I'm gone."

Blade pulled a card from his jacket and held it out. "If anyone approaches you, asks what you told us, or makes you uncomfortable, you call me. Anytime. Understand?"

She took it, eyes lingering on the bolded "Detective B. St. James." "You'll . . . you'll keep my name out of it?"

"Don't worry about that. Just call me if you remember anything else," he said.

Something in his delivery loosened Madison's shoulders a fraction. She backed away and headed for the elevator. She offered a flat smile as the doors sealed her inside.

The air hung dead in the concrete tomb. Somewhere deeper in the garage, a car door slammed.

Tori exhaled, glancing at Blade. "Dr. Stone?"

He nodded once. "Ever heard of him?"

"No, but let's move this conversation to the car." Whatever coolness the poured walls offered couldn't touch the blistering heat outside, and she could feel moisture beading along her neck. Tori dropped into the car, and Blade started the engine.

"Let me make a call real fast."

Blade didn't bother announcing he had calls on speaker with work calls. Everyone on the job expected it. He asked a deputy she didn't know to follow up on Ryan Petersen's story about the golf club. Tori listened, noting how he kept his voice neutral while giving orders. Professional. Kind. The kind of cop who didn't let his rank dictate how he dealt with people.

He hung up, snapped the phone to the magnetic cradle mounted on the dash, and shifted the car into gear. The Charger rolled forward, headlights scything through the dim ramp as they circled out of the garage. Morning light poured in through the Charger's windshield, flattening the dust on the dash into pale gold.

Tori pulled out her phone and typed "Dr. Anton Stone psychiatrist Palm Beach." Results flooded the screen. "Got him. Office is on Worth Street." She scrolled through his credentials. "Surprised I never heard of him. He's published several papers on trauma therapy."

Blade tapped the wheel in a restless cadence, eyes narrowed on the asphalt ribbon cutting north. "What're the odds both Florek and Madison end up with the same shrink?"

"Insurance network?" Even as Tori made the suggestion, it didn't fit. "Still feels off."

"Yeah." He cut a glance at her, then back to the road. "So how do we get Stone to talk?"

Tori angled toward him, knees pressing the console. "We don't. Patient privilege survives the patient."

He flicked his thumb against the leather-wrapped steering wheel. "So subpoena. But unless we've got a hook, judge'll swat us off the docket."

"Which is why we don't ask for Florek's whole file. That's too broad. We go for targeted disclosure. A threat assessment."

That pulled his attention. A quick look, blue eyes sharpening. "A threat assessment?"

"Exactly. It's one of the few cracks in privilege." She'd walked this path before, with offenders, with institutional reviews. "The doctrine flips if danger's imminent. Shrink has to warn if someone's about to hurt a specific person. We argue the reverse. That Florek sat in that office naming someone, a threat closing on him. We show reason to believe Stone might have recorded it."

"So Madison's disclosure about Florek's paranoia, which Madison witnessed, suggests he was in fear for his life."

"Yes." Finally, he tracked. "Florek ends up dead; that means his psych files could hold a name. We don't care about trauma from thirty years ago. We want one thing—session notes that point to a threat. Clean. Direct. That's our line in."

He gave the nod, but his gaze didn't stick with her. Focus shifted inward, something else circling, some other equation pulling at him.

She waved at him. "What's wrong?"

He kept his eyes forward, jaw set. "Nothing. Just a heavy mess to push through. Even for me."

That was odd. Blade didn't usually undercut himself.

She kept watching him. "Out with it."

He didn't answer right away. Kept his focus sharp on the ribbon of asphalt slicing through palm scrub. Then he exhaled slowly. "I was going to ask Kiara to access the Crew file in person, but now that we're on this lead, I think I should call her now before we get buried in the Florek case."

He put the phone on speaker. The first thing to flood the cabin was Kiara's bright, almost singsong voice as she answered with, "Hey, you. I missed you last night."

"Yeah, I missed you too." Blade shifted lower in his seat, his shoulders sinking back, tone dropping into the one he only used with Kiara. "We'll lock in that picnic. But that's not why I'm calling. I've got you on speaker. Tori's with me."

"Oh, hey Tori. You know I love hearing from you guys anytime. This a break in the day, or am I on the clock?"

"I needed to ask you something important," Blade said.

"Important like dinner plans, or important like you're wearing your cop face right now?" Kiara's tone was like syrup over the speaker.

The corner of Tori's mouth wanted to curve upward. Kiara had a tell too. Gentle humor when she was unsettled.

"Cop face," he said. "It's business."

Pause. "Okay . . . what's going on?"

"I need eyes on a file," Blade said. "Millie Beach PD archive. It's a homicide sealed and tagged for IA. I can't touch it. You can."

The silence on the other end stretched long enough for the hum of the Charger's tires to register in Tori's ear.

"Blade . . ." Kiara's voice lost its lilt. "That's—if it's sealed, there's a reason."

"It's connected to something I'm working. Possible . . . corruption."

"Well, yes. I assume if there's an IA seal . . . Are you being investigated?"

"No, no." He hurried to squash that thought. "Not me, but I think someone's life depends on knowing what's in that file."

Kiara let out a soft, uneasy laugh. "What exactly are you asking me to do?"

"I'm asking you because I can't ask anyone else," he said. "I've got a homicide that keeps pointing to people who should be on my side. I don't want to tip off whoever I'm looking at, and you're the only path I've got." He paused a beat. "I'd never put you in this spot if it wasn't necessary."

"This is . . . dangerous, Blade. For you. For me." A beat. "Who's it for?"

He hesitated half a breath. "Someone who deserves the truth."

Tori noticed he hadn't used her name. Hadn't said it was a favor for her.

A faint exhale from Kiara's end. Not quite surrender, not quite refusal. "If I do this, it's between us. You understand?"

"Understood." Blade gave her the case file number.

"I'll . . . see what I can find." Another pause. "No promises. And if I can't—"

"Then you can't," he finished for her.

Kiara said something sweet and affectionate. Tori shut it out. The warmth of it still clung to the air between the seats, syrupy and wrong against the rank bitterness of law firm coffee souring in her mouth.

Blade didn't move, didn't glance over. His stare drilled through the windshield, hands steady on the wheel.

She dragged her fingertip across the fogged glass, carving one last line until it squeaked clear. "That wasn't an easy ask," she said.

"No. No, it was not," he admitted.

She turned back to face him. "She trusts you."

A muscle jumped in his cheek. "I know."

Sweet Kiara, smiling as though danger couldn't touch her. The woman had no idea what she was stepping into. If there was department corruption, she'd be a key witness.

And what was that feeling that cropped up every time Tori heard the woman's voice? Not jealousy. That wasn't it. Was it the threat of collateral damage? Helping them meant clawing through sealed records, trespassing into the kind of secrets men killed to protect. If Kiara got involved, she could lose more than a job.

Blade wouldn't let either happen. All his care went outward, never inward. He'd take the hit without hesitation, the same way he always had, the same way he always would.

But no. Not this time. If Kiara pulled that file and the hammer fell, Tori would plant herself square in its path. Consequences belonged on her shoulders. Hers, not Kiara's, not Blade's. Not this time.

9

DR. ANTON STONE'S WAITING ROOM was designed to lower defenses, with its soft lighting, muted earth tones, classical music barely audible through hidden speakers. It wasn't working on Blade.

The oversized leather chairs were positioned at non-threatening angles. The air carried the scents of lemon polish. Even the magazines fanned across the coffee table avoided anything remotely controversial.

Blade took it all in from his seat by the window, watching the slow drift of a palm frond beyond the tinted glass. Tori had claimed the chair beside him, one leg crossed over the other, winding her fingers through a strand of hair in that unconscious way she had while her thumb culled emails on her phone.

But her threat assessment argument had been solid. Clean legal reasoning backed by established precedent. The judge had signed the subpoena in under twenty minutes.

Still, guilt gnawed at him. They'd used Madison's name to get that signature, and the young woman had asked them to keep her out of it. But this was a homicide investigation, not high school drama. People were dead. More might follow.

"Dr. Stone is finishing up with a patient," the receptionist had informed them twenty minutes ago. "He'll be right with you."

Twenty minutes in therapist time apparently meant something different than twenty minutes in the real world.

"Look at her," Tori murmured, nodding toward the receptionist. "Nine to five, same desk, same view every day. I'd lose my mind."

"Some people like routine."

"Some people like vanilla ice cream too. Doesn't make it interesting." Tori shifted in her chair. "You ever think about what you'd do if you weren't a cop?"

"Nope."

"Come on. Not even when you were a kid?"

Blade considered this. "When I was eight, I wanted to be a gator wrestler."

"Of course you did." Tori grinned. "Very practical career choice for a boy from the Everglades."

"What about you? Before the whole criminal profiling thing?"

"Marine biologist. Wanted to study sharks." She paused. "Guess I still do, just a different kind."

His phone buzzed. Gino's name flashed on the screen. CSU. About time.

"St. James."

"Blade, it's Gino. Bro, I couldn't rest until I figured out what was on that blotter because, dude, you know I love a puzzle." The CSU had that electric edge he got when he'd cracked something. "You got a minute?"

Blade glanced at Tori, then held the phone between them so she could hear. "What'd you find?"

"It was an indentation created when someone wrote on a paper that was sitting on top of the blotter. We used electrostatic detection apparatus. Basically runs an electrical charge across the surface to reveal pressure marks. Like a high-tech version of rubbing a pencil over paper to see what was written on the page above it."

"And?"

"I just texted you the image. Take a look."

Blade pulled up his messages. At first glance, he saw a complex web of lines that formed a six-pointed star.

He showed the screen to Tori, who furrowed her brow and shook her head.

"Looks like some kind of symbol," Blade said. "Any idea what it means?"

"Honestly? Could be anything. Maybe just a doodle. We can't tell who made it. Could've been Florek, absentmindedly drawing while on a call. Or it could've been the killer."

"Why would the killer draw something?" he asked, more to himself than Gino.

"That's the million-dollar question. And if it was the killer, he took the drawing with him because we couldn't find the paper anywhere in the house."

Blade studied the image again. The star wasn't flat. The intersecting triangles created a three-dimensional effect. Was this a wireframe for a physical object? Something about it nagged at the back of his skull.

"You find anything else? Prints? DNA?"

"So far, no prints anywhere. We're still processing samples. Should know more in a few days."

"Keep me posted."

"Will do."

Blade disconnected and took another look at the image on his screen. "Ever seen anything like that before?"

"Not exactly. Reminds me of those three-dimensional stars I used to draw on my notebooks in elementary school." She tilted her head. "Here, gimme your notebook."

He pulled his notebook from his breast pocket and handed it over. Tori flipped to a clean page and drew a giant plus sign. She turned the notebook sideways and drew a smaller X through the center. To Blade, it looked like an uneven asterisk, but he watched as Tori connected the tip of each shorter line of the X to the top of the plus sign.

She held up the paper. "There."

"Looks like a star you'd put on top of a Christmas tree. What do they call those? Capiz star?"

"Yes! That's it." Tori's face lit up. "I'd forgotten the name for it."

"And you call yourself educated." Blade grinned. "Thought you were supposed to be good at math and all that brainy stuff."

"Hey, I'm better with words than numbers."

"Debatable." He slid the notebook into his jacket and raised his phone again, the shape glowing against the screen. His eyes tracked the careful lines. "I guess now we need to figure out if this was a mindless doodle drawn by our victim or a killer signing his work."

"What happened to the original drawing? Did Florek toss it, or did the killer take it?"

Across the room, the receptionist pushed back from her desk, heels quiet on the carpet. "Dr. Stone will see you now," she said, opening a heavy oak door.

Blade stepped into a room built to impress. Leather chairs squared off in tight groupings, not a cushion out of place. Bookshelves climbed to the ceiling, stuffed with journals and gilt-spined tomes that looked only for show. A mahogany desk squatted in the corner, surface clean as glass.

One thing broke the order. A crystal block with a monarch butterfly frozen mid-wing. Afternoon sun struck it and sprayed ribbons of color across the walls, as if even in death the thing wouldn't let anyone forget it was here.

Dr. Anton Stone pushed up from the leather chair, coming around the desk with his hand already extended. His grip waited, steady, while that flawless smile locked in place. Early thirties, hair shaggy long with stray curls brushing the edge of his glasses. Charcoal suit sharp enough to pass for courtroom wear, top button loose for comfort rather than style.

"Dr. Crew. Detective St. James. Welcome."

Blade let his eyes track to the closed door in the far corner. "Thought you had a patient."

Stone angled a hand toward it. "We have an exit. Discretion, of course."

So nobody brushed shoulders in the waiting room. Smart. Blade opened the subpoena on his phone and set it on the desk in front of Dr. Stone.

"We're here for information about a patient who was murdered. Donald Florek," he said.

Stone's gaze hit the screen, and he dropped back into his chair. "This is . . . unusual."

"Murder investigations often are." Tori stood, arms crossed, watching him.

The clock on the far wall marked the seconds with precise tick-tick-tick sounds that seemed louder now, counting down to something inevitable.

Stone lifted the phone with careful fingers, scanning the legal language laid out on the screen. "This is quite specific. 'Any session notes, recordings, or documentation pertaining to threats made against or by Donald Florek during the course of treatment.'"

"That's right," Tori said. "We have reason to believe Mr. Florek discussed specific fears for his safety during your sessions."

"Even if that were true, doctor-patient privilege—"

"Is superseded by court order," Blade finished. "As you can see from the judge's signature."

Stone set the phone down. "Of course. I'll need to review my files." He stood and moved to a locked filing cabinet, producing a key from his vest pocket. "This will take a few minutes.

"I was absolutely horrified when I heard about Donald's murder on the news," he said, pulling out a thick manila folder. "Such a senseless tragedy. I haven't had time to review my notes before your arrival." He gestured to the chairs positioned across from his desk. "Please, make yourselves comfortable. Can I offer you coffee? Water?"

"We're fine," Blade said, settling into the leather chair. The seat was positioned at exactly the right height to make him feel slightly lower than Stone behind the desk. A psychological trick?

Tori remained standing near the bookshelf, her fingers trailing along the spine of a volume on behavioral psychology.

"Donald and I had twelve sessions over the past six months," Stone said, opening the folder. "He was originally referred by his primary care physician for anxiety management." He adjusted his glasses. "He terminated treatment just two days before his death."

Stone's fingers found a specific page in the file. "Session seven, patient reports increased workplace stress. Session nine, patient discusses concerns about professional reputation. Session eleven, patient expresses generalized anxiety about unnamed threats and states he reported information and now believes this was a mistake. Patient described feeling watched. Session terminated early at patient's request."

The clinical tone grated against Blade's nerves. Stone was giving them exactly what the subpoena demanded while revealing absolutely nothing useful. Clinical psychobabble designed to satisfy the letter of the law without violating the spirit of confidentiality.

"That's it?" Blade asked.

"I'm afraid so. Mr. Florek was quite guarded about specifics. He never named individuals or described concrete threats."

The clock's tick-tick-tick drove into Blade's skull. He let Tori take the lead, watching her shift into professional mode as she and Stone began discussing therapeutic approaches and patient resistance patterns. Their conversation drifted into territory that might as well have been a foreign language. Defense mechanisms, transference, cognitive behavioral frameworks.

His phone buzzed on Dr. Stone's desk. Blade grabbed it and checked it, trying not to be rude. A message from his deputy:

Incident report confirms Petersen's story.

Photos and witness statements match his account of the golf accident.

Another lead evaporated. The golf club to the head, the emergency room visit, the alibi that placed Ryan Petersen miles away from Donald's murder. All verified. He'd been hoping for inconsistencies, gaps in the timeline, or a crack in the man's story that Blade could burst wide open.

Instead, he had another dead end. Ryan's injuries were legitimate, which meant they were back to square one on suspects.

The text from his deputy gave Blade an idea. A hail Mary if he ever saw one. "Dr. Stone, does this symbol mean anything to you?" He held up the screen. "Did Mr. Florek ever draw anything like this during your sessions?"

Stone leaned forward, squinting at the display. "May I?"

Blade handed over the phone. Stone pinched the screen to zoom in, studying the intersecting triangular shapes.

"No. Donald never drew it. Not here, anyway." Stone kept his eyes on the screen. "But this . . . this looks like a Keplerian fractal."

Fractal. The word hit Blade like a lightning strike. Damien Sullivan's words slammed back into focus.

He caught Tori's eye, hoping she'd let him run with this. "Keplerian fractals? What exactly is that?"

"Fractals are geometric patterns that repeat at different scales. Johannes Kepler studied star polyhedra. Three-dimensional shapes formed by extending the faces of regular solids." Stone's academic enthusiasm was building. "This particular design resembles a stellated dodecahedron, where pentagonal faces are extended to create star-like projections."

The technical terms made Blade's head spin. He reached into his pocket, fingers finding the texture of his green stress ball. The spiky surface helped anchor his focus while Stone continued showing his sky-high IQ.

Stone held the crystal paperweight up, tilting it until the butterfly inside caught the light. "Fractals. Infinite detail boxed into limits," he said. His thumb traced the ridge of the glass. "Snowflakes. Branches. Insects." He angled the wings toward Blade. "See how the veins fork, same angle, same split, again and again. The colored spots too. Big circles echoing smaller ones. From a distance or with a microscope, it never changes. The whole wing built on repetition. Self-similar. That's fractal geometry."

The monarch butterfly suspended in crystal seemed to pulse with hidden meaning. Blade studied Stone's face, searching for tells. How did a psychiatrist become such an expert on complex mathematical concepts? Was this pure academic interest, or something more personal?

"How do you know so much about fractals?" Blade asked.

"I became fascinated with them when—" He stopped himself, setting the paperweight on his desk. "Well, I can't really say. Confidentiality, you understand. But fractals, once you truly begin to study them, are infinitely fascinating. Some even say they represent God's fingerprint in creation."

Blade had to force himself not to jump out of his chair.

God's fingerprint.

A soft chime sounded, and a light above the door flickered on. Stone glanced at it and stood.

"I'm afraid my next patient has arrived. Thank you for your understanding." He moved toward the exit door, clearly expecting them to follow. "I hope this information proves helpful in your investigation. I'd be happy to have my assistant email the pertinent files."

"Yeah, you do that." Blade pocketed his phone and stood, his mind churning with connections that felt too convenient to be coincidental. Stone's expertise in fractals. His sudden reluctance to explain his interest. The timing of Florek's terminated therapy sessions.

Blade pulled a business card from his wallet and placed it on Stone's desk. "Email those notes today. And expect a few more questions."

Stone nodded, his professional smile returning. "Of course."

Tori stepped forward, extending her hand. "Thank you for your time, Dr. Stone."

As they shook hands, she tilted her head. "This might sound strange, but your voice sounds familiar. Did we have any classes together? Or maybe we've met somewhere?"

Stone's grip lingered a moment too long. "I don't think we attended school at the same time. You look much younger than me, Dr. Crew. Perhaps you heard me speak at a conference?"

Tori's face brightened with recognition. "That's it. I'm sure I heard you speak last year." The thought tugged sideways, like she was looking at the right answer through the wrong window. She filed it away.

They followed Stone through the exit door into a narrow hallway that led to the parking garage. The door clicked shut behind them.

"You thinking what I'm thinking?" Tori asked as they walked toward Blade's Charger.

"Yeah." Blade turned and studied the benign-looking door. "I'm thinking we might have just met our killer."

10

TORI SLID INTO THE PASSENGER SEAT of Blade's Charger, her mind crackling like a live wire. The professional analyst in her was already connecting dots. The Keplerian fractal drawing lifted from Florek's blotter wasn't just some random symbol. It was a thread that tied Donald Florek to Damien Sullivan and his nonsensical warnings about patterns and her parents' murder.

Were they nonsensical? Maybe not if Dr. Anton Stone also studied fractals.

Fractals.

That one word seemed to tie all three together.

And underneath it all, something darker pulsed. A recognition she couldn't place.

"The connections are there," Blade said, starting the engine.

"You're reading my mind." She yanked the seat belt across her chest and clicked it. "Funny thing, though. Dr. Stone drops 'fractals' like he's been studying them for years. But me? First time that word ever hit my ears was yesterday. Out of Damien Sullivan's mouth."

"Can't be coincidence," Blade said. "Stone claims he became interested in fractals because, well, I assume because of his patient, but he didn't actually say."

"I'd say you've found your number one suspect." Tori angled the vent until the blast of cold air hit her face.

"Stone's definitely a person of interest, but I'm not ready to turn the guy's life upside down over fractal talk."

Tori looked out the side window. Stone hadn't hesitated. He'd pulled out that crystal butterfly and offered up the explanation before they'd even asked the right questions.

"If he's the killer, he's a narcissist," she said. "Telling us about the fractals after looking at the drawing would practically be a confession."

"Still, I'll have a deputy run a background check," Blade said. "If he's not the killer, what's the connection?"

She slid her notebook out of her purse. "What if Dr. Stone had a patient tied to my parents' murders?"

"You mean like Sullivan?" Blade lifted his brow. "You're thinking he's our link between past and present."

"I'm thinking we've stepped into something big, but without the case file, nada." She scribbled notes on the page. "Stone counsels someone tied to fractals. Damien mentions fractals in connection with my parents' case. And Florek ends up dead right after seeing Stone about threats . . ."

Blade's phone strobed against the dash. The name "Wells" burned across the screen. He answered on speaker. "Agent Wells. You're on speaker. I've got Dr. Crew with me." A quick glance at Tori. "Talk to me."

"Blade, hey—hope you're caffeinated, because I've got news." Wells's voice boomed out cheerful as ever, like he was announcing a surprise party instead of calling from the Bureau. "Bad news, actually."

Tori's stomach tightened. That tone. A sugarcoat over decay.

"Dr. Forest's dead," Wells continued. "Found in his holding cell this morning. Stab wounds. We have another inmate in custody for it."

Blade's eyes cut to Tori, and she shook her head in disbelief.

"He wasn't in state custody?"

"Correct. They transferred him yesterday to the federal courthouse for jury selection. He was in the holding facility there. He didn't make it to the courtroom." Wells rattled it off like a weather report. "Shame. Guy had answers we needed. But that's how it shakes out."

Blade's breath came sharp through his nose. "Any chance this locks the chain on the organ harvesting ring?"

"Hard to say yet," Wells said. "What I can say is that it doesn't look great for me as head of the task force when a key witness dies before trial." He paused. "But don't wear it, Detective. Keep that chin up. I'll be in touch, and we'll convene the task force soon. Trust me—we'll get there."

The line clicked dead.

Blade sagged back, hands dragging down his face.

Her heart hurt for him. "Blade . . ." She wanted to shove aside her own ghosts and carry some of his weight.

He pulled into a gas station, parking under the canopy. "Can you pull up the coverage?"

Tori's fingers slid across her phone screen and found the local news. A female reporter stood outside what looked like a federal courthouse, microphone poised.

The banner across the bottom read: BREAKING NEWS—DR. WALTER FOREST DEAD IN CUSTODY.

She turned the volume up and pressed play on the video.

"Dr. Walter Forest was found in his cell early this morning," the reporter said. "Forest had been transferred to a federal courthouse yesterday to begin jury selection for his upcoming trial when the attack occurred. According to sources, Forest was stabbed by another inmate while being held in a temporary holding facility. The suspect has not been named, and an investigation is ongoing."

The screen cut to file footage of Forest being led away in handcuffs months ago, his expensive suit wrinkled and his hair disheveled. Tori remembered that day. The day Corbin and Luna nearly died infiltrating Dr. Forest's secret laboratory.

"Walter Forest and his daughter Elizabeth Forest were arrested for their alleged involvement in a human organ trafficking ring operating out of the Chiron BioInnovation Center," the reporter continued. "The charges include trafficking in human organs, criminal assault, medical malpractice, and conspiracy. Dr. Elizabeth Forest died while in custody earlier this year from complications of heart failure. She had been awaiting trial alongside her father. We'll update you as we receive more information."

The video ended. Tori put down her phone. "What does this mean?"

"All those months digging, and the one witness who could've blown the organ ring wide open is murdered before trial?" Blade smacked his palm flat against the steering wheel.

His breaths came clipped, measured. Like he was forcing his lungs to fall in line while the case bled out underneath him.

"Hey." She touched his forearm. "We still have Elizabeth's research notes. The FBI seized everything from Chiron." Not to mention Trinity Brown, a walking, talking science experiment.

"Notes aren't testimony." Blade pulled out a piece of gum and folded it into his mouth. "Forest could have named names, exposed the whole network. Now we're back to circumstantial evidence and secondhand information."

The evidence against Forest and his daughter had been rock solid. Financial records, victim testimonies, the lab equipment seized from Chiron. More than enough to put them away for life. But the FBI had wanted those at the top of the ladder. They'd needed Forest alive to trace the money flowing into his operation, to identify whoever had bankrolled it.

A few midlevel associates sat in federal holding cells, but those arrests felt like swatting flies while the spider remained hidden in its web. Somewhere in the shadows lurked someone with deep enough pockets to fund human experimentation, someone who viewed people as spare parts for the highest bidder. Someone who could afford to eliminate loose ends before they testified.

"Well, sitting here isn't going to help. What's next?" she asked.

He inhaled a deep breath through his nostrils and chewed a few more rounds on the gum. "I'll drop you off at your place, then stop in to chat with Agent Wells. See what's left of our case."

He shifted into drive and circled the parking lot toward the exit. Tori watched his profile as he navigated around a minivan. Another case consuming his evening. Another plan derailed. How was Kiara going to handle it when Blade didn't show? She probably had dinner reservations somewhere with cloth napkins and wine lists, expecting her boyfriend to arrive on time with flowers and apologies for his demanding job. Instead, she'd get a phone call about federal investigations and dead witnesses.

She twisted her fingers in her lap. Kiara deserved better than a man married to his badge. Didn't all women?

Blade pulled into Tori's driveway and cut the engine. He unbuckled his seat belt.

"What are you doing?" she asked.

His brows dipped, head tilting like the answer should've been obvious. "Walking you in."

"Blade."

"Tori." He stepped out of the Charger and waited for her to follow.

She unlocked the door and shoved it open, light spilling across the living room as she slapped on the switch. Blade trailed in behind, palm hovering close to his Glock like he expected company.

"Kitchen first," he said, already angling past her.

She planted herself in the doorway, arms hooked across her chest. "What, you moonlighting as my bodyguard now?"

He rattled the back door, leaned in to check the strike plate, then peeled the blinds apart with two fingers.

"I've been taking care of myself for years, Mr. Macho."

"Humor me," he said, opening her pantry door and glancing inside.

"You gonna check under my bed for monsters too?" She followed him down the hallway, half amused and half irritated by his thoroughness. "Maybe look in my closets for the boogeyman?"

He pushed open her bedroom door and flicked on the light. "Laugh all you want. Your stalker got close enough to lick your ear yesterday."

"Gross." The image hit her like ice water.

That hot breath against her ear, the knife's edge pressing into her throat.

And then there was Forest's death. No way that was random inmate violence. Someone had orchestrated it. Someone with enough reach to eliminate a federal witness.

Blade checked her bedroom windows, testing each lock and lifting the frames to verify they held. She trailed behind him to the guest room, then the hall bathroom.

Thankfully her cleaning lady had come two days ago. Otherwise, he'd be cataloging dust bunnies along with potential entry points.

"All clear," he said, returning to the living room. "Keep your doors locked. Call me if anything feels off."

As he headed for the front door, she caught his arm. "Hey, tough guy. You better watch your six too, all right? Whoever wanted Forest silenced might not appreciate you poking around their business."

He paused, his blue eyes searching her face. Something shifted in his expression. Recognition of the danger they'd stumbled into, acknowledgment that this case had grown beyond a simple homicide investigation.

He nodded once. "I will."

Then he jogged to his car and started the engine before he'd fully closed the door. Tori watched his taillights disappear around the corner before she locked the dead bolt and engaged the security chain.

The house felt too quiet.

She scrolled through her contacts and tapped Luna's name while heading to the master bathroom.

The phone rang twice before Luna answered. "Hey! How'd it go today?"

"Eh. Complicated." Tori squeezed toothpaste onto her brush and wedged the phone between her shoulder and ear. "I heard about Forest. What's it mean for you guys?"

"We're all at the house again. Protective custody. Marshals posted outside, the whole nine yards." Luna sounded almost cheerful about it.

"Ay, that's heavy," she said around her toothbrush. "How are you holding up?"

"Trinity's handling it better this time. Summer's treating it like an extended sleepover. Corbin's like a dad on vacation forcing us to play cards. I almost lost my mind over Phase 10 earlier."

The casual tone didn't fool Tori. Luna was scared. They all were.

She spat minty foam into the sink and rinsed. "What about the gym? The Warrior kids?"

"House parents are still rotating shifts. And Harlee took leave from the ATF to run things. She's handling security and keeping the Warrior program running."

Tori stripped off her work clothes and pulled on running shorts and a sports bra. Tomorrow's three-mile loop would be easier if she could crawl out of bed dressed.

"Harlee took leave?" A federal agent stepping away from her career to babysit teenagers. The scope of this threat crystallized cold and sharp as broken glass.

"Temporary reassignment, she calls it. But yeah." Luna's exhale crackled through the speaker. "Listen, I should go. Trinity's making her famous burnt grilled cheese, and if I don't supervise, we'll be eating charcoal."

"Give everyone my love."

"Will do. And Tori? Be careful, okay?"

The line went dead. Tori set the phone on her dresser and surveyed her reflection. Everyone else was tucked safely behind federal protection or armed security. Luna had Corbin, Trinity, and Summer. Blade had Kiara. Even the Warrior kids had their house parents and Harlee standing guard.

The silence pressed against her eardrums. She'd always prided herself on independence, on not needing anyone's protection or comfort. But watching Luna build her found family, seeing Blade's face soften when he mentioned Kiara . . . Maybe she'd been lying to herself about what she wanted.

Maybe she wanted someone to come home to. Someone who'd notice if she didn't make it through the front door.

She retrieved her Glock from the bathroom and placed it on the nightstand. At least she could read in peace. It was only seven thirty, but she crawled into bed and picked up her book. The words blurred after half a page. Her lids drifted shut.

Outside, a car door slammed, and she reached for the gun before recognizing her neighbor's voice calling his dog.

She pulled the covers up over her head, alone in ways that felt heavier tonight.

Tori snapped awake. Her lungs screamed for air that wouldn't come. A crushing weight pinned her to the mattress. A pillow pressed down like concrete, sealed off her nose and mouth. Her body understood before her mind caught up.

She was going to die.

Training kicked in. Not up. Sideways. Now.

She exploded into a BJJ shrimping escape, her hips bucking hard to the right as she twisted her torso and dragged her knees toward her chest. The attacker's body shifted with her momentum, and she used his imbalance to roll them both off the bed in a tangle of sheets and limbs. They crashed to the hardwood floor with a bone-jarring impact that rattled her teeth.

Her Glock clattered off the nightstand and skittered across the floor into the darkness near the bedroom door.

"Did you miss me?"

The voice slapped her fully awake. The stalker. Here. In her bedroom.

The fear that had flooded her system incinerated. A surge of pure, cold fury sharpened her vision to laser focus.

He blocked the doorway. A dark silhouette between her and escape. The gun lay somewhere near his feet, lost in the shadows.

Create space. Use the environment.

She scrambled backward on her hands and knees, dragging herself toward the primary bathroom. Her bare feet found purchase on the cool tile as she backed against the vanity, the glass shower door to her left, the toilet to her right.

He followed, moving with predatory confidence into the confined space. Moonlight from the bedroom window caught the dark fabric covering everything but his eyes, then the blade in his hand. A hunting knife with a serrated edge.

"Nowhere to run now."

He lunged forward, the knife arcing toward her ribs. She executed a Krav Maga block, her left forearm slamming into his wrist to deflect the strike. The blade's edge sliced a burning line across her skin, and warm blood immediately soaked through her sports bra.

The searing pain only fed her rage.

He drew back for another strike, and she moved. As he lunged again, she dropped low and swept his legs, sending him stumbling forward. She grabbed the back of his head with both hands and drove his face down into the hard porcelain toilet bowl, using his own momentum against him.

The impact made a wet, crunching sound.

Tori bolted from the bathroom, her feet slipping on the hardwood as she dove for her Glock. Her fingers closed around the grip just as she heard him crashing through the bedroom doorway behind her.

She rolled onto her back and fired.

11

THE GLOCK'S BLAST slammed against the walls. The sound ricocheted through Tori's skull. Cordite burned her nostrils. The sharp, metallic scent she'd only encountered during target practice.

The bullet had gone wide. High and right. The framed botanical print above her dresser had exploded in a shower of glass, leaving a spiderweb of cracks radiating from the entry point.

Where was he?

She crouched, gun held close to her chest. She peeked over her mattress and saw the empty window frame. Window raised. Screen in shredded strips. The metal mesh twisted like surgical gauze after a messy procedure.

Gone. Whoever he was. Swallowed by the darkness beyond her bedroom wall.

She didn't pursue. Her hands shook as she kept the gun trained on the empty window frame, finger still on the trigger. Blood dripped from her forearm onto the hardwood floor in steady drops that sounded like a metronome in the sudden silence.

Her head snapped side to side, looking at the wreckage. Sheets snarled on the floor, streaked dark with her blood. The nightstand lay on its face. Jagged shards from the broken frame glittered across the carpet, sharp enough to cut bare skin.

Leaves rustled in the hedge outside the open window. Tori jerked back, the crook of her leg slamming into the bedpost. She dropped onto the floor, tailbone jolted. She scrambled backward into her bedroom closet, yanking the door shut behind her.

She shoved herself into the narrow gap between dresses and storage bins, knees hauled tight to her chest. The dark pressed in, laced with the sweet trace of vanilla. Jasmine. Then spoiled by the tang of her own blood.

Her Glock dug cold against her sternum. Her grip rattled. The weight of her weapon dragged at her hands, an anchor she couldn't put down. Air scraped through her throat in ragged bursts, loud inside the closet, impossible to swallow back.

Four years old again. Hiding from monsters.

A memory crashed over her like a rogue wave. Another closet. Another night. The sound of her parents' screams cut short. Footsteps in the hallway. The metallic smell of blood seeping under the closet door.

The Glock trembled in her grip. Her hands shook so violently she couldn't keep the barrel steady. One wrong twitch and she'd put a bullet through her own foot. Or worse.

She couldn't hold it like this. Not safely.

But what if he came back? Through that gaping window. Through the torn screen that hung like dead skin from the frame.

She forced herself to lower her hand. The gun settled onto the closet floor with a soft thud against the carpet. She kept her palm pressed flat against the polymer frame.

Think. Process. What came next?

Call Blade. Obviously.

Phone. Where was her phone?

On the nightstand.

The overturned nightstand. Back in her bedroom, where glass covered everything and blood stained the hardwood. Maybe even kicked under the bed during the struggle. To reach her phone, she'd have to crawl through the wreckage. Straight into the sightline of that yawning window he'd vanished through.

Her throat constricted. He'd mapped every corner of her house now. The distance from her bed to the bathroom. The angle of approach from the window to where she slept. How long it took her to reach the closet. All the intelligence he needed for next time.

Because there would be a next time.

The Glock's textured grip pressed into her palm. Solid. Real. The only barrier between her and whatever waited beyond this closet door.

Okay, no phone. Now what?

Her smartwatch. The face glowed blue against her wrist, cutting through the closet's darkness like a lifeline. She lifted her palm from the Glock's grip. Her thumb found the side key. One press. Two. Three. The watch beeped and vibrated against her wrist like a heartbeat of hope..

She swiped to activate the SOS feature she'd programmed but never imagined using. The watch pulsed again, confirming the distress signal had transmitted. GPS coordinates, emergency contact alerts, everything automated now. Help would come. She just had to stay alive long enough for it to arrive.

The blood dripped steadily onto the beige carpet beneath her feet. Each drop soaked into the fibers, creating a permanent stain that would never come out, no matter how much she scrubbed.

Great. Now she'd have to replace the whole closet carpet.

Tori reached behind her, fingers searching through the hanging clothes until she found an old gym shirt. Cotton. Soft from a hundred washes. She pulled it free from the hanger and wrapped it around her forearm, applying pressure to the knife wound.

The bleeding slowed. The cut wasn't deep enough for stitches. Just a clean slice across the muscle that would heal in a week or two. But deep enough to remind her how close that knife had come to something vital. An artery. A tendon. Her throat.

She should have listened to Blade last year when he'd suggested extending the hardwood flooring into the closet during her bedroom renovation. "You'll thank me later," he'd said, standing in her doorway with his arms crossed, watching the contractors lay the new planks. "Carpet's a pain to maintain."

Now she'd have to rip out the bloodstained carpet and pray she could find matching hardwood. The original flooring had been discontinued six months after installation. Of course it had.

Time moved like molasses. Each second stretched into minutes. She counted her heartbeats. Focused on breathing. In through her nose. Out through her mouth. The way Stryker had taught her during those early days at the gym when panic attacks had ambushed her without warning.

The front door burst open.

Heavy footsteps thundered across her hardwood floors. Multiple sets. Controlled movements. Professional. Cops clearing a house.

"Clear!"

"Bedroom clear!"

"Kitchen clear!"

"Tori!" Blade's voice boomed through the noise. "Tori! Where are you?"

She opened her mouth to answer. Nothing came out. Five seconds ago, she was worried about the carpet, and now . . . Now she couldn't speak. Her throat had locked completely. Words trapped somewhere between her brain and her vocal cords. Watching shadows move under the door.

Stay silent. Stay hidden.

The rational part of her screamed that these were the good guys. Blade was here. Help had arrived. But she pressed deeper into the corner, making herself smaller. Invisible.

"Bathroom clear!"

"Living room clear!"

Footsteps approached her bedroom. "Tori, it's me."

Blade.

She couldn't hear his movements. Probably going slow, checking behind furniture, under the bed. Looking for threats. Looking for her.

"If you can hear me, you're safe now. We're here."

His voice was closer. Right outside the closet door. She could see the bedroom light flick on through the crack where the door didn't quite meet the frame.

All she had to do was speak. Say his name. Reach out and push the door open.

Her hand remained frozen on the gun. Her voice stayed buried.

The closet door creaked open. Light spilled across her face, forcing her to squint against the sudden brightness. Blade stood silhouetted in the doorway, his massive frame blocking most of the bedroom light behind him.

She must be a sight. Crumpled in the corner like discarded laundry. Gun on the floor. Blood-soaked shirt wrapped around her arm. Eyes wide and glassy with shock.

But Blade didn't speak. Didn't ask if she was okay or demand an explanation. Just snapped his weapon into place and sank to the floor beside her.

The dam broke.

Relief crashed over her like a tsunami, washing away every defense she'd built. The sobs came from somewhere deep inside. Ugly, wrenching sounds that she hadn't heard herself make since she was a child. Her body shook with the force of them. Tears streamed down her cheeks, mixing with snot that she couldn't control.

His arm came around her, pulling her closer. Not romantic or possessive. Just shelter. His hand rested on her shoulder, thumb moving in circles against her collarbone.

She surrendered. Let her head fall against his shoulder. The cotton of his shirt was soft against her cheek, warm from his body heat. He smelled like coffee and the faint trace of his cologne. He simply existed beside her, solid and unmoving as a mountain. And in the quiet safety of his presence, she let herself fall apart.

Blade still didn't speak. Didn't try to fix anything or offer empty reassurances. His heartbeat thrummed steady beneath her cheek. Each beat sent heat through her bloodstream and made her hyperaware of his arm around her shoulders.

The crying continued. She told herself to stop. Get control. Act like the professional she was supposed to be. But her body refused to cooperate. The fear and adrenaline had to go somewhere, and tears were the only outlet available.

A uniformed officer's head appeared in the doorway, took in the scene, and immediately withdrew. The bedroom door clicked shut, leaving them alone in their cocoon of darkness.

Her eyes felt swollen. Puffy. The sniffling wasn't holding back anything anymore. She wiped her nose on the bloodstained shirt wrapped around her arm and let out a shaky laugh.

"Great. Now I got snot all over my evidence."

Blade's shoulders lifted with quiet laughter. "I never liked that shirt anyway."

His voice was gentler than usual. Missing the sharp edge of his classic sarcasm. Worry threaded through every word.

"Plus, I'm gonna have to replace this whole carpet now." She gestured weakly at the bloodstains beneath them. "You know how hard it is to find matching hardwood? The original stuff was discontinued."

"We'll figure it out." He squeezed her shoulder. "Maybe go with something easier to clean next time. Tile. Vinyl. Something that doesn't show blood."

"You suggesting I'm gonna make a habit of bleeding in my closet?"

"With your track record? Probably smart to plan ahead."

The banter steadied her breathing. Grounded her in something normal. Something that felt like home.

"You ready?" Blade asked after a few more minutes.

She nodded, even though she wasn't sure. Ready for what? To face the destroyed bedroom? To relive what happened? To admit that her stalker had escalated beyond anything she'd prepared for?

Tori pushed herself to her feet, legs unsteady beneath her. She reached down and helped Blade up, his weight pulling her forward slightly as he rose. They moved to the edge of her bed, careful to avoid the glass scattered across the floor.

The bedroom looked worse in the light. Furniture overturned. Blood spatter on the walls.

"Can you tell me what happened?" Detective mode engaged.

She stared at that window. The torn screen fluttering in the night breeze. All her security measures had been useless. The motion sensors. The reinforced locks. The alarm system. None of it had mattered when the stalker had decided to come in while she slept. If he could get past all her defenses this easily, what else could he do? Where else could he reach her?

"I don't know how he got in." The words felt thick in her throat. "He might have been here. Under the bed, I think. Or in the bathroom. Somewhere he could watch me sleep."

Blade's gentle concern hardened into skepticism. She could read the calculation running behind his eyes.

Not possible. He'd swept the house. Checked every room, every closet, every potential hiding spot before he'd left. His search had been thorough. Military-grade systematic.

"Maybe he disabled the alarm somehow." The words came out sounding weak.

"Was it the stalker?" Blade's voice carried that detective tone now. Fact-gathering. Building a timeline.

She nodded. Yeah. Had to be. The voice was the same one from her bedroom. She'd know it anywhere. Who else would break into her house? Who else knew her routines well enough to time an attack when she was most vulnerable?

"Did you see his face?"

Tori shook her head, suddenly realizing she was standing there in a sports bra and running shorts. She wrapped her arms around herself. "He was wearing a mask."

But she remembered the knife. Different than last time. Bigger. Not the same weapon he'd pressed against her throat in the gym parking lot. She really didn't want to think about this right now. About what that escalation meant. About how close she'd come to bleeding out on her bedroom floor instead of hiding in her closet with a superficial cut.

But strength was returning. Flowing back into her limbs like blood returning to a sleeping hand. The warrior persona that had carried her through foster care. Through college and medical school, through her residency. Through every challenge life had thrown at her. She could feel it stirring. Ready to fight back.

Blade's phone rang.

He pulled it out, glanced at the screen. Kiara's picture glowed. His thumb silenced the vibration, and he reached to put it back in his breast pocket.

"Answer it."

"Nah. It can wait."

"Don't you make her wait." The words came out sharper than intended. "If you can take her call, you should always take her call."

He looked at his phone like he was thinking better of it. Hesitation flickered across his features. He should jump at the chance to talk to Kiara. The woman he'd been dating for five months. The woman who made him talk in cutesy ways Tori had never heard before.

Finally, he swiped to answer. "Hey, you."

As soon as she heard him say the words, she wanted to kick herself. What was wrong with her? Having him here, focused only on her crisis, felt like the first safe moment she'd had in weeks.

Kiara's honeyed voice drifted through his way-too-loud volume setting, and the sound sliced through whatever fragile connection had been building between them.

Tori's gaze swept her bedroom. The clock, upside down on the floor, said it was only 10:14 p.m.

Numbness crept in from her fingertips. That neurological shutdown she recognized from her residency when the pressure became too much. Emotional anesthesia. Her body's way of protecting her when everything spun beyond control.

She caught fragments of Kiara's words through the phone. ". . . found what you were looking for . . ."

Blade's eyes cut to Tori's. "I'm at a scene right now."

She noticed he didn't mention her name. Didn't explain where he was or what had happened. Just kept it vague. Professional distance.

Pull it together. The warrior persona slid back into place like armor. The terrified woman who'd hidden in the closet was gone. Dr. Tori Crew, behavioral analyst, had returned.

Blade checked his watch. "Yeah, that works. I'll see you then."

Tori realized he was about to ditch her. Leave her with the responding officers to process the scene while he went to meet his girlfriend.

But Blade hung up and turned to her.

She opened her mouth to give him an out. Tell him she'd be fine handling this alone. He should go. Be with Kiara.

Blade spoke first. "You up for seeing the Crew murder book tonight?"

She didn't even think. "Yes."

"Okay then," Blade said. "Let's get you cleaned up."

Blade unwrapped the bloody shirt from her arm. The cut ran three inches across her forearm. Not deep enough for stitches, but it would scar.

Two cuts now. One on her throat. One on her arm.

The stalker had marked her twice, but the second cut would be his last.

12

THE GRAY FOG PRESSED against Stryker like cotton batting, muffling everything. Everything except that steady beep . . . beep . . . beep that marked time in this nowhere place.

Stryker drifted. Consciousness without anchor. Without form. Just awareness. Floating in an endless void. Trapped in a place where memory had no shape and time held no meaning.

Something changed.

A dull pressure settled on his arm. Real. Immediate. The first concrete sensation he'd felt in . . . how long? Days? Weeks?

The pressure increased, fingers wrapping around his bicep.

Then the needle.

Cool metal pierced his skin, sliding deep into muscle. He tried to flinch. Tried to pull away. His body remained a prison. Unresponsive. Dead weight anchored to a bed he couldn't see.

The helplessness crashed over him like a tide. Complete. Absolute. A mind trapped in flesh that no longer obeyed.

Pressure in his veins. The needle pinched as it moved. Pressure again.

"Last one." A voice close to his ear.

The needle withdrew with a wet pop.

"Oops," the voice said. "Sorry about that."

What had gone wrong?

But then . . . a smell.

Sharp. Metallic.

Blood.

The scent hit his consciousness, cutting through the fog.

Not just any blood. His blood.

The copper tang that had filled his nostrils during countless fights, countless crime scenes, countless moments when violence had painted the world red.

The smell was a key turning in a lock.

The gray void shattered.

The beeping monitor faded to silence.

Twenty-six years collapsed in an instant.

The smell of blood hovered in the air. Fresh. Warm. Still spreading across hardwood floors in dark, arterial pools.

Stryker's radio crackled against his shoulder. "Unit 47, what's your status?"

Damien keyed his mic. "We need paramedics. Now." The code for homicide rolled off his tongue. Numbers that meant another family destroyed, another crime scene to process. "And bring child services."

The last part hit harder than it should have. Stryker crouched at the closet entrance, studying the little girl. Her purple princess nightgown was pulled over her knees, and she rocked. Back and forth. Back and forth. The fabric showed cartoon crowns and sparkly wands, innocent images that belonged in bedtime stories, not crime scenes.

Her forehead pressed against her knees, long dark hair falling like a curtain around her face. She hadn't acknowledged his presence. Hadn't even flinched when he spoke.

What did you say to a little girl who may have just witnessed her parents' murder?

He'd arrested child abusers, responded to domestic violence calls where kids cowered in corners. But this felt different. This child had retreated so far inside herself that the outside world might not exist.

"Hey, sweetie," he said. "Can you tell me your name?"

Nothing. The rocking continued.

Behind him, the man's breathing grew more labored. Wet. Rattling. Time was running out for everyone in this house.

Stryker reached toward the little girl, fingers extended. Maybe physical contact would break through whatever wall she'd built around herself.

The moment his hand touched her shoulder, she erupted.

A scream tore from her throat. High-pitched. Primal. Pure terror given voice. She thrashed against the closet wall, small fists beating at the air, eyes wide but unseeing.

"Hey, hey." He pulled his hand back, palms raised. "You're okay. You're safe."

The screaming stopped as suddenly as it started. She collapsed back into her rocking position, forehead to knees, as if the outburst had never happened.

His radio crackled. Paramedics were still five minutes out, but it was already too late for the man and woman behind him. And this little girl was trapped in a nightmare that wouldn't end.

He lowered himself to the closet floor, settling beside her with his back against the wall. Close enough to help if needed. Far enough away that she wouldn't feel cornered.

He didn't speak. Didn't try to touch her again. Just sat in the darkness, matching her rhythm. When she rocked forward, he leaned slightly forward. When she rocked back, he followed.

Sometimes presence was enough. Sometimes sitting with someone in their worst moment was the only thing you could offer.

The little girl's breathing gradually slowed. The mechanical rocking softened into something more natural. Still there, but less frantic.

Sirens wailed in the distance, growing closer.

Damien appeared in the closet doorway, his face grim. He nodded toward the bedroom. "Hey man, we need to do something."

He didn't have to say anything else. In minutes, this house would explode with activity. Paramedics, crime scene techs, detectives, the coroner. Radios crackling, cameras flashing, men and women shouting across a house that should have been filled with Saturday morning cartoons and pancake breakfasts.

The little girl didn't need to see any of that.

Stryker shifted, angling himself to face her more directly. He kept his voice soft, steady. "Sweetie, your daddy and mommy are hurt, and they need some help."

Her head lifted a fraction. Just enough that he caught a glimpse of dark eyes beneath the curtain of hair.

Progress.

"Some very nice people are coming to help them," he continued. "But they need lots of room to work. They have big bags with special tools, and they need to move around without bumping into anyone."

She turned her face toward him. Not fully, but enough that he could see her profile.

"These helpers are really good at fixing people who are hurt," he said. "But while they work, we need to go somewhere quiet where we won't get in their way. Does that sound okay?"

Her eyes met his for the first time. Wide. Dark. Still glazed with shock but present. Aware.

She nodded.

The simple gesture sent relief flooding through his chest. She was still in there. Still reachable.

Stryker swiveled until he could squat in front of her, bringing himself down to her eye level. "Would it be okay if I picked you up and carried you out? I promise I'll be very careful."

For a moment, she just stared at him. Weighing. Deciding.

Then she lifted her arms.

The trust in that gesture nearly undid him. This little girl, who had just lived through only God knew what, was willing to let a stranger carry her to safety.

He scooped her up, and she was impossibly light. His duty belt weighed more than she did. All sharp elbows and bird-thin shoulders, like she might disappear if he held her too tightly.

"I need you to keep your eyes closed, okay?" He placed his hand on the back of her head, guiding her face into his shoulder. "Just like you're playing hide-and-seek. Keep them closed tight until I tell you it's safe to open them."

She buried her face against his uniform shirt, fingers gripping the fabric.

Stryker positioned his other hand over her eyes, creating a double barrier. No matter what, she wouldn't see the blood. Wouldn't see her father's still form on the bedroom floor. Wouldn't carry those images with her for the rest of her life.

He stood, cradling her against his sternum, and moved toward the closet entrance.

Just before they crossed the threshold, she whispered against his shoulder. So quiet he almost missed it.

"What about Nikos?"

The question stopped him cold. Nikos. A name. A person.

The empty crib.

The paramedics came through the front door ready to save lives. Damien pushed past him, moving to intercept them.

"Hold up," Damien said. "This is an active crime scene. We need to preserve evidence before you start tracking through here."

Stryker adjusted his grip on the little girl. The paramedics had protocols for this. They'd know how to handle a traumatized child without making things worse.

"Sweetie," he said, "there's a nice lady here who's going to take you to the ambulance. She needs to make sure you're not hurt anywhere."

The girl's head lifted from his shoulder. Her dark eyes found the female EMT standing in the doorway. A woman with graying hair pulled back in a sleek ponytail and the kind of calmness that came from years of emergency calls.

"Hi there, sweetheart." The EMT stepped forward, hands visible. "My name's Carol. I'm going to take really good care of you, okay?"

The girl looked between Stryker and Carol, processing. Then she nodded.

The transfer happened with surprising ease. Carol lifted the girl from Stryker's arms like she'd done this ten thousand times with her own children, cradling her with practiced efficiency.

"We'll be right outside," Carol said, already moving toward the door. "Take your time in here."

The girl didn't protest. Didn't scream. Just let herself be carried away from the nightmare behind her.

Stryker watched them disappear through the front door, then hurried to where Damien stood blocking the other first responders.

"There might be someone else here," he said. "The girl asked about Nikos."

Damien's eyes flicked around the living room like he expected to see someone standing there among the furniture. "We searched everywhere, man. Top to bottom."

"Not under the beds."

The words hung for a beat. Then Damien turned without another word, heading toward the children's rooms.

Stryker moved in the opposite direction, back toward the master bedroom. He unsnapped his holster but left the weapon seated.

The bedroom felt smaller now, the metallic smell of blood thicker. Stryker stepped carefully around the dark pools spreading across the hardwood, positioning himself on the far side of the bed, the only patch of floor not yet pooling blood.

He crouched down, fingers gripping the dust ruffle.

It was then he heard it. A small, hitched breath. A tiny, almost inaudible whimper from the darkness beneath the bed.

He lifted the fabric.

The smell of urine hit him first. Then his eyes adjusted to the shadows. Two dark eyes stared back at him, wide with a terror that went beyond tears.

A boy. The same dark hair, the same eyes as the girl.

Dark hair was matted to his forehead. Blood streaked his cheek like war paint. More blood, dark and drying, coated his small hand and the handle of the kitchen knife clutched in his fist.

13

CRIME SCENE TECHS MOVED through Tori's space, gathering evidence like ants dismantling a picnic. Blade positioned himself against the kitchen counter, arms crossed, watching the paramedic work on Tori's forearm.

Paul Something-or-other. Clean-shaven, broad shoulders, the kind of easy smile that probably worked on most women.

"You're lucky," Paul said, dabbing medical adhesive along the wound's edges. "Clean cut, no nerve damage. Should heal without much scarring."

Tori sat perfectly still on the couch, her black hair pulled back in a neat ponytail, fresh shirt and jeans replacing the blood-stained clothes from earlier. She'd rebuilt her armor fast.

"Good thing I'm not planning a hand modeling career," she said.

Paul chuckled. "With hands like these? You'd make a fortune."

The flirtation hit Blade like a slap, and his teeth clenched. The reaction made no sense. He had Kiara. Tori was his friend, nothing more. But watching this stranger touch her arm, seeing him lean closer than necessary, it triggered something primitive and protective.

Paul sealed the wound, his fingers trailing across Tori's wrist in a gesture that stretched well past medical necessity. "You'll want to keep this dry for forty-eight hours. No showers, just careful washing around the edges."

"I'll manage."

"I'm sure you will." Paul's smile widened. "But if you need someone to check the bandage tomorrow—"

"She's covered," Blade said, pushing off the counter.

Paul's smile faded. "Right. Of course." He tossed a roll of tape into his medical kit with more force than necessary.

"Detective," Tori said, twisting around to laser him with a stare. "Could you grab me a jacket from my bedroom?"

She was getting rid of him. Fine. He didn't want to stand around and watch anyway. He stomped to Tori's bedroom closet, stepping around a photographer documenting blood spatter on the hardwood. Her clothes hung in neat rows, organized by color and season. He grabbed a lightweight jacket from the end of the rack. Navy blue, practical, the kind she wore to crime scenes.

When he returned to the living room, Paul was gone. Tori sat exactly where he'd left her, hands folded in her lap.

"Here." Blade held out the jacket.

She slipped her arms through the sleeves, careful not to disturb the fresh bandage. "Thanks."

He checked his watch. "You ready?" He kept his voice low, meant only for her. "CSU can handle the rest."

Tori's gaze swept the room one more time. A tech was dusting her coffee table for prints. Another officer photographed the broken lamp near the hallway entrance. Her private space had become a public spectacle, every corner exposed and cataloged.

"Yeah." She stood, testing her balance. "Let's go."

Her steps carried a drag now, measured, like every joint protested movement. The crash from the fight had bled out of her, leaving the kind of weariness that worked its way into the bones.

It was just after midnight. He shouldn't have asked her to ride along, not after the beating her night had already given her. But when she'd locked those eyes on him in the closet, he saw it plain. She'd crawl through glass if that's what it took to chase down what happened to her family. No way he was cutting her out of that.

He nodded toward the door. "Time to get that file."

The warehouse sat at the far end of the lot, nothing but gray slabs and barbed wire, cameras fixed like unblinking eyes. Blade slowed at the gate, badge lifted. The guard studied it, swiped a card, and the barrier ratcheted up. The Charger rolled through.

Tori stayed angled against the seat, arms folded, lashes pressed shut like she'd welded herself away from him and the world outside the glass. He'd kept the silence on the ride over, letting her choose when to talk about what happened before he'd found her in the closet.

He parked and cut the engine. The rumble died, leaving a silence that settled in his ears like cotton. His hand tapped the gearshift on autopilot. Tap, tap, tap. Index, middle, ring.

In ten minutes, they'd walk into that building with Kiara, her career on the line. Not just her job but her reputation. Her clean, safe world where the worst thing that happened was a misfiled court document or a cranky judge. Or a boyfriend who constantly stood her up.

He had no idea why she put up with him. Kiara represented everything that had been missing from those years growing up in the Everglades. She made him picture Sunday mornings that didn't begin with checking over his shoulder. Maybe a house with an actual foundation instead of cinderblocks and rust. Kids who'd never know what it meant to go hungry while their father disappeared for days, chasing the next score that would fix everything and never did.

With Kiara, normal wasn't just some fantasy he'd glimpsed through other people's windows. She was the hope of a future he'd only imagined.

The passenger seat creaked as Tori shifted. She'd been miles away from how she'd brushed off the first attack. No wisecracks. No professional detachment. The second assault had cracked something in her armor, and he could see the fracture lines spreading.

He angled to face her. "You sure about this? After everything that's happened, maybe we should wait. Give you time to process."

She locked onto the building through the windshield, unblinking. Her bandaged arm lay in her lap, jacket sleeve hiding the square of gauze beneath.

"I'm sure."

"Because once we see what's in that file, there's no going back. Crime scene photos, autopsy reports . . . It's not going to be easy."

Tori lifted her eyes to his. No spark this time, no teasing edge, no sharp read on him. She'd dropped every defense, and underneath, where he'd always suspected steel, he found something softer. Something that had been waiting a very long time to stop fighting.

"I couldn't remember."

"What?"

"My entire life, I've had zero memory of that night. I don't remember what my house looked like. Can't picture my parents' faces except from the one photograph I was given in foster care. The same photo that's online. The *only* one online."

Blade's knee stopped bouncing. The crime scene photos would be brutal. He'd seen enough murder books to know. Parents stabbed to death in their own bedroom while their four-year-old daughter hid in a closet. She probably didn't want to see those photos, much less have them burned into her memory forever.

"Do you remember after? The foster homes?"

"Pieces. I read my DHS file a while ago. Nine homes before I ended up with the de Hostos family when I was eight. The case notes said I refused to believe my parents were dead. I had 'behavioral outbursts' and kept running away from foster homes, trying to find them."

"Nine homes." He'd thought his childhood was rough.

"But the de Hostos family never gave up on me." A smile ghosted across her face. "My foster dad, Eugenio, told me if I thought my parents were alive, then he'd help me find them.

"He used to drive me around every Saturday to look for them. I'd sit on my knees and look out the car window while he listened to Julio Iglesias cassettes." She chuckled, soft and bittersweet. "I have no idea how long we really drove around, but it felt like hours. Then sometime around noon, he'd mention he was getting hungry, and we'd stop at the beach and eat empanadillas that Maria had packed.

"When we got home, Maria would sing lullabies in Spanish while she brushed my hair. No questions. No lectures. Just giving me the space to process in my childish ways."

"That sounds really great. Considering." Better than his own childhood, anyway. Foster parents who actually cared enough to drive around looking for ghosts instead of just collecting the state check. "They sound like great people. Why didn't they adopt you?"

"I didn't want it." Tori looked at her hands. "Saying yes to adoption felt like burying parents I wasn't ready to bury."

The truth had more layers though.

"And if I said yes, they'd lose money. The state pays foster families more than adoptive ones. The de Hostos couldn't afford to lose that money." A small shrug. "I thought it would help.

"By thirteen I was running with the wrong kids. Sneaking out. Picking fights. The state was getting ready to move me again." She drew a slow breath. "Stryker found me on the pier that night. He drove out to see Eugenio the next morning. They worked something out with the case worker. Court-ordered placement in the Warrior program. I saw Eugenio and his wife a few times before they moved back to Puerto Rico to take care of Maria's mother.

"We lost touch. They were great, but not my real family." She met Blade's eyes. "That's why I want to see the file. I have no blood family left in this world. I've never remembered anything about them. I just need to see with my own eyes that they didn't abandon me. That they're truly dead and the case can't be solved. Maybe then this aching hole I've had my whole life, the feeling that a piece of me is missing, maybe it will finally go away."

All his doubts about asking Kiara for help, all his worry about crossing lines and bringing Tori here—they evaporated. This wasn't about convenience or shortcuts. This was about a woman who'd spent her entire life wondering if her parents had chosen to leave her behind or if someone really took them from her.

Blade stepped out and rounded to her side. Tori met him at the door before it had fully closed.

He hooked an arm around her shoulders and pulled her in. No quick tap, no throwaway greeting side hug. He locked her against him, anchoring her there, holding on like he could shoulder some of the burden she'd carried since childhood. Inside, he prayed one raw plea.

Lord, fill the hollow she's carried too long.

Headlights swept across the asphalt, slicing through the darkness outside the windshield. He released Tori and saw her swipe at the corner of her eye.

Kiara's sensible sedan parked three spaces over. She climbed out, a smile starting, then slipping. Her eyes cut past him, landing on Tori. He saw it hit her in layers. Her brows tugged down, mouth parting just a fraction. Confusion. A sharp blink. Then the hurt pinched her face before she locked it all away.

"I didn't realize Tori was coming," she said. "I thought you said this was for your case."

Not for Tori. For him. The meaning bled through. She didn't have to spell it out. He caught it clear as a radio signal. She'd shown up believing he needed her help, not because he was running errands for another woman.

He had no choice but to be honest. "The file is for Tori's parents' case. She's the someone who deserves the truth."

"Yeah, of course. I'm sorry, Tori. I'm happy to help." Kiara slipped her arm into his. "Follow me."

He'd be confused by Kiara's sudden shift if he didn't know her like he did. This was straight up Kiara kindness, genuine and unforced.

In all his years with BSO, Blade had never been to the evidence warehouse. The reception area felt like a doctor's office designed by someone who'd never smiled. A bulletproof glass partition separated them from a night clerk who looked like he'd rather be anywhere else.

Blade slid his badge and ID through the metal slot. The motion felt final, like signing a confession. His name would be logged, timestamped, recorded. If Internal Affairs came sniffing around later, they'd know exactly when Detective Blade St. James had accessed sealed files with Records Administrator Kiara Kerns.

The clerk barely glanced at their credentials before sliding a logbook through the slot. Blade signed his name in careful block letters, noting the time. Tori signed next, her handwriting small, loopy strokes he could barely read. When Kiara added her signature, her pen hesitated for just a moment before completing the final stroke.

Point of no return.

The clerk buzzed them through a heavy metal door that sealed behind them with a pneumatic hiss. The hallway beyond stretched like a hospital corridor, all white walls and industrial carpet. Security cameras tracked their movement from ceiling-mounted housings every twenty feet.

"Digital Records Room is this way," Kiara said. Her cardigan brushed against his arm as they walked. "The physical evidence for the Crew case is stored in Section C, but it's sealed with a judicial signature. I can't override that without a court order."

Tori nodded. "What's all in the digital files?"

"Everything that was scanned or photographed. Crime scene photos, witness statements, autopsy reports, detective notes." Kiara glanced back at Tori. "We can view it all on the secure workstation, but no printing. The system logs every document that gets printed, and sealed files trigger automatic alerts."

They passed doors marked with codes and warnings: AUTHORIZED PERSONNEL ONLY. BIOHAZARD. CLIMATE CONTROLLED. The building felt like a tomb for evidence, each room holding pieces of lives destroyed and justice sought.

Kiara stopped at a door marked DIGITAL RECORDS—RESTRICTED ACCESS. She swiped her keycard and placed her palm on a biometric scanner. The lock disengaged with a soft beep.

"Once we go in there and I log into the system, we're committed," she said, her hand still on the door handle. "If anyone reviews the access logs, they'll see I pulled a sealed IA file after-hours with two unauthorized personnel present."

Blade met her gaze. Her green eyes held worry but also compassion. She understood what this meant to Tori. What it meant to him.

"Last chance to back out," he said.

Kiara pushed the door open. "Let's get some answers."

The Digital Records Room felt like a bunker. Three workstations lined the far wall, each equipped with dual monitors and keyboards that looked like they could survive a nuclear blast. No windows. No decorations. Just white walls, industrial carpet, and the steady hum of climate control systems working to preserve digital evidence.

Blade counted four security cameras mounted in the corners, their red recording lights blinking like electronic heartbeats. Every keystroke would be logged. Every file accessed would leave a digital fingerprint leading straight back to Kiara's credentials.

Kiara took the chair at the center workstation. Tori took the one to her left, and Blade pulled up another to her right. Kiara settled at the keyboard.

"Before we start," he said, "we need to confirm the responding officer was Damien Sullivan. That's our priority."

Tori nodded, her bandaged arm resting in her lap. The lights washed the color from her face, making the dark circles under her eyes more pronounced. She'd been running on adrenaline for hours, but the crash was coming.

Kiara's shoulders tensed as she entered her login credentials. The system prompted for additional authentication. A security token from her keychain that generated random numbers every thirty seconds. She typed the code, hit enter, and waited.

ACCESS GRANTED flashed across the screen in green letters.

Blade's palms began to sweat. The database interface loaded, displaying search fields and dropdown menus. Kiara navigated to the case file system. She typed "CREW" in the victim name field, selected "HOMICIDE" from the case type dropdown, and entered the date range.

One result populated: CREW, NIKOS & JI-YEON—DOUBLE HOMICIDE—CASE #98-444-MH.

"There it is." Kiara clicked the case number.

A warning dialog appeared: SEALED FILE—IA RESTRICTED ACCESS. JUDICIAL ORDER REQUIRED. UNAUTHORIZED ACCESS SUBJECT TO CRIMINAL PROSECUTION.

Kiara's finger hesitated over the mouse. Blade could see her pulse jumping in the hollow of her throat. She was thinking about her career, her future, the safe life she'd built for herself. All of it hanging in the balance.

Tori touched Kiara's arm. "You don't have to—"

"No." Kiara clicked OVERRIDE. "Blade is right. You deserve the truth."

The murder book exploded across the screen in a cascade of scanned documents, photographs, and reports. Crime scene photos dominated the first section. Images that made his stomach roil. Blood spatter patterns on bedroom walls. Overturned furniture. Bodies positioned at unnatural angles.

Tori's breath caught, and she gripped the edge of the desk.

"Skip the photos," he said. "Text only. Just the reports."

Kiara scrolled past the crime scene documentation, past the autopsy photos, past the evidence inventory. The responding officer's report appeared, typed on an old police department form with carbon paper smudges.

RESPONDING OFFICERS: SGT. D. BARCLAY, OFF. E. SEGARRA

Not Damien Sullivan.

Tori leaned forward. "Go back to the victim information."

Kiara scrolled to the case summary, and he read the details aloud as they appeared. "Victims: Nikos Stavros Crew, age forty-one, forensic accountant. Ji-Yeon Crew, age thirty-eight, biomedical researcher. Cause of death: Homicidal Violence. Multiple stab wounds."

His eyes landed on the next line, and he glanced at Tori. Her fingers touched her lips, her gaze fixed on the screen.

"Victim three," she whispered. "Unborn female child, approximately thirty weeks gestation." Tori's chin sank. Her hair curtained her face as her shoulders tucked inward. "She . . . she was pregnant."

Blade pushed back from the workstation and went to Tori. His hands found her shoulders, and he swiveled her to face him. Her dark eyes glistened. "Tor, I'm so sorry. How awful."

Behind him, he could feel Kiara's presence, could sense her watching him comfort Tori. Maybe this made her uncomfortable, seeing how naturally he moved to shield Tori from pain. But Kiara would understand—she had to. Right now, nothing else mattered except giving Tori something solid to lean against while she processed another devastating loss.

Tori swiped her nose with the back of her good hand. "I just—I wish I'd known. All these years . . . A sister." Her voice cracked on the last word. "She would've been born in September."

Another loss to add to Tori's collection. Parents she couldn't remember. Ten foster homes she'd cycled through, the last one a family who would have kept her. And now this. A sister who'd never drawn a breath. Never had a chance.

His thumbs traced gentle circles against her shoulders. "I'm sorry."

Inadequate, he knew, but what else could he say?

Tori nodded and straightened, pulling herself together. She turned back toward the screen, but he left one hand on her arm.

"Keep going, Kiara," she said. "I need to see the rest."

"You sure?" Kiara looked between them, but Blade gave her a subtle nod to let her know it was okay. Tori would read it herself if Kiara didn't.

Kiara drew in a breath and read, "Survivors found at scene: Victoria Crew, female. Nikos Crew Jr., male."

Tori's head jerked up to look at him. Eyes wide, mouth parted, locked on those words that punched the air out of the room.

Blade felt the ground shift beneath him, and his fingers tightened on Tori as he stared at the screen. Not just one survivor. Two. Two children found at that crime scene.

"You have a brother?" Kiara asked.

Tori's hand moved to her throat, fingers tracing the scabbed cut there. "I have a brother."

14

TORI FELT LIKE SHE MIGHT THROW UP. A sister. A helpless infant murdered while still in her mother's womb. Who could do such a thing? Who could stab a woman carrying a baby? The room swayed, and she grabbed the edges of her chair to steady herself. But there were survivors—plural.

She stared at the screen until the letters blurred.

Nikos Crew Jr., male.

A brother.

She had a brother.

Two survivors. The truth sat in her chest like a stone, too heavy to lift, too sharp to ignore. Every foster home. Every birthday. Every Christmas morning when she'd wondered if somewhere out there was family who remembered her . . . There had been. A boy who'd survived the same nightmare, who'd hidden somewhere in the same house while their parents bled out in their bedroom.

"Tori." Blade's voice sounded far away. He took his hand off her and tapped the monitor. "Look here. At the date of birth."

She forced her eyes to focus. DOB: 04/15/1994.

April fifteenth. Her birthday.

"I have a twin . . ."

The information sent her spiraling. Not just a brother. A twin. Someone who'd shared her mother's womb. Someone who'd been ripped away before she could even form memories of his face. Her hands trembled in her lap. Years of believing she was alone, of carrying the guilt of being the only one who'd survived.

All of it, a lie.

Kiara looked at her with wide-eyed confusion. "You didn't know? About your brother?"

"No, I never knew." Tori's pulse hammered against her throat. "And I never would have if you hadn't done this. Kiara, I owe you—" She leaned forward, pressing a quick kiss to Kiara's cheek. "I owe you everything for this."

Kiara blinked, touching her cheek where Tori's lips had been.

Blade's eyebrows shot up, but Tori ignored him. The peck had been pure impulse. Completely unlike her. Tori never gushed, never grabbed strangers, never let her emotions spill over like that. But something had shifted inside her. A flicker of life where emptiness used to live.

Blade directed Kiara to open another document, but Tori couldn't pay attention. The world around her diffused. Revelation crashed through her like a tidal wave, washing away years of understanding about herself. All those Saturdays with Eugenio, driving through neighborhoods while Julio Iglesias crooned from the cassette player. The inexplicable pull she'd felt, the certainty that someone was out there waiting for her.

It hadn't been her parents she'd been searching for.

It had been *him*. Her twin.

The psychology textbooks had called it phantom limb syndrome for twins. The persistent sense of incompleteness. The subconscious search for the other half of yourself. She'd studied it. Written papers on it. She just never imagined she was living it.

All those drives through Little San Juan, Coconut Grove, Coral Gables. Had she passed a dark-haired boy on a bicycle? Watched him skateboard past while she pressed her face to Eugenio's passenger window, that phantom ache tugging at her chest?

What did he look like now? Did he have their father's Greek features or their mother's Korean bone structure? Did he search for her the way she'd searched for him, or had he moved on, built a life without the constant ache of something missing?

"Tori." Blade's voice cut through her spiraling thoughts. He'd moved back to his chair, and she hadn't even noticed.

"Sorry." She wiped her palms on her jeans. "I'm here. What does it say?"

"It's Barclay's report." Kiara scrolled, her lips moving as she read. "It's marked as a supplemental report. Filed after the initial investigation."

The timestamp showed 11:47 p.m. Late. The kind of hour when someone filed paperwork they didn't want scrutinized during regular business hours.

"Read it out loud," she said. "Please. I don't think I can focus."

Because whatever Barclay had written in those late-night hours, whatever truth he'd buried in official language and police codes, it would explain why her twin had vanished from her life.

And maybe, finally, she'd understand how to find him.

"Subject: Supplemental Report—Double Homicide, 5486 Flores Drive," Blade read, sounding 100 percent the homicide detective.

"Responding officers discovered two adult victims, both deceased from multiple stab wounds to the torso, neck, and head. Female victim, Ji-Yeon Crew, age thirty-eight, found in master bedroom. Male victim, Nikos Stavros Crew, age forty-one, also found in master bedroom."

Tori's chest tightened. Her parents' names. Their ages. Numbers that reduced their lives to data points in a police file.

Blade continued, "Female child, age four, discovered unharmed in master bedroom closet. Child exhibited signs of severe trauma but no physical injuries."

Kiara reared back in horror.

Tori tried to ignore it. Tried to keep herself from falling apart. "Keep going."

"Male child, age four, located under bed in master bedroom. Subject was armed with kitchen knife and displayed violent, erratic behavior upon discovery. Child attacked responding officer. Considered a threat to his sister. Officer received wounds requiring multiple stitches. Child required physical restraint."

The words hit like punches. *Violent.* Cross to the jaw. *Erratic.* Jab to the ribs. *Threat to his sister.* Uppercut that left her reeling.

"Due to the child's aggressive state and the weapon recovered from his possession, preliminary assessment suggests the male subject may have been responsible for the deaths of both parents. Child has been remanded to psychiatric evaluation pending further investigation."

Nausea reared its ugly head again. The detached way Barclay had reduced her four-year-old twin to a case study in childhood violence. A monster in footie pajamas. It made her sick. "No . . . that's not—he was four years old. There's no way—"

"Tori—"

"A four-year-old doesn't commit double homicide!" Her voice cracked. "He was hiding. Just like me. He grabbed a knife because he was terrified."

"Are you saying you remember?" Blade asked in a soft voice.

"No." But an image popped in her mind anyway. A boy with dark hair and her father's eyes, clutching a bloody knife. Her twin painted as a killer before he'd learned to tie his shoes.

The violation felt worse than the murders themselves. Someone had taken a traumatized child and twisted his survival instincts into evidence of guilt. Had branded him dangerous, unstable, a threat to the sister he'd never even had the chance to protect.

"Find the witness statements." Her hands clenched into fists. "The psych evaluations. Everything Barclay filed after this report."

"Tori, maybe we should—"

"There has to be proof." She stood, her voice gaining strength. "Real evidence. Not just Barclay's interpretation of a scared little boy defending himself."

Because she refused to believe her brother was the villain they'd made him out to be.

"Maybe we should give you some space," Kiara said, pushing back from the desk. "This is a lot to process. Blade and I could step over—"

"No." The word shot out before Tori could think. She glanced at Blade as he got up, catching his steady blue gaze. Something settled in her chest at the sight of him.

"She's right." He pulled Tori under his arm as he had earlier. "We've come this far. Let's keep going. Together."

"I need you here," she said, looking up at him.

The admission surprised her with its clarity, but tucked under her friend's arm she knew. She needed Blade. His quiet strength, his presence, the way he absorbed turmoil without flinching. The same way he'd found her in that closet tonight, offering comfort without words.

"And I need you too," she said to Kiara.

A faint line cut across Kiara's forehead, then disappeared. She dipped her chin once. "I'll find the psychiatric evaluation."

They sank back into their seats, and she studied the blond woman's profile as she scrolled through the files. Watching her, Tori understood why Blade loved her. Kiara carried a quiet grace. Kindness without judgment. The kind that made broken people feel seen.

"Here, I think this is it," Kiara said. "Dr. Jamie Colley, dated October twentieth, 1998."

"By day six of the post-incident reports," Tori said.

"Patient presents with severe behavioral dysregulation following traumatic event," Blade read. "Initial assessment reveals hypervigilance, aggressive outbursts, and persistent delusions regarding threats to his safety. Patient refuses to speak about the incident and becomes violent when questioned about his sister's whereabouts."

He was looking for me. The thought pierced through her. While she had no recollection of him at all, her twin had been fighting to find her.

"Day three," Kiara continued. "Patient attacked orderly with plastic spoon, requiring physical restraint. Exhibits paranoid ideation, claiming 'bad men' are coming to hurt his sister. Refuses medication. Screams for Victoria during night terrors."

Tears burned behind Tori's eyes. He'd called her by name. Even in his terror, even as the system labeled him dangerous, he'd been trying to protect her. And she'd forgotten him.

"Day seven." Blade's voice grew quieter. "Patient's condition deteriorating rapidly. Hallucinations increasing in frequency and intensity. Claims to see 'shadows with knives' in his room. Self-harm behaviors emerging. Patient has bitten through his tongue and clawed at his arms until they bleed."

The clinical language couldn't mask the horror. A four-year-old boy, traumatized beyond comprehension, spiraling into madness while doctors took notes.

"Final assessment," Kiara whispered. "Patient diagnosed with extreme form of early-onset paranoid schizophrenia with homicidal ideation. Prognosis: Poor. Recommend immediate transfer to specialized facility for long-term psychiatric care."

The words hung in the air like a death sentence. Tori's twin, branded insane before kindergarten. Shipped away like a broken toy that couldn't be fixed.

"There's more," Blade said. "A sealed court order."

Kiara's fingers hesitated over the keyboard. "This is marked classified."

"No, don't." Tori reached out, covering Kiara's hand with her own. "You've risked so much already."

Kiara opened the file. "You need to know what happened to him."

The court seal filled the screen. Tori read the header twice before the words penetrated: *In re: Nikos Crew Jr., Minor Child—Petition for Identity Expungement and Protective Transfer.*

"By petition of the guardian ad litem," Tori read, "and because of the unique and severe nature of the child's psychosis, and for the mutual protection of both the subject and his surviving twin, this court orders the immediate legal expungement of Nikos Crew Jr.'s identity."

Expungement. They'd erased him. Wiped him from existence like he'd never been born.

"The subject's name shall be legally changed," Kiara continued. "All birth records, medical files, and identifying documents shall be sealed. The subject is hereby ordered to immediate and permanent transfer to Aletheia Psychiatric Research Institute, Seattle, Washington."

"Hmm," Blade said, pressing his thumb against his lower lip.

"What?" Tori asked. "What's wrong?"

"Probably nothing," he said, dropping his hand. "A label on Florek's folder had 'Psychiatric Research Institute' on it."

Kiara's head tilted. "Aletheia Psychiatric Research Institute?"

"Didn't see the full name. An attorney covered it pretty quick."

Aletheia. The name had triggered something in Tori too. She'd heard it before tonight. Or seen it. "We should check into it. Right now, let's keep going."

"Okay, where were we," Kiara said, moving the mouse cursor over the text. "Okay, here we go. 'Furthermore, pursuant to the Juvenile Trauma Witness Protection Act, all records of the subject's new identity and current location are classified. Access restricted to authorized personnel only. Case closed.'"

"Juvenile Trauma Witness Protection Act," Tori whispered. "That's not real, is it?"

Blade shook his head. "Never heard of it."

Had they made it up? Created fictional legislation to justify disappearing a traumatized child?

"Aletheia Psychiatric Research Institute." Kiara pulled up a web search. "It's still operational. Private facility, specializes in experimental treatments for severe mental illness."

Experimental treatments. Tori's blood ran cold. They hadn't just hidden her brother. They'd turned him into a test subject.

"Twenty-six years," she said. "He's been there twenty-six years."

If he was still alive. If the experiments hadn't killed him. If the boy who'd screamed her name in his nightmares had survived whatever they'd done to him.

Tori stared at the screen until the words blurred into meaningless shapes, her mind churning through fragments of memory and evidence.

Violent, erratic behavior.

Armed with kitchen knife.

Paranoid ideation.

Shadow people.

Something cold began to crystallize in her chest. Not grief. Not loss. Something far worse.

"The knife," she said.

Blade looked up from the file. "What?"

"He knew my routine," she said. "Weeks of surveillance. He knew when I left for work. When I came home. He knew about the gym, about my schedule."

"Tori—"

"Subject was armed with kitchen knife. Patient attacked orderly with plastic spoon. Claims to see 'shadows with knives' in his room." Her voice cracked. "He was obsessed with knives. Always a knife. Never a gun, never anything else. Just knives."

And blood.

A pattern blazed across her consciousness like neon. Was it possible? A four-year-old boy, traumatized by blades. Could he grow into a man who wielded them like extensions of himself?

"The things he said to me." Her breath came in short bursts.

"About shadows. He said I didn't understand the darkness, but he did."

Blade's face went pale. "Tori, what are you saying?"

"Experimental treatments. What if they didn't cure him, Blade. What if they just made him worse?"

The stalker's words breathed into her ear: *"I'm your shadow."*

"The timing." She began pacing, her mind working through the evidence like a crime scene. "A stalker shows up around the time when Damien asked me to come to the prison. And he escalates when we start investigating the Crew murders. When we start asking questions about what really happened that night."

Kiara's eyes widened. "You think your brother's been watching you?"

"He could've been watching me for years." The admission tasted like poison. "Maybe he escaped from Aletheia, maybe they released him. But I think . . . I think he found me."

15

BLADE POPPED A PIECE OF GUM in his mouth, eyes catching the evidence warehouse shrinking in the rearview mirror. Tori sat rigid beside him, shoulders tight as a wire. That file—the psychiatric evaluations, the court orders, the entire timeline—it didn't add up.

"That file bothers me."

Her head swiveled toward him. "What do you mean?"

He drummed his fingers against the wheel. "I've reviewed thousands of case files over my career. This one ticks every box. Looks perfect on paper. But Damien says he was the responding officer that night, and his name doesn't show up anywhere."

"Someone is lying."

"My money's on Damien." He chewed the gum harder and merged onto I-95.

"To fabricate that much information, you'd need serious resources."

"Exactly. Why would Barclay, or anyone really, go to such lengths just to frame Nikos? What's his motive to frame a child?" He let the question hang, but his glance at her told him she didn't want to consider her brother had committed such a horrible act.

"Then why did Damien want to stir all this up again?"

"Maybe boredom. Maybe prison gossip. He heard you're a regular at Union and decided to stir the pot."

Tori stared ahead, processing. "You think he made it all up?"

"I think he's playing head games. Using your trauma to get attention or hoping for some kind of deal or transfer." He clenched the gum between his molars, the anger behind the idea slicing thin. "He's a manipulative piece of garbage. Destroyed his own family. Why not try yours too?"

Her gaze fixed on the road ahead, empty of expression but full of calculation. Blade recognized the effort it took for her to separate the personal from the professional. A twin she didn't remember. A brother responsible for murdering their parents. And a prisoner who talked in circles and probably had them chasing their own tails. Every twitch, every pause, told him she was cataloging it all, testing her own theories.

"I don't know," she said finally. "He was convincing. If he hadn't sent us after the file, I'd still be in the dark about Nikos."

Before they pulled him away, Damien had sounded . . . desperate.

"What did he shout as they dragged him out?"

Tori's eyes closed. "He said it started with them. My mother knew about the fractals."

"Right. Then he mentioned it was the start of a pattern."

"And he said Barclay lied. The official report's a cover-up." She opened her eyes. "He said Barclay created a second murder book."

Blade's fingers froze on the wheel. *Second murder book.*

"You think there's something to it?" she asked.

That doubt stuck like a splinter. Damien's desperation hadn't felt staged. Warning? Or the manipulation of a con artist working an angle? "I hate to admit it, but yes. Sounded like he was trying to warn you about something bigger."

"We need to talk to Damien again."

She'd read his mind. "Yeah, and if there's a second murder book, we find it. No more surprises."

"Speaking of surprises, where are we going? You missed my exit."

Blade glanced at the highway signs flashing past. "No way you're going home tonight."

Tori's head snapped toward him. "Excuse me?"

"Excuse me? Excuse you. Your house is a crime scene mess after someone tried to kill you. I'm not leaving you alone." He kept his eyes on the road. "You can crash at my place."

"I don't need a babysitter."

"Good thing I'm not applying for the job. The pay's terrible and the hours are worse."

She crossed her arms. "I can just stay with Harlee."

"Right. Wake up Harlee at this time of night and see how that goes for you. She's a bear when her sleep gets interrupted. She'll rip your face off before you finish explaining why you're standing on her doorstep."

"Yeah, well, your girlfriend isn't going to love the idea of another woman sleeping over."

He shrugged. "It's no big deal. You've crashed there plenty of times. Remember our Lord of the Rings marathon? You made it through exactly half of *Fellowship* before you were snoring on my sectional."

"I was not snoring." Her indignation was exactly what he'd hoped for.

"You sounded like a freight train with a deviated septum."

"That's impossible. I have excellent nasal passages." She shifted in her seat. "I was resting my eyes."

"For four hours."

"It was a very long movie," she said. "And the books were better anyway."

"The books were better? Tori, we're talking about Peter Jackson's masterpiece. The battle sequences alone—"

"Were overly dramatized. Tolkien's prose captured the mythology in ways the movies never could. The films turned Faramir into a weak-willed—"

"They're classics, Crew. Cultural touchstones."

"They're three hours of walking and talking about jewelry."

His phone buzzed against the center console. Kiara's name lit up the screen.

He didn't want to answer. For the first time all day his shoulders had dropped below his ears. This easy banter with Tori felt like breathing after holding his breath all day.

Why was everything so easy with her? So natural.

He glanced over, caught himself smiling, and snapped his eyes back to the road.

"You going to answer that?"

"She'll leave a message."

The buzzing stopped.

"You feel bad," Tori observed.

"I feel practical. She's probably calling to see how you're doing. I'll call her back once we're settled and I'm not driving."

"Settled at your place. Where I'm apparently staying whether I like it or not."

"You could always sleep in your car. I hear the back seat of a Honda Civic is surprisingly comfortable."

"I drive a Range Rover."

"Even better. More room to stretch out."

She laughed. "You're impossible."

"I'm thorough. Brother or not, your stalker knows where you live, knows your schedule, knows how to bypass your security system. He's escalated from watching to breaking and entering to attempted murder." Blade's voice hardened. "I'm not giving him a third shot at you."

The laughter faded from her face. "When you put it like that . . ."

"Plus, my couch misses you. It's been asking about you."

"Your couch talks?"

"Only to special people. It's very selective about its conversations."

"What does it say about Kiara?"

The question caught him off guard. He'd never thought about it before, but Kiara rarely came over. She preferred her own space, her own routine. Their relationship existed in careful compartments. Dinner dates, weekend day trips, planned activities that fit neatly into schedules.

"Kiara isn't on speaking terms with my couch," he said.

Tori didn't respond.

Probably the best place to leave it.

They drove in comfortable silence for several miles. Blade took the exit off A1A toward his condo on the narrow strip of island tucked between the Intracoastal and the Atlantic. His phone buzzed with a text. He ignored it.

"You know," Tori said as they pulled into his parking garage, "I held my own tonight."

"I know you did. But handling something alone and having backup aren't mutually exclusive concepts."

She unbuckled her seat belt. "Fair point."

"Besides, someone needs to make sure you don't wake the neighbors with your snoring."

"I told you I don't snore."

"We'll see about that."

Blade unlocked his front door and stepped aside, letting Tori enter first. Her easy agreement to stay over felt less like surrender and more like absolute trust.

She kicked off her shoes and rubbed her temples. "I'm wrecked. I've got to get some sleep."

"You know where the guest room is." He grabbed two water bottles from the kitchen and tossed her one.

"Thanks." She headed down the hallway, her shoulders sagging with exhaustion.

He retreated to his bedroom and tried to shut down for the

night, going through the motions. Gun on the dresser, badge beside it. But the case notes pressed against the back of his mind. Before he knew it, 3:33 a.m. blinked at him from the nightstand. He gave up and reached for his phone. Corbin wouldn't appreciate the hour, but he always answered logic with logic, and he needed that now.

"King."

"It's Blade. You awake?"

"Now I am. What's going on?"

"I need to run something by you, but first—you cannot breathe a word of this to anyone. I accessed a sealed file through unofficial channels."

A pause. "Go ahead."

Blade gave him the rundown: the psychiatric evaluations, the court orders, the transfer to Seattle, the diagnosis of early-onset paranoid schizophrenia. Every detail from Nikos Crew Jr.'s file.

"Hold on," Corbin said when he finished. "You're telling me they had a complete psychiatric workup on a four-year-old within six days? Multiple evaluations, a formal diagnosis, and a sealed court order for transfer to a specialized facility?"

"That's what the file shows."

"Blade, I've worked juvenile cases. Getting a psych eval on a traumatized child takes weeks, not days. And early-onset paranoid schizophrenia in a four-year-old? That's extraordinarily rare. Most psychiatrists won't even diagnose personality disorders in children that young. Plus," Corbin continued, "my father may have been a calculated piece of work, but I'm praying that he's walking a new path these days. Maybe this is about redemption."

"So you think—"

"My gut says the file may've been manufactured. The question is who did it, and why."

"Okay, so I'm not crazy. I just had to talk it out."

"That's what I'm here for, brother."

Blade thanked Corbin and hung up.

He pulled back the covers, but his feet stayed planted on the cold hardwood. If someone had fabricated the file, then the real killer walked free and a four-year-old boy had been framed for murder.

Blade padded into the kitchen only a few hours later, following the rich aroma of coffee that had pulled him from sleep. Tori sat at the kitchen island with her laptop open and hunched over a well-used legal pad, scribbling notes. She had her lips pinched in concentration. Her hair was twisted into some messy updo, and she wore one of his gray undershirts over leggings.

The sight of her made him hold the stare a bit longer. To really look at her. Something about the way the morning light caught the curve of her neck, the focused intensity in her posture, the casual intimacy of her wearing his clothes—

He shook the thought away and reached for his favorite mug. "Did you cut my shirt?"

She glanced down at the hem, which now hit her mid-thigh instead of somewhere around her ankles. "You're a giant. It was either cut it or put a belt around my waist and wear it as a dress."

"And you chose scissors?"

"I didn't have my belt."

"That's destruction of property."

"That's practical problem-solving." She looked back at her laptop screen. "Besides, you have like twenty identical shirts. You won't even notice."

"I'm a detective. I notice everything." He poured coffee into his mug and took the first sip, savoring the bitter warmth. "What are you working on?"

"It's too early to call Aletheia, so I'm cross-referencing the timeline from the file against what Damien told us. Something about the psychiatric evaluation bothers me. The deterioration happened too fast, even for trauma-induced psychosis."

The doorbell rang.

Blade froze, coffee mug halfway to his lips. He'd completely forgotten to text Kiara back. The missed calls. The unanswered messages.

Dread washed over him as he opened the door to find Kiara on his doorstep, looking cheerful and ready for work. The warm, sweet smell of pastries wafted from a white bakery bag in her hands. Her blond hair fell in perfect waves, her green eyes bright with morning energy.

"Good morning, sunshine. I brought you—"

Her gaze flicked past his shoulder and landed on Tori, who had moved to stand by the couch, still wearing his shirt. The warmth in her eyes chilled instantly, replaced by a cool, polite mask.

"Kiara, I can explain—"

"No need." She stepped inside, her voice maintaining its gentle cadence despite the frost in her expression. She placed the bag of pastries on the counter. "After what Tori learned last night, it's understandable she'd need a shoulder to cry on."

"I wasn't crying," Tori mumbled.

His eyes snapped a warning look to her. Not now.

"I just wanted to drop by on my way to work," Kiara said. "Make sure Blade ate something because I know he doesn't always take care of himself." She attempted a smile that didn't reach her eyes. "Coffee isn't a meal, you know."

"Kiara, listen—" He scrambled for words that might fix this.

"Blade, could we have a minute?" Kiara's eyes flicked toward Tori then back to him. "Just us."

Tori snapped the laptop closed and pulled her cord free. She stacked her notepad and laptop under one arm. "I need a shower anyway." Eyes down, she cut across the living room. The guest room door snicked shut, leaving him and Kiara alone.

"Let's sit." He touched her elbow, guiding her to the couch.

Every half-formed excuse collapsed before it left his throat. An apology would never make up for the way he'd dodged her calls, dragged her through Tori's entire case last night, then didn't bother mentioning Tori would be sleeping over. Kiara didn't deserve this.

He sat beside Kiara, and she scooted over, putting space between them.

She studied his face, probably cataloguing the exhaustion. "You look terrible."

"Thanks," he said on a laugh. "Exactly what every guy wants to hear."

She didn't smile. Her gaze dropped to her hands, and he noticed her blush pink nail polish. So perfectly innocent. So perfectly her. The thought of his own stupidity made him feel like pond scum.

"Kiara, there is nothing, and I mean nothing, going on between me and Tori."

She looked up at him, green eyes clear. "That's just it. There's a whole universe between you two. A shared history I could never be a part of."

"That's not—"

"Please." She held up a hand. "This isn't about anything you've done wrong. I'm not accusing you of anything."

The words hit him wrong. She deserved better than his lip service. Better than him fumbling through damage control. Better than whatever this was.

"You're a good man." She squeezed his hand once, then let it go. "But your heart belongs to someone else. I suspect it always has." She laughed without humor. "I don't understand why you two can't see it when everyone else can."

Words gathered, then died on his tongue. He wanted to tell her she was wrong, beg her not to end things. But part of him—the part that had felt something shift when Tori had broken down in his arms last night—knew she was right.

"You and Tori . . . there's something between you two that I could never compete with," she whispered. "And I shouldn't try. You deserve the person who already owns your heart, even if neither of you has admitted it." She swallowed, offering him a sad smile. "You're in love with her, Blade. You just can't see it yet."

In love with Tori?

"Don't be upset. This really is for the best."

She stood and wrapped him in a hug that smelled like her vanilla perfume. "Open your eyes, Blade. Tori's actually an amazing woman."

Her kindness cut straight through him. Anger would have been easier. Jealousy he could have fought against. But this gentle understanding, this graceful exit from his life, left him hollowed out and grateful and ashamed all at once.

He walked her to the door, his feet heavy on the hardwood.

"Take care of yourself." She kissed his cheek, then was gone.

Blade closed the door behind her and leaned against it, staring at the bag of pastries on his counter. The white paper bag sat there like a symbol of the normal life that had just walked out his door.

16

TORI SWITCHED OFF THE BLOW DRYER and flicked her hair back, shaking it out. She couldn't get over the look on Kiara's face when she'd walked in, taking in the obvious overnight situation.

Great. She'd probably just torpedoed five months of Blade's happiness.

It didn't take a psychiatrist to know that women didn't like it when their boyfriend's best friend was another woman. Especially when that woman ended up wearing his clothes at seven in the morning.

God designed men and women to be in relationship. A symbiotic way of meeting each other's needs. And it was only natural for men and women to be drawn into something beyond friendship when they spent extended time with someone of the opposite sex.

The cut on her arm burned like a brand. She shook two Tylenol from the bottle Blade kept stashed in the drawer and sucked water from the tap to swallow them both.

The mirror reflected back dark hair and dark eyes. Complete opposite of the woman Blade loved.

One day, Kiara would draw that line. One day the ultimatum would come.

Maybe that day was today.

Blade would choose Kiara. How could he not? The man had earned peace after everything life had thrown at him. A quiet home. Kids chasing a golden retriever through a backyard. Dinner that didn't come from a takeout bag. She could step aside for that.

She just hadn't pictured Kiara as the one handing him that dream.

Kiara was too . . . soft. Too removed from the ugliness he faced every day. He needed someone who understood the darkness, who could stand beside him in it.

Someone like—

Tori froze. "Like *me*?"

She shook her head. Stupid. The two of them? That was crazy talk. She had to pull her thoughts back to work. That's what mattered right now.

She cracked the bedroom door, peering through the narrow gap. Blade leaned against the counter, sipping his coffee with his shoulders locked in a straight line that screamed damage control. Kiara was nowhere in sight.

"Coast clear?"

"Yep."

She settled back at the island and opened her laptop. The same man who could stare down armed suspects without blinking had been wholly derailed by a pastry bag and whatever had happened with it.

"I'm sorry. That was—"

"You were right." He set the mug on the counter and stared at the dark swirl inside. "Except I didn't end it. She did."

Her mouth wouldn't form words. Ended it? That gentle, perfect woman?

"What? No, Blade—"

"It's fine." He turned toward the sink, rinsing his mug. "Better this way."

"It's not fine. You love her."

"Love? No." He slapped the water faucet off and spun around. "And I want you to drop it, Tori."

The finality in his tone slammed the door shut on any argument she might make.

But she knew him. The dismissal was his way of shoving the pain down deep where it couldn't interfere with the job. It was eating him alive, and she couldn't let him stay in that headspace. She needed her partner sharp, focused. They had work to do. A brother to find, Florek's murder to solve.

Time to speak the only language they both understood.

She grabbed her legal pad and placed it on the counter in front of him. The lattice diagram she'd sketched earlier covered the page. Boxes and arrows connecting their three active cases.

"Look at this."

His eyes locked onto the diagram, and she watched him shift into work mode.

"We've got three cases," she said, pointing to the labeled boxes. "Crew murders, Florek homicide, stalker. All connected one way or another."

She tapped the stalker box. "The file says Nikos showed aggression, obsession with knives, paranoia. My stalker has similar traits and attacked me with a knife both times. But he didn't just attack—he studied me first."

Blade leaned closer, his focus sharpening. "The waiting. The watching."

"Exactly. Classic paranoid behavior but organized. Methodical."

"The file says Nikos has schizophrenia. But stalking requires control. Planning. How does that fit?"

"That's what bothers me." Tori traced the arrow connecting the boxes. "Paranoid schizophrenia with homicidal ideation doesn't usually present as methodical stalking behavior. Most cases show disorganized thinking, impulsive violence, auditory hallucinations driving the aggression. My stalker waited weeks. Learned my patterns. Chose specific moments to approach. That's not psychotic break behavior. That's calculated predation."

"Either the diagnosis was wrong—"

"Or someone wanted us to think it was right." The pieces clicked into place. "What if the psychiatric evaluation was fabricated? What if they needed a reason to disappear a four-year-old witness who saw something he shouldn't have?"

"You don't think Nikos is your stalker anymore?" Blade asked.

"Actually it still fits." She tapped the Crew name on her paper. "Two children witness the horrific murder of their parents. One child develops dissociative amnesia. Complete memory block of the trauma. The other child becomes obsessed with blood and knives."

"And his sister."

She nodded. "The early-onset schizophrenia diagnosis is incorrect at best. A lie at worst. Something to hurry the case along. Made it easier to disappear him without questions."

"It's hard to believe a four-year-old could overpower two adults and stab them to death. Even with that alphabet soup of psychiatric labels they slapped on him." Blade leaned across the counter and grabbed Kiara's pastry bag, pulling out something that looked half donut, half croissant. He offered her the bag.

She normally avoided pastries and sweets. Not worth the sugar crash that always left her sluggish. But the buttery smell was irresistible. She picked one with whipped cream and a strawberry on top. Fruit was healthy, right?

"Dissociative amnesia protects the psyche from unbearable trauma. That's how my brain coped." She licked sugar from her thumb. "But Nikos's brain processed it differently. Instead of blocking the memory, he fixated on it. The violence became his baseline normal."

Blade nodded, chewing. "Makes sense. So, what's our next move?"

"Investigation's your department. I analyze behavior."

"Right, except we're not supposed to know any of these details. Sealed file and all that." He wiped his fingers on a napkin. "But I've got two ideas. First, we talk to our favorite tech nerd, Jett. Maybe he's got some new software up his sleeve that can help us track down what name Nikos's using now."

"And the second?"

"The Damien problem. Every call, letter, visit between us gets monitored. We can't just walk in there and tell him we've seen the file and ask him about the second murder book."

He was right. The urge to call Damien this morning had been strong. She'd even pulled up the prison's number on her phone before second-guessing herself. Every word would have been recorded, analyzed, flagged for review. "So what's your big idea for that one?"

"We use the same methods criminals use." Blade grinned. "It's called the Privilege Channel. We use the attorney-client privilege to pass information to Damien and back."

"That's genius! I could kiss you, but I'd need a stepstool." She punched him in the arm instead.

He laughed, rubbing his bicep. "We'll set it up."

Tori pointed back to the Florek box. "Now let's get a plan for this one too. What do we know so far?"

"Knife attack, personal and prolonged. No forced entry. Valuable items left behind." Blade reached for her pen. "May I?"

She handed it over, and he started filling in details around the Florek box. His handwriting was clean, angular. Cop writing.

"Defensive wounds suggest he fought back," Blade continued, scribbling. "Blood spatter shows the killer paused mid-attack. And the scene presented like a crime of passion slash rage."

"But it wasn't."

"No. Too controlled. Too calculated." Blade dragged a line from *Florek* to *Stalker*. "He followed the same drill. Watched the mark. Mapped the hit."

"Attacked with a knife." Her mouth stopped working. Breath

snagged, half formed. The question shoved through anyway. "Could the stalker have killed Florek?"

Blade stilled, eyes cutting toward her, then he scrawled another note—*trace link: Florek/Crew.*

"Wait—no. I didn't know Donald Florek."

"Doesn't matter," Blade said. "Could've been nothing more than the wrong glimpse. Grocery store. Parking lot. Stalker sees, twists it, decides it means something."

"I don't talk to strange men in grocery stores or parking lots."

Blade dragged his pen across the page, blocky strokes, jotting: *Verify her claim.*

Her mouth twitched before she could stop it. "Your handwriting—so dramatic. Like every letter's bracing for a fight."

"Better than your bubble letters."

"Those are not bubble letters."

"They look like they belong in a middle school girl's diary."

"Shut up." But she was smiling now, and so was he. The tension in his shoulders had eased.

She took the pen and drew another arrow, this one connecting the *Crew* and *Florek* boxes to a central point labeled *Fractals.* "Sullivan mentioned patterns. Dr. Stone identified the symbol as Keplerian."

Blade studied the diagram. She could practically see the gears turning.

"Can you pull up those photos you took at Florek's house and drop them to my iPad?" he asked, already pushing back from the counter.

"Sure." Tori minimized her timeline document and opened her photo gallery. The crime scene images filled her laptop screen, graphic thumbnails of the violence that had torn through Donald Florek's living room.

Blade jogged down the hall, his footsteps slapping against the tile. A drawer screeched open, then slammed. Plastic rattled.

Something dropped, thudded, got shoved aside. He reemerged a beat later, iPad gripped in one hand.

"Why does the battery always seem to be dead on this thing?" He held up the iPad, squinting at the black screen. "I can't find my charger."

"Who needs the babysitter now?" Tori grinned, reaching for her laptop in her bag and grabbing a cable. "Here, but I want it back."

He plugged in the cable and then jammed it into the port. The screen lagged, black and stubborn, until the tablet finally lit. His lock screen filled with a color photo of him and Kiara framed by a bleeding sky over water. Her gaze snagged on the image. She dragged her eyes back to the icons, locking her focus on the job instead of the picture.

Blade climbed onto the chair beside her. She could smell his soap. Something clean and masculine that made her hyperaware of his proximity.

She pushed the photos across to his tablet. Blade picked up his stylus, unlocked a drawing app, and the screen lit with a grid of tools.

"Okay, let's see what we're working with." He flipped through the gallery of photos she'd sent. He tapped the wide shot of Florek's living room and overlaid one from the original crime scene. The overturned furniture, blood spatter, and Florek's mangled body filled the screen in high resolution.

Tori watched as he created a new layer. His fingers moved across the screen like he'd done this a thousand times before. He pulled up the Keplerian fractal image Gino had sent earlier.

"I can lower the opacity and create an overlay," he explained, adjusting settings with quick taps. "See if there's any correlation between the symbol and the scene layout with and without the victim."

The fractal appeared as a translucent geometric pattern over the crime scene photo. Blade used a combination of the pencil and his fingers to resize the overlay, making the Keplerian fractal larger and smaller, testing different proportions and angles.

Tori leaned closer. “How do you know how to do this?”

“I dabble in drawing.” His voice carried a hint of defensiveness.

Her eyebrow hitched up, the kind of lift that pinned him in place without a word.

“What? It relaxes me.” He shrugged, still focused on the screen. “Gives my hands something to do while watching TV.”

As he moved the fractal image around the crime scene, rotating and adjusting, something began to emerge. The geometric lines seemed to align with elements in the room, but not quite.

“Hold on.” Her pulse quickened. “Can you zoom in on the lower part of the photo?”

Blade tapped the screen, enlarging the section that showed Florek’s body and the surrounding furniture.

“Here, let me—” She reached for the screen, her fingers brushing his as she pinched to zoom further.

“Twist to rotate,” he instructed. “Like this.”

Their heads bent close together as they worked, adjusting the overlay. She felt her eyes going wider as the pattern began to align. The Keplerian geometric lines traced along the positioning of Florek’s body, followed the edge of the overturned couch, connected to the coffee table’s corner, drew a perfect line along the fireplace mantel, and terminated exactly where the bloodied book had been placed.

They both stopped and straightened, the significance hitting them simultaneously.

The Keplerian image overlaid nearly perfectly with the crime scene. Every major element—body, furniture, evidence—fell along the fractal’s lines forming a hexagon with additional internal lines forming triangles.

“What did we just stumble into?” she whispered.

The crime scene hadn’t been the result of a frenzied attack or even a calculated murder designed to look passionate. It had been choreographed. Arranged according to a specific mathematical pattern that required advance planning, precise measurements, and an understanding of fractal geometry that went far beyond casual knowledge.

Blade's jaw tightened as he stared at the screen. "This wasn't just murder. This was . . . art."

"Sick art." Tori's stomach churned. "Someone killed Donald Florek and then arranged his body and the scene according to this pattern. They turned his death into some kind of geometric statement."

"Which means our killer isn't just methodical." Blade saved the overlay image to his tablet. "They're educated. Sophisticated. And they wanted us to find this connection."

"Why?"

He met her eyes, and she saw the same realization reflected there. "Because they're not done."

17

BLADE STARED AT THE IPAD SCREEN, the geometric patterns of the fractal overlay searing his retinas. The patterns lined up exactly where his gut had told him they would. Hours of dead ends and false starts and now he had traction.

Exhaustion gave way to the energy that came with a solid lead. Or maybe it was his third cup of coffee, or the butter and sugar from the pastries working their magic. Either way, his mind sharpened, cutting through the fog of the last twenty-four hours.

Kiara's words from that morning still rode shotgun, though. No shouting, no tears. Just that level, gentle tone of hers, steady enough to gut a man.

"You're in love with her, Blade. You just can't see it yet."

He hadn't argued, but maybe he should have. Wasn't that what women wanted? A guy to fight for them? But the look in her eyes said it didn't matter what he claimed. It was already over. And if he was honest with himself, he knew it was the right thing to do.

Still, he'd find a way to make sure Kiara didn't get burned for helping them. She'd risked that nice, clean record of hers pulling the Crew file. It was the kind of favor that could cost her a career if anyone upstairs came sniffing. He owed her for that, no matter where they stood.

Later. Right now, a murderer was out there, probably planning his next move.

Wrong. They'd found his signature.

He flicked a glance at Tori. A faint smear of gauze peeked out of her sleeve where her arm had been patched. She hadn't noticed him watching, too deep in whatever web of data she was spinning. They were in sync. Two investigators with a clear mission to track a highly intelligent killer who turned murder into mathematical patterns. If they were going to catch him, Blade had to get his head in the game.

"This guy's organized. The scene is too perfect for this to be his first time." He tapped the image on his iPad. "We need to find out if there are other victims."

"Agreed. Learning more about his pattern can help us figure out how he chooses his victims and what his timeline looks like," Tori said.

"I need you to take what we know and build me a picture of the kind of unsub who would do this. Education level, background, psychological drivers, the whole package."

"You got it." She used a band from her wrist to put her hair up in a fast ponytail as she talked. "I'll call Harlee and see if she can bring me some clothes."

Blade pushed back from the kitchen island, already reaching for his phone. "I'm going to make some calls while this lead is hot. Get people moving on this."

He scrolled through his contacts and found the number for the Florida Department of Law Enforcement's Pattern Analysis Unit. Three rings, then a man answered.

"Kobilinsky, Pattern Analysis."

"Larry, it's Blade St. James, Broward Homicide. I've got a fractal-aligned staging thread from a homicide. I need a cross-case MO search—Florida-wide, N-DEx if possible. Give me five to ten matches with case numbers, agencies, dates, and a concise 'why this is a match' for each."

"Fractal-aligned staging?" Larry's voice sharpened with interest. "That's a new one. What are we looking at for parameters?"

"Sharp force trauma, knife or similar weapon. Clean crime scene. Victim is a professional, lives alone, no forced entry. Scene shows extensive blood spatter, but killer took time to arrange elements in a specific geometric pattern. The staging isn't random. It's geometrical."

"Okay . . ." He drew the word out.

"I know. It's confusing." Kobilinsky's mind might explode if Blade started talking about dodecahedrons like Dr. Stone had. He figured this was more of a show than tell situation. "Just make sure to note any cases where the geometry matches the fractal overlay we pulled from the crime scene. I'll email it over right after this call. We'll want timelines aligned as well."

"Got it. We'll pull MO correlations. Weapon, staging, victimology, entry and exit patterns, and any geometric consistencies. If we find patterns that repeat across unsolved cases, we'll flag them. Expect a preliminary hits list in twenty-four to forty-eight hours, with a matrix you can skim in briefing."

"Copy that. I'll run it through the system and cross-reference with similar staging elements. If this guy's been active elsewhere, we'll find him."

Blade ended the call and immediately opened his email, attaching the fractal overlay images from the iPad. His fingers thumped the screen as he typed a brief explanation of the geometric correlation they'd discovered.

The coffee had kicked in fully now, sharpening his focus to a razor's edge. Twenty-four hours ago, the Florek case had felt like a dead end. Now they had a thread that could unravel an entire pattern of murders.

He glanced at Tori, who was already deep into her laptop, building the psychological profile. Her fingers flew across the keyboard, translating their discoveries into a framework that would help them understand their killer's mind.

His phone buzzed with a text from Larry:

Got your images. Running the search now. This is fascinating. Geometric staging is rare. Will prioritize.

Blade set the phone down and cracked his knuckles. Time to see how deep this rabbit hole went.

Blade scrolled through his contacts again, finding ADA Rene Garrison's direct line. The prosecutor answered on the second ring.

"Garrison."

"Rene, it's Blade St. James. I need legal guidance on a multi-jurisdictional MO search. We've got a potential serial with geometric staging patterns."

"Geometric staging?" Papers rustled in the background. "That's specific. What's your evidence foundation?"

"Solid. Crime scene analysis shows deliberate arrangement following a geometrical pattern. We're still processing the scene for non-victim DNA."

"You said 'potential' serial," Garrison said. "What makes you think this isn't isolated?"

"The crime scene appears ritualistic with the arrangements. This level of organization and the geometric staging suggest experience." Blade paced to the window, watching a kite surfer below. "I've got Dr. Crew building a psychological profile, and we're running a cross-case search through Pattern Analysis to see if there are similar murders."

"Smart approach."

"Thanks. But I need to know how to handle discovery when the hits come back. If we find matching cases across jurisdictions, what's my protocol for evidence sharing and case coordination?"

"Good question. Document everything through official channels. Any cross-jurisdictional matches need to go through the proper task force protocols. I'll draft a memo outlining discovery requirements for multi-agency coordination."

"Appreciate it, Rene."

"Thank you for calling ahead, Blade. You'd be amazed how many detectives make my job infinitely harder by not asking for guidance until they're already knee-deep in legal complications. What else?"

Blade walked back across his living room. "I need help pursuing a warrant for Donald Florek's office at the law firm. CSU lifted an impression from his home office blotter that turned out to be a geometrical drawing. The crime scene was staged to follow the pattern drawn at his desk. We need to eliminate whether Florek drew these doodles anywhere else."

Rene's silence stretched for several seconds. When she spoke again, her tone had shifted to full prosecutor mode. "That's interesting. If the victim was drawing the same patterns found at his murder scene, it changes everything. Either he was communicating with his killer, or the killer had access to his private workspace."

"Exactly. The law firm stonewalled us on attorney-client privilege grounds. But if Florek was documenting these patterns himself, that's not privileged communication."

"No, it's not. Personal notes, doodles, calendar entries—none of that falls under privilege protection. We can craft a narrow warrant for geometric drawings, mathematical notations, and similar non-client materials."

Blade pumped his fist. "What's our timeline?"

"I can have a warrant application ready by noon if you get me the CSU report on the blotter impression. Include photographs, measurements, and any expert analysis on the geometric properties. The more specific we are, the better our chances with the judge."

"Done. I'll have Gino rush the documentation, and I'll email the overlay we created with the victim."

"Good. One more thing, Blade. If this pattern holds across multiple jurisdictions, we're looking at federal involvement eventually. FBI's Behavioral Analysis Unit will want in once the scope becomes clear."

"Actually, Dr. Crew consults for BAU regularly. She can liaison when the time comes. And I'm in touch with Special Agent Sebastian Wells in the local field office."

"Perfect. That'll streamline coordination." Papers shuffled again on Rene's end. "My recommendation? Stay ahead of it. Once you hit three confirmed victims with matching MO, have Dr. Crew reach out to her contacts at Quantico. Better to bring them in as partners than have them take over later."

"Understood. Three victims, then we loop in the feds through Agent Wells."

"Exactly. Keep me posted on the warrant progress and any Pattern Analysis hits. This could get big fast."

"Will do. Thanks again, Rene."

Blade ended the call and turned back toward the kitchen, where Tori's fingers still flew across her keyboard. Every few seconds, she'd pause to scribble notes in the margins of a legal pad. Black-rimmed glasses perched on her nose, magnifying her dark eyes as they tracked across the screen.

Since when did she wear glasses?

His mouth almost shaped a crack about the glasses, but she didn't lift her head, apparently locking every ounce of focus on the profile stacking on her screen. Work mode. No breaking that.

He headed down the hall, pushed into his bedroom, and thumbed Gino's number.

The line clicked alive. "Gino here."

"It's Blade. I need that blotter impression report expedited. Full documentation, photographs, measurements, and expert geometric analysis if you can swing it. ADA Garrison needs it for a warrant application."

"You got it. The impression is clean. Definitely deliberate drawing, not accidental marks. I'll have everything packaged and delivered within the hour."

"Perfect." Blade stood in his doorway and glanced at Tori, still absorbed in her profile work. "One more thing. Can you run a comparison between the blotter impression and our crime scene staging photos? I need to know if they're identical or just similar."

"Already on it. Preliminary comparison shows significant correlation, but I want to run it through some new AI software before I commit to an exact match."

Blade smiled. Gino's thoroughness had saved cases before. "Rush it, but don't sacrifice accuracy."

"Never do."

The pieces were falling into place. Legal framework, evidence analysis, pattern recognition. All the elements needed to build a case against a killer who thought he was too clever to be caught.

Blade brushed his teeth and swiped deodorant before heading back to the kitchen. He stopped across the counter from Tori, who was still deep in her profile. With the glasses, she looked like a professor, all serious concentration and academic focus.

"I'm going to call Damien's attorney, Janice Lebowitz. See if she's willing to communicate with him for us."

Tori looked up. "That's not something you can ask over the phone."

"It's not?"

"First of all, we can't risk a digital trail." She leaned forward on her elbows. "You need to deliver this sensitive, off-the-books request in a way that leaves no electronic trace. Second, you're asking a lawyer to risk her career and potentially her life to act as a covert operative."

He nodded slowly. "Right."

"We need a face-to-face meeting in a neutral location," Tori said. "Coffee shop, her office, somewhere public but private. That's the only professionally sound and paranoid-enough choice."

"Paranoid-enough," Blade said. The phrase worked. He flicked his gaze at her face. "When'd you start wearing glasses?"

"They're blue light blocking, not prescription. Protects my eyes when I'm staring at screens for hours. I don't always use them, just when I'm tired."

"You should take a nap while I meet with Janice."

"You seriously think I'm sitting this out?"

"What was I thinking?" Blade smiled and scrolled his phone to Janice's contact. She answered on the third ring.

"Janice, it's Detective Blade St. James, Broward Homicide. I need to meet with you about Damien Sullivan. Something that can't be discussed over the phone."

A pause. "That sounds ominous."

"It's complicated. Are you available today?"

"I have one more case on the docket at the north regional courthouse. Should wrap up in an hour, but I'm starving. Haven't eaten all day."

"Can we meet at that Mexican place around the corner from the courthouse? Dos Hermanos."

"Best carnitas in the county. I can be there in two hours."

"Perfect. See you then."

He grinned at Tori. "See? I can charm a woman when I need to."

"Oh please." She rolled her eyes. "You offered food to a hungry lawyer. That's not charm, that's basic survival."

"Hey, it worked."

"Because she's hungry, not because you're irresistible." Tori stood and stretched, her borrowed shirt riding up slightly. "But you're not taking me to get tacos dressed like this."

His undershirt, her jeans from yesterday, hair in a ponytail. She looked like she'd been through exactly what she'd been through.

"Right. Harlee's bringing clothes?"

"Should be here soon." Tori gathered her notes and laptop. "Then we can head out. This meeting with Janice could change everything."

Tori disappeared down the hall. Blade planted his elbows on the counter. Now he had to figure out how to ask Janice Lebowitz, of all people, to funnel them intel. That wasn't a playbook move. It was reckless. But options weren't on the table.

If there really was a second murder book, the only shot at prying it loose lived in Janice's hands.

18

BLADE WATCHED TORI SIGNAL the waiter for another basket of chips and salsa. Her second refill. He shook his head and grinned.

"Seriously? You're gonna clean them out of tortilla chips."

"Can't help it that you've been starving me." Tori crunched through another chip loaded with salsa verde. "Besides, this is authentic. Not that jarred stuff you probably keep in your fridge."

"I can't believe a woman who weighs maybe a hundred and ten pounds soaking wet can put away more food than I can." Blade gestured at the empty basket between them. "Where does it all go?"

"Fast metabolism. Plus, I grew up eating real food. Maria made empanadas every Sunday. Pernil on special occasions. Arroz con gandules that could feed half the neighborhood." Tori rolled the words like she was back in Little San Juan, each name of a dish landing with the rhythm of home.

The smell of sizzling fajitas drifted from the kitchen, mixing with fresh cilantro and lime. Blade's stomach growled.

"What about you?" Tori asked. "What did the St. James family feast on?"

"Cornbread. Lots of cornbread." Blade scraped the bottom of the chip basket for a crumb and popped it in his mouth. "Eight kids, two parents working dawn to dusk. Cornbread stretched everything. Cornbread with beans. Cornbread with whatever fish we caught. Cornbread with more cornbread when times got really tight."

"That explains a lot about you."

"Yeah? Like what?"

"Why you never order bread at restaurants."

Of course she noticed. Tori noticed everything. It was a detail Kiara, after five months, had never picked up on. He loved her thoughtfulness, but no matter how many times he mentioned his dislike of bready foods, she continued to bring them. Case in point, the pastries she brought this morning.

Well, that didn't matter anymore. She wouldn't be bringing him carbs or anything else now.

He reached for his water glass. A flash of light near the entrance caught his eye. Janice Lebowitz swept through the door, navigating the crowded restaurant like she owned the place, her blond hair defying both gravity and the humid Florida air. He stood and waved her over.

She sauntered to their booth with the confidence of someone who'd never met a courtroom she couldn't command. Late fifties, probably on a first-name basis with her plastic surgeon, but not overdone. Professional polish with just enough edge to remind you she'd clawed her way to the top.

Janice slid into the booth beside Tori just as their waiter appeared.

"¡Janice!" the waiter said. "¿Cómo estás, mi amor? ¿Lo de siempre?"

"Sí, Carlos. Y tráeme el queso blanco también."

Tori jumped in without missing a beat. "Yo también, por favor."

They chattered with the waiter in Spanish, and Blade caught maybe half the exchange. Something about cheese, definitely. And he was pretty sure he heard the word *tequila* somewhere in there, which made him nervous about what Tori had just ordered.

When this was all over, he should ask Tori to teach him Spanish. His patrol days had given him enough to handle basic situations, but conversations like this left him feeling like a tourist in his own county.

"Detective St. James." Janice extended a manicured hand across the table. "You sounded mysterious on the phone."

"Thanks for meeting us on short notice."

Blade studied her face as they shook hands. Friendly enough, but he caught the exhaustion lurking behind her professional smile. The skepticism that came with decades of cops sending her clients to jail. This wouldn't be an easy sell.

He couldn't lead with the conspiracy theory. Had to build trust first.

"How's your caseload these days? I know defense attorneys are swamped with the backlog."

"Brutal. Three trials next month, two appeals pending, and a rich client who thinks calling me at three a.m. constitutes legal strategy." Janice's laugh held no humor. "But that's not why you dragged me to my favorite taco joint."

Carlos returned with a fishbowl-sized margarita for Janice and bowls of white queso for both women. Blade wondered if he should wait until she finished the drink before making his pitch, but time was working against them.

"Your client Damien Sullivan reached out with information about a cold case. Problem is, he's in administrative segregation. Warden's refusing visitors and phone calls."

"Administrative segregation usually means he ticked someone off." Janice dipped a chip in the queso. "What kind of information?"

Blade played his next card. "The Crew murders."

Janice's chip stopped halfway to her mouth. Her gaze shifted to Tori, and Blade watched recognition dawn in her eyes. The professional mask slipped for just a moment, replaced by something deeper. Empathy. Understanding.

She wasn't looking at just another cop and consultant anymore. She was looking at the surviving daughter of a case that had made headlines across the state.

"Honey, you might need this drink more than I do." Janice pushed the margarita toward Tori.

"I'm good, thanks."

This was his opening. Blade leaned forward, lowering his voice to avoid being overheard.

"Janice, I'm going to tell you something that could end careers. Maybe lives. We believe there was a cover-up. Chief Barclay buried evidence. Damien claims there's a second murder book with the real investigation. We think he's the only person who knows what was in it and where it is."

Janice lifted the margarita and drew out a slow drink, the rim leaving a smear of melted salt on her lip. She lowered the glass with care, squared it against the table's edge.

"Let me make sure I understand what you're asking. You want me to go into a maximum-security prison, meet with my client under the protection of attorney-client privilege, and ask him about evidence that may or may not exist in an unsolved case that he was supposedly involved in but that has been sealed six ways to Sunday for a quarter of a century."

Blade dragged a thumb across his jaw, mouth flattening into something like a grin.

"I might not have been so concise, but you got it."

Janice scraped the salt from her lip with her tongue, then locked on Tori. She launched into Spanish, fast and seamless, too quick for Blade to grab more than a word here, a phrase there. Tori matched her, steady and sure.

He tracked what mattered. The body language. Janice cocked her brows like a question. Tori answered with a clipped nod. The rhythm between them shifted. Light at first, then heavy, both of their faces sharpening, the easy edges gone.

His lungs stalled. The noise in the restaurant blurred to a low hum. His focus stuck on Tori, on the tug-of-war written across her face. Rule-follower versus justice-chaser. If she gave the wrong answer, their whole case went down with it.

Janice nodded and patted Tori's shoulder. "I'll do it. But on my terms. I go in as his legal counsel. Everything stays under privilege. I ask your questions, I bring back his answers. Only if he agrees."

She pointed her chip at Blade like a weapon. "But if this goes sideways, if this blows up in our faces, I will deny this conversation ever happened. I will throw you both under the bus so fast it'll leave skid marks. Are we clear?"

Blade nodded. "Crystal."

"Good." Janice crunched on her chip. "I'll check my calendar and see when I can make the trip."

Tori swallowed the bite she'd been chewing. "That's the other thing. It's going to take up your entire day. Eight hours round trip, not to mention the time you'd spend inside."

Janice swirled the ice in her margarita. "I don't know when I could do it. My calendar's packed solid through next month."

Carlos appeared with a fresh basket of chips and pulled out his order pad.

Blade jumped at the interruption. The smell of those fajitas had been torturing him for the past twenty minutes. "I'll take the chicken fajitas. Extra guacamole."

Tori studied the menu like she hadn't been demolishing chips for the past half hour. "Wow, I'm not even sure if I'm hungry."

Blade pressed his molars into the inside of his cheek, holding back the grin that wanted out. She ordered the ceviche anyway and handed her menu to Carlos. Janice ordered tacos, then changed her mind at the last second.

"Fajitas sound perfect," she said. "Same as Detective St. James."

Carlos scribbled their orders and disappeared back toward the kitchen. The moment he was out of earshot, Tori cut her eyes to Blade. Her look said she wanted him to take over and make this happen.

"I appreciate you taking this on," Blade said. "I wanted to make this easy for you, so I've lined up a private plane to shave down the hours."

Janice's margarita stopped halfway to her lips.

Tori's eyes widened for a split second. He hadn't told her about the plane. He must've arranged it while she was out of the room. A backup move he expected they'd need.

Janice set down her drink. "It must be really important if you arranged a plane."

"It is," Blade said. "A car will be waiting at the airport to take you to the prison. Tori and I will wait at a nearby diner."

Janice picked up a chip and studied it like it held the secrets of the universe. "When do you want to go?"

"The plane is ready and waiting."

Blade's shoulders locked still. Janice didn't speak for a full thirty seconds. Her gaze flicked to her phone. The screen glowed with a color-coded column of stacked obligations. Days full of what he assumed were hearings, meetings, and client calls all crammed one on top of the other.

She lifted her glass and wet her lips with the margarita. Then she set it down, punched a number, and pressed the phone to her ear.

"Maria? It's Janice. I need you to rearrange my schedule. Cancel everything for the rest of today."

Blade's shoulders loosened. Janice was clearing the deck. She was doing it.

"I don't care what you have to move. Reschedule the Bailey deposition for next week. Push the Lawson meeting to Friday. And call Judge Patterson's clerk. Tell them I need a continuance on the Silva hearing. No, I can't tell you where I'll be. Just handle it." Janice ended the call and laid her phone face down on the table. "There. My afternoon just freed up."

She raised her margarita in a mock toast. "To justice. And to hoping we don't all end up in prison for whatever we're about to do."

Blade lifted his water glass. "To finding the truth." He looked at Tori, not Janice.

She met his gaze, and for a split second, the noise of the restaurant faded away. He saw the exhaustion, the worry, but underneath it, a flicker of something else. Gratitude. Trust. It was a silent acknowledgment of the massive risk he was taking, not just for the case, but for her.

The ice clinked as their glasses met across the table. Around them, the restaurant hummed with families sharing meals, couples on dates, and friends catching up over drinks.

None of them noticed they were sitting feet away from a conversation that might crack open a conspiracy and a killer decades in the making.

19

THE BRIGHT LIGHTS in the Waffle House cast everything in a warm, welcoming glow. Tori stared at the slice of triple chocolate pie in front of her, the fork suspended halfway to her mouth.

"I can't believe you ordered dessert." Blade shook his head, amusement flickering in his blue eyes. "You were practically comatose for the entire flight. I had to check your pulse twice."

"I was not comatose." She took a bite of the pie, savoring the rich chocolate. "I was digesting. There's a difference."

"You snored."

"For the last time, I do not snore."

"The pilot asked if we needed to make an emergency landing."

Her smile broke loose anyway. Blade kept needling, and for a breath, the worries of the day lifted. She let out a laugh, fork scraping ceramic, then her gaze slipped down. Two phones rested on the scarred Formica, screens black, waiting.

No calls. No texts.

"I've never seen a Mexican food coma up close before," Blade continued, stirring sugar into his coffee. "All that salsa verde and those baskets of chips. Plus the ceviche. And the rice. And the—"

"Okay, okay. I get it." She waved her fork at him. "But I needed something sweet. And caffeine." She gestured to her steaming mug. "This is strategic fuel."

The coffee was terrible. Bitter and thin. But it was hot, and it was keeping her hands busy. Otherwise, she'd be drumming her fingers on the table or biting her nails or doing any of the dozen nervous habits that betrayed how wound up she really was.

Had they given Janice enough questions? The list felt comprehensive when they'd created it, but now, sitting here rolling it through her head, every gap seemed glaring. What if Damien decided to play word games the way he had with them? Or launched into another lecture about fractals and mathematical patterns instead of answering direct questions about the night her parents died?

What if the warden refused to let Janice see him at all?

"She's probably in there right now," Blade said, as if reading her thoughts.

Tori nodded, not trusting her voice. Janice had texted forty minutes ago: *"Cleared security. Going in."* Nothing since.

She forced herself to look away from her phone to the counter, where a waitress topped off sugar shakers. A trucker perched on a red vinyl stool chuckled at something she'd said. The cook behind the grill took a swig from his soda, then pressed a mound of shredded potatoes flat with his spatula. At a corner booth, a family with two kids debated whether to share waffles or pancakes.

"What if he doesn't talk to her?" The words tumbled out before she could stop them. "What if he just sits there and talks about God's fingerprint the way he did with us for the first ten minutes?"

"He'll talk." Blade's voice carried quiet confidence. "He reached out to you, remember? Through Corbin. He wants something. And Janice knows how to work people."

She took another bite of pie, but it tasted like cardboard now. The sugar rush she'd been hoping for felt more like a crash waiting to happen. "What if we're wrong about everything? What if there is no second murder book? What if Damien is just—"

"Playing games?" Blade finished. "Then we'll figure that out too."

But what if they were chasing shadows? What if she were putting everyone she cared about at risk? Blade had already lost Kiara.

Her phone buzzed.

Tori lunged for it, but it was just a spam text about how much money she owed to the toll authorities. Tori's heart hammered against her ribs as she set the phone back down.

"She said she'd call as soon as she was out," Blade said.

"Or she might just show up here." Tori pushed the pie around on her plate. "Janice doesn't strike me as the type to waste time with phone calls when she could just drive over."

"True."

The bell above the door chimed as someone entered. Tori's head popped up, but it was just another trucker.

Twenty-six years of questions. Twenty-six years of wondering what really happened that night. And now, somewhere behind the concrete walls and razor wire of Union Correctional, a woman in a cheetah-print dress was getting the answers Tori had been searching for her entire life.

Or walking into another dead end.

The silence stretched between them, broken only by the soft clink of silverware against plates and the distant hum of the grill. Tori pushed the chocolate pie around her plate again, her mind spinning in circles she couldn't escape.

"Is gator wrestling a real thing?" The question popped out before she could stop it. "Like, do people actually make money doing that?"

Blade paused with his coffee cup halfway to his lips. "Random question."

"I need a distraction." She gestured at her phone. "And I was thinking about your whole swamp childhood thing. So, is it real or just some tourist-trap nonsense?"

A slow grin spread across his face. "Oh, it's real. My uncle Ricky used to make decent money at it during tourist season. Couple hundred bucks a show if he was lucky."

"Are you serious?" She set down her fork. "People pay to watch someone wrestle an actual alligator?"

"Tourists eat it up. Uncle Ricky had this whole routine. He'd start with the smaller ones, maybe six or seven feet, work his way up to the big boys. Twelve, thirteen feet." Blade reached over and stole a bite of her pie. "The trick is knowing where to grab them. Get behind the front legs, clamp down on the snout, and don't let go."

"That's insane." But she found herself picturing it. Blade in the mud, all that controlled strength focused on something that could kill him with one snap of its jaws. "Although I have to admit, seeing you tackle a twelve-foot gator might be amusing."

"Amusing?"

"Educational. I could study your technique. For science."

"Uh-huh." He took another bite of her pie. "You'd probably be taking notes. 'Subject demonstrates poor decision-making skills. Recommend psychological evaluation.'"

Despite everything, she laughed. "I would not."

"You absolutely would. You'd have your little notebook out, documenting my risk-taking behaviors and maladaptive coping mechanisms."

"Okay, maybe I would." She reclaimed her fork before he could steal more pie. "But only because wrestling prehistoric death machines would definitely qualify as abnormal behavior."

She leaned into the banter and felt a real smile curling at the corners of her mouth. They were just two friends sharing terrible diner food instead of two people whose worlds had been turned upside down by murder and conspiracy and family trauma that had shaped their entire lives.

"Do you still see them? Your brothers and sisters?"

The easy smile faded from Blade's face. He stared down at his coffee cup. "No."

"Not at all?"

"Not since I was fourteen." His tone carried professional distance. "They made their choice. I made mine."

She waited, recognizing the pain behind those simple words.

"After everything went down, my parents decided I was too much trouble." Blade stole her fork again and raked lines in the chocolate with the tines. "They had seven other kids to worry about, and I was the least of their worries."

"Blade—"

"It's fine." But the tightness around his eyes said otherwise. "Better this way. Clean break."

She understood that logic. The brutal mathematics of survival that foster kids learned early. Sometimes cutting ties was the only way to move forward. But understanding it didn't make it hurt less.

"You want to know the funny thing?" Blade's laugh held no humor. "I was the good kid before that night. Quiet, stayed out of trouble, helped with the younger ones. I was fishing off that pier, waiting for my parents to finish some business deal, when I heard you scream."

They'd never talked about the details of what that night had cost him. All these years, she'd carried the guilt of the reckless choices that put her at that pier. The violence that followed.

"I was such a mess back then," she said. "Angry at the world. Running with this crew that made me feel tough, shoplifting, staying out all night. I thought I was so smart, so independent."

"You were a kid."

"I was an idiot." She wrapped her hands around her coffee mug, seeking warmth. "The guy who attacked me was connected to the gang I'd been running with. I was tired of it. Tried to walk away, and they decided to teach me a lesson about loyalty. If you hadn't been there, if you hadn't acted . . ."

"But I was there."

"And it destroyed your life. Your family, your future, everything you'd planned—"

"Tori, look at me."

She did and found those steady blue eyes that had anchored her through more storms than she could count.

"That night didn't destroy my life. It changed it. There's a difference."

"How can you say that? You lost everything."

"I lost a family that was willing to throw me away the second things got complicated. I lost a future that probably would have involved running bait lines and patching airboat engines until I was too old to work. But Stryker found me. And I found the program. I found a purpose."

"You found me," she said quietly.

"Yeah. I found you."

His hand crossed the table, big and warm, closing over hers. He pried her fingers from the mug and kept them locked inside his grip. Two broken kids who'd somehow managed to piece each other back together, one shared moment at a time.

"Stryker saw something in both of us," Blade said. "Two sides of the same coin, he used to say. You were running toward danger, I was running toward justice. Both of us were running from pain."

"And he convinced a judge to give us both a chance."

"Best thing that ever happened to us."

The booth felt smaller than it had five minutes ago. She studied his hand over hers. Years of history in that grip. The connection wasn't just friendship. It was deeper and more essential than oxygen. Blade was the other half of her story, the missing piece that completed her.

The bell over the door chimed, and she pulled her hand back. Some observations were better left unexamined.

Janice stood framed in the doorway, her cheetah-print dress a violent splash of color against the diner's muted tones. She strode over with her usual confident swagger and slid into the booth beside her.

Tori pushed the pie plate out of the way. "What happened? What did he say?"

Janice's laugh came out shaky and bitter. "That man is either completely insane or scared out of his mind. Maybe both." She lifted an empty coffee mug to signal the waitress.

"What I'm about to tell you can't leave this table. Not to his son, not another detective, not to anyone. He made me promise," Janice said. "He claims that people have already died to keep this buried, and they won't hesitate to kill again."

Tori looked at Blade, and they both agreed. Not a word.

"The warden didn't want to let me in. First, she tried to block the visit because it was outside visiting hours. Then, because Damien's in confinement. But I told her I needed a signature for an official document."

The waitress slid in, tipped the pot, and filled the mug. Janice dropped a manila folder onto the table, popped it open, and spread the flap wide. One sheet sat inside, heavy with type, her letterhead stamped sharp across the top.

"It's a waiver of attorney-client privilege. Allows me to break confidentiality with the two of you."

Tori stared at the document. "Brilliant."

"This ain't my first rodeo." She smiled and tucked the paper back into the folder. "You know, the entire time I defended Mr. Sullivan, he claimed his boss had it out for him."

"You mean Chief Barclay?" Blade asked.

Janice nodded and lifted the mug. Coffee sloshed against the rim, but she managed a sip before it spilled over the edge. "But during our conference today, he never said the name. Not once. He said they were listening, even though it's illegal for a warden or prison staff to listen to an attorney-client conference without permission."

"If Sullivan believed someone was monitoring privileged conversations, his paranoia might not be paranoia at all."

"True, but it probably happens more than we'd like to believe. It's also difficult to prove." Janice added a splash of cream and stirred her coffee. "Either way, Damien didn't name names today.

He spoke in generalities. But I saw him draw *B* on the table with his finger when he talked about his boss. I'm sure it's Barclay."

Tori remembered Damien's finger tracing lazy circles on the metal table between them. All those seemingly random circles. Was he trying to communicate something she'd missed?

"I started with your first question," Janice continued. "Damien swears he was the responding officer to the Crew homicide, no matter what the murder book says."

"What about the fractals?" Tori leaned forward. "The patterns?"

"I asked that next, but he wanted to start at the beginning." Janice took a sip of coffee and shook her head. "You know, after all these years I've represented this man, this was the first time Damien admitted he was a dirty cop."

Everybody in Millie Beach had heard the rumor. Sullivan wasn't clean. Hearing it laid out now only made her feel worse for Corbin growing up with a father who'd sold off his own badge.

Janice continued, "Damien said he was part of a larger operation. Paid to look the other way on certain arrests, lose evidence. Sometimes plant evidence. It paid well, and he needed the money."

"I suspect he also enjoyed the power trip," Blade said.

The waitress appeared with the coffeepot, steam curling from the dark liquid as she topped off each mug. Janice's manicured hand dismissed the offered menu with a sharp gesture, and the waitress gathered the empty pie plate before retreating.

"At some point, Barclay started using leverage instead of money," Janice said. "Photos, recordings, documentation of everything Damien had done. Classic blackmail. Do what I say, or I'll destroy your life. He was called into the office three days before the shooting, and Barclay laid into him. Damien knew he was in trouble, knew Barclay was planning something. So he took precautions."

"What kind of precautions?" Tori asked.

"Damien isn't as impulsive as everyone thinks. A mean drunk, yeah. But he was smart enough to keep records. Handwritten notes, copies of evidence, everything he needed to prove corruption at the highest level. His insurance policy. But Damien made a huge mistake." Janice tapped the table with her index finger. "One night, he'd been drinking, and he mouthed off to Barclay about it. Said he had enough evidence to take everyone down. You can imagine what happened when he sobered up."

"He realized what he'd done," Blade said.

"And the danger he'd put himself in," Tori added.

"You've nailed it," Janice said. "So the night before Barclay fired him, the night before the shooting, Damien hid his insurance policy."

Her heart hammered against her ribs. If Damien had kept track of everything he'd covered up or hidden, he might have information about her parents' murder. Maybe even her brother's new legal name. Proof that Damien had been there that night.

"Okay, so where's this evidence?" she asked. "Did he tell you?"

"Sorta." Janice let out a soft laugh. "He said, 'The man who saved Tori can find it in the bag from the first fight.' Does that mean anything to you?"

"Does he mean Stryker? He's the man who saved me. Has he been sitting on this evidence all these years?"

Blade was shaking his head even as Tori finished her sentence. "No way. Stryker wouldn't look the other way on this."

"Well, Damien didn't have a chance to explain about that or the fractals. And I'm sorry, but he didn't tell me anything about your brother," Janice said. "The warden interrupted our meeting, saying I'd had plenty of time to get my signature and confer with my client. She adiosed me right out of there."

"Sounds familiar," Blade said.

Hard to picture Janice giving ground to anyone. "She really just cut you off? Can she do that?"

"Warden runs that place, so yeah." Janice leaned back and crossed her arms. "But I made sure Maggie Quick understood.

If she stuck her ear where it didn't belong, I'd end her." Her smile showed teeth.

The coffee's dark surface reflected Tori's face back at her, blurred and distorted.

The man who saved her. The bag from the first fight.

Damien, with his stupid cryptic messages. Leads that only took them in circles. Questions that only led to more questions.

"We need that notebook," she said.

Blade nodded. "Yeah. We do."

20

THE SOUND CUT through the gray fog like a blade through silk. Voices. Two voices, familiar but distant, as if filtered through water.

"I wish Stryker would just wake up."

He was awake. He was listening. *Speak again.*

Who was that? It sounded like . . . Tori?

More words drifted past, syllables he couldn't grasp, meanings that slipped away before he could hold them. His body remained a prison, unresponsive to every command he sent down broken neural pathways. His entire life he'd had reflexes. Control. Lightning-fast reactions that had kept him alive in the ring, on the street, in uniform. Now, nothing.

"Stryker saved us both."

Who had he saved? When?

The voice registered now—deep, steady.

Blade.

He remembered. Blade who came and prayed over his broken body. Blade who read that ridiculous book of dad jokes while Stryker fought to move even a finger. The kid who'd become a man, who'd become a brother.

The fog rolled back in, thick and suffocating, dragging him under. Consciousness slipped away like sand through his fingers.

Then he was listening again. How long had he been gone this time? Minutes? Hours? Days? He had no anchor to time anymore, no way to measure the spaces between awareness. He was so tired. Bone-deep, soul-crushing exhaustion that made even thinking feel like lifting concrete blocks.

The woman's voice again. Tori. "Did he know I have a brother? Why wouldn't he tell me?"

The question was a lightning strike in the dark. It didn't just register; it detonated. The gray fog shattered like glass. The beeping monitor vanished. The antiseptic smell, the weight of the blanket, the tube in his throat, all of it dissolved.

A little boy, Tori's mirror image, cowered under the bed. Dark hair, same delicate features. His eyes locked on Stryker, wide and unblinking, carrying more than terror. Not the hollow stare his sister wore. This gaze carried blame, as if the blood on the knife had glued shame to his skin.

The boy gripped the kitchen knife with both hands. Blood slicked the steel, smeared down his wrists. His pajama top sagged heavy, dark patches spreading from the collar all the way to the cuffs, the same cartoon print as his sister's gown, only his drowned in red.

Stryker froze, the scene locking into place. A kid with a bloody knife, him with a drawn Glock. Wrong picture.

He shoved the pistol back into the holster and dragged both hands up, palms open, nothing to threaten.

"Easy," he said. "You're safe now."

The boy pressed himself deeper into the shadows, the knife trembling in his grip. A whimper escaped his throat, high and broken.

Stryker lowered himself to his stomach so he was at eye level with the child under the bed. The hardwood floor was cold against his chest, sticky in places where blood had pooled and begun to congeal.

"Are you okay? Where are you hurt?"

The boy's lips moved, but no sound came out. His eyes darted between Stryker's face and the doorway behind him, as if calculating escape routes. The knife never wavered.

"My name's Stryker. What's your name?"

"Nikos." The word was barely a whisper.

"Nikos. That's a good name. A strong name." Stryker kept his voice gentle. "Can you tell me what happened?"

The boy's face crumpled. "They wouldn't stop screaming."

A shadow fell across the room. Heavy footsteps thudded in the hallway.

"King!"

Stryker tipped his head toward the doorway. Commander Barclay filled it, shoulders squared, eyes cutting across the room. They tracked the sprawled bodies, the overturned chair, Stryker on his belly. No recoil. No startle. Just a quick read, like he'd walked into exactly what he expected.

Stryker got to his feet, instinctively creating a barrier between Barclay and the hidden child. A thin cut ran down the left side of Barclay's face from ear to jaw. He'd seen similar scratches on the commander's hands and neck before. Occupational hazards from the German shepherds he raised at home for police training. But this one seemed deeper. Fresher.

"Sir, we have another survivor. A male child. He's under the bed."

Barclay stepped inside, and his gaze flicked past Stryker, locking on the shadow beneath the bed. His jaw shifted, tightened. The faintest flicker crossed his face. Like he'd just settled on a verdict.

"Good work, King." His voice boomed loud enough to announce himself to whoever lingered in the hall. "Looks like you found our perpetrator."

Stryker's gut bucked hard, his breath catching before he could haul it steady. "Sir?"

Barclay moved closer, his presence filling the room. "The boy attacked his parents, then went after his sister. She hid in the closet. He crawled under the bed with the murder weapon when he heard your sirens."

The narrative was insane. Impossible.

He opened his mouth to object, but Barclay's attention had already shifted to Damien, who stood frozen in the doorway.

"Sullivan. Get that kid out of there. Bag the weapon."

He expected Damien to object, but he didn't move. His skin blanched gray, eyes fixed on some middle distance. Not a word. Not a shake of the head. Nothing.

If his partner wasn't standing up for the kid, then Stryker would. "Sir, that's a four-year-old child. A victim. He's terrified."

Barclay stepped in hard, chest nearly brushing Stryker's.

"You are a patrolman who responded to a call." The commander's breath was hot in Stryker's face, carrying the stench of coffee and cigarettes. "You will hand your preliminary notes to Officer Sullivan. You will not speak to anyone else about what you think you saw in this room. Do I make myself clear?"

"Sir, I—"

"This family's tangled up in things way above your pay grade, King. The boy—he's dangerous. Unstable. Best outcome for this child is if he disappears into the system where he can get the help he needs."

Stryker locked his fists at his thighs, blood surging fast, body begging for action. One strike, one shove, and he could clear the rot out of this room. But Barclay's words jammed him where he stood.

"You've got a future, King. Don't burn it. This is bigger than one family circling the drain."

Barclay drove his hand down on Stryker's shoulder, not friendly.

Ownership. Control. Fingers drilled into muscle, hard enough that he'd carry the mark into tomorrow.

"This is mine now," Barclay said. "You're done here."

Behind them, Damien had dropped to his knees beside the bed. "Come on out, son. Nobody's going to hurt you."

Stryker heard the boy's terrified whimper, the sound of feet scuffling against hardwood as Damien dragged him from his hiding place. The knife struck the hardwood, bounced once, then spun flat with a metallic ping that hung in the air.

"Mommy!" The boy's scream cracked the air, sharp as glass. "I want Mommy! Mommy!"

Stryker turned, muscles coiled, but Barclay shoved him down the hall. "Walk away, King. Now. That's an order."

He heard the threat in Barclay's tone. The kind of threat that promised more than a write-up or lost stripes.

Damien locked his arms around the kid, absorbing the wild fists hammering his chest. The boy clawed and twisted, shouting, "Victoria! Where's Victoria?"

Damien caught one tiny wrist, folded it into his palm, holding him steady. "She's safe. She's going somewhere safe."

This wasn't right. None of this was right. Barclay's fingers dug into his shoulder blade, the grip promising consequences that stretched far beyond this blood-soaked house.

Right and wrong had died the moment they'd crossed this threshold.

Barclay finally released his grip, stepping back with a satisfied nod. "You did good work tonight, King. The department won't forget it."

The bedroom door swung shut with a solid click. Whatever truth was in there stayed locked with the dead.

Stryker stood frozen in the hallway. His fingers curled hard enough that the nails cut his own palms, the only thing keeping the shake out of his hands. His vision blurred, and he caught the tear with his thumb before it could fall. Stryker King did not show weakness. Not to them, not to anyone.

His boots were heavy on the hardwood as he walked toward the front door. The other officers barely glanced up. Just another night. Just another case.

He pushed through the door into the humid Florida night. The red and blue lights of the patrol cars washed over him, painting the world in colors of emergency and order. The cops, the paramedics, the neighbors standing in the street and peering from their windows. He didn't see justice. He saw a machine. A machine that the department's chain of command controlled.

Two bodies lay cooling in that bedroom. Parents who would never see their children grow up. A little girl sat in an ambulance outside, probably still rocking, still silent, with nothing but a caseworker between her and a lifetime of foster homes.

She would spend decades trying to outrun this night. The nightmares would follow her through every placement, every new bed, every attempt at normal. And her brother. What would they do to that terrified little boy? Lock him away in some institution where the truth would die with him?

He looked at his own hands now covered in blood. The same hands that had just tried to save a man's life and comfort a child. Hands that could KO a man with a single hit but had no power in this situation.

Not if he could help it.

He couldn't stop what had already happened. But he could watch. He could wait. And when those children got chewed up and spit out of whatever system they were being sent to, he would be there.

21

BLADE LEANED AGAINST THE WALL, the green spike ball rotating between his palms. The soft rubber spikes pressed into his skin, giving his restless fingers something to focus on while questions without answers cycled through his head.

Tori stood beside the hospital bed, working the tangles from Stryker's salt-and-pepper hair and giving him an update that Blade was 90 percent sure he couldn't hear. "Luna's doing great with the evening classes. You'd be so proud of how she's stepped up. The kids listen to her, you know? She's got that same way you do of making them believe they're worth something."

Two nights ago, Blade had found her huddled in her closet, shaking so hard she couldn't speak and eyes wide with terror that went bone-deep.

The spike ball stilled between his palms. People didn't just bounce back from trauma like that. Not without serious work. Not without someone believing in them enough to make the healing possible. Stryker had done that for her. Given her a place to rebuild, a purpose that mattered, kids who needed what she had to offer. Plenty of survivors never made it past the wreckage. Tori had done more than survive. She'd become someone who could anchor others. Anchor him.

His fingers tightened around the spike ball until the rubber points bit into his palm.

"The man who saved Tori can find it."

The words had been circling his head for hours, wearing grooves in his thoughts like the spike grooves in his hand. Stryker was the key. But what good was a key when the lock was trapped behind closed eyes?

He studied Stryker's profile. The weight had melted off him. Muscle mass gone. Oxygen tube under his nose. IV needle taped to his hand. A pale blue hospital gown. All of it had taken his friend, his mentor, and made him into something fragile.

Stryker would hate this. The man had never worn anything that showed weakness. Not even a Band-Aid when he'd split his knuckles on the heavy bag.

"Scars tell stories," he'd always said.

This wasn't a story. This was a nightmare.

They needed Stryker to wake up. They needed his strength. His wisdom. His guidance. Instead, they had Damien Sullivan's riddles and a mentor who looked like he was sleeping but wouldn't wake up, no matter how loud they called his name.

"Why now?" Blade spoke the question that had been gnawing at him. "Why is Damien bringing this up now?"

"Isn't it obvious?" Tori glanced up. "Fear. Damien's a coward, and self-preservation has always been stronger than his conscience. He's kept his mouth shut because he knows Barclay's reach is long."

"You're not buying his 'new man' thing?" He made air quotes.

"Damien's seen Corbin become the man he never was. A good agent. Honorable. Maybe it's eating at him."

"Yeah."

Tori set the hairbrush on the nightstand and arranged Stryker's hair around his shoulders.

"It'd be hard for Damien to ignore how he wrecked his own legacy while Corbin built something honorable in spite of it," Blade said.

"Damien's probably worried about Corbin. He shined a light on some dark people and could be in danger."

But still, Blade thought, *he's a coward*.

His phone buzzed against his hip, and he glanced at the screen. Larry Kobilinsky. He answered on the second ring.

"St. James."

"We've got three high-confidence matches for your geometric staging query." Larry's words came rapid-fire, the excitement of a breakthrough. "Tampa PD 2023, Orlando PD 2024, and a weird one from St. Johns County Sheriff's Office from earlier this year."

The spike ball dropped from his hand, bouncing once on the linoleum before rolling under Stryker's bed. The ball stayed where it landed. He'd get it later. Three more victims. Three more crime scenes staged like mathematical art.

"Email me everything you've got." Blade pushed off the wall. "Photos, reports, witness statements. The works."

"Already sending."

"Thanks, Larry. I owe you."

He ended the call and turned to Tori. "We've got more victims."

She leaned down and kissed Stryker's forehead. "We'll be back soon. Rest. We've got everything covered."

He gave Stryker's arm a gentle squeeze, feeling the muscle that had once been iron-hard now soft beneath the hospital gown. "Hang in there, brother. We're getting closer."

They hurried toward the door, leaving Stryker to his quiet battle.

Blade swiped his badge at the War Room door, the electronic lock disengaging with a sharp click. The lights flickered on automatically, illuminating their investigation hub. Whiteboards covered three walls, dense with timelines and suspect photos.

Coffee-stained files created precarious towers on every available surface.

Tori claimed the workstation nearest the main display screen, her laptop coming to life before Blade had even settled into his chair.

"Tampa first," he said, clicking open Larry's email attachment.

The crime scene photos loaded pixel by pixel, revealing a horror that made Blade's jaw tighten. Judge Doreen Kagay, seventy-three, found in her study. Blood spatter painted the walls in arcs that spoke of prolonged violence. Overturned furniture. Shattered picture frames. The same brutality they'd seen at Florek's house.

"Living alone," Tori murmured, scanning the report. "Retired. No forced entry."

He opened the Orlando file next. Software developer Scott Kaufman, forty-five. The photos showed an apartment that looked like a war zone. Underneath the disaster, a similar staging. Furniture positioned just so. Personal items moved to specific locations.

"This one's still active," Blade said, scrolling through the case notes. "Victim was killed by his roommate, Cole Miller. Trial starts next month."

"What evidence do they have?"

Blade scanned the forensics section. "No murder weapon. Roommate was covered in the victim's blood. Lots of fingerprints. Unidentified male DNA found in the kitchen and bathroom. Loads of circumstantial, including Cole had been having an affair with Kaufman's girlfriend."

"Oldest story in the book," she said. "But what about that male DNA?"

"Looks like they dismissed it as a visitor once they zeroed in on the roommate."

"Dismissed it?" Tori blinked. "That's sloppy work."

"Or convenient work. Why bother testing every known male visitor when you have enough evidence to nail the roommate? That's a job for the defense." He pulled up the St. Johns County file. Sasha Robie. An elderly woman. Retired records clerk from the state court system. Another brutal scene. Another case closed with a convenient suspect.

Tori leaned into the glow of the monitor, her cursor hovering over a crime scene photo from Tampa. "Blade, look."

On Judge Kagay's mahogany desk, amidst the papers and files stacked and scattered across its surface, sat a yellow legal pad. The original investigator had dismissed the scribbles on the top sheet as "victim's personal notes, no evidentiary value."

Blade saw what the Tampa detective had missed. Geometric lines forming an intricate pattern that seemed to repeat.

"Pull up Florek's sketch," Tori said.

He opened the image from Florek's desk blotter. Different, but related. Where the Tampa drawing was a simple Star of David with smaller stars nestled in every point, Florek's was a web of intersecting triangles radiating outward.

"They're related," Tori said, her fingers flying across her keyboard. "Look." She pointed at the screen. "Keplerian fractals. 'Self-similar patterns created by iteratively applying geometric transformations based on regular polyhedral.'"

"English, please," he said. "Heck, I'd even take Spanish at this point."

Tori grinned. "Think of a snowflake. Each branch has smaller branches that look exactly like the big one. Fractals repeat the same pattern at different sizes. Instead of branches, our killer's using platonic solids."

"That's less opaque." But it still wasn't quite clear. "In my world, platonic doesn't describe shapes. It only describes our relationship."

Tori's fingers froze above her keyboard. Her eyes widened, then narrowed as she processed his words, a flush creeping up her neck. "Just . . . here. Look."

She overlaid the Tampa symbol on the crime scene. The match was unmistakable.

"The killer's signature," he said.

"He was still perfecting it back then."

"Which is why he forgot the drawing."

"Three years of evolution." Tori pulled up all four crime scenes side by side. "Tampa was crude, experimental. Orlando more refined. St. Johns showed real sophistication. And Florek . . ."

"Florek was his masterpiece."

Three years of practice. Three years of refining technique while bodies piled up. The killer hadn't just been murdering people. He'd been learning, evolving, treating each crime scene like a rough draft toward some perfect final composition.

The smoking gun they'd found wouldn't just solve Florek's murder. It might free an innocent man and expose a predator who'd been hunting for three years.

"You should call Orlando PD," Tori said. "Cole Miller might be innocent."

Blade was already reaching for his phone. "I'll put Deputy Gregory on it. I need to call the ADA."

He speed-dialed Garrison's direct line.

"Garrison."

"Rene, we have him. It's a serial. We have a second crime scene with a matching fractal symbol drawn by the victim. Two more possibles. I need that warrant for Florek's office. Please."

Silence stretched for three heartbeats. He could practically hear the gears turning in Garrison's prosecutorial mind. "How confident are you in the connection?"

"Dead certain. Four victims, three years, same geometric signature. The killer's been perfecting his craft."

"I'll have the warrant in your inbox within the hour."

He hung up.

"Grab your stuff," he said, already pocketing his phone. "We're heading to the law firm."

Tori closed her laptop with a decisive snap. "McCrary's not going to be happy."

"McCrary can file a complaint with my supervisor."

The drive to the high-rise took ninety minutes through downtown traffic, and the elevator ride to the fifth floor felt endless. When the doors opened, Rich McCrary stood waiting in the lobby, his professional smile replaced by cold fury. His expensive suit couldn't hide the rigidity in his spine.

"Detective St. James. I assume you have the proper paperwork this time."

Blade pulled up the warrant on his phone and turned the screen toward McCrary. McCrary's eyes scanned it, his jaw working like he was chewing nails.

"This is harassment," McCrary said. "My clients have privileges—"

"Your employee's been murdered," Blade cut him off. "This isn't a witch hunt. It's a homicide investigation."

The CSU techs filed past them. Blade directed them toward Florek's office while he and Tori carted file boxes to the conference room.

The same room. The same massive painting dominating the wall.

The itch started immediately. Stronger now. More insistent. Like a tuning fork vibrating in his skull.

"I need another look at this," Blade said, setting down the boxes.

What was it about the painting that pulled him in?

Patterns within patterns.

The lines and spirals seemed to shift, each curve leading to another, smaller version of itself.

Tori stepped beside him. No questions. No commentary. Just the quiet understanding of a partner who knew when to let him work. Her shoulder hovered inches from his, close enough that he felt her breathing rhythm match his own.

This wordless collaboration had become second nature. No need to explain his process or justify the time spent staring at what others saw as decoration. She trusted his instincts the same way he'd learned to trust her analytical mind. The partnership freed him to sink deeper into the visual puzzle, to let his subconscious make connections his rational mind might miss.

"There's something in this painting. Can't pinpoint it yet."

He let his eyes go unfocused. Not looking at the swirls of blue and green paint, but through them. Searching for the pattern within the pattern.

The colors shifted. Depth emerged where none should exist. And then—

Blood rushed faster through his veins.

Hidden within the layers was a face. Hollow eyes. Slack mouth. The unmistakable features of Judge Doreen Kagay from the Tampa file photo.

"What in the world . . ." Was he seeing this for real, or had he imagined it?

"What's wrong? What do you see?" He felt her rise on her toes beside him.

"I don't want to influence you. Tell me if you see something weird."

"Like your face?"

He shot her a look.

"Sorry." She stepped closer, her expression shifting from playful to focused. Then she gasped. "Not your face, but a face. Tell me I'm not seeing—"

"Shh." Blade glanced toward the doorway.

Tori clamped her hand over her mouth.

"We have to play it cool," he said, even though his pulse hammered at his collar.

"What does it mean?" Tori whispered.

"Not sure yet, but follow me."

He headed toward the lobby, forcing his stride to stay casual. Ryan Petersen passed them in the hallway with a wave. The bruises had shifted to a sickly green-yellow that made Petersen look jaundiced.

In the lobby, Blade approached the reception desk and stopped short. The woman behind the counter wasn't Madison. This young woman wore clear glasses and a polite smile. He'd been distracted by McCrary when they'd arrived and hadn't noticed her.

"Excuse me," Blade said, flashing his badge. "Where's Madison?"

The woman looked up, blinking. "Madison? I'm sorry, I don't know who that is. I'm Kristin. I'm just a temp. How can I help you?"

Blade glanced at Tori. Had Madison been fired for talking to them? The timing felt too convenient. "How long have you been here?"

"Couple of days." Kristin adjusted her glasses. "Is there something I can help you with?"

"Actually, yes." He gestured toward the painting behind the reception desk, forcing enthusiasm. "I'm really drawn to these paintings. Who's the artist?"

Kristin followed his gaze. "Oh, I'm not sure."

"Is the information lying around back there?" He peeked over the counter-height desk. "You know, in case a client wants to know."

"Uh." She glanced around, more confused than searching. "I don't think so. But I can look up the delivery record if you'd like."

"That'd be great."

While Kristin clicked through her computer, Blade studied the painting. His eyes searched for another hidden face, but either he was looking too hard or it wasn't there. The swirls of color remained just swirls.

Tori nudged him and leaned close. "Bottom left. Follow the blue spiral down."

He shifted his focus, and there it was. The angular features of Scott Kaufman, the software developer from Orlando. The face emerged from the brushstrokes like a photograph developing in a darkroom.

"Here we go," Kristin said. "They came from Gallery Showcase in the Miami Design District."

"Would it be okay if I took a picture?" Tori asked. "I have a few friends who would just love to see these."

"I don't see why not."

Blade's phone vibrated against his hip. He'd been so focused on the paintings that he'd missed several calls. The screen showed Corbin's name. He couldn't wait to bounce this off him, but later.

When Tori finished photographing, they thanked Kristin and returned to the conference room. His phone buzzed again.

"Your phone's been going off," Tori said.

"It's Corbin." He answered with a grin. "Brother, you're not going to believe this—"

"Blade." Corbin cut through his excitement.

The grin died on his face. "What's wrong?"

Tori moved closer, close enough to hear.

Silence stretched for three heartbeats before Corbin spoke again.

"My father was murdered."

22

TORI CLOSED THE CONFERENCE ROOM DOOR with a soft click. Damien Sullivan. Murdered. Probably because of them.

She turned back to the painting. A massive abstract composition mounted on the wall the way some people mount a taxidermy trophy. She stepped back to take in the entire piece.

The brushstrokes pulsed with violent energy. Broad sweeps that mimicked arterial spray. Aggressive slashes that echoed knife wounds. The massive canvas allowed the artist complete freedom to recreate the crime scene. Each mark documented process, not just product.

"He was reliving them," she said.

Blade moved to stand beside her. "I'm sorry, Corbin, I can't talk here. I'll call you back in twenty."

"Each fling of the brush is another strike of his victim." She traced the violent arcs with her eyes.

The pattern matched what she'd seen at Florek's house. The blood spatter on the walls, the trajectory of the attack. The pivot of a shoulder guided the sweep of the paint. The killer traced the memory of the resistance he'd felt when the knife hit bone.

"Come with me." Blade's hand found her elbow. He glanced at the security camera in the corner of the ceiling.

He guided her toward the door, and she had to pull her gaze away from the canvas. She forced herself to look at the floor. If she looked at the painting again, she'd start counting the slashes.

In the hallway, his stride remained measured.

"We need to be chill," he said under his breath, nodding to a passing paralegal.

They stopped at Florek's office, where Gino crouched beside the desk, photographing papers arranged on the carpet. Crime scene tape crossed the doorway.

"Gino." Blade crooked a finger, and the tech walked over. "Take over in the conference room. We've got to go."

Gino looked at Tori. "Everything okay, bro?"

"I'll text you."

Gino's eyes flicked between them, reading the undercurrent in Blade's tone. He'd worked enough crime scenes to recognize when something shifted.

"Got it." He straightened, already reaching for his equipment bag. "I'll handle it."

Tori grabbed her work bag from the conference room and followed Blade to the lobby. While they waited for the elevator, she returned to the painting behind the receptionist's desk, looking at it with new eyes now. The geometric staging hummed beneath the brushwork. Different style, same violent energy.

Was the killer here? Walking these halls, admiring his gallery? The thin skin under her eye began to twitch. She pressed a finger there, but it didn't stop. How many people looked at these paintings, never knowing they were looking at death?

She pulled out her phone and typed quickly:

We need to find Madison.

The elevator arrived with a soft ding. She hit send as they stepped inside, watching the lobby through the closing gap. Too many eyes. Too many ears.

Blade's phone buzzed. He glanced at the screen and read her message.

"Yes, we do," he said.

The elevator doors sealed shut.

"Damien—" Blade started.

"The paintings—" Tori said at the same moment.

They stopped. Blade pushed the heels of his hands into his eyes.

She was feeling the same way. They had some great leads, but right now, those leads were tangled around them like fishing line in a hurricane.

She reached over and rubbed a circle on his shoulder. "We can do this. We just decide what to pursue first."

He looked at her with a faint redness in one eye. "Coffee?"

She laughed, the sound surprising her. "Yes. Definitely pursue coffee first."

Once they arrived at the car and got in, Blade shifted into drive and pulled out into the afternoon sunshine. Tori opened her laptop on her knees, using them as a makeshift desk, and flipped to a fresh page on her legal pad.

"Time to brain dump. Give it to me."

"Damien first," Blade said, merging into traffic. "I was right to be nervous about him. Corbin said he was killed walking to the showers. Somebody didn't want him talking."

She focused on the pen in her hand. "I feel awful about that, but let's not deal with feelings until we've processed the facts."

"Okay." Blade exhaled. "So Damien talked about fractals, and we've confirmed our unsub has a fascination with fractals."

She scribbled notes as he spoke. "The painter hid the faces of the victims in the paintings. Trophy keeping."

Blade pulled into the drive-through line of a local café. "There were only two paintings we saw. Where are the rest?"

"Yeah, that's the first question." Tori drew a column header: *Questions.* She wrote: *Where are the other paintings?*

"Let's start there." Blade texted Gino:

> Check for other paintings in the office like the one in conference room or lobby. Let me know if warrant needs expanding.

The response came as a thumbs-up emoji.

They inched forward in the line. Tori added another question: *How many victims total?*

The car ahead of them ordered three lattes and a breakfast sandwich. She watched the exhaust from their tailpipe curl into the humidity. The world was moving on. People were buying breakfast while she and Blade were chasing down a murderer who kept a gallery of death.

The smell of coffee hit before the cup did. Blade handed her a cup. The heat through the cardboard sleeve stung her palms. She welcomed the bite of it.

"I think our next stop is the art gallery," she said as Blade pulled away from the window. The coffee was hot and strong, just how she liked it. "We figure out who the artist is. The drive gives us an hour to work."

Blade nodded, merging back into traffic. "Agreed. But first, we need to bring the FBI in. See if they'll approve you as our consulting behavioral analyst."

"If they agree, I'll clear it with my supervisor."

"When we catch this guy, it'll be the best research sabbatical in the history of sabbaticals." He pulled out his phone, putting it on speaker as he dialed.

One visit to the prison. That's all the field research for her book was supposed to be. She hadn't expected the prison visit with Damien to be anything other than a mind game. Boy, was it.

She looked at her reflection in the window. Her hair was frizzy from the humidity, and her eyes looked sunken. She looked like a woman who spent too much time drinking coffee just to buy more hours in the day.

The call connected after two rings. "Agent Wells."

"Sebastian, it's Blade St. James. Mind if I put this on speaker? Dr. Tori Crew is with me. She's been consulting on this case."

"Not at all. What's up?"

"While running down a lead that spun out of the Florek homicide, we may have stumbled into a serial. Still too early to tell."

"Outstanding work, Blade." Sebastian's voice carried genuine warmth, the sound of someone pleased to hear from a colleague. "How can I help?"

Tori sipped her coffee, studying Blade's careful phrasing. He was holding his cards close.

"At the moment, we're holding steady. We'll loop you in once she's verified a serial pattern."

"Brilliant idea. I've heard of Dr. Crew. She's a fantastic consultant. Wish we had her on our team."

Tori rolled her eyes. They were always saying that, but spotting a unicorn on I-95 had better odds than landing a Behavioral Analysis Unit position. Besides, she'd never leave Florida. This was home. Blade, the beaches, her chosen family.

"Okay, Blade, keep me in the loop. If you need federal resources, you call me first. I'm there for you. We'll keep the circle small."

Blade agreed and disconnected.

Tori smiled. "Well, that went well."

An hour later, they parked across the street from the Gallery Showcase, the late afternoon sun glinting off its glass facade.

Tori stepped into the Gallery Showcase and felt the temperature drop ten degrees. The space stretched before them like an aircraft hangar painted white, every surface gleaming under track lighting that could illuminate surgery.

The current exhibit dominated the walls—black and white portraits blown up to massive scale. A grandmother's weathered hands filled one frame, each line and callus rendered in sharp detail. A teenager's pierced face took up another entire wall.

"Interesting," she murmured, studying a portrait of a construction worker whose smile revealed a gold tooth. The photographer had captured something raw and honest in each face. Real.

Nothing like the violence hidden in those law firm paintings.

A woman approached from the back of the gallery, her heels clicking against polished concrete. Sleeveless hot pink dress, perfectly styled dark hair, the kind of composed elegance that Tori expected in an art gallery.

"Welcome to Gallery Showcase. I'm Laelanie Ferreira."

Blade stepped forward with an easy smile. "I'm Blade, and this is my girlfriend, Tori."

Tori blinked. Girlfriend? She recovered quickly, sliding her hand into the crook of his arm and leaning against his shoulder. The gesture felt surprisingly natural.

"We're interested in meeting an artist," Blade continued. "Tori's really into abstract work."

"Of course." Laelanie's smile widened. "What kind of pieces speak to you?"

She pulled out her phone, swiped to the photos, and handed Laelanie the phone. "Something like these. They're so powerful."

She watched Laelanie's face as the woman studied the screen. No shock. No horror. Just a flicker of professional recognition.

"I recognize these," Laelanie said, handing back the phone. "But I'm sorry, I have no idea who the artist is."

Tori let her shoulders dip, stretching the sigh into her bones, leaning into the letdown harder than she needed to. "Really? They're incredible. We heard they came from this gallery."

"The paintings are shipped here for treatment and mounting," Laelanie explained. "We handle the preservation work, frame them properly, then ship to whatever address we're given. Very anonymous process."

Tori looked at Blade. "I really wanted to meet them. Maybe even commission something."

Laelanie's expression brightened. "Oh, I might be able to help with that. Let me show you something."

She gestured toward the back of the gallery. "We keep detailed records of our preservation work. Perhaps we can trace the shipping information."

Tori squeezed Blade's arm as they followed Laelanie deeper into the gallery. Anonymous shipping. That meant paper trails. Records.

Maybe even an address.

"It's understandable you'd be drawn to those pieces," Laelanie said, navigating around stacked canvases and shipping crates. "They're abstract fractals."

Tori's foot caught on a wooden frame leaning against the wall. Blade's hand shot out, steadying her before she could fall.

"Oh yes, watch your step," Laelanie called over her shoulder. "There's junk everywhere back here."

Tori's heart slammed upward like it wanted out. "What's an abstract fractal?"

"Well, back in ninety-eight or ninety-nine, a physicist proved that Jackson Pollock's drip paintings follow fractal patterns." Laelanie stopped at a cluttered desk, waking up her computer with a mouse click. "That just means that paint splatters repeat at different scales, just like you see in nature when you look at flowers or shrubs."

The screen flickered to life, displaying a shipping database.

"Some people think you can authenticate a Pollock using mathematical equations, though that's debatable." Laelanie's fingers moved across the keyboard. "But I can see how these pieces would be soothing. There's something about abstract fractals that speaks to us."

Tori gripped Blade's arm tighter. Fractals. Mathematics. The same obsession that connected Damien Sullivan to their killer.

"Ah, here it is." Laelanie's finger traced across the screen. "The paintings are shipped from The Mandelbrot Group."

"Mandelbrot," Blade corrected gently. "Like 'bro,' not 'brot.'"

"Right, thank you." Laelanie smiled, but Tori barely heard the exchange.

Mandelbrot.

Damien's rambling about fractals. Dr. Stone's casual lecture on Keplerian patterns. The mathematical staging of each crime scene.

She forced her breathing to remain steady, her expression mildly interested rather than electrified. She'd been reading about the Mandelbrot set. The most famous fractal equation in mathematics. Self-similar patterns repeating infinitely, beautiful and terrifying in their complexity.

Just like their killer's methodology.

She flicked a look at Blade. His gaze locked on hers, sharp and lit with the same strike of recognition. He pinned his jaw shut, muscle ticcing once.

"Oh." Laelanie's voice brightened with discovery. "Looks like we have a painting that just came in from them. Would you like to see it?"

"We'd love to," she managed, her voice steady despite the adrenaline flooding her system.

Laelanie guided them through a maze of shipping crates to a sterile viewing room lined with adjustable track lighting. White walls, white floor, white ceiling. Everything designed to eliminate visual distractions.

"This keeps the dust away and gives us perfect color temperature," Laelanie explained, lifting a wrapped canvas from a shipping box.

Tori clasped her hands behind her back, fingers interlaced so tightly her knuckles ached. The woman moved with infuriating slowness, smoothing her white cotton gloves before peeling away each layer of protective paper with museum-quality care.

Rip it off already.

But the gloves were a blessing. No fingerprints contaminating evidence. No blown cover requiring explanations about chain of custody.

The final layer of tissue paper fell away.

Tori's breath caught. Violent brushstrokes erupted across the canvas. Aggressive slashes of crimson and black that mimicked arterial spray. The same strokes she'd studied in the conference room painting.

She scanned the chaotic composition, searching for the hidden pattern. There. In the lower right quadrant where the paint formed a spiral of decreasing circles.

Donald Florek's face emerged from the fractal geometry. Eyes wide with terror. Mouth open in a silent scream. The killer's latest trophy.

Tori's gasp escaped before she could stop it.

"I know, right?" Laelanie beamed, misreading the sound entirely. "This one's even more breathtaking than his last. The artist is really growing in his craft."

Growing. Tori's stomach lurched. Each murder refined his technique. Each victim taught him something new about staging, about violence, about transforming death into art. Laelanie was right. This . . . this . . . Mandelbrot killer was perfecting his masterpiece, one corpse at a time.

"It's incredible," Blade managed, clearing his throat. "Where is this headed? I'd love to see more of his work in person."

Laelanie consulted the packing slip. "Interesting. The final destination is TBD. The Mandelbrot Group has instructed us to hold it until they provide shipping instructions."

Tori's heart sank. A dead end wrapped in a breakthrough. They had irrefutable proof connecting the murders. Florek's terrorized face stared back at them from the canvas. But the killer remained a ghost, hidden behind corporate anonymity.

"How frustrating," she said, forcing disappointment into her voice instead of the rage building in her chest. "We were hoping to meet this artist."

"I'll keep your information on file," Laelanie offered. "If they contact us again, I can pass along your interest."

Perfect. Another waiting game while the killer planned his next fractal masterpiece.

23

THE SAND SHIFTED beneath Blade's feet with each punishing stride, his lungs burning as he drove himself harder along the deserted shoreline. Three miles into his run and the image still blazed behind his eyelids. Florek's terrified face hidden in those violent brushstrokes, staring back at them like an accusation.

Another dead end.

His feet pounded the packed sand at the water's edge, salt spray misting his face. The Mandelbrot Group. A corporate shell hiding their killer behind layers of bureaucracy and legal protection. Meanwhile, the psychopath—the Mandelbrot Killer as Tori had dubbed him—was out there planning his next masterpiece, selecting his next victim to transform into fractals and fear.

And Blade couldn't stop him.

The failure gnawed at him worse than the stitch developing in his side. Four victims. Four families destroyed while he chased shadows and corporate records. The killer stayed three steps ahead, orchestrating each scene with geometry while Blade stumbled through the aftermath like a rookie.

No wonder Kiara had dumped him. Normal guys didn't stand over a body staged like a math equation. They didn't skip dinners for diagrams of blood spray. They didn't let their cases fracture their relationships.

He reached his turnaround point and pivoted, driving himself back toward his condo. His quadriceps screamed in protest, but he welcomed the burn. Physical pain was clean. Manageable. Unlike the mess churning in his gut.

How could he be so close to answers but feel miles away?

Tori deserved answers after all these years. After all she'd endured. The murder of her parents. The nightmares and foster homes and years building walls so thick even he couldn't break through them. And now her brother—her twin—might be hunting her with plans to finish what had begun that night.

He should have connected the dots sooner. Should have protected her better. Should have been the detective Stryker believed he could become instead of this broken version stumbling through cases he couldn't solve.

His legs gave their opinion first. The trembling started at his knees and worked up. He slowed to a walk at the surf's edge, hands on his hips, head down, gasping. The waves hit the shore and hit it again. Relentless. A1A hummed somewhere behind the dunes. The patio music from across the Intracoastal had long since faded. Just him and the water and the air scorching his lungs.

Utterly alone under a canopy of stars that offered no answers.

The nausea came without warning. He doubled over, hands dropping to his knees, vision swimming. Sweat dripped from his face onto the wet sand. His body was collecting on a debt he'd run up over too many miles and too little sleep.

A flicker at the edge of his vision.

Blade's head snapped up. A man sprinted directly at him across the sand, closing the distance with unnatural speed. Instinct fired before thought. Not a jogger. The figure ate up the sand in clean, lethal strides, every step too balanced, too honed. Predator closing.

Dark workout clothes. A balaclava covering everything but his eyes. The figure barely disturbed the sand beneath his feet, as if he weighed nothing at all.

The raised hand registered a split second before Blade saw the knife.

"You think you can take her from me?" The voice cut through the night air like shattered glass. Blade's blood turned to ice.

The stalker.

Blade twisted his torso violently to the right and brought his left arm down in a desperate sweeping block. No technique. No form. Just flesh and bone thrown between himself and the steel racing toward his gut.

The six-inch blade punched through his jacket and sank deep into the meat of his left bicep. Pain exploded through his nervous system like white lightning, every nerve ending screaming in protest. The attacker used his momentum to rip the knife free, tearing muscle and fabric in one savage motion.

Blood, hot and slick, soaked through his sleeve and dripped onto the sand.

Blade stumbled backward, his mind reeling from the shock. He clutched his bicep, feeling the torn muscle beneath his fingers, the pain radiating down to his fingertips in waves. His left arm hung useless at his side, already a dead weight.

The fight had just started and he was already compromised.

The masked figure circled him like a predator, knife held low and ready. No words. No taunts. Just cold calculation behind those dark eyes visible through the mask's openings.

Blood continued to flow from the wound, warm rivulets running down his forearm. The metallic taste of adrenaline flooded his mouth as his body prepared for what was coming next.

The stalker pressed forward without hesitation, his knife arcing in a vicious horizontal slash aimed directly at Blade's throat. The blade caught moonlight as it cut through the air, a silver line of death seeking flesh.

Blade planted his feet and swept his right arm outward in a

classic 360-degree block, his forearm smashing into the attacker's wrist with bone-jarring force. The knife arm flew wide, the strike missing his neck by inches. Blade drove his right leg forward, his running shoe targeting the stalker's lead knee with everything he had left.

The kick connected with a satisfying thud. The stalker grunted, his body folding slightly as the joint buckled under the impact. But the soft sand beneath their feet absorbed the force like a cushion, robbing the strike of its devastating potential. The man stayed upright, already recovering.

The stalker came back immediately, his knife transforming into a blur of silver death. Short, vicious stabs punctured the air like a sewing machine needle, each thrust aimed at Blade's chest. No wild swings. Nothing wasted—each strike measured, precise, and meant to kill.

Blade gave ground, backpedaling toward the water's edge where the sand packed harder under the constant wash of waves. His feet slipped twice in the loose granules, his injured left arm throwing off his balance. The stalker pressed his advantage, closing the distance with each retreating step.

The first stab came at his sternum. Blade twisted his torso, the knife missing by millimeters. The second thrust targeted his ribs. He deflected it with his right forearm.

On the third attack, Blade pivoted hard to his left and trapped the stalker's knife arm against his own body in a tight clinch. His right hand clamped down on the attacker's wrist like a vise while his damaged left hand, screaming in protest, reinforced the grip. Blood from his bicep wound made his fingers slick, but he held on.

Got him.

They were chest to chest now, a brutal, grunting struggle for control of the weapon. Blade used his weight advantage, driving forward with his legs, trying to wrestle the smaller man off-balance. If he could get him to the ground, pin him in the sand, he could control the knife and end this.

The stalker's head snapped forward like a battering ram.

Pain detonated behind his eyes, white-hot and blinding. Cartilage crunched as Blade's nose flattened under the impact. Tears streamed down his cheeks, mixing with blood that poured from his nostrils. The world tilted sideways, his grip loosening for one critical moment.

The stalker wrenched his arm free from the clinch with surprising strength, his wiry frame belying the power in his movements. As Blade stumbled backward, trying to clear his vision through the haze of pain, the knife came around in a wild backhand slash.

Blade ducked, but not fast enough.

The knife caught him high across the upper chest and collarbone, slicing through jacket and skin in one agonizing line. Fire raced along his nerve endings as the steel parted flesh, adding a third injury to his growing collection. Blood began soaking through his shirt, warm and sticky against his skin.

Two down. How many more before he couldn't fight back?

The stalker circled again, breathing hard but still controlled. Still calculating. The knife in his hand dripped with Blade's blood, dark drops disappearing into the sand at their feet.

Blade pressed his right hand against the chest wound, feeling the warmth seep between his fingers. His left arm hung useless, the bicep wound throbbing with each heartbeat. His nose felt like someone had driven a spike through his skull.

He was losing this fight.

The mask hid most of the stalker's face, but his eyes glinted with the recognition of wounded prey. He stalked forward, knife slanted low and ready. His eyes flicked on the widening stain of Blade's blood spreading dark across the sand.

Blade staggered toward the waterline, his chest burning like molten metal. Each breath sent fresh waves of agony through the collarbone wound. His left arm wouldn't lift, fingers numb and unresponsive. Blood loss was making him lightheaded, his vision swimming in and out of focus.

He needed distance. Time to think.

His foot snagged a rope of seaweed, the slick coil wrenching his ankle sideways. His balance vanished. Leg shot wide, body pitching. His right knee slammed the sand and the shock ricocheted up through his frame.

The stalker's lips curved into a smile visible beneath the mask's fabric. He raised the knife high overhead, gripping it like an ice pick, the tip pointed downward for maximum penetration. Death gleamed in the steel as he lunged forward.

Blade's hand hit wet sand. Without thinking, he scooped up a massive handful of the heavy, waterlogged grit and hurled it upward with everything he had left.

The sand cloud exploded into the stalker's face like a shotgun blast. Wet granules filled his eyes, nose, and mouth. He screamed and stumbled backward while clawing frantically at his mask.

Blade exploded upward from the sand, adrenaline drowning out every scream of pain from his wounds. He drove forward like a missile, wrapping his arms around the stalker's waist and lifting him clean off his feet in a textbook double-leg takedown. They crashed into the shallow surf, salt water mixing with blood as Blade slammed him onto his back.

Full mount. Weight distribution perfect despite his injuries. The stalker flailed beneath him, still clawing at his sand-filled eyes, the knife cutting wild arcs through empty air.

Blade trapped the knife wrist against the wet sand with his damaged left hand. Fire tore through him. His right fist came down twice. Precise hammer strikes to the jaw. The first blow stunned. The second made the stalker's body go limp.

The moment his weight shifted to wrench the knife away, the stalker's eyes snapped open. Not unconscious. Not even close. Just waiting.

His hips bucked upward with explosive force, sending Blade down hard into the surf. Before he could recover, thumbs drove into his eye sockets like twin daggers.

Pain detonated through his skull—absolute, blinding agony that wiped out every coherent thought. His vision disappeared behind a wall of white fire. He rolled away, gasping, his strength hemorrhaging out with his blood. Every wound screamed as salt water invaded torn flesh.

Splashing. The stalker scrambling to his feet in the shallow waves.

More splashing. Coming closer.

Blade clawed at his eyes, trying to clear his vision, but saw only darkness punctured by dancing spots of light. His left arm wouldn't respond. His chest felt like molten metal.

This is how it ends.

A single gunshot cracked through the night, sharp above the crash of waves.

The stalker cried out. Scrambling footsteps retreating fast through the dunes behind him.

Blade blinked frantically, salt water and grit mixing into a painful paste. His vision returned in blurry splotches. A silhouette stood at the beach path's edge. Pistol held ready in a perfect Weaver stance.

Tori.

The adrenaline abandoned him like a retreating tide, taking with it every scrap of strength that had kept him upright. His legs dissolved beneath him. He collapsed backward into the surf, salt water rushing over his wounds like liquid agony. The world tilted sideways, stars wheeling overhead in dizzying arcs.

Splashing footsteps crashed toward him.

Tori's words sliced through the fog closing in around him. "Harlee, Blade was attacked."

A clipped silence. A phone. She wasn't talking to him. "Meet me at his condo."

The sound drifted. The pressure in his ribs dragged him down, deeper into the black that kept pulling.

"Hurry—it looks bad."

He tried to answer, maybe crack a joke. Prove he still could. His tongue stuck to the roof of his mouth. Nothing came out. Salt water filled his ears, and the world narrowed to the failing drum of his own blood.

Tori dropped to her knees in the wet sand beside him, her hand pressing against his chest above the wound.

"Blade! Blade, look at me!"

He forced his eyes to focus through the haze of pain. Her face swam into view. Terrified but fierce. His best friend. The protector. The woman who had just saved his life when everything else had failed.

Every wall he'd built between them crumbled to dust in that moment.

If he'd possessed the strength, he would've pulled her down to him and kissed her until the world made sense again.

Instead, he managed a single word through cracked lips. "Tori."

Then, blackness.

24

BLOOD SPREAD through the salt water like red ink, and Tori's heart seized as Blade's eyes rolled back. His body went completely limp, sinking deeper into the surf.

No. No, no, no.

She lunged forward as waves crashed around them. Her hands found his shoulders, pulling him up and into her lap before the next wave could wash over his face. His head lolled against her, dead weight, and panic clawed up her throat.

"Blade! *Blade*!"

His chest barely moved. Blood poured from the knife wounds, mixing with salt water and sand. Too much blood. Way too much.

This was her fault. Her stalker. Her brother. Her nightmare that had reached out and destroyed the one person who'd never left her side.

She pressed both hands against the worst wound on his chest, trying to stem the bleeding. "Jesus, please. Please don't take him. I can't—" Her voice cracked. "Blade, you have to stay with me. You hear me? You don't get to leave."

His eyelids fluttered. A weak cough sent salt water spraying across her face and arms, but she'd never been so grateful to be soaked. He was breathing. Fighting.

"That's it. Keep breathing. Just keep breathing."

The chest wound looked horrific at first glance. Torn fabric, blood everywhere. But as she examined it closer, her medical training kicked in. The knife had hit muscle, not nerves. Not organs. Deep enough to bleed like crazy, but not deep enough to kill. The bicep wound was worse, still bleeding freely, but manageable.

Her free hand fumbled for her phone. "I'm calling 911. Just hang on—"

"No." His voice came out as barely a whisper. His hand splashed the water, trying to catch her wrist. "Can't trust."

She hesitated. Of course. The dispatcher would route the call to the closest unit. A Millie Beach patrol car. Barclay's people.

If Barclay was dirty—and everything pointed to exactly that—then calling his department was handing them both to the enemy.

"What about this crime scene?" She gestured at the bloody sand around them.

"What crime scene?" Blade's mouth quirked up in a ghost of his usual grin. "Tide's coming in. Washed away." His eyes found hers, more focused now. "Get me upstairs before he comes back."

The vulnerability of their position crashed over her. They were sitting ducks on an empty beach, Blade bleeding and defenseless, her Glock the only thing standing between them and a killer who could return any second.

"Can you walk?" She shifted position, getting her feet under her.

"You planning to carry me?" Despite the pain etched across his face, that teasing note crept into his voice. "I'm six-four, Crew."

"Shut up and lean on me."

She got her shoulder under his good arm and hauled him upright. He swayed, gritting his teeth, but stayed on his feet. Together they slogged through the sand toward the condo building, leaving a trail of blood and salt water behind them.

The lobby's pristine travertine floor became a danger zone as they dripped their way to the elevator. Tori jabbed the button repeatedly, her eyes scanning the entrance for any sign of movement.

In the elevator, Blade sagged against the wall, his breathing shallow but steady. "Did you see his face?" she asked.

"He was wearing a mask, and it happened too fast." Blade's jaw tightened. "Good fighter, though. Knew what he was doing."

The elevator dinged as they reached his floor. Tori got him inside and steered him straight to his bathroom, where he collapsed onto the closed toilet seat.

"Don't move." She sprinted to the guest room, grabbed her medical kit from her bag, and raced back.

"Doc Crew making house calls." He managed another weak smile.

"Haven't done this since my residency." She hopped onto the bathroom counter and opened the medical kit, then snapped on latex gloves and assessed the wounds again. "Good news. I don't think you need real stitches. Medical adhesive should hold you together."

"Should?"

"Trust me."

"Always do."

The shoulder wound sealed cleanly under the medical adhesive, but the bicep cut fought her. It was deeper than she'd hoped, and the edges kept wanting to pull apart as Blade's arm moved.

"Hold still." She pressed gauze against the bleeding. "This one's tricky."

"How tricky?"

"You'll live." The adhesive caught, drawing the torn muscle back together. "But no MMA for a while."

"There goes my weekend plans."

She braced Blade's arm against her thigh to keep the muscle from twitching, then pinched the ragged edges of the cut on his bicep together. The second strip caught and held, the skin closing neat as a seam. Her fingertips pressed hard to test the seal, then reached for the next one.

He'd taken this cut for her.

The fact shoved against her focus, but she slammed it back. Instead, she locked in on the burn of antiseptic clogging her nose and the rip of adhesive tearing free from the package under her fingers. Strip to wound, seal the edges, move to the next. Nothing else stayed in frame.

Blade tipped his chin, mouth quirking even as sweat ran along his temple. "You're the only woman I know who hauls a trauma kit everywhere she goes."

"Probably the only one who needs to." Tori positioned the strip and pressed it into place. "And I wouldn't need one if I had a best friend who wasn't too stubborn to call EMS when someone tries to gut him like a fish."

Blade's lips twitched. "Says the woman who told me it was 'just a scratch' when that stalker put a knife to her throat and sliced her arm."

"Touché."

He winced as she smoothed the edges of another strip. "How's your arm, by the way?"

"Better than yours. At least mine still works." Her gaze snagged on his. His eyes were puffed, rimmed red, matching the crooked mess of his nose. He grinned anyway, like he hadn't been half beaten. Tomorrow his body would remind him they weren't teenagers taking hits on the mat anymore.

"Looks worse than it is," he said. "Though I have to say, for someone who works for FDLE, your marksmanship needs work. You completely missed your target."

"Who says I missed?" She reached for the final Steri-Strip. "Some of that blood might be his. Hard to tell in the dark."

"Fair point. Should be a blood trail if you actually hit him."

"I wouldn't have had to shoot him at all if you'd been able to take him down properly." She took her time peeling the backing, drawing out the moment before the final strip sealed his wound.

Blade's chuckle rumbled through his chest. "I was unarmed against a knife in the dark after a long run. Think I held my own pretty well."

"Sure. If your definition of 'holding your own' includes getting carved up like a Thanksgiving turkey."

The antiseptic's clean scent mixed with the brine of the ocean still clinging to his skin beneath the coppery tang of drying blood. His breathing had steadied, no longer the harsh, shallow gasps that had punctuated the first few minutes of her work. The only sounds now were her controlled exhales and the whisper of medical tape against skin.

Tori placed the final Steri-Strip and smoothed the edges. Her knuckle brushed against the warm, uninjured skin of his shoulder.

Electric.

Her clinical detachment evaporated like morning mist. She wasn't seeing Blade the patient sitting on the bathroom stool. This was Blade. Shirtless. Wounded. Close enough that she could feel the heat radiating from his body despite the air conditioning's steady breeze.

His jaw flexed as he dragged air through clenched teeth. A lock of dark hair slipped loose and dangled across his forehead, careless, like the rest of him lived in fight mode and had no time for mirrors.

Those blue eyes locked on her. Pinning. Steady. She forgot the rhythm of her own lungs.

He took that knife because of her. Went down hard in the surf because of her. Willing to die—because of her.

Her thumb continued to caress the Steri-Strip. Checking her work, though it wasn't about the wound anymore. The skin under her touch radiated heat. Alive, stubbornly alive, when earlier she'd thought she'd lose him to the dark.

Her gaze locked with his again, and his blue eyes sent heat climbing up her neck.

"I guess you're all set," she said.

He didn't move. Neither did she. The air barely seemed to either.

Warmth surged up her throat, flushed her ears, and she didn't dare breathe. Her lips parted. She tilted her face toward his. The space between them disappeared to nothing.

She jerked backward, the spell broken as abruptly as snapping fingers. No. Not like this. Not with blood under her fingernails and adrenaline still crackling through her veins. Words first. Understanding first. They'd been running from a stalker, chasing down a killer. They hadn't even had time to figure out what *this* even meant.

She hopped off the counter, putting three feet of bathroom tile between them. Not nearly enough distance.

"You may want to wear a sling on that side for a while." Her voice came out too bright. "Might heal faster."

She cranked the faucet handle and let cold water rush over her hands. The soap dispenser required two pumps. Then three. The scrubbing gave her something to focus on besides the way Blade's eyes had held hers.

The doorbell's sharp chime shot through the moment like a rocket. Both of them flinched.

His hand reached for his hip, searching for a weapon that wasn't there. He winced, palm pressing against the bandaged bicep.

"Stay here." Blade shoved upright, shoulders tight, moving stiffly as he headed for the door.

Tori stayed rooted at the sink, soap sliding off her fingertips and dripping in tiny constellations onto the basin. Better she kept her mouth shut. No blurting out words that would only tangle things between them. Blade was her friend. Her partner. Nothing else. No matter how her heart insisted otherwise.

From the living room came the scrape of his tired voice. Another layered over it, female, precise in upbeat rhythm.

Harlee.

She'd almost forgotten she'd called her and asked her to come. Tori stepped out of the bathroom and almost walked into Harlee.

Harlee's smirk stretched wider as her gaze bounced between them. "About time you two figured things out."

Tori's stomach dropped to somewhere around her ankles. Harlee wasn't the only one who teased about what a great couple they'd be.

"Don't start." Blade's voice came out rough, exhausted. "I'm in too much pain for jokes."

The smugness melted from Harlee's expression, replaced by genuine concern as she took in the extent of his injuries. "That looks bad. Are you okay? What happened?"

Blade braced a hand on the counter, shoulders tight. "Guy came at me on the beach. Sprinting out of the dark."

Harlee's eyes flared, and she stepped closer. "You need a hospital."

He flicked a glance at Tori, lifted his bandaged arm with a wince. "Already handled."

"It looked worse in the dark. Once we got up here, I realized the cuts weren't deep."

Harlee's gaze cut back. "You get a good look at this guy?"

Blade's jaw flexed once. He gave a short shake of his head.

"I fired," Tori said. Her fingers worried the hem of her sleeve. "It was too dark to be sure if I hit." The image of Blade and the dark figure about to bring the knife down. Her blood flashed hot then cold. She could've hit Blade.

"Please tell me you called this in," Harlee said.

"We didn't call local PD." Tori crossed her arms. "Didn't really want to deal with Barclay and his possible corruption issues."

"You can't just let this psycho run around loose." Harlee's voice carried that edge it got when she was gearing up for a fight. "He's escalating. First your house, now this."

"I'll call it in now." Blade headed toward his bedroom. "But I'm calling my people at BSO, not Millie Beach."

The bedroom door clicked shut behind him, leaving Tori alone with Harlee's penetrating stare.

"All right." Harlee dropped onto the couch, arms folded. "What's really going on here?"

"What do you mean?" Tori perched on the edge of the coffee table, maintaining distance.

"Something changed between you two. I can feel it from across the room."

Tori opened her mouth to deny it, to insist nothing was happening between them. But the memory of Blade's eyes holding hers in the bathroom stopped her cold. The electricity when her knuckle had brushed his shoulder. The way her heart had stopped when she'd found him bleeding in the surf.

Truth was, she'd been fighting it for weeks.

"I don't know." The words came out smaller than she intended. "Maybe it's the stalker. Maybe it's the case. Everything feels . . ."

"Different?"

"Yeah."

Harlee's expression softened. "Tori, everyone knows you two belong together. Seems like the only ones who don't realize it are you and Blade."

Heat climbed Tori's neck. "It's not that simple."

"Why not?"

Because friendship was safe. Because she'd already lost everyone who mattered. Because crossing that line meant risking the one relationship that had never failed her.

Because she was terrified.

"Because Blade only ended up in the Warrior program because of me." The words hurt to say aloud. "He nearly ruined his life protecting me from that knife attack when we were kids. Went to juvie for it."

Harlee's eyebrows pulled together. "So?"

"So I already destroyed his life once. And now I did it again with Kiara." She picked at the bandage on her arm. "Maybe there's still time for him to patch things up with her. She's good for him. Safe."

"Kiara's a great woman," Harlee said, pushing to her feet. "But she's so not the one for Blade."

The certainty in her tone froze something behind Tori's ribs.

"I'm gonna head out. Big project at work, and it looks like you two have things handled." Harlee moved toward the door.

Tori followed. "Thanks for coming."

"It's what family does. We have each other's backs." She pulled Tori into a quick hug at the threshold. "And listen, Blade might have been the man who saved your life that night at the pier, but I'm pretty sure that whole incident saved his life too."

Harlee wasn't talking about his heartbeat. Without that night, Blade would have stayed an alligator-wrestling swamp kid instead of becoming a man with a badge. Saving her gave him the only exit ramp he was ever going to get.

The door clicked shut, leaving Tori staring at polished wood and wondering what had gotten into Harlee. First the wise-old-man-type advice, then the hug. Physical affection wasn't Harlee's usual speed.

But it was the other phrase that suddenly blazed through her consciousness like a lightning strike.

The man who saved your life that night at the pier.

"The man who saved Tori can find it."

Damien's riddle. The message from prison that had sent them chasing shadows, assuming he'd meant Stryker.

But Stryker had found her *after*.

The man who had *physically* saved her life, the man who had pulled her from the darkness that night—

She didn't walk. She ran. Across the living room to Blade's bedroom. She burst through the door without knocking.

Blade stood beside his bed, struggling to pull a fresh T-shirt over his head, movements stiff with pain from his wounds. The fabric caught on his bandaged bicep, and his mouth pinched.

"The pier. The message from Damien." The words spilled out of her, breathless and ragged. "It wasn't about Stryker. It was you."

She took a step closer.

"You're the man who saved me."

25

BLADE STRAIGHTENED HIS SHIRT and turned, the fabric settling against his bandaged wounds. The pull forced a sharp flinch through him.

"I'm the man who . . ."

The realization struck him with stupid, blinding clarity. Of course. Why hadn't he seen it? Fourteen years old, running toward screams on a pier. A girl with terrified eyes and a man with a knife. The moment that had defined everything that came after.

He had been the one to save Tori that night.

The bag. Damien's message.

"It has to be in the evidence bag from that night," he said.

He started moving toward the living room, looking for his keys, his phone. Action was escape. Movement meant he didn't have to think about how Harlee's assumption had been right. He'd almost kissed Tori. Almost ruined everything.

"Blade. Stop." Tori's hand caught his gently. "Look at me."

He froze, turning back to her.

"We're not going to talk about the case. Not for five minutes," she said. "We're going to sit down and talk about what just happened here. We can't move forward until we do."

"What are you talking about?" The denial was a half-hearted defensive block.

"Something Harlee said. About that night at the pier saving you as much as me. That's why you do this, isn't it? Why you risk everything to save people around you. It's always been about that night at the pier."

He wasn't sure what Tori was talking about, but he eased onto the couch. The knife wounds pulled against the bandages with each movement, and grit from the beach still scratched behind his eyelids every time he blinked.

He was exhausted. This week had stretched him past his limits. Every time he thought he had a lead on a case, a bigger lead erupted on a different one. Answer one question only to end up with three more. The pattern never broke, just shifted, multiplied, demanded more than he could give.

And now they were digging up the past he'd buried and tried to forget.

He lifted his head to look at Tori. The cut at her neck had healed to a half-moon scab, dark as a dirty fingernail. She'd kept the gash on her forearm wrapped in flesh-colored gauze, but he'd seen the knife wound. He'd seen the blood. And he'd felt like a failure.

"That night . . . it changed everything," he said. "I saw what that guy did to you. How he'd thrown you on the sand and straddled you with a knife to your throat. I made a promise to myself then. Never again. Never on my watch."

Tori sank onto the couch beside him. "I spent my whole life trying not to feel like a victim, but you . . . you spent your whole life trying to be the antidote. For me."

She inhaled like she was preparing to release something.

"That night at the pier . . . I remember everything. The way you didn't hesitate. You heard me scream and you ran toward the danger, not away from it."

Blade kept his eyes fixed on his hands, but her words pulled at his memory.

"You were just a kid yourself. And you killed that guy. To save me." She paused, letting that settle. "You were a hero, but no one saw it that way. You were forced to pay the price, and that was more than just six months in juvie. You lost your entire family. You saved my life, but it cost you everything. And I never thanked you properly. Not just for saving my life, but for what it cost you."

The gratitude blindsided him.

"No." He looked at her, meeting those dark eyes that he'd memorized all these years. "I didn't lose everything. I found my purpose."

Tori's expression softened. "You found me."

The simple truth of it hit him. She wasn't just right, she was completely, devastatingly right. Every choice he'd made since that night had been about her. Not consciously, but with the kind of bone-deep certainty that guided a man's life without him even realizing it.

He studied her face in the lamplight. Really looked at her.

Not the terrified fourteen-year-old from the pier. Not his colleague or his friend or the woman who could make him laugh when things got too dark. He saw Tori. The woman who had been the one constant in his life. The person who understood his silences and matched his intensity and never asked him to be anything other than exactly who he was.

The truth hadn't shifted. He had. What once blurred sat sharp now, stripped of fog, undeniable in its clarity. Kiara hadn't been his future. She'd been his hiding place. A safe harbor where he could pretend he wanted the life everyone said he should want. But his heart had made its choice eighteen years ago under a dark pier.

Blade stared at his hands, shame crawling up his throat like acid. Maybe he hadn't technically been unfaithful to Kiara, but something inside him had been divided all along.

"Kiara must be convinced I'm like every other man I despise. A no-good cheater and liar." He rubbed his face. "No wonder she dumped me."

"Anyone who's met you knows you're not that guy." Tori nudged his knee with hers. "Your name might sound big and tough, but deep down you're a softy."

"I can hold my own." But even as he said it, he thought about how close he'd come to dying on the beach tonight. The stalker's thumbs digging into his eye sockets, the knife slicing through skin. Without Tori's intervention, he'd be fish food by now. "Thanks for saving my life, by the way. I owe you."

"Nah. We're even. Just stop being mushy."

"Mushy? I'm expressing gratitude."

"Exactly." She grinned. "Next you'll be writing me a thank-you card with little hearts on it."

"Hearts are Corbin's thing. I'd use skulls."

"Much more dramatic."

Tori shifted closer, her fingers tracing the line of his jaw. "I think we're finally starting to see what everyone else has been seeing for years."

The words should have required some kind of response, but his brain had gone blank. All he could manage was, "Yeah."

She leaned in, and when their lips met, something dormant in his chest ignited. The kiss was soft, tentative, but it felt like his soul had been holding its breath his entire life and could finally exhale.

When they broke apart, reality crashed back. The case. The evidence bag. The killer still out there.

"I wish I could stay here with you," he said, brushing her hair back behind her ear. "For the rest of my life." He pressed his lips to hers and pulled back just enough to whisper, "Your five minutes are up."

She smiled as they kissed again, then she nodded. "There will be time for more talking, but first—the job."

Blade closed his eyes. He needed a minute to gather his thoughts. Sort through Damien's cryptic words. The bag from the first fight.

"Damien must've hidden his blackmail notebook in the evidence from my case."

Tori tilted her head. "How would he have access?"

"Did you forget who arrested me that night?"

She blinked. "Damien Sullivan?"

He nodded.

"What are the odds?"

"Pretty good. Back then Millie Beach only had three full-time officers and ten commissioned. It's not much bigger now, which is why major crimes generally fall to BSO."

"So, Damien would've had access to hide his notebook in your evidence bag, but isn't that evidence gone by now? Destroyed? Your juvie record was expunged when you turned eighteen."

"They don't always destroy evidence when there's been a death. Especially a homicide." He stood, energy returning. "But if the evidence is still there, we have another problem."

"You were a juvenile. It's going to be sealed."

"Kiara was our only key to accessing sealed evidence, without a warrant."

"And since she dumped you . . ."

He tried to give her the same don't-go-there look she always gave him.

"Okay, that's not funny," she said. "But we're locked out. We don't need a key. We need a battering ram."

He saw the spark in her eyes ignite with an idea.

"We need a lawyer who is now personally invested in seeing this conspiracy burn to the ground. We need Janice."

"Yes." He pulled up Janice's contact, his thumb hovering over the call button. "It's pretty late. Should we wait until tomorrow?"

"Remember her client who calls at three in the morning? She answers for him, maybe she'll answer for you."

"Right." He pressed the button and listened. Janice answered on the first ring like she'd been sitting on the phone.

"Janice? It's Blade. I need you to work a miracle."

"After yesterday? I'm fresh out of those." Her laugh carried no humor. "But I'm curious. What do you need?"

"Access to evidence from 2008. We think Damien hid his blackmail book in the evidence from my juvenile case."

The silence stretched so long, he checked if the call had dropped.

"Blade, listen to me. Juvenile cases are sealed tighter than Fort Knox. We're talking about a judicial order that would require showing imminent threat, conspiracy at the highest levels, and evidence of ongoing criminal activity. The bar is astronomical."

Hope leaked out of him. Another wall. Another dead end in a maze designed to protect the guilty.

"There has to be something—"

"Even if I could convince a judge, which is a massive *if*, the evidence is archived in a secure facility with protocols that would make the Pentagon jealous. We'd need—"

"Damien Sullivan."

"Blade, I am not going back—"

"Didn't you hear? He was murdered by another inmate."

The line went dead quiet. Blade counted heartbeats waiting for Janice to process what he'd just told her.

"I don't understand. He was in protective custody. And why hasn't anyone called me about my client?"

"Look, I don't have all the answers. All I know is our primary witness in a decades-old conspiracy involving police corruption is dead, and the evidence that could expose his killers might be locked in the evidence warehouse."

Another silence stretched until Blade's lungs burned from holding his breath.

Janice swore, then apologized. "This changes everything. Witness elimination. Pattern of violence. Active conspiracy." Her voice gained momentum, her legal gears spinning faster. "I can petition the ADA for emergency access. Imminent threat. Preservation of evidence in an ongoing criminal enterprise."

"Will it work?"

"It's still a long shot. But it's a shot."

Twenty minutes later, Janice called back.

"Someone must looove you." Janice drew her words out. "Joint privilege review. Tomorrow morning. The ADA's office will meet us at the warehouse. We get supervised access to the sealed evidence."

Victory surged through him, electric and fierce. They had a path forward. "Thank you. We'll see you there."

He disconnected and turned to Tori, who had been working on her laptop. More distraction than work, he suspected. "We're going to the warehouse tomorrow morning. The DA's office is meeting us there."

The personal wreckage could wait. They were one step closer to the truth.

The next morning, Blade stood with Tori and Janice beside a metal table, watching ADA Rene Garrison flip through a thick folder of court orders. The woman's gray suit matched her muted expression.

"This is highly irregular," Garrison said for the third time. "The restrictions are non-negotiable."

Janice nodded. "Understood. My client acknowledges the limitations."

Blade's jaw tightened. The restrictions felt like handcuffs. He could observe. He could identify items that belonged to him. But he couldn't touch anything without permission. Couldn't remove anything. Couldn't even photograph the contents.

He wanted to get his hands on Damien's notebook, and if it was in that evidence box, they'd have to try and stop him when they came to it.

The clerk, a thin man named James Fiske, wheeled in a gray storage box marked with evidence tags and judicial seals. Blade shoved his hands in his pockets and rocked forward on his heels. A single cardboard container held the physical remnants of that night.

"Box 894," Fiske announced, setting it on the table with reverent care. "Sealed August 2008. Contents logged but not inventoried since initial processing."

Tori stood beside him at the table's corner. The evidence box would dredge up memories for her too. Blood on sand, screams in the dark. He didn't want either of them to relive that night. He wanted Damien's notebook and nothing else. *Get in, get out, move forward.*

Fiske used a box cutter to break the evidence seals. The box opened to reveal several plastic bags, each tagged and dated. Blade's stomach lurched as he recognized fragments of that night.

"Victim's clothing first," Garrison directed.

Fiske lifted a bag containing a blood-stained shirt and jeans. He broke the seal and, with gloved hands, laid the pieces on the table. The fabric wasn't as big as he remembered. The man he'd killed had been smaller than Blade was now. Not the giant his memory had constructed.

Next came Blade's own clothes. The sight of his bloody shirt and jeans reminded him of just how far he'd come. The fabric was cheap, worn thin from too many washings. Gaping holes in both knees. A torn belt loop. Poor kid clothes that screamed desperation and hand-me-downs.

Fiske reached for the next sealed bundle. Tori's clothes. Cutoff shorts and a tank top smeared with dark stains. Not her blood. Thank God for that. The clothes looked impossibly small. Like they belonged to a first grader. Evidence of how badly overmatched she'd been against a grown man twice her size and three times her strength pinning her down.

Fiske searched every seam, every pocket, recording the absence of anything hidden before folding the clothes with the care of a mortician and sealing them into fresh plastic. His pen scratched across the log sheet. Another bag cataloged, another piece returned to evidence purgatory.

Tori's gaze stayed locked on the empty fabric until her lips parted, wordless. That crushed look in her eyes was heavier than the box itself. "Where is it? It has to be here."

Janice placed her hand on Tori's. "Have a little patience. We've got several more bags to check. We're here, we may as well be thorough."

She was right. Still, the itch crawled up Blade's shoulders. Another dead end, another possibility slipping through their fingers.

Fiske bent and lifted the clear plastic bag containing the knife.

Blade forced himself to look. Like Tori's clothes, it was smaller than he remembered. Too small to end a man's life, yet he'd driven it home with the strength it took to kill a gator. Every ounce behind it. That truth had put him in handcuffs, charged as a killer before anyone saw past the weapon in his hands.

He shook his head. Stryker had rescued him. Convinced an understanding judge to grant the lifeline—

His hand shot out before reason caught up, and he grabbed ADA Rene Garrison's arm.

"The judge. Who was the judge on my case?"

She blinked, startled, then pulled free, fumbling through her folder. "It was juvenile court. Judge Doreen Kagay. Why?"

His heart froze for a beat. "Because she's dead. Murdered. Two years ago."

"Wasn't she murdered in Tampa?" Tori asked.

Garrison froze, papers half raised. "She . . . she retired. Moved to Tampa to be near her grandchildren." Her stiff composure faltered as her gaze flicked between them.

Janice shook her head like she was trying to shake something loose. "What does that mean?"

Fiske cleared his throat. "Perhaps we finish the evidence review first. Then we discuss implications."

The box waited.

But Blade's skin had gone cold. The judge who had shown him mercy, who had approved his placement in Stryker's program instead of state detention, was now dead. Murdered in the same brutal fashion as Florek. The geometric staging, the prolonged violence, the personal nature of the attack.

The killer wasn't just targeting random victims. He was eliminating everyone connected to—

He looked at Tori.

The evidence box suddenly felt like a tomb. Not just of physical remnants, but of people. Damien Sullivan. Judge Kagay. How many others were already dead? How many more were marked for execution?

Fiske held up the plastic bag containing the knife, its blade still stained dark after all these years. "I assume we don't need to unseal this one?"

Garrison nodded quickly. "We'll agree to that."

Fiske set the weapon aside and pulled another box from the cart. This one was smaller, marked with different tags. "Defendant's personal belongings," he announced, reading from the paperwork clipped to the lid. "Items were to be returned to defendant Blade Tiger St. James upon his release but were never claimed."

Blade felt everyone's eyes turn to him. He shifted his stance, the bandages under his shirt pulling against the knife wounds.

"What? I never knew about this," he said.

He caught Tori's sideways glance.

"Tiger?" she mouthed, one eyebrow arched.

He gave her a crooked grin and focused on the evidence.

Fiske broke the seal and reached inside. When he pulled out a battered brown and green plastic tackle box, recognition hit Blade like a punch to the gut.

"Oh yeah. I do remember it." His voice softened. "That's my tackle box."

The box looked exactly like he remembered. Cheap plastic with a broken latch that never quite closed right. Scratched and faded from years of use before that night. His fingers twitched with the urge to touch it, to flip open the compartments and see if his hooks and sinkers were still arranged the way he'd left them.

"I'd been fishing from the pier when I heard Tori screaming. I dropped my pole and ran. Left everything behind. I'm surprised my brothers didn't snag it and bring it home. But our parents had taught us that cops weren't the good guys and it was every man for himself."

Garrison's eyebrows lifted.

How did you explain a father who hollered at his kids to duck down when a cop passed them on the highway or a mother who taught them to be quiet and hide whenever someone knocked on their trailer door?

As an adult, he'd figured it out. His mom had been writing hot checks, floating money they didn't have to keep food on the table. His father had been caught killing gators without the proper tags, trying to feed eight kids with whatever the swamp provided. Both parents had been constantly at risk of being picked up on outstanding warrants.

No wonder they'd bailed when he got arrested. The St. James family survival strategy had always been simple: Avoid law enforcement at all costs. When their third-born son ended up in handcuffs for killing a man, even if it was to save a girl's life, they'd cut him loose rather than risk exposure, and he was just now figuring it out.

Fiske opened the tackle box. The rusty hinges squeaked like old bones. Inside, the compartments were exactly as Blade remembered. Organized with the obsessive care of a boy who owned almost nothing and treasured what little he had.

Hooks sorted by size. Lead sinkers arranged by weight. A few lures his father had given him for his thirteenth birthday. And there, tucked into the bottom compartment beneath a tangle of fishing line, he saw it.

"My wallet." A cheap Ocean Pacific trifold with fraying edges. His brother's, originally. Or maybe his dad's. He couldn't remember anymore. "I forgot I even had that."

Fiske looked to Garrison, who nodded. The clerk placed the wallet on the table.

Blade stared at the worn fabric. When he slid the wallet into his back pocket, he'd felt rich. Adult. Important.

"May I?" he asked Fiske.

Fiske glanced at Garrison, who nodded. Then he said, "If you can provide proper identification, I can turn these items over to you right now."

"You should've had this years ago," Garrison said.

Blade pulled out his driver's license and handed it over. Fiske's pen scratched across the release form, copying information. Each stroke felt like another layer of bureaucracy peeling away from that night. When Fiske finished, Blade didn't bother putting his license away. He grabbed the wallet and ripped the Velcro open with a grin.

"They don't make Velcro like this anymore."

"Good thing," Tori said. "That thing's loud enough to wake the dead."

He chuckled and checked the largest compartment first. A single dollar bill sat folded inside, creased from years of pressure.

"That's not going to cover my fee," Janice said.

He chuckled again and dug deeper. He found his old school ID with a grainy photo of a chubby kid with too-long hair and wide eyes. Then his fingers found the photograph tucked behind it.

The image stole his breath.

His parents stood in front of their trailer, his father gripping an alligator by the tail. A second, even larger gator lay dead at their feet. His mother, visibly pregnant, held a baby on her hip while Blade and two of his brothers straddled the dead reptile like conquering heroes.

The laughter that escaped him was half sob, half joy. He'd forgotten how young his parents had looked, how proud his father's stance was, how his mother's smile could light up even the grimmest of circumstances.

"Can I see?" Tori asked softly.

Blade nodded and passed the photograph to Tori, his gaze

already shifting to the wallet's remaining compartments. The ache in his chest caught him off guard—raw and immediate, like touching a live wire. These people in the photo, frozen in their moment of triumph—they belonged to someone else's life. He'd built himself into something different, something better. The forgiveness had been real, the moving forward complete. So why did his throat feel like it was closing?

He focused on the wallet's inside pocket. Empty. The opposite side yielded nothing either. The final compartment where he hid his coins required prying the stubborn Velcro apart. The sharp ripping sound blasted through the quiet room. He dumped the contents into his palm.

Three nickels, a dime, six pennies. And something that didn't belong.

A tarnished brass key, no bigger than his thumb, sat among the coins like an intruder. The metal was worn smooth at the edges. He'd memorized every inch of this wallet as a kid, counted these same coins a hundred times, dreamed of the day he'd have enough money to fill every pocket.

This key had never been there.

"I've never seen this before."

Janice leaned forward, studying the key through her reading glasses. "Looks like a safe deposit box key. See the number etched on the side?"

"I never had a safe deposit box," Blade said. "I didn't even have a bank account."

Tori's eyes met his across the table, and he saw his own realization reflected there.

"The notebook," she breathed.

"Damien must've hidden it while cataloging evidence." He held the key up and stared at it. "We have to find the box that matches this key."

26

TORI STEPPED BACK from the whiteboard and studied the complex web of connections she'd mapped across the surface. Red lines linked her parents' murders to Florek's brutal death, blue arrows connected the Mandelbrot paintings to their victims, green circles highlighted the key players who surfaced in every thread.

They'd transformed the Kingdom MMA office into a makeshift command center, gathering the sharpest minds Tori trusted to crack this case wide open. Well, Corbin and Luna had joined virtually through video since they were still in protective custody. At least she had their expertise.

"Here's what I think." She capped the marker and glanced at the faces around the room. "Our unsub is Nikos Crew Jr., and he isn't just my stalker. He's the Mandelbrot Killer. A serial killer."

Harlee leaned back in her chair and swiveled side to side, tattooed arms crossed, her focus riveted on the whiteboard. "You're saying witnessing his parents' murders at such a young age twisted his trauma. He's recreating the crime over and over?"

"That's my read on it," Tori said. "Not as his sister or a survivor of the same crime. I'm analyzing as if he were any other subject on the board."

Corbin's image pixelated on the TV for a moment before resolving. "The psychiatric evaluation said he showed violent tendencies, right?"

"But schizophrenia? At age four?" Luna glanced at Corbin sitting beside her on the screen. "That's a stretch."

"The patterns fit," Jett said, pushing off from Harlee's desk. "But why the geometrical staging? Why the personal nature of the attacks?"

Tori turned back to the whiteboard and traced the fractal pattern with her finger. "The geometry isn't random. It's control." She faced the group again. "Nikos witnessed pure chaos that night—blood, violence, his parents dying. The fractals represent his attempt to impose order on that trauma. Each murder recreates our parents' death, but he stages it afterward using mathematical precision. The fractals are his way of making sense of senseless violence."

"Self-similar patterns at every scale," Jett said.

"Yes," Tori said. "Just like his compulsion. He can't stop reliving that night, so he forces others to experience it. Then he relives the murders but transforms them into something beautiful and controlled."

"The paintings," Luna said.

Harlee swiveled her chair to face the group. "But how does a four-year-old in Seattle become a serial killer targeting people in Florida?"

"He didn't stay in Seattle." Tori moved to the monitor, pointing at the timeline she'd constructed. "Look at the dates. The psychiatric facility transfer happens in 1998. The first Mandelbrot murder is 2023. That's twenty-five years to plan, to research, to become someone else entirely."

Luna leaned forward on screen. "You're talking about a decades-long revenge plot."

"Exactly." Tori turned back to the board. "He's been watching, learning, identifying everyone connected to that night. Everyone who played a role in separating us."

"Hold up." Blade's fidget spinner stopped mid-rotation. So today it was that instead of the spiky green ball. Whatever kept that brilliant, scattered brain of his on track.

The room's attention shifted to him. He set the spinner on the table and leaned forward.

"I need motive. Real motive, not just psychological theory." His good hand gestured toward the board. "Based on this, I can understand Judge Kagay. But why Florek? Why Kaufman? What's the connection between them?"

Tori felt the frustration of having pieces that almost fit.

"We're missing something," Harlee said. Her fingers began flying across her keyboard. "Some connection we haven't found yet."

Corbin's voice cut through the speculation. "What about the missing painting? Sasha Robie?"

"We haven't located it yet," Blade said.

Tori stared at the board, at the web of connections that felt so right but remained frustratingly incomplete.

"We have to find the notebook first," she said. "Damien's insurance policy. Whatever he documented about that night, it might give us the missing piece. How our unsub is choosing victims."

"Or how they are connected," Jett said.

"The key," Blade said, pulling it from his pocket. "We track down every bank in a fifty-mile radius of where I lived. Someone has to have a record of this box."

"I can help with that," Harlee said. "Financial institutions keep digital records going back decades now."

Blade's phone buzzed against the table. He glanced at the screen, answered with his usual crisp "St. James," then winced as he pushed himself up from his chair.

Tori tracked his movement as he walked to the far corner of the room, his voice dropping to a murmur she couldn't quite catch. Harlee's fingers clicked across her keyboard as she discussed cross-references with Jett. Something about boxes that hadn't been accessed since 2008, digital archives, pattern matching algorithms.

But Tori's attention stayed locked on Blade. His free hand rubbed the back of his neck. And twice, maybe three times, his gaze found hers across the room.

The call involved her.

Blade ended the conversation and walked back to the group.

"We have to go," he said. "BSO just arrested a man who walked into Broward General with a gunshot wound. Nine millimeter. Matches the caliber of your Glock."

Luna leaned forward on screen. "Is it the stalker?"

"That's what we're about to find out," Blade said.

Harlee's chair squeaked as she swiveled around. "Whoa. You might be about to meet your brother for the first time."

Tori's heart skipped, then hammered against her ribs. The room tilted slightly, but she straightened her shoulders and compartmentalized the fear. Professional distance. She was FDLE's behavioral analyst first, the shooter second, sister last.

Tori stood in the BSO corridor, staring at the reinforced glass of Interview Room B.

"You don't have to do this right now," Blade said quietly behind her.

Her reflection stared back at her from the glass. Professional blazer, notebook clutched against her chest, the scab across her throat barely visible above her collar. She looked composed. Steady. Everything she didn't feel.

"Yes, I do." She turned to face Blade. "If he is Nikos, if he's my brother, I need to understand what happened to him. What turned a terrified four-year-old into this."

He moved in, closing the space between them, and caught her hand. His grip pulled her back from the edge.

"Hey. Look at me." His words carried the same quiet command that had pulled her through the darkest nights.

She met his blue eyes, finding the steady anchor she'd always found there.

"You survived that night when you were four," he said. "You survived foster care, the streets, everything that came after. You became someone who helps people, who fights for justice. That's who you are."

"And he became a killer."

"Maybe. We don't know for sure yet. Whatever he became, that's not on you. That's not your responsibility to carry."

She nodded, though the heaviness pressing behind her eyes refused to budge. "I keep thinking about what Damien said. About patterns. What if seeing our parents murdered was just the beginning of his pattern? What if he's been killing ever since?"

"Then we stop him," he said with absolute certainty. "Together. Like we always do."

She drew a deep breath, straightened her shoulders.

"Ready?" Blade asked.

Tori gripped her notebook tighter and nodded. Time to meet the monster who might share her DNA.

She pushed through the heavy door into the BSO interview room and claimed the consultant's chair and angled herself slightly back from the metal table to maintain professional distance. Deputy Worth Edwards settled into the lead detective's position across from her, his posture relaxed.

"Remember, you're here to observe," Edwards said. "Redirect questioning if you see an opening. Only take the lead if you spot a way through his lies or denial, capiche?"

"Sure." She'd done this a thousand times. "I'm here to watch for tells and cracks in his story."

She glanced at the one-way mirror, where Blade stood behind the glass. The glass showed nothing but the reflection of the room and her own face staring back, but his presence steadied her racing pulse.

The door opened with a metallic click. A uniformed officer guided Jeremy Hoult into the room, and Tori's breath caught.

This wasn't the terrifying monster who'd attacked her in the dark. Hoult was small, maybe five-foot-eight, with pale skin that looked yellow under the harsh lighting. His left arm hung in a blue sling, and his entire frame trembled like a chihuahua in a thunderstorm. Dark circles shadowed his eyes, and his brown hair stuck to his forehead with sweat.

He looked like a victim, not a killer.

The Mandelbrot Killer was organized, controlled, sophisticated. Hoult appeared to be falling apart.

She searched his face for recognition, for some flicker of the brother she'd never known. There was something. A tilt of his chin, maybe the shape of his jaw. But he didn't look like what she'd imagined Nikos would become.

Edwards straightened in his chair. "Mr. Hoult, I'm Deputy Edwards with the Broward Sheriff's Office. Before we begin, I need to read you your rights."

Hoult's trembling intensified as Edwards recited the Miranda warning. Tori watched his micro-expressions, cataloging each flinch and nervous swallow.

"Do you understand these rights as I've explained them to you?" Edwards finished.

Hoult stared at an empty spot on the floor. "I want a lawyer."

Tori blinked. An amateur would have started talking immediately, either protesting innocence or trying to explain away evidence. Asking for counsel was a sophisticated move, the kind of decision made by someone who understood the system.

Edwards leaned back in his chair. "Interview terminated at 11:47 a.m."

The uniformed officer stepped forward to escort Hoult back to his cell. As he stood, Hoult's gaze found Tori's across the table. For just a moment, something flickered in his expression. Recognition, maybe, or calculation.

Then he was gone.

Tori stood and paced the length of the interview room, her sneakers squeaking against the polished concrete floor.

"How can you be so calm?" she asked Edwards, who remained seated with his hands folded on the metal table.

Edwards shrugged. "I'm used to this dance. Twenty-three years on the job teaches you patience." He glanced at his watch. "Schmitt will be back soon, and then we'll see what story Hoult and his attorney cook up."

"This waiting is killing me."

"Why don't you go get some coffee? Clear your head before round two."

She shook her head. "No thanks. I don't want to miss even one moment of this interview."

Edwards raised an eyebrow. "Then get me one. Black."

Tori gave him a look that could have melted steel, but she headed for the door anyway.

Blade intercepted her in the hallway and fell into step beside her. "That guy doesn't look like a serial killer to me."

"What exactly do you think serial killers look like?"

"I don't know. More intimidating? Less like they'd blow away in a strong wind?"

"Ted Bundy was charming and handsome. Jeffrey Dahmer looked like an accountant. Dennis Rader was a church deacon." She pushed through the double doors into the bullpen. "They don't wear signs advertising their hobbies."

Blade chuckled, wincing slightly. "My job would be a lot easier if they glowed in the dark or something."

"Wouldn't that be convenient." She located the coffeepot and poured Edwards his black coffee. The bitter aroma cut through the stale air. "Unfortunately, monsters tend to look disappointingly ordinary."

Blade's hand touched her shoulder, stopping her midstride. "Hey. You doing okay with all this?"

Tori met his eyes and found genuine concern there, not the polite inquiry of a colleague but the worry of someone who'd seen her at her worst and stayed anyway. She'd been so focused on the case, the analysis, the professional distance that she'd forgotten someone actually cared about her well-being.

"Yeah, I'm good."

"Really?"

"Really," she said, meaning it this time. "Thanks for asking."

She retraced her steps to the interview room, where Edwards accepted the coffee with a grateful nod. They settled into another stretch of waiting, the minutes crawling by with agonizing slowness.

After what felt like forever, the uniformed officer brought Hoult back in, followed by his attorney. A thin man in his fifties wearing a rumpled suit and carrying a battered briefcase. His gray hair stuck up at odd angles, and his tie hung slightly askew. Tori spotted what looked like salsa staining his khaki pants.

The attorney nodded at Edwards. "Good to see you again, Worth."

"Troy." Edwards gestured toward Tori. "This is Dr. Crew from FDLE. She's here for observation."

The attorney set his briefcase on the table with a thunk. "I've had a brief consultation with Mr. Hoult. I understand he's been Mirandized and we're ready to proceed."

Edwards pressed record on the digital device. "Interview resumed at 1:03 p.m. Present are Deputy Edwards, Mr. Jeremy Hoult, attorney Troy Schmitt, and Dr. Tori Crew observing." He looked directly at Hoult. "Do you understand your rights as previously explained?"

"Yes, sir," Hoult said.

"Great," Edwards began, "let's talk about last night. Can you tell me where you were around ten thirty p.m.?"

Hoult straightened in his chair, his trembling subsiding as he launched into his response. "I was working the night shift at Waffle House. Started at six p.m., clocked out at two thirty a.m."

Tori watched his body language shift. The nervous energy disappeared, replaced by confidence. His voice steadied, his hands stopped shaking, and he made direct eye contact with Edwards for the first time since entering the room.

"Which Waffle House?" Edwards asked.

"The one at Black Creek Road. I'm a dishwasher there." Hoult's words came smoothly now, each detail delivered without hesitation. "I can give you my manager's number if you want to verify."

Too eager to provide verification.

"How did you get to work?" Edwards continued.

"Broward County Transit. Route fifteen. Caught the five twenty bus at the stop on Oakland Boulevard, transferred at the Federal Highway station, arrived at work by five fifty."

Cross streets, exact times, specific route numbers. When people told the truth about routine activities, they approximated. "Around five thirty" or "I think it was the five twenty bus." Hoult's timeline had been rehearsed.

"And after work?"

"Same route in reverse. Except I was walking home from work. These two guys jumped me. They wanted my wallet. I tried to run, but one of them had a gun. He shot me when I wouldn't stop."

Edwards leaned back in his chair. "Did you get a good look at these men?"

"It was dark. They wore hoodies. I couldn't see their faces."

Tori studied Hoult's expressions as he delivered his story.

No genuine confusion in his eyes, no frustrated searching for information. Instead, she caught a flicker of satisfaction when Edwards wrote something in his file.

The story was too clean, too detailed in some areas, and conveniently blank in others. Hoult thought he'd constructed a bulletproof alibi, but his coworkers said he'd had a two-hour break. Time that nobody could account for. The break would probably line up with the window of Blade's attack. If that was it, Hoult was done.

At least for the attack. She wasn't so sure Jeremy Hoult had the same qualities she'd identified in the Mandelbrot Killer's profile. Smart enough to construct an alibi with a vague robbery. Not smart enough to fill every gap.

She tapped her index finger once against the metal table.

Edwards caught the signal without missing a beat. "Tell me about the bus driver that night. The one who picked you up at Oakland Boulevard."

Hoult's eyes flicked toward his attorney for a split second before returning to Edwards. "Just a regular driver. Middle-aged guy, I think. Nothing special about him."

The fractional hesitation screamed deception. He hadn't thought to memorize details about the bus driver.

Tori leaned close to Edwards's ear. "Cognitive interview. Make him tell the story backward."

Edwards nodded and shifted his approach. "Jeremy, I want you to help me understand your route home better. Let's start from when you reached your front door and work backward. What was the last thing you did before going inside?"

Hoult blinked twice, his practiced confidence wavering. "I . . . unlocked my door."

"And before that?"

"I walked up the steps to my apartment."

"How many steps?"

Hoult's hand moved to the hem of his sling, rubbing the fabric between his thumb and forefinger. "Three, maybe four."

"Before the steps?"

"I walked across the parking lot."

Edwards maintained steady eye contact. "From which direction?"

"From . . ." Hoult's gaze darted around the room, landing anywhere except Edwards's face. "From the street."

"Which street?"

The rubbing motion intensified. Hoult's breathing quickened, and a thin sheen of sweat appeared on his forehead despite the room's air conditioning.

"I don't . . . I don't remember."

Tori recognized the signs of extreme cognitive load. When people told the truth, working backward felt natural. They simply reversed the sequence of actual memories. Fabricated stories collapsed under the weight of maintaining consistency in reverse order. Hoult's script hadn't prepared him for this approach.

"Before you reached the street, where were you?"

"Walking from the bus stop."

"Which bus stop?"

Hoult's left leg bounced under the table. "The one near my apartment."

"What's the name of that stop?"

"I . . . there's no name. It's just a stop."

Edwards leaned forward slightly. "Describe what you saw when you got off the bus."

"It was dark. I couldn't see much."

"Streetlights?"

"Maybe one or two."

"Working or burned out?"

Hoult's composure cracked. His answers became monosyllabic, contradicting details he'd provided minutes earlier. The confident man who'd recited bus routes and transfer stations had vanished, replaced by someone scrambling to maintain a story that no longer made sense.

"I don't remember every little detail," Hoult snapped. "I was tired from work."

Schmitt placed a restraining hand on his client's arm. "Perhaps we could take a short break?"

Edwards ignored the attorney. "Before the bus stop, you were on the bus. Tell me about the ride from Federal Highway to your neighborhood."

"It was just a normal bus ride."

"How many other passengers?"

"I don't know. A few."

"Sitting or standing?"

"Both, I guess."

"Where did you sit?"

Hoult's rubbing motion stopped abruptly. His hand clenched into a fist. "I stood."

"The entire ride?"

"Yes."

"But earlier you said you were tired from work."

The contradiction hung in the air like smoke. Hoult stared at the table, his chest rising and falling in rapid, shallow breaths.

Tori caught Edwards's attention and gave him a slight, sharp nod. Time to close.

Edwards's voice remained calm. "Jeremy, I think we both know you weren't on any bus last night. Your alibi at Waffle House has a two-hour hole in it. And you weren't robbed by two men in hoodies."

Hoult's attorney started to object, but Edwards continued.

Edwards leaned forward across the metal table, his kind eyes hardening into something sharper. "Let's talk about your sister, Jeremy."

Hoult's breathing turned ragged, shallow gasps that bounced his shoulders. The color drained from his face, leaving him pale as parchment.

Tori felt her own pulse race. She'd expected Edwards to press the stalking charges, to challenge the timeline inconsistencies. Not this. Not yet.

"What's her name?" Edwards coaxed.

Hoult's lips trembled. "Victoria."

His gaze found hers across the table, and the anguish in his expression sent ice through her veins. Gone was the nervous defendant, the skilled liar, the calculating predator. What remained was something broken and desperate and achingly familiar.

Then the dam burst.

"She was so little," Hoult sobbed, his words tumbling out in a torrent of grief. "Four years old, just like me. We had matching purple pajamas that Mom bought us for our birthday. Victoria's was a purple nightgown. She loved that thing. Wore it every night."

Tori cocked her head and stared at Hoult. The sobbing from the killer across the table felt wrong. Like someone had flipped a switch. Serial killers didn't fracture like this. They didn't pivot from calculated lies to raw hysteria in seconds. Especially killers who stabbed their victims with such violence, then staged their bodies with a fractal signature.

But the purple nightgown.

He was faking it. She could see deception all over this guy, but what exactly? No one outside the sealed case file could've known about the purple nightgown she'd worn that night. Not her foster parents. Not even Blade.

Yet Hoult spoke as if he'd been there.

"We shared a room." Tears rolled down Hoult's face. "Bunk beds. Victoria always made me check under her bed for monsters before she'd go to sleep. I told her I'd always protect her from the scary things. But I couldn't protect her that night. I hid under the bed when the bad man came. I left her alone in the closet while he hurt Mommy and Daddy. I was supposed to take care of her, and I failed."

Each detail hit Tori cut after cut. The shared bedroom. The matching pajamas. The promise of protection. Details that were too specific to be fabricated. Details that only her brother could know.

Jeremy looked directly at her through his tears. "I've been looking for you my whole life, Victoria. I never stopped hoping I'd find my sister."

The man who'd shadowed her steps, broken into her home, drawn her blood. He was the same four-year-old who used to crawl under her bed, hunting monsters for her.

And her brother had become the very thing he'd once promised to protect her from.

A monster.

27

THE UNIFORMED OFFICER'S HAND CLOSED around Hoult's elbow. The cuffs clicked against the metal chair as Hoult stood, his movements loose and cooperative. Hoult allowed himself to be led through the doorway, his shackles scraping against the floor. Schmitt gathered his papers, but Tori remained frozen at the table, staring at the empty chair where her supposed brother had just confessed to stalking and trying to kill her.

Every detail Hoult had delivered matched the file they'd read. Purple pajamas, shared bedroom, bunk beds.

Blade didn't buy it. Too clean. Too rehearsed. Someone had fed Hoult those details, coached him through each memory like lines in a script. Blade flattened his palm against the observation window, the glass cold against his skin.

Through the barrier, he could see Tori hunched forward, her hands trembling against her thighs. She'd swallowed it whole. The lie had landed its punch.

Edwards poked his head into the observation room. He nodded toward Tori through the glass. "She needs a minute."

"Yeah, I see that." He stepped back from the window, needing a moment himself.

He dialed Harlee's direct line. She picked up on the first ring.

"What's up, Tiger."

"Tori told you about that, huh?"

"Totally," Harlee said, keyboard clacking in the background. "How'd it go?"

"I'll tell you later. I need a few things. Off the books. Urgent."

Her typing stopped. "Go."

"I've got our office running a DNA comparison between Jeremy Hoult and Tori using his stored sample, but I need everything you can dig up on Aletheia Psychiatric Research Institute in Seattle. Patient records, staff directories, anything from 1998 to 2024. If Hoult's name pops up, I want to know immediately. I also want you to see if there's a connection to the Mandelbrot Group."

"That's a tall order for—"

"There's more. Nikos Crew Jr. had his name changed. We've got to figure out what it is now. And Officer Edgar Segarra, Millie Beach PD. Died ten months after the Crew murders. Shot during a traffic stop. No witnesses, no arrests."

Harlee took a sharp breath. "You think this is connected?"

"I think something is going on. I just need to prove it."

"How long do I have?"

Blade watched Tori through the glass. She pressed her palms against her eyes, her entire body shaking. The confession had shattered something fundamental inside her. The brother story offered closure wrapped in poison.

"Fast as you can manage. And Harlee? This stays between us until we know for sure."

"Copy that."

The line went dead. He pocketed the phone and returned to the window. Edwards had entered the interrogation room, his hand gentle on Tori's shoulder. She looked up at him with gratitude, accepting comfort from a man who'd just delivered her greatest hope and deepest nightmare in a single package.

Tori stood and gathered her notebook, her pen, her composure.

The professional mask slipped back into place, but cracks showed around the edges. She'd found her brother and lost him in the same breath. A monster wearing the face of her deepest longing.

The observation room door opened. Edwards stepped inside, his expression troubled.

"She wants to see him again."

"That's not happening."

"She says she needs closure."

Blade turned from the window. "She needs the truth. And that wasn't it."

Edwards studied his face. "You sound certain."

"I am certain. Question is whether I can prove it before she destroys herself believing a lie."

Edwards checked his phone. "Blood type's right, but we'll do a preliminary kinship DNA to confirm. Should have results within seventy-two hours."

He caught up to Tori as she pushed through the maze of desks. Around them, the station continued its routine. Phones rang. Printers churned. A drunk in holding sang off-key somewhere down the hall. His hands wanted to reach for her, pull her close, promise they'd figure this out. But Tori needed space to think. Always had.

They stopped at the elevator bank. He pressed the down button and searched for the right words.

"You did good in there. Real good."

She turned to face him. Her eyes locked on his, something broken flickering behind them. "He remembered our room. The purple pajamas. Everything."

The elevator dinged. The doors slid open to reveal Sergeant Acker carrying a stack of case files. He stepped out, glanced at Tori, then at Blade.

"Heard you caught a break on your case," Acker said.

"Something like that." Blade pressed the down button again. The elevator had already moved on.

The elevator returned. They stepped inside. The moment the doors slid shut, Tori collapsed against him. He wrapped his arms around her and held on despite the fire shooting through his bicep. Her head found the exact spot where Hoult's knife had bitten deep. He gritted his teeth, swallowed the pain.

They stood like that for a full minute before she remembered and jumped back. "Ay. Your cuts."

"It's fine. I think we both needed that."

She ran a finger under her eye, checking her reflection in the mirrored ceiling. "What would a girl do without waterproof mascara?"

Blade didn't think she needed mascara at all, but he didn't mention it.

His phone buzzed. A text from Harlee.

Found Madison. She's fine. Took personal days. Her parents just retired and moved down from New York. She's been helping them unpack a condo in Boca. Very Florida.

He exhaled and held the phone out for Tori to read.

She let out a breath too. "Good. She deserved to stay out of this."

"Yeah." He pocketed the phone. One less thing to carry.

The doors opened to the main lobby, where civilians waited on hard plastic chairs and desk sergeants processed paperwork.

Kiara stood near the information desk. Her blond hair shimmered in the afternoon light streaming through the glass doors. She wore a navy dress that he'd complimented last week, back when their biggest concern was where to eat. She looked so normal. So untouched by the violence that had consumed his last forty-eight hours. At least she hadn't seen him hugging Tori in the elevator.

Her eyes locked on his across the lobby.

"Hey." Kiara waved and crossed toward them.

They stopped beside a bulletin board covered in community

announcements. A child's laughter drifted from somewhere near the front desk. A mother bounced a drooling toddler on her hip while she filled out paperwork. Dealing with basic problems. Parking tickets. Noise complaints. Things that could be fixed with the right forms and the proper signatures.

A simple apology would never make up for the debt he owed this woman. He'd dodged her calls. Left her hanging for days without a word and canceled dates time and time again.

"Kiara—" His throat tightened. The words he should say—denials, explanations, promises—all died before they reached his lips. She deserved better than lip service. She deserved better than him.

"You look terrible." Her green eyes swept over him, probably cataloging the exhaustion.

"Thanks. That's what every guy wants to hear."

She didn't smile at his attempt at humor. "I heard you were attacked. How are you doing?"

He shifted, his bicep protesting the movement. "Stiff, but fine. How are you doing?"

She blew out a breath, her hands fidgeting with her purse strap. "Yesterday, I was called into HR. Someone filed an anonymous complaint about me accessing the sealed IA file after hours. I was placed on indefinite administrative leave. They took my credentials and walked me out."

"Kiara, I'm so sorry." He moved in, half a step, as instinct overrode reason. "I'll make a call. Tell them it was my fault. I twisted your arm, pressured you—"

"Please don't do that." She cut him off with a raised hand. "I knew the risks when I helped, and I did it anyway."

A uniformed officer walked past, his radio crackling with dispatch codes. Blade watched Kiara's face, seeing the kindness in her eyes. The way her mouth curved downward, not in anger but in understanding.

"Kiara, I'm so sorry," Tori said. "You don't deserve this. You risked everything to help me learn the truth about my family. I owe you for that."

"No, you don't. I'm just glad you found answers about your family." Kiara pulled Tori into a gentle hug that surprised him. "I really hope you guys figure everything out—about your brother and everything else."

Her eyes found Blade's over Tori's shoulder, and he understood she meant him and Tori also.

Kiara stepped back, smoothed her dress, and walked toward the exit without another word.

The automatic doors closed behind her with a soft whoosh.

Tori slipped her hand into his. "You okay?"

"Yeah." He exhaled hard. Kiara's kindness made it worse. "She loses her career for helping us and still walks out like she's thanking the world for the chance."

"We'll find a way to make it right for her."

Yeah. He wanted to believe that. Especially now, with the truth staring him right in the face. Kiara had been right all along.

He'd been in love with Tori and never knew it.

"C'mon," he said, tugging Tori's hand. "Let's go."

They walked through the glass doors into the afternoon heat. The asphalt radiated warmth through his boots as he crossed the parking lot. His Charger sat in the shade of a dying palm tree, its black paint dulled by dust and salt air. He really should run it through a car wash.

He opened the driver's door and slid behind the wheel. The leather seat scorched his back through his shirt. The car was idling from his remote start, but the air-conditioning hadn't done much to cut through the heat.

Tori thumbed across her phone screen and tapped rapid fire on the keyboard. Whatever she typed stayed between her and the phone.

"Seems like our only path forward is that key," he said, backing out of the parking space.

"Your wish is Jett's command. Harlee says they've found something and to meet them at the gym." She buckled her seat belt. "Vamos, Tiger."

He laughed, shaking his head. "If you think that's funny, wait till you hear my siblings' names."

Minutes later, Blade pulled into the lot and parked behind the Kingdom MMA building. He studied the peeling paint as they walked toward the entrance. "Remind me to get this place painted."

Tori nodded, running her finger along a strip of loose paint. "Stryker spent so much on the inside remodel, he didn't have anything left for outside."

"Yeah." Blade pulled the door open, holding it for her. "Be nice for him to wake up and see it looking good."

They jogged up the metal staircase and pushed through the office door.

Jett looked up from his workstation. The ultrawide monitor glowed around him, displaying code that scrolled too fast to read. Harlee sat across the room, her fingers dancing across a mechanical keyboard that clacked like machine gun fire.

"Tell me you found something useful," Tori said.

Harlee spun her chair toward them. "We ran Damien's financials backward and forward. No safe deposit box payments anywhere."

Blade dropped into the nearest chair. "What about his wife? Michelle?"

Harlee looked at him like he'd asked what color the sky was. "We checked that. Both sets of parents. Came up empty."

Jett rolled his chair toward Blade, wheels squeaking against the concrete floor. He handed over a sheet of paper covered in technical diagrams and specifications. "I uploaded photos of your key to my analysis software. Found the manufacturer, the type, everything."

Blade studied the printout. Numbers and measurements filled the margins alongside close-up photographs of the key's teeth and grooves.

"Bad news is it's super common," Jett continued. "Good news is it's a specific model from First National's old security system. I eliminated several banks right off the bat, but it didn't narrow things down much."

"Damien would've used a bank nearby," Blade said. "Somewhere he had regular access."

"Exactly. That's why we shifted gears and did things the old-fashioned way." Jett grinned and pointed toward the code streaming across his monitors. "With a twist."

Harlee swiveled back to face them. "We built an AI agent."

"With Corbin's permission," Jett added, "we cloned his voice."

Blade's eyebrows shot up. "You did what?"

"My AI agent is calling every bank in Florida. Corbin's cloned voice tells them he's a Special Agent with FDLE, his father passed away, and he's got this key with a number but doesn't know where it goes."

"Don't worry," Harlee said. "We programmed in a sad son voice."

Jett took over the explanation, his hands moving as fast as his words. "Once we eliminate the box by name, AI Corbin says his dad was a criminal and there's a possibility he used a different name." He tapped the paper in Blade's hand. "These are the banks that refused to give any information."

Harlee held up another sheet. "But these are the ones that gave us the name of whoever owned that box number."

Blade looked at the second list. Longer than he'd expected. "How does that help us?"

"Because we ran those names against a database of known aliases for Damien Sullivan," Jett said. He pulled a folded sheet from his shirt pocket and handed it to Blade. "Only one hit."

He unfolded the paper. A single name stared back at him, written in Jett's careful handwriting. His heart hammered against his ribs.

He grabbed Jett by the face and kissed the top of his head. "I love your brilliant brain."

He turned toward Harlee, arms spread wide.

"Touch me and die, Tiger," she warned, but she couldn't hide her grin.

Blade laughed and handed the paper to Tori. She scanned the bank name and address, her eyebrows lifting.

"Half hour drive," she said. "Not bad."

He pulled out his phone and dialed Garrison's number, hitting speaker as it rang.

"ADA Garrison."

"Rene, it's Blade. I've got you on speaker. I need a warrant for a safe deposit box. We've got probable cause based on a known alias for Damien Sullivan and the identity of the box holder. The deceased's son, Corbin King, will consent to the search." He glanced at Jett to make sure.

Jett gave him a thumbs-up and rolled his chair closer to the phone.

"The alias complicates the identity issue," Garrison said. "The court will likely want bank records or lease documents as supporting proof that Sullivan actually used this identity."

Harlee spun in her chair and shot both thumbs up.

"We have supporting documentation," he said.

"Good. Send it over. Give me half an hour and I'll see if I can get it signed."

The line went dead. Blade pocketed the phone and checked his watch. Three forty-seven. The afternoon was burning away, but they finally had a solid lead.

Tori stretched in her chair. "Think Damien actually hid his blackmail book in the box?"

"Only one way to find out. And the bank will be closing soon." He stood and grabbed his jacket from the back of his chair. "Either way, we're about to get answers."

28

THE GRAY FOG PRESSED against him like wet cotton, muffling everything except the drone of a television. The anchor's voice cut through the haze, sharp and clinical.

"... murder at Union Correctional Institution. Damien Sullivan, serving life for a workplace mass shooting that claimed the lives of four officers ..."

Damien Sullivan.

The name yanked Stryker backward through time like a fishhook through his skull.

Rain drummed against the patrol car's roof in a steady rhythm that matched his thumb tapping his thigh. Stryker sat alone behind the wheel, watching the convenience store through streaks of water that blurred the neon signs. The duty belt dug into his hip where the seat belt crossed it. The department needed to redesign these seats. Cut deeper wells, extend the buckles. Stop jamming duty belts into officers' ribs every shift.

A year without Damien as his partner. A year since Barclay had pulled his former partner into day shift, promising promotions and better assignments. Stryker knew what that meant. Bigger fish to fry. More important cases to bury.

The radio crackled to life, the dispatcher's voice tinny through the static.

"Unit 47, respond to domestic disturbance." She rattled off the address. "Multiple prior calls to this location."

"Speak of the devil," he muttered to himself.

Yeah, he knew that address. Sullivan. Six calls in eight months, and each one had carved something deeper out of Michelle Sullivan's face. The bruises had spread like storm clouds, and her stories had worn thinner than paper.

"Unit 47, copy. En route."

He reached for the volume knob and turned it down until the radio became background noise. The wipers scraped against the windshield as he pulled out of the lot, slapping water away before the next sheet hammered down.

The modest Florida house sat in darkness when he arrived. Porch light out. Damien should know better. The front door stood wide open behind the metal screen door. The neighborhood slept around him, windows dark, driveways empty except for the occasional sedan.

The silence bothered him more than shouting would have. Domestic calls usually came with noise. Screaming, breaking glass, neighbors complaining. This quiet felt wrong, like the pause before a scream.

Rain soaked through his uniform shirt as he approached the front door. Cold water ran down his neck. He positioned himself to the side of the doorframe, hand resting on his holstered weapon.

"Millie Beach Police. Damien Sullivan? Mrs. Sullivan?"

Nothing.

His fist slammed against the aluminum door frame. The metal clanged through empty rooms, but no one stirred. No shuffle of feet across linoleum. No muffled responses from the back bedroom. Just rain drumming the roof and the refrigerator's electric wheeze.

Protocol demanded he wait for backup. Secure the perimeter.

But he'd heard Michelle Sullivan's voice crack over the phone too many times. He'd seen the fear in her eyes when she insisted everything was fine, just a misunderstanding.

Stryker opened the screen door and stepped inside.

The stench hit him first. Whiskey and cigarettes mixed with something sour that might have been vomit. Michelle Sullivan lay sprawled across the couch, one arm dangling toward the floor, knuckles brushing an overflowing ashtray. Her face was turned toward the cushions, but he could see the fresh bruise blooming purple-black across her left cheek. The color of rotting fruit.

A soft shuffle made him turn.

A boy peeked around the hallway doorframe. Sandy blond hair stuck up at odd angles, and when the boy's mouth opened slightly, Stryker caught the gap where front teeth should be. Six, maybe seven years old. The kid's eyes were too wide, too alert for this time of night.

The same terror he'd seen in that closet. The same way that little girl had pressed herself into the corner, trying to disappear into the darkness.

Stryker's mouth went dry. He stepped over Michelle's outstretched arm and eased toward the hallway.

"Hey there." Stryker crouched down to the boy's eye level. "Where's your daddy?"

The boy didn't let go of the doorframe, but his finger pointed toward the master bedroom.

"Okay. I'll be right back."

Stryker found Damien on the floor beside the bed, not on it. A lit cigarette dangled from his mouth, ash scattered across his uniform shirt. The ember glowed orange in the dim light, close enough to his skin to leave burns. Passed out cold, reeking of whiskey.

He pinched the cigarette out before Damien set himself on fire.

When he returned to the hallway, the boy hadn't moved. Still clinging to that doorframe like it was the only thing keeping him upright.

Calvin? Caleb? No, those weren't right.

Corbin.

Stryker dropped to one knee. The boy's skin had gone chalk-white, and a streak of grime marked his left cheek. His T-shirt sagged off his shoulders, the neckline pulled and darkened with stains.

"Corbin, right? I work with your daddy. I want to make sure everyone's okay. Can you tell me what happened tonight?"

The boy's grip tightened on the doorframe. His mouth opened, then closed.

"It's all right," Stryker said. "You're not in trouble."

"They got into a fight," Corbin whispered.

"What was the fight about?"

A shrug. But as the boy shifted, Stryker caught sight of the bruises. Finger-shaped marks wrapped around Corbin's arm. Another bruise peeked out from the neckline of his T-shirt. About the size and shape of adult thumbs pressed into small shoulders.

"How'd you get those bruises on your arm?"

Corbin's eyes went wide, and his pupils dilated with sudden panic. He turned and bolted across the room, his bare feet slapping against the tile. The closet door slammed.

"Well, well. Look what we got here."

Stryker rose and turned. Damien Sullivan leaned against the hallway wall, bloodshot eyes, cigarette ash dusting his badge hanging crooked on his chest.

Cold rage settled in his stomach. Not the hot flash of anger he might feel during an MMA fight, but something visceral. Deep-seated. This wasn't just a domestic disturbance. This was a cop. His former partner. Beating his family.

"Damien Sullivan." His hand drifted to his cuffs. "You're under arrest."

Damien barked out a laugh. "For what? Having a drink in my own house?"

"Domestic battery. Child abuse." He pulled the cuffs free. "Turn around."

"You got some nerve, King. Coming into my house, making accusations." Damien shoved away from the wall, stumbled a half step. "That boy falls down all the time. Kids are clumsy."

"Those are grip marks, Damien. Fresh ones."

"Prove it."

"I said turn around." He caught Damien's wrist, twisted, drove him chest-first into the wall.

A photo dropped, shattering on tile. Damien swung back with his elbow. Stryker ducked, pinned the arm up behind him. The first cuff snapped shut as defiance turned to heavy breathing. The steel clicked home with a finality that he hoped Corbin would hear.

Damien's forearm was thick as a fence post, forcing him to wrestle the second restraint wider, though it wouldn't quite latch.

"You have the right to remain silent—"

The screen door squeaked open behind him.

The temperature in the room dropped ten degrees. He didn't need to turn around to know who had entered. The air itself seemed to thicken, pressing down on his shoulders like a lead blanket. Sergeant Dean Barclay's presence filled the space, sucking oxygen from the room.

Barclay stepped closer. His boots scraped against the tile. The sergeant's eyes locked onto the dangling cuff in Stryker's hand, then shifted to Damien's face.

"Domestic battery and child abuse charges." Stryker kept his stance square, shoulders back. "I'm placing Sullivan under arrest."

Barclay's jaw worked side to side. His gaze flicked to Damien, held there for three seconds too long. Damien's chin dipped once. Stryker caught the signal that passed between them. They were men who'd done business before. Dark business.

Damien's lip curled into a smile. Like he'd been expecting this interruption all along.

Stryker's fingers locked around the loose cuff. Damien could expect whatever he wanted. This ended now. No more wife beaten bloody. No more kid cowering in corners. Stryker snapped the second cuff around Damien's wrist and cranked the ratchet until metal bit flesh.

"King, I need a word." Barclay's hand landed on Stryker's shoulder, fingers pressing down like a vise. "Outside."

The pressure guided him toward the door, but Stryker planted his feet. "Sullivan's under arrest. I'm reading him his rights."

"Outside. Now."

The grip on his shoulder increased until Stryker's collarbone creaked. He had no choice but to move, leaving Damien cuffed in the hallway.

Rain pounded the porch roof and drove needles into Stryker's cheeks. Barclay shifted, blocking the door. Water dripped from the sergeant's cap, pooling shadows where his eyes should be. Just two black sockets staring back.

"You know what the blue line means, King?"

Stryker's jaw muscles bunched. "It means we protect and serve the community."

"No." Barclay stepped closer. "It means we protect each other. Brotherhood. Family. You don't turn on family."

"Damien's beating his wife and kid. That's not brotherhood. That's—"

"Maybe you've taken one too many hits to the head in that ring." Barclay leaned forward until his breath fogged the space between them. "Maybe you're not thinking clearly anymore. Maybe you need to decide which career you want to keep."

Stryker's lungs forgot how to work. The walls of the cramped porch alcove pressed inward, the sergeant's bulk filling every inch of escape route.

Through the screen door, he caught movement. Corbin peered

out from his bedroom door, face pale as milk in the dim light. The boy's eyes held a flicker of hope, like maybe this time would be different. Maybe this time someone would help.

He clenched his molars until his temples throbbed. A headache bloomed behind his eyes, sharp and insistent.

"Uncuff him, King."

The words felt like swallowing broken glass. Stryker looked at his hands, at the key ring hanging from his belt. At Barclay's face, carved from granite and just as unforgiving.

He walked back inside.

Damien grinned and stretched his fingers as the metal snapped apart. Barclay stepped closer and dropped a hand on Damien's shoulder. He steered him toward the hallway, their heads bent together. Words spoken in hushed fragments. Dates, names, what needed disappearing.

The closet door gaped open like a wound. Corbin's face collapsed, hope draining from his features until only recognition remained. The boy understood now. No one was helping. No one ever would.

Stryker locked eyes with the boy. A contract sealed without words. *This isn't finished.*

Outside, he dropped behind the wheel and yanked the door shut, hands on the steering wheel for a long second before turning the key. The window shuddered in its frame. His fists hammered the steering wheel until his knuckles cracked open. Blood smeared the crevices of his fingers. Beating the car wasn't going to help. He dropped his head and pressed his forehead against the wheel as rain machine-gunned the roof.

"God, what do I do?"

Barclay commanded this place. But God commanded everything else. The storm settled into a steady drum. Then came the whisper, threading through his chest.

Choose a different way. When the time is right, rescue the ones they abandon.

Good and evil sprouted from the same soil. You couldn't separate them until the end.

Stryker lifted his head. Rain hammered the windshield, blurring the house into watercolor streaks. The voice had come before. Cutting through doubt, demanding action when the department demanded silence. When the brass ordered him to look away while people suffered.

He reached for his badge. His fingers worked the pin loose from his shirt, and he held it in his palm. The shield caught what little light filtered through the storm clouds.

He opened his hand and let the badge tumble onto the passenger seat.

29

THE DIGITS ON THE WALL CLOCK crawled forward like they were swimming through molasses. Four fifty-five.

Five minutes until the vault closed, and Rene Garrison still hadn't shown.

Tori knocked her knees together, a jittery beat syncing with the clock's tick. Beyond the glass wall, Blade paced lines across the marble lobby. Left, pivot, back again. His shoulders rode high, one fist flexing open and shut.

Liz Reynolds looked up from her computer screen and pushed her long blond hair behind one ear. She was pretty, with freckled skin and the kind of no-nonsense attitude that said she'd heard every excuse in the book and wasn't about to fall for anything.

"I'll have to close the vault in five minutes," she said. "Is your warrant coming or not?"

"She'll be here." But traffic had strangled them on the way over. What should've taken thirty minutes stretched to forty. Rene might not make it. "If she's late, can you wait just five more minutes? Please?"

Liz shook her head. "Federal regulations don't bend for anyone, hon. I've got protocols to follow, and my supervisor breathes down my neck about closing procedures."

"I understand."

But the waiting. Every second stretched like an eternity while crucial pieces of her life hung in limbo. Information about Aletheia, the Mandelbrot Group, Stryker's condition, who killed Damien and why. All of it just out of reach. And now, familial DNA results that could reshape everything she thought she knew about herself.

Days. It could take days. Like Tori wouldn't spend every one of them looking at her own hands and wondering whose they resembled. Wondering whether Jeremy Hoult's eyes were shaped like hers. Whether the thing that made him violent lived somewhere inside her too.

Her fingers drummed against her thigh. The same restless energy that had her bouncing her knees earlier now demanded some other outlet. Some way to burn through the questions that circled her mind like vultures.

The bank's front door chimed.

Tori sprang to her feet. Garrison strode across the lobby, warrant folder in hand. She swept into the office at four fifty-eight, slightly breathless.

"Sorry. Traffic was a nightmare."

Liz reviewed the warrant. Tori watched her eyes scanning every line before nodding. "This'll work. Let's go."

The vault door stood like a monument to security. Thick steel bars behind reinforced glass. Liz's key turned with a solid click, and the electronic lock disengaged with a soft beep. Inside, rows of safe deposit boxes lined the walls in perfect formation.

"Box 894." Liz ran her finger along the numbers until she found it. "Dual key system. You've got one, I've got the other."

Liz inserted her key, twisted, and stepped back for Blade.

Tori stopped breathing as he inserted his key into the slot. His massive hands blocked her view of the mechanism, and she couldn't tell if the key had turned or if the box would remain locked forever.

Then he looked at her with that grin she'd known since she was a teen.

The box slid out smooth as silk. A long metal rectangle that could hold a life's worth of secrets. Liz carried it to the table in the center of the vault.

"I'll give you privacy." She stepped just outside the vault door, close enough to maintain protocol but far enough to respect the moment.

Blade pulled on latex gloves and handed Tori a pair. "May need to preserve prints and DNA."

The gloves felt cold against her sweaty palms. This was it. They might finally get answers.

Blade lifted the lid with his good arm, wincing slightly from the knife wound. Tori stood on her toes, craning her neck, but she was too short to see anything except empty metal space. Her heart plummeted.

Blade's face fell. "It's—"

"Empty?"

"No. Wait." He reached in with his uninjured arm and pulled out a stack of manila file folders. Then his hand disappeared again and emerged with a black leather notebook, the elastic closure strap wrapped diagonally to hold a pencil against the side.

Damien's blackmail book.

The sight hit her like a lightning bolt. Pure, triumphant adrenaline flooded her system. It was real. Damien hadn't been lying. All those years of doubt, of wondering if her parents' deaths would remain unsolved forever. Vindication washed over her in waves.

"It's actually here." She reached for the notebook with trembling hands. "Let me see it."

It was thick, stuffed with loose papers and photographs wedged between pages. The leather cover was worn smooth from handling.

She opened to the first page, steeling herself for whatever horrors lay inside.

The handwriting slanted right in pencil strokes that were

smudged and faded in places. But the first thing she saw was a loose sheet of spiral notebook paper. The pocket-sized kind Blade carried.

Her eyes scanned the note.

Barclay's going to frame me for something big. I can feel it coming. If anything happens to me, this book has everything. —D.S.

"What's it say?" Blade leaned closer.

"It's true. Damien knew." Her voice barely worked. "He knew Barclay was going to frame him before it happened."

Garrison looked up from the file folders. "Damien thought Barclay would frame him for the workplace shooting before it even happened?"

Blade frowned. "That's awfully convenient. Write a note predicting your own frame-up, hide it away for someone to find later. Sounds like premeditation to me."

Tori shook her head. "If this was all fabricated, if he made this up, why didn't he pull this out before trial? He went to prison for life, Blade. He never used this to defend himself."

"She's got a point," Garrison said, flipping through the folders. "And you both need to look at what I'm seeing here."

Garrison spread photographs across the table. Crime scene shots. In one photo, a bloody footprint was clearly visible on white tile. In the next photo of the same location, the footprint was smeared beyond recognition.

Another set showed a stack of drugs and cash on a table. The second photo showed the same table with a much smaller pile.

Garrison turned one photograph over. "Case numbers on the back. Looks like evidence tampering to me."

"Crime scene manipulation," Blade said. "Damien was documenting every time Barclay altered evidence."

"There must be hundreds of photos here," Garrison said,

spreading more images across the table. "This isn't just a few bad cases. This is institutional."

Blade pulled out a stack of police reports from beneath the photographs. "Look at these. Copies of the originals and the filed versions."

Tori took the first set. The original report described a domestic violence call with multiple witnesses and clear evidence of assault. The filed version painted a different picture entirely. Mutual combat, insufficient evidence to prosecute. Both reports bore signatures at the bottom.

Her stomach clenched. "Damien's signature and Barclay's. When he was still a sergeant."

"Check this one." Blade handed her another pair. A drug bust that originally netted fifty kilos of cocaine and three hundred thousand in cash. The filed report listed ten kilos and twenty-five thousand.

Where had the rest gone? Into whose pockets?

The third set made her throat close completely. A sexual assault case. The original report detailed a victim's statement, physical evidence, and a suspect in custody. The filed version dismissed the charges due to "credibility issues" and "insufficient evidence."

"They destroyed this woman's life," Tori whispered. "Made her look like a liar when they had everything they needed to prosecute."

Garrison photographed each page with her phone. "We'll need the FBI on this. This level of corruption requires federal intervention."

"Special Agent Sebastian Wells offered to help with anything we needed. He's been briefed about the possible serial killer."

Garrison nodded. "Good call, but we do this together. We verify everything quietly, build an airtight case before Barclay catches wind. One leak and he disappears."

"Got it," Blade said.

Tori flipped through more notebook pages, searching for any

mention of her parents' case. The entries were chronological, starting in 1995. She skimmed a few.

March 1995: Barclay asked me to lose a piece of evidence. Said the guy was connected and it would go away clean. I told myself it was one time.

November 1996: Third time this year Barclay's had me bury something. Each time it gets easier. That scares me more than the thing itself.

June 1997: Overheard Barclay on the phone. Names I didn't recognize. Something bigger than dirty cops covering for each other. I asked him about it. He looked at me a long time before he answered. Said I was either in or I wasn't. I told myself I was already in.

Her parents died in 1998. She found the October entries and read.

October 12, 1998: Barclay called me in. Says there's a situation with the Crew thing and it needs to be handled. Scene needs to be clean when it's done. No witnesses. Told Barclay I'd help bury it.

October 14, 1998: King and I responded to the call at 5486 Flores Drive. Possible burglary in progress, neighbor reported male subject fleeing. I had no idea what we were walking into. Barclay made it sound like the hit would be clean and simple, but we found the parents butchered in the master bedroom. Male vic was still alive when we got there, throat cut but breathing. King tried to save him while I secured the scene. There were kids. Nobody said anything about kids. I found the girl child in the closet. King found the male child under the bed with the knife. No way the boy did it, but Barclay insisted on the report as written. Had me sign off on the psych eval recommendation for the boy. Barclay took care of the rest.

October 15, 1998: Stryker asking too many questions. Barclay reassigning him effective immediately.

Tori couldn't speak. Couldn't breathe. The words on the page swam together until only one name remained in sharp focus.

King.

Stryker had been there. That night. He'd been there when Damien found her in the closet, terror-stricken. He'd seen Nikos under the bed with the knife, covered in their parents' blood. He'd known about her twin brother for twenty-six years and never said a word.

The notebook slipped from her trembling hands and hit the table with a dull thud. All those years at the gym. All those conversations about family, about loss, about moving forward from trauma. He'd sat across from her, watching her struggle with the gaping holes in her memory, and kept his mouth shut.

The vault walls pressed closer, stealing her air.

Stryker had saved her that night, but he'd also betrayed her every day since.

30

BLADE SHUFFLED through the stacks of papers. Original police reports. Photos. Decades of secrets sat stacked in this vault for years, but this was it. The proof they needed to bring down Barclay and expose the whole rotten system.

"We got him." He looked up, expecting to see triumph reflected in Tori's face. Instead, she'd gone bone-white, her lips parted in shock.

"What's wrong?"

Tori's hand went to her mouth, and she just shook her head. With her other hand, she pointed a shaky finger at the journal.

His eyes tracked the loops and slashes of Damien's handwriting over Tori's shoulder. One name jumped off the page like a slap.

Stryker King.

As he read the journal entry, the context registered.

King and I responded to the call . . . I found the girl child in the closet. King found the male child under the bed.

He shoved his own reaction aside and focused on Tori. Her features buckled, eyes wide then vacant, as if something vital had been ripped clean out of her. Betrayal.

"Tori, don't jump to conclusions just yet." He pressed a steadying hand against her back. "We need to—"

His phone vibrated against the steel table, the sound an intrusion into Tori's private devastation. His eyes dropped to the screen, expecting Harlee's name, but his blood turned to slush.

DEAN BARCLAY glowed on the display.

Blade's thumb hovered over the decline button, but rejecting the call wouldn't make this go away. He glanced at Tori, still reeling from Stryker's betrayal, then at Garrison, whose face had gone rigid with understanding.

Men didn't call in this moment unless they were sure the board was theirs. Unless they wanted to rub it in. Confidence bred sloppiness. Sloppiness left cracks.

He hit speaker. "St. James."

"Detective." Barclay's voice filled the vault. "I trust your field trip was productive."

The casual arrogance made Blade's teeth grind. "I don't know what you're talking about."

"Safe deposit box 894. First National on Federal Highway." Barclay chuckled. "You really thought that little AI stunt was clever, didn't you? Cloning a voice to harass every bank in Florida creates a massive electronic footprint. One my network has been monitoring for years."

Of course. Barclay had been watching them, waiting for this exact moment. He'd known about the blackmail, he just hadn't known how to find the evidence. And now they'd led him straight to it.

Blade closed his eyes for a beat, then, "What do you want, Barclay?"

"I want whatever you found in that box. I want Damien's notebook."

"What makes you think I'd give you anything?"

"I received a fascinating anonymous tip," Barclay said. "About a pretty Records Administrator named Kiara Kerns. Something about accessing sealed IA files after hours. Granting access to an outside officer. A felony. It would be a terrible shame for such a bright, honest young woman to have her life ruined."

Blade's throat shut down. Air fought to get past it. He snapped his gaze to Tori—she stood stiff, palms pressed to the table, eyes locked on him like she'd just watched him pull the trigger on Kiara's life. Heat crowded his ribs, grinding in from every angle.

Barclay said, "I've sent you a picture. Take a look."

His heart hammered wild. What had he done to Kiara? If he'd touched even one hair—

The image detonated across the glass. It wasn't Kiara.

Stryker.

His mentor was strapped in a wheelchair, head lolling. A purpling bruise spread across his cheekbone, fresh as a punch an hour ago.

Blade's hands shook, the phone nearly slipping from his white-knuckled grip. "You abducted a man from his hospital bed? How?"

"I didn't abduct him, I reclaimed him. He was my sergeant long before he was your mentor," Barclay said with a bark of laughter. "I came to see him. More than once. Practically a regular. This time my people handled the transport while the duty nurse was too busy dealing with a 'coding' patient three doors down to notice a wheelchair leaving the floor. It's amazing what a well-timed distraction can buy."

"Snatching a man from an ICU bed is a new low, even for you," Blade said, his heart hammering against his ribs as he looked at the image of his mentor. "You've got my attention. Now tell me what you want before I lose my patience."

"You have my property, Detective," Barclay said. "As you can see, I have yours."

Blade's fingers balled tight, every muscle in his arm primed to drive it straight through the phone and rip the man's throat open. "Just tell me what it's going to take to get him back."

"The old Mayfair department store on the causeway," Barclay

said. "You have one hour. Bring the book. Dr. Crew can be your plus-one, but not another soul, understand?" A pause. "If I see one uniform, a single cruiser, or a federal agent . . . King dies. And I promise you, Detective, the evidence against Ms. Kerns is already in the right hands. The frame will stick, and her fate will be one worse than death. Promise."

The line went dead.

Blade locked his eyes on the phone, running plays that collapsed before they started. Barclay hadn't left him room to maneuver. A cage. One wired so tight every angle hit trip wire.

Garrison had her hands slicing the air, her lips firing off protocol and channels and official paths, but all of it scattered useless, like static. The only sound that mattered lived inside his skull. Barclay had known exactly where they were, exactly when they'd found the evidence, and he'd been ready.

Fifty-seven minutes.

"We have to go." Blade shoved the notebook into an evidence bag.

Garrison's words finally registered. "—need to coordinate with the FBI and—"

"No time." Blade cut Garrison off, already moving toward the exit. "We have fifty-six minutes and it'll take every one to get there."

"Detective, you can't just charge off with evidence and face Barclay alone." Garrison stepped between Blade and the vault door. "This is a crime in progress. We need to coordinate law enforcement response."

He stopped dead, his hand already reaching for the exit. "I am law enforcement." He turned back. "There's more than enough evidence in those files. Take them straight to your office and secure them, but don't tell anyone what's going on until I've had a chance to talk to SAC Sebastian Wells."

"Blade—"

"No one. I'm not letting local law enforcement get involved." He gestured at the scattered documents. "I don't know how deep this corruption goes. Could be half the department on Barclay's payroll. Maybe even BSO."

Garrison's jaw worked, legal training warring with the reality staring them down. Finally, she nodded. "Two hours. Then I'm calling in the cavalry whether you like it or not."

Blade was already moving, Tori beside him, her face still pale but her stride steady. They hit the bank's lobby at a jog, ignoring the curious stares from customers.

Fifty-three minutes.

The Charger's engine roared to life as Blade peeled out of the parking lot, tires screaming against asphalt. The city streets blurred past. Familiar territory that suddenly felt alien, hostile. Every shadow could hide Barclay's eyes.

Tori sat beside him, checking her Glock. She ejected the magazine, counted rounds, slapped it back home.

The clock on the dashboard glowed: 5:27 p.m. Forty-three minutes to reach the causeway. Blade tromped on the accelerator and raced off.

"We have to think," Tori said. "What's Barclay's weakness?"

He nodded at the battered notebook resting across Tori's knees. "That's it. His weak spot."

"We're really handing Damien's notes over? You think he lets us leave after that?" She shook her head. "No way."

They both knew them getting out alive wasn't part of Barclay's plan.

"Barclay buried half his life setting pieces in place, shielding himself, tying off loose ends." Blade shifted his grip on the wheel, eyes fixed on the traffic. "He choreographed every move. Every one but this."

Tori looked up from her weapon. "What?"

"He's expecting me to follow his rules. Walk into his trap like a good little soldier." Blade pulled out his phone. "I'm calling Wells."

"The FBI? Barclay said—"

"I know what he said, but he's our only shot. Barclay has eyes in the department, maybe even IA. He knows we've got FDLE and BSO at our fingertips, but a federal ghost team? That's the one backup he won't be looking for."

Blade hit the call button before doubt could creep in. The phone rang twice before Wells's cheery voice answered.

"Hey, Blade, good to hear from you. I know I owe you a—"

"Chief Dean Barclay has kidnapped Stryker King." No preamble. No wasted words. "He's forcing a meet at the old Mayfair department store. Threatening to kill him if he sees any backup. It's a trap, Sebastian. I need a covert team. Your best. Untraceable."

Silence stretched for three heartbeats. Then Wells's voice returned. "Okay, Blade. I'm on it. Give me the details."

Blade laid out the situation in clipped sentences—the notebook, the evidence, Barclay's threats against Kiara. Wells absorbed it all without interruption.

"I'll handpick the team," Wells said. "We'll be ghosts. Thermal imaging, long-range overwatch, entry teams on standby. He won't see us coming, but neither will you."

"Great." The vise around Blade's ribs eased, just enough to let his lungs drag in more air than they had all day.

"Call me two minutes before you go in," Wells continued. "We'll be in position. We've got your back."

The call ended. Blade dragged his gaze from the asphalt just long enough to catch Tori watching him.

"Wells has us," he said.

She gave a sharp nod. "Then we have a chance."

The Charger ate up the miles toward the causeway, carrying them toward whatever waited in the shadows of the abandoned department store. But now they weren't walking into Barclay's trap alone.

We're coming, Stryker. Hold on.

The Mayfair department store loomed against the darkening October sky like a concrete vault. Five stories of broken windows and graffiti-scarred walls, surrounded by a parking lot that looked like a war zone. Weeds pushed through cracks in the asphalt, and rusted shopping carts lay scattered like the bones of some retail apocalypse.

Blade pulled the Charger into the lot, broken glass crunching under the tires. The building's main entrance gaped open, a black mouth waiting to swallow them whole.

The Charger's engine ticked as it cooled, the only sound in the desolate parking lot.

He pulled out his phone, thumb finding Wells's number. One ring.

"We're here. Going in."

"We're in position. Go." Wells's voice was reassuring.

Blade slid the phone into his pocket and took the notebook from Tori. He shoved it into his back jeans pocket, the motion sending knives of fire through the gash in his bicep. Weak side. Liability. If he couldn't even muscle open the Charger's door, how was he supposed to shield her when someone came out swinging?

Tori lifted her hand between them, palm open. A scatter of red and white pills pressed into the crease of her skin. "Here, take these."

"What's that?"

"Acetaminophen and ibuprofen. One-two punch." Her eyes didn't move from his face. "Takes the edge off without fogging you. You'll need that arm functional."

He didn't waste time debating. Dropped the pills on his tongue, chased them with the stale water from yesterday's bottle he'd forgotten in the cup holder.

"Thanks, Doc."

Blade stared at the building's black entrance. Every instinct screamed at him to turn around, drive away, let the FBI handle this. But Stryker was in there.

And so was the man who'd destroyed Tori's family.

"I want you to stay here and wait for Wells before you go in," he said without looking at her.

"Not happening."

"Tori—"

"We've been through this before." Her chin lifted in defiance, ready for a fight. "I'm not staying behind while you walk into a trap."

Blade turned to face her, memorizing the way her dark eyes held no fear. Only courage. If something happened to her in that building—if Barclay hurt her—

He wouldn't survive it.

Somewhere between the stalker attacks and the evidence warehouse, between watching her patch his wounds and seeing her devastation over Stryker's decision to hide the truth about her brother, Blade had figured out that he couldn't live without her.

"We go in together," she said. "Watch each other's back. Just like always."

He wanted to argue. Wanted to lock her in the car and face Barclay alone. Instead, he nodded.

"Stay close," he said. "Trust the plan."

Their boots cracked over loose concrete, each step snapping through the silence. The stench rolled out of the dark. Mildew. A sour tang that clung wet to the back of his throat. Inside stretched an empty husk of a store, shadows swallowing the floor, splintered racks jutting up like bones.

Blade's Glock cut left, steady. Tori's barrel tracked right.

The wide floor opened before them, tiles fractured like old teeth, steel frames with their guts rusted out.

Too much space. Too many places to hide a man.

Barclay wanted them in here. Wanted them hunting.

Blade pivoted, weapon raised toward the blind wedge behind a ruined counter. Drawers hung open like slack mouths, nothing moving in the dark beyond. He flicked his fingers, quick signal toward the rear. Tori caught it, pressed on creeping along a pillar.

A soft glow filtered down from the upper floors. Tori spotted it first, her hand rising in a silent signal. She pointed upward, two fingers indicating the second floor. He followed her signal and saw electric light spilling through the dead escalators. The long jaw of metal teeth ran up between the floors.

They approached the frozen escalators, metal steps locked in place like broken teeth. Blade went first, testing each step for noise before committing his weight. The steel held under his boots. Tori followed three steps behind.

The second floor opened into another cavern of retail decay. But this level felt different. Lived in. The light source became clear as they rounded a concrete pillar. Work lamps on tripods with harsh white beams cutting through the dark.

It took him a moment to comprehend what he was seeing. The space had been transformed into an artist's studio. A massive canvas dominated an easel near the windows, draped in white cloth as if waiting for a reveal. Smaller paintings leaned against the walls in neat rows. Paint supplies covered every surface. Brushes, palettes, tubes of color squeezed and abandoned. Splatters of red, blue, and yellow decorated the floor and walls like abstract blood spatter.

Barclay. Barclay himself was the Mandelbrot Killer.

He turned to share the revelation with Tori, but she was already moving toward the covered canvas. Her weapon remained ready as she approached the easel.

"Tori, wait—"

She grabbed the cloth and yanked it away in one swift motion.

The face on the canvas stared back at them. Maggie Quick.

"The warden," Tori said.

Half finished but unmistakably her, painted with the same detail as the hidden portraits they'd found at the law firm.

Blade's stomach dropped. "He killed her."

"Or he's about to."

Blade swung his weapon across the room. Canvases lined every wall. Stacks of paintings leaned against each other. Abstract fractals that probably concealed more faces, more victims. He kept his sights locked on the threat, no room to peel back the fractals and find the buried faces in the paint.

This wasn't just a studio. It was a trophy room. A monument to decades of murder disguised as art. How many people had Barclay killed?

The warden's painted eyes seemed to track Blade's movement as he studied the canvas. The paint still looked wet in places. Fresh. Recent.

A crash echoed from the back of the store. Metal against concrete.

Blade snapped toward the crash, Glock up, sights carving empty air.

"Detective."

The word landed from behind.

Blade's muscles locked. He angled his shoulders, ready to pivot.

"I wouldn't." The clean snap of a safety clicked off. "Dr. Crew and I are having a moment."

Blade rotated anyway, and his world collapsed into a single, devastating image. Tori, statue-still, her weapon half raised but useless. Barclay's service pistol pressed against her temple, his forearm wrapped across her throat.

The crash had been a feint. A distraction designed to exploit the one moment when their attention would be divided. Barclay hadn't ambushed them. He'd lured them into a kill box of his own design and waited for the perfect opening, and it was Blade's fault.

Professional curiosity had created that opening. His need to understand the art, to explore the evidence, had given Barclay the split second he needed.

"Drop your weapon, Detective," Barclay growled. "Slowly. Kick it away."

"Don't do it," Tori said.

Blade's Glock dragged at his grip, heavier than steel had a right to be. His body screamed to keep it, to fight, to do anything but give the man leverage. But Tori was a step away from execution.

He crouched. Set the weapon down. Nudged it with his boot until it scraped across concrete and vanished into the dark.

Barclay's mouth tugged upward, that warped grin more vicious than a snarl.

"Good. Now we can talk."

31

THE MUZZLE BRANDED HER TEMPLE, a circle of cold metal that wasn't just steel. It was a gravestone marker. Every wrong turn, every second she froze, every gut signal she'd shoved aside pressed into her skull with that barrel. She'd given Barclay the opening. She was the weak point. The moment she'd turned toward that canvas, she'd handed Barclay everything.

Barclay leaned close and breathed in, savoring her stillness the way a hunter measured the twitch before the strike.

Blade's eyes shattered her. Across the studio he had his palms up, face locked into tactical stone, but his eyes screamed his fury. Stripped of all options, all forward momentum. A man built for action rendered helpless.

They would both die here, and then Barclay would finish Stryker.

Her lips shaped the word across the gap—*sorry*.

Blade cut her off with a single head shake, short and hard.

Barclay lifted his chin. "Your phone. Kick it to the wall. Now."

Tori watched Blade's hands move, but his eyes never stopped calculating. Even now, he searched for angles, for that sliver of hope that would crack this situation open. His phone hit concrete with a hollow clatter.

"You too," Barclay said, squeezing her tighter. His breath was hot against her neck. Like the stalker's had been.

She clenched her jaw and let her Glock tumble from her hand, then her phone. The clatter cracked through the room. Her only equalizers, gone.

Barclay's arm yanked her head back until her vision tilted. She heard him kick her items away, but she couldn't track where. Couldn't see anything except the stained ceiling tiles illuminated from the harsh work lamps burning in the corner.

"Well, well, well," Barclay said against her ear. "Stryker King's mighty proteges are still just children playing with adult consequences. The two of you thought you were so smart. Digging into the past. But you never understood the bigger picture, did you?"

"You murdered my parents," she said, straining against his forearm. "Damien. All those other people. It's just one big game to you, isn't it?"

Air scraped thin through her throat. Black spots freckled the edges of her sight. The ceiling tilted above her, water-stained and indifferent. The paintings she'd seen on her way in might as well have been a thousand miles away.

Barclay's grip loosened just enough for her to breathe, but not enough to move. He wanted her conscious for this.

"You kids were weeds I never pulled. Grew up wild in the cracks I left behind." Barclay laughed. "And look at you now—one badge, one doctorate. Life turned out pretty fine for you both. What's there to whine about?"

Tori's stomach twisted. He talked about their lives like they were proof of his benevolence.

"Then Damien had to ruin it. He told me he wanted to purge his guilt, even if it meant exposing the corruption and bringing us both down." Barclay's laugh held no warmth. "I thought framing him for those officer murders at the precinct was the perfect solution. A life sentence was better than the grave he'd earned. Should've gone with my gut. Made it a mass shooting and suicide. But after all those years he spent looking the other way and helping me bury messes, I suppose I felt I owed him a life."

Damien's notebook was right. He'd been framed for the shooting. Whatever corruption had stained his badge, he hadn't killed those officers. Barclay had.

"But that's over. I took care of him for good now."

"And my brother? What about him? Did you take care of him too?"

"Never mind about him." The gun barrel pressed deeper into Tori's temple, metal warming against her skin. Barclay leaned closer and whispered, "You'll never find him."

Across the studio, Blade shifted. Not his normal restless energy, but a predator measuring distance. She caught the micro-movement of his right foot, sliding closer to where his Glock had fallen. Blade could kill Barclay with a paintbrush if he had an opening.

She had to give him one.

"The paintings," she managed, forcing admiration into her voice. "They're brilliant. The way you staged the crime scenes with the geometric patterns." She turned her head slightly, trying to meet his eyes. "You're the Mandelbrot Killer."

Barclay's laugh cracked through the studio.

"Interesting moniker. A bit dramatic, though." He dismissed the artistry with a wave. "It's all necessary, if theatrical, housekeeping. But, I guess you can say that Stryker has his proteges, and I have mine. I just find ways to use them a bit more creatively."

Tori barely registered Barclay's nonsensical chatter. Blade's eyes locked onto hers, and she read the message there.

Opening. Be ready.

Barclay dragged her back a foot, repositioning for better control.

"You may be pretty smart, Barclay," Blade said, taking half a step. "But you made one very big mistake."

Barclay's grip tightened. "And what would that be?"

"Your mistake," she said, pressing her temple harder against the barrel, "was letting me within reach."

Her heel smashed down, crushing the bones in Barclay's instep. She could feel the crack jolt up her leg. She snapped her head aside, slipping the barrel by inches. Barclay jerked and screamed. A guttural sound ripping loose as the gallery walls caught the noise and hurled it back.

She didn't pause to savor it. Her elbow rocketed up and back, targeting the soft space between his ribs. Air punched out of his lungs in a wet grunt that sprayed against her neck. His grip loosened for a half second.

Tori twisted hard left, using his forward momentum against him, spinning out of his grasp like water through fingers. She over-rotated. Her feet tangled and she crashed to the concrete floor. Her shoulder slammed first, then her hip. Pain shot through her arm.

She scrambled backward, putting distance between them, concrete scraping her palms. Her eyes blazed as she gained her feet, ready to fight again.

Barclay pivoted and ran, his limp barely slowing him down as he disappeared through a doorway into the adjacent room.

Tori and Blade dove for their weapons. Her fingers closed around her Glock's grip as Blade snatched his service weapon from where it had skittered under a canvas.

They came up armed, training their weapons on the empty doorway.

"Side exit," Blade barked, nodding toward the doorway in the far corner.

Tori's chest heaved as adrenaline flooded her system. The taste of copper filled her mouth. She'd bitten her tongue during the fall, and she was pretty sure the cut on her arm had broken open. Her shoulder throbbed, but everything moved correctly. Functional damage only.

"He's setting up another ambush," Tori whispered, keeping her gun trained on the doorway, finger indexed along the frame.

Blade moved toward the wall, using the shadows for cover. "Be careful. He has Stryker."

Tori pressed her back against the doorframe and nodded to Blade. His fingers counted down—three, two, one—and they moved as a unit around the corner.

The training kicked in. Pie the corner. Check your sectors. Trust your partner. But the reality felt nothing like the simulations at the FBI's National Academy at Quantico. Her heart hammered against her ribs, and sweat made her grip slippery. Every shadow could hide another gun. Every step forward increased the chance she'd freeze at the wrong moment, hesitate when Blade needed her to act.

He trusted her. That had to be enough.

They rounded the corner and froze.

The sight punched through her chest like a fist through paper. Stryker sat slumped in a wheelchair, his salt-and-pepper hair falling across his forehead, hospital gown hanging loose on his frame. Leather restraints around his wrists and chest held him upright. Without them, he'd collapse to the floor like a broken marionette. His breathing was shallow.

The man who'd earned MMA championship titles and built warriors looked like he might shatter if someone spoke too loudly.

He shouldn't be here. Moving him from the hospital could trigger another stroke. The stress alone, his blood pressure spiking, his heart racing, it could kill him fast as any bullet.

Barclay stood behind the wheelchair, his service weapon pressed to Stryker's temple. The same spot where he'd held the gun against her minutes ago.

This wasn't a chess move anymore. This was checkmate.

"Drop your weapon," Blade's voice boomed. "Now."

"That's not how this works." Barclay's finger rested on the trigger, casual as a man adjusting his tie. "You see, if you kill me, you convict your girlfriend."

Blade's eyes flicked to Tori for a split second. Confusion, then understanding, then something that looked like the world ending.

Barclay didn't mean her.

"The moment Ms. Kerns's credentials opened that sealed file, it triggered a deep-system script," Barclay said. "I had my programmer create something special. It's not just dumping files. It's fabricating a history. Creating a digital trail that proves that Kiara's been the one covering cases and switching files for months."

Blade's weapon never wavered, but Tori watched something die behind his eyes.

"You're lying," he said.

"Am I?" Barclay's smile widened. "Right now, there's a data packet sitting in a buffer, waiting for my heartbeat to stop. The moment I die, it uploads to a DOJ server. Kiara Kerns becomes the architect of a massive conspiracy and cover-up."

Tori saw it all in Blade's expression. The anger at being trapped. The devastation of watching someone innocent get destroyed. The terrible calculation of a man who'd spent his life protecting people, now forced to choose between them.

"I'm the only one with the abort code," Barclay continued. "Kill me, and she goes to federal prison for the rest of her life. But cooperate, and maybe we can work something out."

Stryker's head lolled forward, and Tori's chest tightened. Even unconscious, he was running out of time.

Barclay's attention shifted to Tori. The gun never moved from Stryker's temple, but his focus became a weapon all its own.

"You're still chasing ghosts, aren't you, Victoria?" The name rolled off his tongue like poison. "Worried about poor Jeremy Hoult?"

He said the name with a sneer that made it sound like Jeremy was something he'd just scraped off his shoe.

"Or should I call him Nikos Jr.?"

Her grip tightened on the Glock. "Hoult isn't my brother. The DNA test will prove that." Had to prove that.

"Maybe not, but he'll go down as the . . . what did you call him? Mandelbrot Killer?" Barclay smiled. "I do like that name. Poor Jeremy was just a kid needing a mentor. A mentally unstable man who became obsessed with a woman who'd interviewed him years ago, then convinced himself he was her long-lost twin brother."

Tori's stomach dropped. The confession in the interrogation room. Hoult's detailed knowledge of her childhood, the purple pajamas, the shared bedroom. "You fed him information about me."

"The beauty of it is how believable it all sounds," Barclay went on. "A man who used art therapy to restrain his urges to kill finally breaks free and comes looking for his sister. When she rejects him, he snaps. Starts killing people connected to the investigation into their parents' murders."

Her hands trembled. The narrative was airtight. Hoult's obsession with her was real—that part didn't need fabrication. His mental instability was documented. His presence at her house, the attacks on her and Blade, all of it would support Barclay's story.

Tori's heart pounded so hard her chest started to hurt. All she could do was shake her head.

"Even you believed him." Barclay's smile turned vicious. "So desperate for a brother, you opened the door and let the monster right in."

"He is not my brother!" The words tore from her. "You just twisted him into thinking he is."

Barclay wobbled his head side to side. "Maybe, maybe not. His DNA might not match yours, but it will match what's found at the crime scenes."

"No." Tori snapped the word. "No one will believe you. You manipulated Jeremy, just like you manipulated the narrative around my parents' murders. Nikos didn't kill them. You did."

The words hit their mark. Barclay's perfect control cracked like glass under pressure. His face contorted, the mask of calm authority replaced by something raw and ugly.

"Of course he didn't do it!" The roar tore from his throat, rage pouring out like blood from a severed artery. "A terrified boy with a kitchen knife was a gift! A perfect frame for a job that needed to be done right!"

"You butchered them and shattered two kids' lives. Framed one. Shoved me into the system like trash."

Tori advanced, two steady strides, Glock locked on his forehead. "Keep spinning lies. It doesn't matter. We've got the evidence that nails you clean."

"It's your mother's fault. She discovered the pattern. Figured out that the Mandelbrot set was the key to regenerative cardiac tissue. The future of organ transplantation. Her research was worth millions!" Fury burned in Barclay's eyes. "She could've been rich beyond imagination, but she wanted to publish it. Give it away to the world."

Her stomach hollowed. Her parents were tangled in something bigger than anything she'd ever let herself picture.

"Ji-Yeon forced my hand," Barclay continued. "I gave her multiple opportunities to fall in line. But Nikos convinced her to go public. So I did what had to be done."

The room fell silent except for her own labored breathing and the echo of Barclay's words. Her parents' murders laid bare.

Bootsteps hammered through the building. More than one set locking in rhythm.

"I heard every word, Dean. It's over."

Tori recognized that voice. Special Agent in Charge Sebastian Wells.

They'd done it. Wells had heard everything. Barclay's confession, his threats against Kiara, his orchestration of decades of corruption. All of it.

Wells walked toward them, unhurried, two agents flanking him in plain clothes. No tactical gear, no badges showing. Weapons drawn but lowered.

He nodded to Blade. "Give me the book. It's federal evidence now."

Blade's face showed exhausted relief. The notebook shook as he extended it.

Wells took the notebook. He examined the worn cover for a moment, then looked up at Barclay with something that might have been disappointment.

He walked past Blade.

Past her.

Stopped beside Barclay.

Wells didn't reach for handcuffs. Didn't signal his agents to move in. Instead, he held out the notebook like an offering.

"I believe *this* belongs to you, sir."

32

BLADE SAW IT IN SLOW MOTION. Wells extending the notebook. Barclay reaching for it. The leather-bound record of corruption and murder changing hands like a business transaction.

Wells chuckled, the sound echoing hollowly against the concrete pillars. "You look wounded, Blade. But you should be proud. We knew Damien had buried that notebook, but the man was a drunk and a coward. He'd never been able to pin down the exact location, knowing they listened to every word. We needed someone with a personal stake to sniff it out."

Barclay pocketed the notebook.

He'd been played. They'd all been played.

Blade cataloged the situation.

Barclay behind Stryker's wheelchair, one hand gripping the handle, the other pointing his gun near Stryker's skull. Wells stood a few feet to Barclay's left, arms in front in a compressed ready position. The two on the wings held the room.

Left side, a man with a towering frame and copper beard. Big Red.

The other held square shoulders and a bald head, feet planted wide. The man was a dead bolt between them and the exit. Lock.

Even if he could fire before they reacted, he couldn't take four targets simultaneously. Not from this position. Not with Tori in the line of fire.

No cover. No backup. No miracles.

There was only one variable he could change.

Only one way to shift the equation in her favor.

Blade's finger itched to pull the trigger.

Blade narrowed his eyes, putting the pieces together. "You orchestrated the timing of Damien's little confession through Corbin to get us moving."

Barclay adjusted the gun he held at the back of Stryker's head. "After all those years, Corbin finally visited his old man in prison. Guess he helped Damien find religion, and suddenly his conscience was a problem again. Started trying to convince the warden to turn on me too."

"He wanted to save his soul. We just wanted our insurance policy back." Wells took a step toward Tori, and Blade tensed.

"You needed Tori and me chasing that notebook so you could reclaim it before it could actually burn you."

"You were never in control here, Detective. We simply let you off the leash long enough to fetch the one thing we couldn't find ourselves." Barclay patted his pocket. "Thanks for doing the heavy lifting."

Blade stared down his sights, drifting between Barclay and Wells. The heat of his rage nearly matched the fire in his wounded bicep. He had to stop this, but how?

"So that's the cost," Blade said. "You turned the whole state into a graveyard just to keep Barclay out of a prison jumpsuit?"

"You really think it's that simple, Blade? A corrupt old chief and a dusty blackmail book?" He gestured to Barclay, palm flat up. "This man is not a criminal. He's a patriot."

"The Nexus Initiative," Blade said.

Wells paced the narrow space between a concrete pillar and where Barclay stood behind Stryker's wheelchair. "He built an organization that protects the interests of this country when the politicians are too weak to act."

"The organ harvesting isn't a crime," Barclay said. "It's a pragmatic solution. Hearts for senators. Livers for tech innovators. Kidneys for defense contractors. We preserve the people who shape the world."

Blade didn't bother arguing. There was no reasoning with zealots. Instead he flicked a gaze to the flanking agents.

"What about the paintings?" Tori asked.

"I'm the artist," Wells said, gesturing back through the open doorway.

Blade could see it now. The Bureau's golden boy. Sharp suit, charming grin.

The smiling mask most serial killers wore.

Sebastian Wells was the Mandelbrot Killer.

"The Mandelbrot set is the signature of God. I'm the hand that draws it." Wells patted his chest. "Dean provides the targets. I transform their exits into something beautiful."

"You didn't just paint fractals," she said. "You recreated the crime scenes."

Wells tilted his head. "Did I?"

"The victims are hidden in the layers," she continued. "The spirals repeat the geometry of the kill site. The angles. The blood patterns. You're reliving every kill."

Tori took a slow step sideways, her gaze moving from Barclay to Wells.

"Every brushstroke lets you revisit the moment you had complete control over someone's life," she said. "The fear. The power. The final second."

A smile crept across Wells's face.

"Finally," he said softly. "Someone who appreciates the work."

"The faces. Hidden in the fractals," Blade said. "Your victims."

Wells gave a small bow.

"I prefer to think of them as my stigmata."

"Then why were they hanging in Florek's law office?"

Wells glanced at Barclay.

Barclay chuckled. "Because Donald Florek was a problem. Our head legal counsel brought him in to work some magic with our shell accounts." He shook his head. "McCrary underestimated him."

Rich McCrary, senior partner of the law firm where Florek worked.

Where they'd first seen the faces in the paintings.

Blade didn't interrupt. He wanted everything laid out, because when he found a way out of here, these men were going to prison forever.

"Florek was smart," Wells said, picking up the thread. "Too bad he did the one thing you should never do when you suspect powerful people of powerful crimes."

"He went to the FBI," Blade said.

Wells spread his hands. "He came to me."

Florek's crime scene strobed though his mind. He shook it loose. "You're sick."

"I'm an artist," Wells said.

As if that was all the license he needed to murder.

A soft sound rasped through the room.

Blade's attention snapped to the wheelchair.

Stryker's head lifted and dropped forward again. A faint groan slipped past his lips.

Blade tightened his grip on the Glock. "What does he have to do with this?"

Wells followed his gaze.

A slow smile spread across his face.

"Everything." Wells moved to the wheelchair.

Barclay took a half step back, giving Wells the space. His gun dropped from Stryker's skull to his side.

Wells grabbed Stryker by the chin and lowered his face to within inches of his. "Stryker always had a soft spot for the broken, didn't he?"

Wells pushed Stryker's chin away as he released his grip. "I was his first project, long before he had a fancy name like the Warrior program. I was just a kid from juvie he thought he could save with a Bible and a boxing ring."

Wells's smile was thin and sharp. "But I wouldn't listen. I didn't want to be *reformed*. Stryker saw the darkness in me and got scared. He kicked me out before you and Tori ever even arrived."

The casual use of their names made Blade's skin crawl.

"To him, I was a failed experiment." Wells flicked a strand of Stryker's hair.

He turned to Barclay. "But Dean? Dean saw potential where Stryker saw a monster. He recognized my . . . unique ritualistic needs. He didn't try to pray the darkness away. He taught me how to sharpen it. Helped me climb the ranks of the Bureau, giving me a badge to hide behind while he pointed me at the people who threatened our mission."

"That's right, son." Barclay's hand landed on Wells's shoulder with paternal pride. "Sebastian had certain impulses. I gave him targets that served our mission. Channeled his artistry toward eliminating threats."

"Enough of your resume," Blade said. "Why did Damien have to die?"

Wells smiled like Blade had finally asked the right question. "We save the lives that matter. The leaders, the innovators, the architects of our future. Your parents, Tori, were a part of that. Then they became a threat."

The rational tone made it worse. Lives reduced to equations. Children orphaned for balance sheets.

"Just like Dr. Forest and his daughter?" Blade asked.

"Dr. Forest thought he could freelance," Wells continued. "Use our infrastructure for his personal crusade. We couldn't allow that kind of exposure."

"I suppose that's why you left the medical ethics book at Florek's house," Tori said. "A little message to what happens to those who don't follow *your* ethics?"

"I was hoping you'd see it. Did you know that your mother contributed a chapter?" Wells studied her for a reaction.

Tori didn't move. Didn't blink. The only thing that gave her away was the slight adjustment of her finger on the trigger of her Glock.

Heat rose behind Blade's eyes, but he filed everything away and kept his sights steady. Wells was trying to get inside her head. Make her react.

She wouldn't give him the satisfaction.

Neither would he.

But Sebastian Wells would've been a teenager when the Crews were murdered.

Blade lifted his chin at Barclay. "You killed them. It was you who stabbed Nikos and Ji-Yeon while Tori watched. Then you pinned it on her brother. You started all this."

"The Crew murders weren't the beginning," Barclay said, shaking his head. "No, this is centuries of groundwork. Building networks. Placing assets. Destroying others."

Then he smiled.

Wells tilted his head, almost sympathetic. "We could make Kiara's file-access problem disappear. Logs can be edited. Cooperate, Blade. She walks. Refuse, and she goes down for federal computer fraud."

Blade's jaw locked. "Don't you threaten her."

His gaze flicked to Tori. She wasn't looking at him. Her focus remained locked on Stryker, something fierce and protective burning in her dark eyes.

She would die for that man. He knew it the way he knew his own heartbeat.

He caught her eye for a fraction of a second.

When I move, you get Stryker. Go.

He saw understanding in the slight widening of her eyes, the almost imperceptible nod.

His Glock was useless at this range. A shot would go wide or hit Stryker.

He moved.

Barclay never saw it coming. Blade drove a shoulder into his sternum and slammed him into the concrete wall. Both weapons hit the floor. Wells spun, trigger finger moving, but Barclay was in the way.

One heartbeat. That's all it bought.

It was enough.

Blade's fist found Barclay's jaw. The chief's head snapped back. Blade didn't wait to see how it landed. Jab to the body, cross to the chin, the combinations that had dropped men half Barclay's age. The old chief was thick through the chest and shoulders, but he was eating every shot, his guard coming up too slow, legs going uncertain beneath him.

Blade could feel it. Another thirty seconds, and Barclay would fold.

Barclay drove a desperate fist into Blade's wounded side.

The beach knife wound tore open. Pain detonated through his side, and his hands dropped for one involuntary second. It was enough for Barclay to clinch, grabbing Blade's collar, using his weight to slow the assault.

Across the room Tori had Stryker's wheelchair moving, one hand on the grip, Glock up in the other. She muscled him behind a concrete pillar and planted herself in front of him.

Wells opened fire toward her position, shots cracking off the concrete above her head. Tori dropped below it, returned two shots from the low position, then moved again.

Blade broke the clinch with an elbow to Barclay's forearm, stepped back, reset. Barclay's left eye had swollen nearly shut. His lip was split, breathing labored. He was done and he knew it.

The rifle butt caught Blade behind the knee.

The leg buckled. He took the fall on his shoulder, rolled, and a boot came down where his face had been. Big Red stood over him, rifle barrel dropping toward his skull. Point blank. The concrete was cold against Blade's back.

He could see his Glock on the floor. Ten feet away. It might as well have been a mile.

Barclay wiped blood from his mouth with the back of his hand. "Finish it."

The shot came from behind the pillar.

Big Red's chest opened up. He dropped straight down, rifle clattering off Blade's leg.

Blade rolled away from the body as Wells swung his weapon toward Tori's position, firing fast, rounds popping off concrete.

Blade was already going for his gun. His knee screamed where he'd landed, the leg threatening to give again with every stride.

Barclay and Wells scrambled for the far side of the room, using the support pillars for cover. Blade reached his Glock, scooped it, came up behind a pillar of his own.

A gun barrel pressed against his temple from the other side of the concrete.

Lock.

He'd forgotten about Lock.

Pure instinct. Blade's left hand shot up, fingers finding the slide, ripping it backward and off the frame in one motion. The pieces hit the floor. Slide one direction, frame the other.

Lock stared at the disassembled weapon for a fraction of a second.

The knife came out.

Blade still had his Glock, but the space between them was nothing. Two feet, maybe less. Lock knew it. A knife at this range beat a drawn pistol every time, and the way he moved forward said he knew exactly how to do that math.

Blade backed off the trigger, shifted his grip, used the Glock's frame as a blocking tool on the first slash. The second got through, raking across his forearm. He dropped the gun without meaning to, fingers going slick.

Now they were even.

Lock pressed forward, every step cutting off Blade's angles. He was fresh. Blade was bleeding from three places, his knee threatening to buckle every time he pivoted, the beach wound screaming across his ribs with each breath.

He caught a thrust on his forearm, deflected it wide, drove a palm strike into Lock's nose. Felt it give.

Lock's eyes watered but he didn't slow. An elbow strike caught Blade's jaw. He tasted blood. Another drove into his collarbone, and his shoulder went briefly dead. Lock pivoted behind him, and the forearm locked across his throat.

Blade clawed at it. Drove his elbow back into Lock's ribs. Once. Twice. The grip didn't change.

His vision began to gray at the edges. Across the room through the narrowing tunnel of it he could see Tori. Wells had her pinned from the left, Barclay had worked around from the right, and she had nowhere to move without leaving Stryker exposed. Her Glock tracked between them, buying seconds she didn't have.

She couldn't see everything at once.

Nobody could.

Wells fired. She ducked left. Barclay fired. She ducked right. Back and forth, walking her into a corner one shot at a time. They weren't trying to hit her yet. They were herding her. The moment she ran out of bullets, it was over.

She needed someone to pull one of them off her.

Blade was that someone. He'd always been that someone.

His fingers found Lock's forearm and couldn't move it.

The gray closed in, sounds going hollow and distant, his body slacking.

He was going to die here, listening to the gunshot that killed her.

33

MUZZLE FLASHES STROBED through the dust. The air tasted like pulverized concrete. She had two of them working her from each side. Wells from the left, Barclay cutting off the right with the pistol Wells had tossed him. Rock peppered her shoulder like hail as another round bit into the concrete.

She was pinned. Where was Blade?

Wells and Barclay had a pattern. Controlled bursts on the left, Barclay covering the gaps on the right, walking her into a corner one shot at a time. One magazine against two shooters with an unconscious man at her back.

This wasn't working.

Across the room, she saw Wells's agent drop Blade's body like a sack of sand. The sound hit Tori in the center of her chest. For a second, she wasn't sure if he was alive, but then Blade's foot twitched. His hand slid under his back, fingers searching for a weapon.

A chunk of concrete popped under her boot. More were scattered around her feet. One the size of a golf ball. One a softball. In the Kingdom parking lot, Stryker had spent an afternoon trying to teach her to pitch. She'd nearly taken out his side mirror. He'd laughed and told her she had the arm of a pitcher and the aim of a blind man. The memory pressed against the back of her throat, and she pushed it down hard. Stryker was three feet behind her in a wheelchair. Her turn to save him.

Barclay's shots kept coming. Wild. One-handed. The rounds landed two feet wide. He had one working eye and a shoulder Blade had pulverized. He couldn't hit her if she stood up and waved.

But he could hit Stryker. Stryker was a stationary target.

She picked up both stones.

Lord, I need a David and Goliath here. Please.

Wells's gun went quiet. He was reloading.

She hurled the small rock into the steel beams overhead. It rang hollow and loud.

Wells's eyes went up. His hands paused on the reload.

She stood and threw the big chunk at his face with everything she had. The concrete connected. The magazine spun away across the floor.

Tori came out from behind the pillar at a dead run, boots loud on the concrete.

Barclay fired, but his shot went wild.

"Wells."

He looked up.

She fired two shots. Center mass. He stumbled back, hit the wall, and slid. His wide eyes found hers.

"Impossible," he whispered.

The agent over by Blade snatched his knife off the ground.

"Blade!"

Blade's head came up. Groggy. His hand came from behind his back with his gun. He fired from the ground.

The agent standing over him dropped.

"Sebastian!" Barclay was beside Wells. Pistol gripped in his good hand, he patted Wells's slack face. "No. Sebastian, no."

"It's over, Barclay." Tori stared at him down her sights.

"You," Barclay snarled, getting to his feet.

His gun came back up, aimed for her. He fired three shots, fast and wild.

Tori kept moving. Her ears rang with the shots.

Click. Click. Click.

The pistol's slide locked. Empty.

He threw the gun at her and she dodged it, closing the distance in three strides.

She jabbed once, the impact running all the way to her elbow. Then she drove her right leg forward, hip rotating through the arc. Her boot connected with his midsection.

The teep folded him. Barclay went down backward, then rolled, grappling for Wells's gun. She kicked the pistol into the dark and stood over him with her own Glock pointed at his face.

He looked up from flat on his back. His eyes were wet and his mouth was working, but whatever he was trying to say had already left him.

"You should have died with them," Barclay finally spat out.

"Shut up." She adjusted her finger on the trigger, ready to fire.

This man had killed her mother before Tori was old enough to know her voice. Killed her father before she could memorize his face. She'd spent her life believing she was alone because of what he chose to do one night in October.

"Do it." His eyes drifted to Wells's body. "Shoot me. You know you want to."

The Glock sat heavy in her hand. The child who had hidden in that closet wanted to pull the trigger. She wanted to erase him the way he had erased her family.

"Do it!" Barclay shouted.

She looked at him and saw the evil she'd studied in textbooks. He was like a weed growing wild among the wheat, choking the life out of everything he touched. She wanted to rip him from the dark soil he lived in.

If she pulled the trigger, she became just like him.

She lowered the gun.

"It's not my job to judge you. That's for God."

She turned away.

Ten feet away, Stryker was still in the wheelchair, head dropped forward but breathing.

Blade was standing there too. Blood soaked through his shirt in a dark map of the last hour. He crossed the space without a word. She met him halfway. His good arm pulled her against his chest. He smelled like blood and sweat. She pressed her face into him anyway.

His hand moved over her hair.

"You're bleeding," he said.

She pulled back to look at him. His nose was crooked. His eye was swelling shut. He looked like he'd been through a war, and he had. For her. "So are you."

"No, Tori. You've been shot."

She looked down.

A dark stain had soaked through the left side of her shirt. Three inches of torn fabric where the bullet had clipped her, the skin beneath it raw and weeping. Barclay's wild shot. She hadn't registered it.

It burned now.

She pulled the fabric aside. Clean entry, clean exit. The skin around it already purpling. "Through and through."

Sirens outside. Ambulance. Cops. Real ones this time. Garrison didn't bluff about calling for backup.

Blade stripped off his outer shirt and folded it into a pad, pressing it tight against her side. She put her hand over it to hold it.

"You're going to need this cleaned and packed properly."

"When the paramedics get here," she said.

There was one more thing she had to do.

She limped over to Barclay, squatted, and fished Damien's notebook from his jacket.

Barclay laughed from the floor, clutching his shoulder. "You think you've won? There are others. You haven't touched the surface of this network. You're done."

"No," Tori interrupted. "You are."

34

THE PARAMEDIC HAD BEEN PATIENT for about as long as Blade was going to allow. She'd been talking at him for ten minutes. Pressure here, hold this, don't move that. He'd complied, but when she reached for the saline flush, he put his hand over hers.

"I'm good."

She gave him the look that all paramedics gave people who said they were good when they were clearly not good.

"Sir, you have a broken nose, two cracked ribs, a laceration on your bicep that needs stitches, and your knee—"

"I know what I have." He stood. His knee made its opinion known immediately, but he kept moving. "Where's Dr. Crew?"

She pointed.

Tori was sitting on the edge of a gurney, a second paramedic working on her side. She had her chin up and her eyes on the ceiling. She didn't see him coming until he was three feet away.

She looked at him the way she had in the closet after the stalker attack. Like she was checking to make sure he was real.

"Give us a minute, will you, Deb?" Tori asked the paramedic.

The woman applied one last strip of tape to the gauze on Tori's wound and pulled her gloves off. "I'll be back in a few minutes."

He eased down beside her, their shoulders brushing. Across the room, techs crouched, dropped yellow placards, swept flashbulbs across blood and broken glass. The adrenaline had burned down to nothing, leaving behind a bone-deep exhaustion that put lead into every muscle.

"Nice shooting," he said.

"You too." She glanced at his knee, his nose, the bandage already dotted with blood on his arm. "You look terrible."

"I've looked worse."

"No," she said. "You really haven't."

That made him chuckle. He hadn't lost her. He knew exactly what she was to him. He just hadn't said it out loud yet.

"You know what I keep thinking about?" Tori asked.

"What's that?"

"How quiet it is now." She gestured toward the CSU team setting up their equipment. "All that gunfire, all that noise, and now it's just . . . work. Regular police work."

Blade watched a technician photograph Wells's body. "Feels weird, doesn't it? Being on this side of it."

"Yeah. Usually I show up after all the shooting."

"Usually, we don't have to do the shooting."

She turned to look at him. "You okay with that? What happened in here?"

"Are you?"

"I asked you first."

Blade considered the question. Three men were dead. He'd been in a fight that could have gone either way. Tori had killed two people to save his life and Stryker's.

"Yeah," he said finally. "I'm okay with it. They made their choices."

"Good answer." Tori's eyes locked on him. Her skin close, her breath right there.

He wanted to pull her in for a long kiss. Tell her how much he loved her. Get down on his bruised knee and ask her to marry him. But he shoved the want down.

Not here. Not like this.

Instead, he kissed her forehead and let her lean into him. Blade felt the connection. A love that had survived everything life had thrown at them.

His eyes drifted to where Stryker lay on a stretcher. IV lines snaked from his arm. An oxygen mask covered his nose and mouth.

Stryker's eyes fluttered.

Blade's knee screamed as he jumped to his feet.

"Tori, look."

Stryker's eyelids twitched. They opened a sliver. Barely there then gone. Like a body trying to drag itself back from somewhere deep.

His eyelids cracked open, but Stryker didn't move. They were already by his side at the gurney.

Tori's hands wrapped around Stryker's with the kind of desperation that made Blade's chest ache. "Stryker? Stryker, can you hear me?"

Stryker's eyes tracked to Blade's face, recognition flickering. His mouth moved, but no sound came.

"Don't try to talk," Blade said. "Save your strength."

The older man's gaze shifted to Tori, to the paramedic, to the officers in the corner, then back to Blade. Questions lived in those eyes. Questions that would have to wait.

"We've gotta get moving," one paramedic said. "This man needs to get to the hospital."

Tori stepped back and said, "Call Corbin King, he's a Special Agent with FDLE. He has medical power of attorney."

They took Corbin's number and rolled Stryker toward the exit. His eyes were closed again.

More voices rang through the building, shouting orders. Two grim-faced FDLE investigators Blade recognized and trusted had taken control of the scene. No BSO uniforms. No FBI. Not yet.

Crime scene tape had gone up. Photographers documented

everything. The studio that had been a serial killer's shrine was now little more than evidence.

Blade gave his statement to Special Agent Marsha Bondi, a twenty-year veteran of the FDLE whose word carried weight in court.

The facts came out clean and simple. A detached account that felt like a story about someone else. The knife attack on the beach. Acting on Garrison's intel that brought them here. The confrontation with Dean Barclay and Sebastian Wells. Shots fired in self-defense and defense of others.

Marsha recorded it on her phone, stopping him now and again for clarification.

When Blade had finished, Marsha released a loud sigh. "Well, this is one for the books. I'll need to get Dr. Crew's statement."

"She's with the EMTs." Blade nodded toward the gurney, where Tori had returned to have the paramedic clean the cut on her arm she'd reopened along the way.

"And the older gentleman? The one they took to the hospital?"

"Kidnapping victim. I doubt he can give a statement. He's been in a coma for months."

Marsha stared. "Oh—okay then. I'll coordinate with the hospital."

For years, Tori and Blade had trusted a man who'd held a secret.

Stryker had walked away from that crime scene in 1998 knowing exactly what Barclay had buried. He'd watched Tori train in his gym for years, watched her chase a past she couldn't remember, and never said a word. One day he'd have to answer for that. But the man had been in a coma for nearly a year and he'd just survived a kidnapping.

The reckoning could wait. Healing came first.

35

TORI PRESSED HER BACK against the molded plastic chair in the ER waiting room, trying to ignore the kid three seats down who'd been sniffling for the past hour. Each wet, congested breath made her skin crawl with imaginary germs.

Half an hour ago, some guy had stumbled through those doors clutching a baggie packed with ice and his own severed hand. Gator bait, the nurses whispered. He'd dangled raw chicken too close to those prehistoric jaws.

The coffee in her hands had gone cold an hour ago, but she kept holding the cup anyway. It gave her something to do with her fingers. The liquid looked like motor oil and tasted worse. Bitter enough to strip paint. Her stomach cramped with hunger, but the thought of the vending machine sandwiches made her nauseous.

Blade was beside her, arm tucked in a sling. He sat close enough that she could feel the heat radiating from his body through the thin hospital air. Not touching. They hadn't touched since Blade had been properly stitched up over an hour ago.

The trauma team had cleared her for shock an hour back. She'd given her statement to Marsha Bondi right there in the bay, hooked to a saline line, the bullet graze freshly packed. Two shots fired.

Both clean. Self-defense and defense of others. Marsha had taken it down in that flat, careful voice she used when she already knew the case would hold, and then she'd left Tori with the fluorescent hum and the smell of iodine.

Stryker was stable. Still unconscious, but the doctors said that was normal. Expected. His body needed time to heal from whatever Barclay had done to him during those missing hours.

The adrenaline had burned off somewhere around midnight, leaving behind an ache that went deeper than muscle and bone. Everything hurt. Her forearm where the stalker's knife had found its mark. The bullet graze. Shoot, even her eyelashes hurt.

She needed to move, needed air that didn't taste like other people's germs and bad decisions.

"I'm going outside," she said, standing.

Blade was already rising. "Mind if I come?"

"Yeah. Sure."

The automatic doors whispered open, and Florida humidity hit her like a wet blanket. Thick, muggy, soup-like atmosphere that clung to her skin and made her lungs work harder. But it was better than the recycled sterility inside.

The rumble of a motorcycle engine cut through the night. Harlee's Kawasaki swept into the parking lot, headlight carving a bright arc across empty asphalt. She killed the engine, slid off, and jogged toward them, helmet tucked under one arm.

"How is he?" No preamble. Straight to the point.

"Stable," Blade said. "CT came back clean. No new swelling. He's unconscious, but—"

"I need to see him."

"You can't. Not yet," Tori said. "ICU restrictions. We have to wait until they call us."

Harlee's face softened. "Right. Sorry. I just—" She shook her head, regrouping. "I have news. Had to deliver it in person."

Tori's stomach dropped. More bad news. Had to be. Nothing good ever required in-person delivery at two in the morning.

"Edwards called. He tried to reach you but—"

"I turned my phone off," Blade said, reaching into his pocket to find it. The screen flashed white as it powered up, and he slid it into his sling.

"Mine's dead," Tori said.

"Anyway, when Edwards ran Hoult through the FDLE DNA investigative database, he popped. The file said Hoult had a forensic evaluation for a competency hearing performed by one Dr. Crew."

Tori shook her head slowly. "I don't remember that."

"It was a while ago, and you've seen how many patients?"

"Countless," Tori said.

"Edwards ran a rapid DNA and got the preliminary results." Harlee paused.

The world tilted sideways. Tori braced herself against the brick wall. Did she want a brother like Hoult? A damaged, violent man who'd stalked her and tried to kill Blade? Maybe not, but she wanted answers.

"Is Jeremy Hoult my brother?"

Harlee's lips flattened. "There's zero percent probability that Jeremy Hoult is your biological brother."

The hope Tori hadn't even realized she'd been clinging to evaporated.

Gone. Truly gone.

She looked at Blade. He didn't say I told you so. Didn't offer empty platitudes about it being better this way. He just watched her with those blue eyes full of shared sorrow, understanding exactly what this lie had cost her.

When he lifted his good arm, she ducked under it and let him hold her despite his injuries. Let herself lean against his chest while the Florida night pressed close around them.

She felt Blade's phone buzzing in his sling, and he released her to fish it out. Garrison's name lit up the screen.

"Take it," she said, wiping a tear with her index finger. "Put it on speaker."

Blade swiped to answer. "Garrison."

"I've been trying to reach you for an hour. I've got updates. Big ones." Garrison's voice carried the exhaustion of someone who'd been working nonstop. "Where are you?"

"Hospital. Tori and Harlee are with me. You're on speaker."

"Good. You all need to hear this." Papers rustled in the background. "First, Hoult confessed everything. And I mean everything."

Tori straightened, pulling away from Blade's chest. "What did he say?"

"Barclay's people approached him in prison. He had been obsessed with you ever since that competency hearing years ago. Barclay manipulated him. Fed him every detail from the fake file."

"So he never thought he was my brother?" The words tasted bitter.

"I'm sorry, no. He was playing a role. Barclay needed a distraction to keep you from listening to Damien, so he activated his patsy," Garrison said. "Hoult admitted to the stalking and the attacks on you and Blade. He said Barclay promised him protection, maybe even a way to be reunited with you for good if he played his part."

Blade's jaw tightened. "Reunited how?"

"We're not going there. The important thing is Hoult's talking. He's giving us names, dates, everything we need to dig deeper into this conspiracy."

"What about Barclay?"

"Singing like a canary, trying to cut a deal. But we have Damien's blackmail book, so we may not need to make one." The satisfaction in Garrison's voice was unmistakable. "Barclay says he can lay out the entire command structure of the Nexus Initiative, which is what he calls his organ trafficking ring."

"What about the other victims?" Blade asked. "Kaufman. Kagay. We never closed the loop on how they connected."

"Looks like Scott Kaufman was on the payroll of a shell company that is connected to the Chiron BioInnovation Center. It's buried deep, but it's there. He knew enough about the technology and the money to be dangerous, and eventually Wells decided he was more dangerous alive than dead."

Blade asked, "Judge Kagay and the records clerk?"

"That's a little simpler. Small county, one criminal court judge. For thirty years, every case that touched Barclay's operation went through Kagay's desk, and every single one went his way."

Tori thought about Sasha Robie, the murdered records clerk, and how easily that could have become Kiara.

"I can't believe it," Tori said. "Wells and Barclay destroyed anyone in their paths."

"Yes, and the investigation isn't over either. Barclay mentioned a medical examiner and at least one other officer," Garrison said. "I'm sure more names will rise to the surface. We also have names of the shell companies used to launder money. We're executing federal warrants in six states as I speak."

"Six states? How big was this thing?"

"Bigger than we thought. We found encrypted communications on Sebastian Wells's laptop proving he used a federal backchannel to contract the hit on Dr. Forest while in custody. He even scrubbed his own DNA profile, though I haven't heard how he pulled it off. We're still sorting through the data, but it's over. The ring is finished."

The tightness in Tori's chest loosened, but her focus shot to the next danger waiting in line. "What about Kiara Kerns?"

Blade looked at her with something that might have been gratitude.

"The frame Barclay threatened? That one's going to take some time," Garrison said. "She's in the clear, but the digital forensics are complex. We're trying to locate whoever hacked into the records department and who programmed the dead-man's switch."

Harlee nudged Blade and pointed to herself.

"I know tech experts who can help," Blade said. "ATF Agent Harlee Bay here with me, and you might know Jett Nu."

"Nu? The one who creates the intelligence software?" Interest sparked in Garrison's voice. "Are they available?"

Harlee gave a thumbs-up.

"They'll be happy to make themselves available," Blade said.

"Perfect. We'll make sure Kiara gets cleared. I'll coordinate with your people tomorrow—today, actually."

This wouldn't make up for everything Kiara was going through. The accusations, the betrayal she felt, the career uncertainty. But it was a start.

"What happens now?" Tori asked. "With the investigation?"

"We keep digging. There are still loose ends. Other victims, financial trails, accomplices we haven't identified. But the core conspiracy is broken. Barclay and Wells were the architects."

"And my brother? My real brother?"

"That's still an open question. We know Nikos Jr. existed. We know he was taken that night. Finding him . . ." Garrison paused. "That's going to be a different kind of investigation. One that might take time while we jump through the legal hoops."

Tori nodded, even though Garrison couldn't see her. Time. She'd waited her whole life already. She could wait a little longer.

"Get some rest," Garrison continued. "All of you. We'll reconvene in the morning with fresh eyes and clear heads."

The call ended, leaving them standing outside the hospital. Harlee had her phone out, probably texting Jett about the digital forensics.

"You didn't have to ask about Kiara," Blade said quietly.

"Yes, I did." Tori looked up at him. "She didn't deserve what happened to her. None of us did, but her especially."

The automatic doors whispered open behind them. A nurse emerged, her scrubs wrinkled after a long shift.

"Family of Stryker King?" she called.

They turned as one. Family. Not by blood, maybe, but by

choice. By shared trauma and stubborn loyalty and the kind of love that survived bullets and betrayal.

"He's awake," the nurse said.

"Wait." Harlee's voice cut through the humid air before they could reach the automatic doors. "I didn't get to finish before Garrison called."

Tori stopped midstride and swung toward Harlee. The woman's gaze snapped from her face to Blade's and back again.

"I did something without asking." Harlee's fingers twisted around her helmet strap. "After we got your DNA sample, I ran it against genealogical databases. All of them. Looking for any biological matches."

The blood drained from Tori's face. "You should have asked."

"I know. I'm sorry. But I took a shot, and it paid off."

Tori's heart stopped for a beat. Then slammed against her ribs so hard she could hear it in her ears. The parking lot tilted sideways. She gripped Blade's arm to keep from falling.

"What did you find?"

Harlee's voice went soft. "I found a full biological sibling."

Real. Not Jeremy Hoult's manufactured delusion. Not another lie from Barclay's playbook. A real family somewhere out there, carrying the same DNA that had survived that horrible night.

"Where?" The word scraped out, and she wasn't even sure it was the right one.

Harlee pulled an envelope from her jacket and held it out.

Tori took the envelope and stared at the thing like it might explode. Everything she'd wanted to know sat right there in her hands.

Blade's smile reached his eyes for the first time in days.

"Don't you want to open it?" Harlee's brow pinched.

Tori tucked the envelope against her chest. "Later."

"But—"

"My real family is inside that hospital, waiting for me." Tori looked at Blade, then tapped the envelope. "This . . . this can wait."

36

THE FIRST THING WAS SOUND. A soft, rhythmic beeping. Distant. Then voices. Muffled. Like listening underwater.

A woman's voice, low and steady. Tori. A man's, a deep rumble. Blade.

His eyelids dragged like sandbags, every twitch a battle.

He pried one open, and light knifed in. White. Searing. Splitting across his skull. Needles drove behind his eyes. He slammed them shut again.

His stomach pitched sideways, threatening to heave.

A hand closed over his. His fingers twitched.

The motion drew in a sharp breath. Tori.

He dragged his eyes open again, lashes scraping dry. White glare bled into outlines, then into faces crowding the bedside. Tori clutching him. Blade standing tall, shoulders squared like he could take the hit for him. Harlee hovering back, arms knotted across her chest. Jett restless, shifting from foot to foot. Luna angled sharp, watchful. Corbin standing rigid, jaw locked.

All of them. His kids. His family. Here.

But where was here? The smell was antiseptic. The bed was wrong. He tried to speak, but only a dry, rasping sound came out.

"Stryker? Can you hear me?" Blade.

He wanted to nod. To speak. A tear escaped the corner of his eye, tracking a hot path into his hairline. Frustration. He couldn't move. He couldn't talk.

"You've been out for almost a year, Stryker. A whole year." Harlee.

A year? The word didn't compute. A year was a lifetime. Where . . . where had he been for a year?

His gaze found Tori. She was the anchor in the disorienting sea. She looked different. Older.

He saw an envelope in her other hand. A plain, white envelope that she held like it was both a treasure and a bomb. He didn't know what was in it, but he saw the question in her eyes.

Memories bounced around the silent chambers of his mind, and with them came the cold, hard face of Dean Barclay.

He knew what he must do. Tell her. About everything. He squeezed her hand again, trying to pour a lifetime of apology and explanation into that single point of contact.

His throat felt like it was full of sand. He forced a sound out, a dry whisper. "T-t-t-t."

"He's saying your name, I think," Jett said.

Yes. Her name. Tori. He owed her the truth, no matter how much it hurt. He looked around at the faces of his family, then back to her. He needed them all to hear this. To understand the burden he'd carried.

"Tori." His voice was a broken rasp, each word a struggle. "That night . . . in . . . house . . ."

Why was this so hard? Each word exhausted him. He paused, gathering strength.

"Bar . . . clay . . . found me . . . with . . . Nikos."

"Stryker, stop. You don't have to do this. Rest."

But he saw the flicker of pain in Tori's eyes.

"Yes . . . I . . . do."

He closed his eyes. Felt himself drifting.

"Turn the lights off. It might help." Luna.

He pulled his eyes open. Darker. Better.

"Barclay . . . said . . . Nikos saw . . . face . . . A witness." He took a shallow breath. "The people . . . worked for . . . don't leave . . . witnesses. Not . . . even . . . children."

He looked directly at Tori, trying to make her see the impossible geometry of the choice he'd faced.

"He gave . . . me . . . a choice."

Another tear rolled down his cheek.

"He said . . . he can make the boy . . . disappear . . . into the system . . . brand him a . . . psy . . . psychotic . . . or . . . have him . . . eliminated. Made me . . . choose . . ."

The ugly words hung in the air. Tori held his hand as tears fell down her face.

"He looked at me . . . said . . . Your choice, King. One child gets life . . . One child goes away . . . or he would put both . . . both in the ground."

The silence stretched. He watched Tori's face, bracing for the impact. The anger. The hatred. The final, deserved accusation of betrayal.

But it didn't come.

He watched her process not his betrayal but the impossible choice. The burden he'd chosen to carry so she wouldn't have to. The hurt in her expression melted away, replaced by a dawning, devastating understanding.

Her hand covered her mouth. Shoulders rounded, as if something heavy finally settled into place. "Oh, Stryker." The words broke out, carried by breath more than sound. "You saved us. You saved us both."

It wasn't an accusation.

It was an absolution.

The forgiveness was so complete, so immediate, it stole the air from his lungs. The twenty-six-year-old weight on his soul finally, blessedly, lifted.

"I couldn't stop him," he whispered. "But I could . . . I could make sure you both lived."

"You did." Tori's tears fell freely now. "You did everything you could."

He saw Blade place an arm around Tori and hold her.

Harlee wiped her eyes with the back of her hand. Jett stood straighter, like a burden had lifted from his shoulders too.

His gaze drifted to Corbin and Luna, arms linked.

Luna was here.

When had she come home?

"How long?" he asked, his voice gaining strength. "How long in the hospital?"

"Eleven months, two weeks, four days," Blade said. "But who's counting?"

Stryker tried to smile. "What did I miss?"

"Everything," Tori said.

She squeezed his hand again, and he squeezed back.

Stronger this time.

37

THE ICE CLINKED against Tori's glass as she lifted it, condensation cool against her palm. The afternoon sun warmed her shoulders through the thin fabric of her sundress, but the breeze off the water carried just enough chill that she was grateful for the denim jacket draped over her lap.

"Okay, that one." She pointed her glass toward a gleaming white yacht moored three slips down. "*Sea-duction*. Really?"

Blade followed her gaze. "I picture . . . a thick mustache. Expensive shirt half unbuttoned to show off the gold chain buried in his chest hair."

She snorted.

"What about that one? Number five down there." Blade pointed. "*Knot Working*."

"I picture a captain's hat with scrambled eggs on the brim and a man who calls everyone 'matey.'" She took a sip of sweet tea, the tartness making her pucker.

Blade shook his head. "Probably has a trembling chihuahua that gets seasick."

"I always wanted a dog." She traced the rim of her glass with her finger. "But I pictured myself with something massive. Like, as big as I am. One I could train as an emotional support dog, take with me to help patients relax."

"I can see that."

"Maybe a chihuahua wouldn't be so bad. One of those with long hair and pointy ears. Could keep my lap warm during those long movie marathons."

"That you'd both sleep through."

"Don't start." She threw a wad of the straw wrapper at him.

"I always pictured you with a rottweiler," Blade said, grinning. "But I can totally see the chihuahua. Sassy. Fits in your purse. Wears cute outfits. And the best part, small dog, small poop."

Laughter bubbled up from deep in her chest. Real laughter. When was the last time she'd done that? They'd been so buried in the case, in survival mode, that it felt like ages.

Heat collected in her ribs, and her fingers twitched against the tabletop, an impulse screaming to close the short distance, to lay her hand over his. Anchor him, anchor herself.

If she were honest, really honest, she was stalling. Buying time to gather courage to admit her feelings.

To her, Blade wasn't just her protective big brother anymore, the one who'd teased her about movie marathons and made her laugh until her sides ached. He was the man whose hand she wanted to reach for across the table. The man whose smile made warmth bloom in places she'd kept carefully guarded. The man she'd fallen head over heels in love with. The man she wanted to spend the rest of her life with.

And he deserved to know.

She checked her watch instead. Five minutes late.

Down the sidewalk, a family of tourists had discovered the fish-feeding station. The father dumped a handful of pellets into the water while his kids shrieked with delight as dozens of fish swarmed to the surface, their mouths opening and closing in a frantic ballet.

"Look at that," Tori said, watching a little girl in a pink sun hat drop her entire cup of fish food at once. The water churned white with feeding fish. "Kid just created a riot."

"Reminds me of the bullpen when someone brings donuts."

She laughed and nodded to the pelican who landed on the dock railing near their table, eyeing their shrimp and crab dip appetizer.

"Don't even think about it," Blade told the bird.

"He's calculating his odds. Wondering if he can take you."

"Smart money's on the pelican."

The breeze shifted, bringing the scent of salt and sunscreen and fried shrimp from the kitchen. Tori shrugged into her jacket, not because she was cold but because the gesture felt comforting.

Three weeks since the Mayfair. Three weeks since Stryker had opened his eyes and the world had shifted back into focus. The envelope from Harlee still sat on her kitchen counter. Tori had only opened it two days ago. Every morning she'd walk past it at least ten times before her coffee finished brewing just trying to work up the courage.

Blade looked past Tori, and she watched the smile that spread over his face. "Here he comes."

Tori turned and saw the man walking toward her in khaki shorts and a linen shirt, wearing dark Ray-Bans and a smile she recognized. Her body did its own thing by standing up.

Dr. Anton Stone reached out before he was even in touching distance and pulled her into a solid hug that didn't let up. "This is incredible," he said into her hair. "Utterly, impossibly, amazingly incredible."

Tori took a deep breath, grounding herself in the reality of hugging her twin brother. All she could say was "I know."

When he finally released her, he didn't let go of her hand, like he was afraid he'd lose her forever. He greeted Blade, saying he was a little surprised to see him here.

As they sat and scooted chairs up to the table, Tori explained that Blade was her best friend. She almost said he'd been like a brother, but she couldn't say it because all she saw now was the only man she could ever love.

Blade took over. "We sorta grew up together, but there's plenty of time to talk about that. First, we should get Anton a drink and order some real food because the dip isn't cutting it for me."

Tori's stomach fluttered with nerves. She wasn't sure she could eat, but she ordered a tuna poke bowl knowing that Blade would finish whatever she didn't eat.

"I'll have the same thing," Anton said. Tori thought he looked nervous, his academic composure gone. He was just a man at a life-altering meeting.

Tori coaxed Anton into telling his story.

Anton had no memory of the trauma, only a lifetime of feeling like a piece of him was missing. He had vague memories of being in a "scary hospital for kids" until a kind psychiatrist, who couldn't find a reason for his committal, adopted him. His wife couldn't have children.

He was raised with love, with every advantage. But he always knew he was adopted, and his parents had said they knew very little about his background. He put his DNA in every database hoping to find a relative, a clue to his past. He just never imagined he had a sister, much less a twin.

It wasn't a tearful Hollywood reunion. It was quiet, hesitant, profound. Two strangers, bound by blood and tragedy, taking the first, tentative step toward becoming family.

Tori had no memory of their shared past either, but she too had felt like something was missing. She told Anton that one day they would talk about it, maybe even write about twin connections, but for now, she just wanted to know Anton the man.

As Tori sat across from Anton, this quiet, kind, intellectual man who was the antithesis of the monster she was led to believe her brother had become, a thought bloomed in her mind like light breaking through storm clouds.

The enemy had come in the night and sown weeds among the

wheat. And from the moment she read the case file, she'd believed the lie. That the wheat had been twisted into something monstrous. That her brother had become a creature of violence and madness.

But Stryker had understood the wisdom of the harvest. He hadn't tried to rip the weeds from the soil in his haste to protect her. He'd simply sheltered the field and waited, knowing that truth would separate itself from deception when the season was right.

And now, here he was. Not a weed. Not a tare. The good seed. Grown true despite the darkness that had tried to choke it out.

"You're staring," Anton said, his smile gentle.

"Sorry. I'm just . . ." She shook her head.

"The files made it sound like I was a very disturbed child."

"Fabricated," Blade said. "All of it. Part of a cover-up to hide what really happened that night."

Anton's hand tightened around his water glass. "What really happened?"

Tori glanced at Blade, then back to her brother. "Our parents were murdered. You and I were witnesses. The people who were supposed to protect us betrayed us. One was the real killer."

The color drained from Anton's face. "Witnesses."

"You were four years old, hiding under the bed with a kitchen knife because you were trying to protect me." Tori's voice caught. "You weren't a killer. You were a terrified little boy who loved his sister."

Anton stared at the table for a long moment. When he looked up, his eyes were bright with unshed tears. "I always wondered why I became a psychiatrist. Why I was drawn to helping adults work through a childhood filled with trauma. Maybe some part of me remembered."

"Maybe," Tori said softly.

The waiter brought their food, but none of them moved to eat. The moment felt too fragile, too sacred to interrupt with something as mundane as lunch.

“What happens now?” Anton asked.

Tori looked at this man who shared her genetics, her earliest memories buried so deep neither of them could reach them. Then she looked at Blade, steady and patient beside her, the anchor she’d never known she needed.

“Now we figure out how to be a family,” she said.

38

THE SAND SHIFTED beneath his bare feet, cool and yielding after the heat of the day. Blade matched Tori's pace along the shoreline, the same stretch where the stalker had cornered him weeks ago. Cold grit under his back. Knife steel flashing down. Heat ripping through his shoulder. The reel unspooled, sharp as ever, but it slid off him now, weightless. Just facts. Just something that happened to someone else.

Tori splashed through the ankle-deep surf beside him, her sundress hem darkening with salt water. She didn't care. The woman who used to flinch at getting sand between her toes now kicked at the waves like a kid.

"You realize you're destroying a perfectly good dress," he said.

She grinned. "It's just fabric."

Just fabric. Three weeks ago, she would have hiked the hem above her knees and tiptoed around the water. Now she waded right in. Anton's visit had changed something in her. The brother who was a stranger, the family that existed in theory but not in practice—somehow meeting him had loosened something that had been wound tight for years.

The sun hung low behind them, a molten orange ball sinking

toward the Intracoastal on the western side of the island. The Atlantic threw back streaks of amber and rose like watercolors on wet paper. Beautiful.

But he couldn't stop watching her instead.

She stopped walking and turned to face him. The dying light caught in her hair, creating a golden rim around her face. Her smile was different now. Smaller, sadder, more real than the bright one she'd worn for Anton.

"Thank you," she said.

"For what?"

"For not giving up. On finding him. On me." She slid her hand into his. "Always."

Her fingers were damp from the salt water, warm from the sun. The contact sent electricity straight up his arm. Years of friendship, of careful boundaries, of pretending this moment would never come. All of it crumbled.

He pulled her closer, just a step, until he could smell the coconut sunscreen on her skin. The surf filled the silence between them, washing and retreating, washing and retreating.

"I need to tell you something," she said. "About Anton. About having a brother who's basically a stranger. It's weird, you know? Sharing DNA with someone who doesn't know that I hate mustard or that I still sleep with a night-light."

He nodded. Waited.

"But watching him today, seeing how he looks at the world . . ." She paused, her thumb tracing across his knuckles. "It made me realize how much I don't want to be strangers with the people who matter."

He led her up the beach to a spot above the tide line where the sand was dry and soft. They sat facing the water, watching the sun melt into the horizon. The sky deepened to purple and gold.

"You know what Kiara said when she broke up with me?"

Tori went still beside him. "What's that?"

He picked up a handful of sand and let it run through his fingers.

"She said my heart belonged to someone else. That I was in love with you and just couldn't see it."

Tori's breathing changed. Shallow. Careful.

"She was right." He turned to look at her. "You know that, don't you?"

Her eyes searched his face. Hope flickered there, mixed with fear and something that looked like relief. "Blade . . ."

"My life didn't change the night I killed that man at the pier." The words came easier than he'd expected. "It changed the moment I heard you scream. Every choice I've made since has been about getting back to you. I love you, Tori. I always have."

Tears welled in her eyes, but her smile broke through them like sunlight. "I love you too, Blade."

The space between them disappeared. Her hand curved around the back of his neck, fingers threading through his hair. Every nerve ending in his body came alive.

This was Tori.

He closed the gap, dropped his mouth to hers, and claimed the kiss.

Her lips were warm, soft, tasting like the strawberry lip balm he'd seen her wear since high school. The kiss started gentle, tentative. A question. Then she pressed closer, and the question became an answer.

His arms circled her waist and pulled her against him until he could feel her heartbeat through the thin cotton of her dress.

Time stopped. The world narrowed to this one moment. Her mouth on his, her arms clinging to him. The way she fit perfectly against him like she'd been designed for this exact spot.

When they finally broke apart, neither moved away. Her breath whispered warm against his cheek. Her forehead rested against his, and in her eyes he saw himself whole. The man she'd been waiting for all these years while he'd been too scared to believe he deserved her.

"So." She traced lazy circles on his chest. "What happens now?"

He captured her hand, pressed it flat against his heartbeat. "Now we stop pretending we're just friends."

"Good. I was getting tired of that anyway."

He kissed her again, deeper this time. Her hands fisted in his shirt, anchoring him to this moment, this choice, this woman who'd always been his home.

The waves rolled in, crashed, and pulled away, washing away everything that came before. Only this remained.

Only Tori.

Epilogue

THE KNOCK ON GARRISON'S DOOR came in three sharp raps. A pause, then the handle turned.

Tori sat up straighter in her chair. Beside her, Anton did the same. That unconscious mirroring thing twins apparently did, which still caught her off guard every time. Blade's hand slipped from hers as he leaned back in the chair on her left.

The man who entered wore a charcoal suit that screamed federal authority and a face that belonged on currency—all angles and no warmth. His hair was silver-gray, cropped military short, and his eyes swept the room like he was cataloguing threats.

"Deputy Director Mario Platt, Department of Justice." He didn't offer his hand. "Ms. Garrison, thank you for arranging this."

Garrison nodded. "Of course."

Platt remained standing, hands clasped behind his back. "I'm sure Ms. Garrison has informed you that Barclay is cooperating fully. He confirms he murdered the Crews on direct orders from a ranking member of the Nexus Initiative."

No preamble. No small talk. Platt cut straight to it.

"We've been going through Wells's recovered files, and this runs deep. It's going to take us a while to unravel it all. Especially how you, Dr. Stone, played a role in this." Platt looked at Anton, whose eyes went wide.

He put his hand to his sternum. "Me? I wasn't involved. I—"

"Not directly." Platt cut him off with a wave. "After Barclay framed you for your parents' murder, he had you transferred to a research facility in Seattle. The intake notes labeled you a juvenile psychopath. Obviously we know this was all fabricated. You were four years old."

"I remember the building," Anton said. "Not the rooms. Just the building."

"The doctor who eventually pulled you out wasn't supposed to. He saw what the charts said and what you actually were and didn't see a match. He took you home. He probably saved your life."

"My adoptive father." Anton's voice was barely there.

"Yes. He never knew the Aletheia facility was part of a larger network that kept tabs on you the entire time. Let me ask you, why did you open your practice in Florida?"

Anton glanced at Tori like she might have the answer, but she'd been wondering the same thing. And after everything that had happened, she had a feeling it wasn't pure coincidence.

"Well, my father suggested I go to his alma mater for my education. When we toured the campus, I thought it was beautiful. Especially the water. The alumni status helped financially, of course. After I graduated, I just stayed."

Platt nodded. "That's what I suspected. What about your retainer with McCrary's firm?"

Anton shifted. "Well, I guess the surveillance will tell you that Rich was a patient. It came up that he'd known my father, and he liked me so much he wanted all his staff to see me exclusively."

Anton's head dropped into his hands. "They knew who I was the whole time."

"From the day you set up the retainer," Platt said. "They picked you because they could control you. McCrary sent his employees from the firm to give Wells access. We've swept your office, and it appears you were under surveillance for quite some time."

Anton went very still. "Someone was listening . . . All my sessions?"

"Every one. The recordings were in Wells's files. They're sealed now under federal privilege protocol, but they exist."

"That's just . . ." Anton's hands flexed in his lap. "It's not just an invasion of my privacy. It violates patient privilege in the most egregious way."

Tori watched him. She couldn't say anything without making it about her, so she waited.

Anton looked at her. "They knew who I was."

"They brought you in," Tori said. "They wanted you specifically. A psychiatrist they could use to keep tabs on their people."

"Florek." Anton's voice was flat now. "He was going to expose the shell accounts. They were listening to him talk to me about it. They killed him because of what he knew."

"All part of the Nexus Initiative," Platt said. "It's a cabal we've been tracking for years. Barclay and Wells are just the tip of the iceberg."

Tori's chest tightened. They were right. All of it. Every instinct, every connection, every sleepless night chasing shadows that turned out to be monsters.

Garrison leaned forward. "Dr. Crew, Detective St. James, you did it. You brought them to justice. We can't thank you enough."

The words should have felt like victory. Instead, they settled over Tori like a blanket she couldn't quite pull tight enough.

"That's not the real reason we called you here," Garrison said.

The temperature in the room seemed to drop ten degrees. Garrison's pen stopped clicking. Blade's hand went still on his knee. Even the air conditioning seemed to quiet.

Platt's professional mask didn't slip, but his focus narrowed, laser-sharp, onto Tori and Anton. He pulled out a chair and sat, folding his hands on the polished table. "In Barclay's confession, and in the files we recovered, we found a discrepancy in the original Crew murder file. Another lie. They were all lies."

Tori's pulse spiked. She'd lived with the weight of her parents' deaths for twenty-eight years. She'd accepted the brutality, the randomness, the way evil could slice through a family and leave only fragments. What more could they possibly—

Platt slid a document across the desk.

A birth certificate. Official seal, crisp edges.

Tori's fingers trembled as she picked it up. The names jumped out at her immediately:

Nikos Stavros Crew and Ji-Yeon Park Crew. Her parents. The date of birth made her stomach lurch.

October 12, 1998.

Two days before the murders.

Her mind flashed to the autopsy report she'd read weeks ago.

Victim three, unborn female child.

The line had haunted her, the idea that she'd lost not just her parents but a sibling who never got the chance to breathe.

"The report was a lie, Dr. Crew." Platt's voice cut through her thoughts like glass. "Your mother wasn't pregnant when she died. She had just given birth. Barclay's first official act for the Initiative wasn't just murder. It was kidnapping."

The oxygen seemed to vanish from the room. Tori's lungs locked, as if her diaphragm had forgotten its most basic function. Her eyes dropped back to the birth certificate, scanning for details she'd missed.

The time: 3:47 a.m.

Weight: 6 pounds, 2 ounces.

Length: 18 inches.

And then the name.

Isadora Jinri Crew.

The paper slipped from her fingers and fluttered to the floor.

Isadora.

Not a possibility. Not a maybe. Not a victim who died with her parents.

A sister. Stolen. Alive.

The room spun around her. Blade's hand found her shoulder,

steady and warm, but she couldn't feel it. Anton leaned forward, his face pale as he processed the same impossible truth.

"They took her." Her voice came out as a whisper. "They murdered our parents, and they took our sister."

Platt frowned. "We believe so, yes."

"Why? Why would they steal a baby?" Anton asked.

Anton's eyes fixed on her, searching for something she didn't have to give. Her gaze shifted to Platt instead, the only place left to look.

Platt's expression darkened. "We don't know for sure. But the children of Nexus members are considered assets. Their 'research,' as your mother called it, was about more than regenerative tissue. It was about potential. And they believed Isadora had the highest potential of all."

The silence stretched like a wire about to snap.

Tori reached down for and retrieved the birth certificate, her hands steadier now. The shock was crystallizing into something harder, more focused. She looked from the paper in her hands to Anton, whose dark eyes reflected her own.

Finally, she turned to Blade. His eyes carried it all. Grief for what she'd lost, fury at what had been taken, and an unspoken promise that whatever came next, she wouldn't face it alone.

The wound was immense, ripped open just as another was beginning to heal. But the pain wasn't defeat.

It was fuel.

"She's out there," Tori said. "Isadora is out there, and I'm going to find her."

Not a hope. Not a wish.

A promise.

READ ON FOR A SNEAK PEEK
AT THE FIRST BOOK IN

THE KING LEGACY SERIES

AVAILABLE NOW
WHEREVER BOOKS ARE SOLD

1

LUNA ROSATI COULD DISAPPEAR into any crowd, any city, any life. Except this one. This life. It had a way of pulling her back. Like a riptide dragging her under.

10:42 a.m. and the man who held the key to the life she'd left behind was twelve minutes late. She'd convinced herself she was ready for this moment. Now that it hovered before her, Luna wasn't so sure. Not about finding her daughter—that was nonnegotiable—but about facing everything she'd left behind.

She stared out the diner's picture window, her gaze fixed on the empty street, bracing for the moment her carefully constructed life would change.

The morning sun glinted off a passing car, and an elderly couple strolled by. Both moved without any hustle or bustle. Millie Beach was mostly locals. No surprise there. It wasn't exactly a popular vacation destination. The small beach town had all the crime of Miami and none of the beauty.

Eighteen years ago, she'd walked away from this place and vowed never to return. But vows made in storms weren't always kept in the calm. Which was why she was sitting in the back corner of the same rundown diner from her childhood, watching the street through the glassy expanse up front.

The dumpy place hadn't changed a bit. Same faded tan linoleum. Same yellowed Formica tabletops. Same cracked red vinyl chairs. Everywhere she looked, same, same, same. Except the deepened lines etched into the faces of the waitstaff.

Age and a two-pack-a-day habit had not been kind to Marge. The owner frowned from her perch in the kitchen. She'd never liked newcomers. Preferred to keep it to the regulars.

A younger version of Marge appeared at Luna's table. "What'll you have?" The square name tag on her grease-stained shirt said her name was Angie.

Wow, this was Marge's daughter? The woman had aged double time. Strands of gray laced her dark curls. Dark-brown sunspots speckled her weathered face. Indelible kisses from the unrelenting sun reflecting off the ocean in a town where sunblock was for tourists.

Luna picked up her plastic-covered menu, feigned a glance, and dropped it. "Lemonade for now. I'm waiting for a friend."

Angie narrowed her eyes. "You waitin' on Stryker?"

"You know him?"

"'Bout the only one who comes in this time a day. Tourists don't come in for a while yet, and you don't look like a tourist. I get a feelin' I seen you somewhere before."

Luna caught the lie before it slipped out. Years of deception and faking her identity were more natural than truth. But she didn't need a cover here. Not in the town where she grew up. Here she could be herself. Here she could be Luna Rosati. "Yeah, I'm waiting for—"

The bell over the entrance tinkled when a man pushed the glass door open.

Luna looked up, and something inside her fractured. She could hear it. The sound like stepping on a glass pane. A resounding crack that broke open everything she'd worked so hard to keep bottled up all these years.

"Spoke too soon about the tourists." Angie knocked her swollen knuckles on the table. "Be right back with that lemonade."

Angie's words drifted over her unabsorbed. She couldn't take her eyes off the guy she used to know, now standing there all grown up. Hair shaved into a classic crew cut. A far cry from the boy with the unruly mop of sandy blond hair she'd remembered. The khaki-colored linen suit hung on his broad shoulders with a confidence that shouted law enforcement.

Funny, the last time she'd seen him in a suit was at his father's murder trial.

Corbin King removed his sunglasses and scanned the room with intense brown eyes. His Adam's apple rolled when his eyes met hers.

She didn't dare move.

With nonchalance, he strolled over and snagged the vacant seat opposite her. His elbows found a comfortable spot on the table, fingers intertwining while still cradling his sunglasses.

Her tongue skimmed her dry lips, primed to seize the conversation first if anything came to mind. There was nothing to say. But also, everything.

His dark eyes penetrated her. "What are you doing here?"

A dozen cutting remarks tumbled through her mind ranging from "How dare you?" to "Please go away so I never have to see you again." The reflexive restraint honed during her tenure at the CIA barred any of those from slipping past her lips.

Instead, she said, "I'm meeting Stryker."

Corbin looked over his shoulder at the empty restaurant. "Here?"

She didn't respond.

Angie set a glass of lemonade on the table with a clink and smiled at Corbin. "Get you anything, doll?"

She hadn't called Luna a doll.

Corbin dropped his sunglasses on the table and leaned back to look at Angie. "Coffee. And a few moments of your time, if you don't mind." He reached into his breast pocket and withdrew a black wallet. A deft flip revealed his credentials. Florida Department of Law Enforcement. "I have a few questions for you."

Impressive. Corbin had done well to work his way into Florida's version of the FBI.

Angie flicked her eyes between Luna and Corbin, and she coughed a phlegmy laugh. "Am I in trouble, Officer?"

"No, ma'am. Just have a few questions about a missing person. Can we chat in private when I'm done with my friend here?"

"Sure. I guess I ain't goin' nowhere." She sauntered back to the kitchen, shoulders squared and a touch of extra height in her stance.

"What are you doing here, Luna?" The honeyed tone he'd used on the waitress morphed to granite.

"Since when does the FDLE investigate missing persons?"

"Since when do you talk to Stryker? Or any of us, for that matter?"

"Why do you keep answering questions with another question?" Although she knew good and well she'd started it.

The squiggle of a blue vein bulged at Corbin's temple, and she kind of enjoyed it. "Since we gave our baby up for adoption. Since you cut me out of your life." His finger stabbed the table to punctuate each sentence. "Since you left town without a word and never looked back."

Another crack formed. His words knifed her heart. Images of a teen beggar girl on the streets of Pakistan played through her mind. The one with dark hair and eyes that mirrored her own. The girl's striking resemblance to herself had brought Luna back to the time when she held a tiny life in her arms. The baby girl she'd given up—not because she wanted to, but because she refused to let her child suffer the life she'd had.

The daughter she'd brought into being was somewhere out there in the world, and she needed Stryker to tell her where.

The pang cut deep, but Luna gathered her composure and locked her emotional armor down tight. She wasn't the only one who'd walked away. "You broke up with me, Corbin. You told me you didn't want to be a father. You made that choice. I just made sure our daughter had a future."

The skin around his collar flushed crimson. She could see his neck straining. "I can't believe you—"

A sharp glint of light flashed through the storefront windows. Whatever Corbin was saying faded into nothingness. She watched Stryker emerge from his rusty old Jeep parked across the street. His hair, a blend of salt and pepper, hung in a knot at the nape of his neck. Aside from the silver strands, he looked like the same athletic man she'd known when she was a teenager.

Years melted away. She saw the man who'd seen the good in her, even when she was a mess of anger and bad choices. The man who'd taken a lost and confused girl and forged her into something stronger, something more. He'd pulled her back from the edge, shown her a different path. And somehow, against all odds, the rebellious girl who'd once cursed every cop in sight had become a government agent.

He'd challenged her, pushed her, never let her give up on herself. And she hadn't. Would he still recognize that girl in the woman she'd become?

A black SUV slammed to a halt outside. Doors flew open. Three dark figures jumped out, faces swallowed by masks, bodies muted by black tactical gear.

Guns. They had guns.

Luna was on her feet before she knew what was happening. Her brain put it together on the fly. *Outside. Help Stryker.*

Corbin's chair scraped back. Clattered over. He was on her heels.

Stryker wouldn't go down without a fight. With his reflexes, he could disarm a shooter and break a few bones faster than she could blink. His resistance would buy them the priceless seconds they needed to get outside.

One man pointed a Taser at Stryker and squeezed the trigger. Two barbed probes shot through the air and embedded into the back of Stryker's neck, sending fifty thousand volts of electricity screaming through his body. The other two men caught him under the arms before he hit the sidewalk and hauled his limp body into the back seat.

Luna and Corbin burst outside. Shouts. A woman screamed. But Luna's eyes were laser focused on the dark vehicle. The doors slammed shut.

Corbin had his gun out. "Police! Stop or I'll shoot!"

The SUV's engine roared. The vehicle lurched forward, tires shrieking, grabbing traction. It fishtailed, sideswiping two parked cars. Then it swerved back on course, speeding down the street. It blew through a stop sign and disappeared around the corner.

Bits of red and yellow confetti littered the street and sidewalk. Luna crouched and used her fingernail to scrape up a few of the tiny round dots.

Corbin sprinted half a block chasing after the vehicle before he stopped. Feet set shoulder width apart. Knees flexed. Arms extended and ready to fire.

She marched over and slapped her palm on the muzzle of his gun to shove the barrel down. "Put that away. You can't shoot into a busy street at a fleeing vehicle."

He was breathing hard. "No plates. They wore masks. Should be able to get surveillance footage and interview witnesses." Like her, Corbin was already thinking of the next steps.

She had her phone out, thumb hovering over the screen. The secret code used to send secure cables to the Agency wouldn't work on this plain smartphone. The only person whose number was stored in this one had just been kidnapped.

Corbin muttered something Luna couldn't hear. He had a hand

on his waist. The tail of his blazer was pushed back, showing the gun in its holster on his hip. He rattled his name, badge number, and their location into his phone. "I'm reporting a confirmed kidnapping in progress. Requesting immediate backup and notify detectives."

With Stryker gone, she had no reason to stay. Time to start searching for him. She did an about-face and went back inside.

Angie was on the phone in hysterics. It'd be a wonder if the dispatcher could make sense of the gibberish behind her sobs. Luna marched to the table and picked up her purse. Paused long enough to drain her lemonade and toss a twenty on the table before heading back outside.

Corbin fell into step beside her, phone still pressed to his ear. "Where are you going?"

She kept walking.

"Hey, you can't leave a crime scene." He grabbed her shoulder and spun her around.

She caught his hand in a wrist lock and rotated his forearm until his knees buckled. "You've gotten slow in your old age." She flashed a thin smile and shoved him, releasing her hold.

Corbin stumbled a few steps. The look on his face was almost worth the agony of seeing him again. She turned and headed for her car.

The last person she'd ever wanted to see was Corbin King. Not here. Not now. Not ever.

"Luna! You can't just walk away. Luna!"

Stryker was not only her mentor but a father figure. She wouldn't stand by and let someone hurt him. Besides, he was the one who'd arranged the adoption. Handled everything himself, outside the system when she was too young and emotionally wrecked to question the details. Back then, she hadn't wanted to know. Convinced it was better that way. But that had changed.

Now, without Stryker, she had no way to find the only blood

relative she had left. And after everything she'd lost in Pakistan, she could not afford to lose anything else.

The weight of it all didn't matter.

She would save Stryker.

She would find her daughter.

And she would do it without Corbin King.

Dear Reader,

Thank you for joining me on this journey through Fatal Pattern, *Tori and Blade's story. Tori has lived in my head for years, and writing her meant going back to places I had not visited in a long time.*

I aged out of foster care at age eighteen. I know what it's like to be the kid who refuses adoption. I know that the state pays more when a child stays in care than when they're adopted and what that knowledge does to a kid who already feels like a burden. I know what it's like to love people who feel like home and still hold them at arm's length, just in case. I struggled with all of these things myself. Tori carried that struggle for me on the page, and the de Hostos family carried the love I knew. If any of this is your story too, I'd love to hear from you. There are more of us in this community than you might think, and your story should be heard.

Fatal Pattern *also took me deep into the strange and beautiful world of fractal mathematics. The Mandelbrot set is an attempt to explain God's design woven into creation itself. In broccoli. In coastlines. In lightning. In your own circulatory system, where fractal branching allows blood to reach every cell in your body. Researchers are studying this same math right now to regenerate cardiac tissue, actual lab-grown patches that could one day mend a damaged heart. Beautiful work. Worth a great deal of money. And as Tori's mother discovered, worth killing for.*

This book opens with Matthew 13:24–30, the parable of the wheat and the weeds. A man sows good seed in his field. While everyone sleeps, an enemy sows weeds. The servants want to rip them up at once. The master says no. Let them grow together until the harvest. Stryker spent years living that parable. He knew where the weeds were. He didn't pull them, because pulling them would have destroyed the wheat alongside. Tori. The program. The lives he had built around her. He sheltered the field. He waited. And in God's time, the harvest came.

That part wasn't just for Stryker. If you are carrying a truth that feels too dangerous to act on yet or are watching evil flourish next to good and wondering when justice is coming, I've been there too, and I pray this story gives you a little more peace with the wait.

I'd love to stay connected with you, dear reader. You can find me on Facebook and Instagram, where I'm most active. Come say hi, tell me what you thought of Tori and Blade, and let me know which character you'd like to see next as The King Legacy series continues.

Thank you for letting these characters into your life.

Blessings,
Kate Angelo

P.S. There's one scene I had to cut from the final manuscript. If you'd like to read it, subscribe to my newsletter at KateAngelo .com, and it's yours.

Acknowledgments

To God, thank you for the endless ideas. For the curiosity that won't shut off, even when I want it to. For giving me a brain that loves both stories and equations and somehow finds a way to braid the two together on the page. Thank you for letting me write stories about broken people you're still building, because that's the only kind of story I know how to tell.

To Jerry, my husband. You put up with the deadline panic, the staring-into-space episodes, the questions about explosions and technology asked at the dinner table with a perfectly straight face (I should probably also be thanking your sixth-grade physical science teacher). You're my biggest cheerleader, my loudest promoter, and the person who reminds me to eat when a chapter is consuming me. There is no version of this book, or this life, without you. Thank you for choosing me again and again.

To my Cheese, Tacos, and Alibis crew. For the long talks about cheese and tacos (obviously). For helping me with all the plot ideas and finding the words when they refuse to come. (It was *car*. The word I couldn't remember was *car*.) For being the first to choose my coffin when I disappear from our chat for twenty-four hours and you automatically presume I'm dead. I love you all.

To the Museum of the Bible, especially Jerry P., Yancy, and Simon. Thank you for the most awe-inspiring place to write whenever I'm in DC and for being wonderful fans of my work. I can't wait until I'm famous enough to have my book signing in your halls.

To my family. For being so gracious with me all the time. For being so inspiring. The laughs, the hugs, the stories you tell, the photos you share, the tech we talk about, all of it refills my soul with creativity.

To my team at Revell. Kelsey, Lindsay, Karen, and Laura, thank you for championing this book through every step of getting it into readers' hands. Working with you is the gift I never stop being grateful for.

To Kristin and Barbara, my line editor and proofreader. You both have keen-eye superpowers. Thank you for finding what I'd been staring past for months.

To Dan, Teresa, and Shannon, who showed me what it looked like to love a kid who wasn't sure she was lovable. You're in every page of Tori's story.

And to you, dear reader. Thank you for being here. A book's journey doesn't end when you finish it. Its life grows when you share it. Thank you for carrying stories with you into your world and sharing them wherever you go.

Kate Angelo is the *Publishers Weekly* bestselling author of *Hunting the Witness*, Selah Award winner of *Deadly Holiday Hijack*, and Amazon Top 100 Bestseller of *Driving Force*, in addition to *Girl Lost*. Kate works alongside her husband championing stronger marriages and families. Her journey from foster care to bestselling author fuels her fast-paced romantic suspense, where flawed characters discover hope and healing through life's fiercest trials and relationships. When she's not putting fictional people through the wringer, she's out creating real-life happily-ever-afters at conferences and events nationwide. Learn more about Kate at KateAngelo.com.

Sign Up for Kate's Newsletter

Keep up to date with Kate's latest news on book releases and events by signing up for her email list at the website below.

KateAngelo.com

FOLLOW KATE ON SOCIAL MEDIA

Kate Angelo Author   @KateAngeloAuthor   @TheKateAngelo